CATCHING STARS

This edition published in ***2018*** *by*
OF TOMES PUBLISHING
UNITED KINGDOM

Cover art by Jo Painter
Cover design by Eight Little Pages
Interior book design by Eight Little Pages

CATCHING STARS

CAYLA KEENAN

OFTOMES PUBLISHING
UNITED KINGDOM

Dedicated to my Dad:

my very first reader, without whom I never would have been brave enough to share this story.

PROLOGUE:

MADDIX

Maddix wasn't afraid of witches. There was no reason to be afraid. Everyone knew magic was dying. Even the Kingswitch, the most powerful *sahir* in their land—in *any* land—was rumored to be losing his abilities. The stories said something in their Oldlands, whatever gave them their magic, was dying and sucking the witches dry in the meantime. Though he had no way of knowing what was true, Maddix relished the thought that the *sahir* might one day be as mortal as the rest of them.

Another widespread rumor suggested they were being called back into the Dark. It was common knowledge that the witches came from across the sea, but some said they sold their souls in return for power. Their starcursed magic had spread from generation to generation until it was a veritable plague throughout the Three Kingdoms. But now, their contract was up.

How it happened didn't matter to him. Maddix was of age and a proud member of the Kingsguard. He had only been given his pin a month ago, but it had been the proudest moment of his life. Finally, he was free to roam Pavaal as he pleased and would be given the respect he rightfully deserved. With any luck, he would rise quickly through the ranks; maybe even make it to Ayrie Palace. He had his whole life ahead of him, and Maddix didn't need anything as troublesome as witches mucking it up.

He didn't understand why the King hadn't taken a leaf from the Vandelian's book and exiled the lot of them. Witches served no purpose; they hadn't in centuries. For no reason but that they'd been born with magic, they lived in the Palace, basking in luxury and wanting for nothing. All the while, the rest of the Aestosi had to fight just to survive.

As a child, he would sneak out of the Gull and watch as the Kingswitch and the other *sahir* from Ayrie Palace paraded through the merchant sectors, hoping that if he got close enough, their magic would rub off on him. He'd been young and stupid then. Now he knew better.

It didn't matter now—witches and their starcursed privilege. He was of age, a man with a profession that afforded him dignity and honor. Darek, his roommate in the barracks, said some of the Guards went their whole careers without any kind of magical incident. Maddix was confident he would be just as lucky. His star would look out for him, like it always had. Without it Maddix might have been like the other boys at Northside Orphanage, jumped into carrion gangs before they were even of age.

At the moment, though, Maddix would suffer carrions and witches alike if it meant there was something to do. From sundown to sunup, he didn't do much more than stand around and watch the empty streets. Sometimes he prowled around the block, but this tiny corner of the city was quiet in a way that drove Maddix out of his mind with boredom It was easy duty for greenblood Guards, but stars above, Maddix couldn't imagine anything more tedious than guarding grain storehouses all night.

It wasn't as bad as guarding the nobility, with their well lit, scrupulously clean streets, but the merchant ring of the city wasn't much better. The Gullet was where the *real* action happened, and only the toughest, most seasoned Guards took on the gang-ridden streets in the very heart of Pavaal. There, the Guard's control was tenuous at best and the threat of violence hung in the air like the stench from the river. New Guards generally avoided it for their own safety.

Maddix had requested the Gull as his assignment. He'd grown up in the slums, and there was no better place to cut his teeth than against the carrions. Naturally, that request had been denied, and Maddix had been posted with the merchants.

"Ey, greenblood," a senior patrolman said, rounding the corner. Maddix shook himself, emptying his head. "Report."

"Nothing out of the ordinary, sir," Maddix said, snapping a textbook salute and fighting the urge to reach for the black star pendant that hung around his neck. It was just a bauble, found with him as an infant, but it was as good as any other good luck charm.

"Good work," the other man said, clapping Maddix on the shoulder. "You're the greenie who requested the Gull, didn't ye?"

"Yes, sir," Maddix replied, still holding the salute in place.

"At ease," the patrolman said with a chuckle. "Good for you. That's the kind of spine we need in the Guard these days. You keep this up and you'll make rank in no time."

It occurred to him that the senior Guardsman might have been poking fun, but having his dream said aloud for all the sky to hear made Maddix stand straighter. He glanced at the man's face, seeking to thank him by name, but darkness swathed most of it in shadow, and Maddix was sure he would have remembered an officer with a shiny scar on his top lip.

"Thank you, sir," Maddix said, puffing out his chest. The Guardsman nodded and inclined his head before marching out of sight.

You'll make rank in no time. The words echoed in Maddix's ears, buoying him through the rest of his shift. Some of his classmates envied Maddix's easy post, but he couldn't wait to be reassigned. Maddix couldn't prove himself in combat if he never saw any.

Not that Aestos had seen an actual war in years. Centuries, even. Vandel and Kaddah, the kingdoms to the north, had been embroiled in a shadowy war for as long as Maddix could remember, though Aestos had never been brought into the conflict. No one wanted to go to battle with a kingdom with witches instead of a standing army. They would decimate anyone in their path with their Dark magic, and so Vandel and Kaddah left Aestos well enough alone.

Settling against a warehouse wall, Maddix thought of glory on the battlefield. He had grown up on stories of Aestos, before the witches came from their homeland across the sea. The Aestosi had been warriors then, fighting off warlords and invaders who wanted to steal their land. Kaddah had been plagued by famine and drought for as long as anyone could remember, and Vandel was mountainous and inhospitable. Aestos had plenty of fertile farmlands and more than enough food, something the neighboring kingdoms sorely lacked. Warrior kings led deadly armies into battle to defend their borders, and only the strong survived. They were feared and revered throughout the Three Kingdoms. It was nothing like today, where decadence chipped away at their fearsome reputation.

Maddix entertained himself with fantasies of being born in a different age, of fighting invaders and usurpers, instead of standing around and waiting for something exciting to happen.

A loud clatter shook him out of his thoughts and Maddix jerked upright, unsheathing the sword at his hip.

"Bleedin' stars!" an unfamiliar voice shouted from just around the corner. Maddix lurched into motion, his heart breaking into a gallop. Finally, something to report. A chance to prove he was worth more than just watching warehouses.

"Hey!" Maddix yelled, announcing himself. At first glance, it looked as though the alleyway was empty, save for one man. He had fallen onto the cobbled streets, his arms clutching his middle like he was trying to hold himself together. Frothy blood foamed out of his mouth.

Maddix blinked and another figure appeared in the cramped alley. A dark hood obscured its features, and the shadows around it seemed to writhe and dance like living things. Faces appeared in the swirling darkness, drowning souls gasping for air, each one twisted in screams of agony.

"Help me," the man gasped, and Maddix finally tore his eyes off the shadows, holding his sword at the ready.

"You there!" Maddix shouted at the hooded creature, trying to keep his voice from trembling. "Stop, in the name of the King!" The figure turned towards him, and Maddix's heart dropped into his boots. There was no face under the hood, nothing human, just an empty void.

Demon, Maddix thought, his mind flooding with terror. Ice gripped his insides and froze the breath in his lungs. All his thoughts of proving himself and making rank vanished. The figure shifted, and it was across the alley in the blink of an eye, all without making a sound.

Maddix tried to run, tried to call out for help, but he couldn't force his legs into motion. As the creature came closer, the darkness receded enough to reveal red eyes that glowed like embers. Somehow, Maddix shook off the icy stillness and struck out with his weapon. The demon didn't flinch or stumble, standing perfectly still as the steel passed through it as if it were as insubstantial as smoke. Its eyes glowed red, and a clawed hand reached out, seizing Maddix by the throat. He choked, fighting the grip on his neck, but the hand lifted him off the ground with terrifying ease.

"Stop," Maddix wheezed, black spots dancing across his vision. His legs kicked uselessly. "Please."

The hooded figure only drew him closer, crimson eyes aglow, and Maddix's skin blistered where the demon touched him. He was burning, without smoke or fire, burning from the inside out.

Without warning, the creature released its grip, and Maddix fell to the ground. He landed on his side and pain cracked through his chest. Maddix forced himself to breathe and his ribs protested; at least one was broken, maybe two. It didn't matter. He had to move, and he had to move *now*. With the last bit of strength he had left, Maddix crawled along the pockmarked street to where he'd dropped his sword.

Something came down hard on his wrist, and he heard the *crack* as the small bones broke. The pain was a distant thing, as though it wasn't his at all. Somewhere, someone was screaming. It might have been him. The fire within him surged anew, driving him into the smallest corner of his mind and trapping him there.

"Rise," the creature said in a voice that rasped like a snake's. Maddix's body rose of its own accord, yanked upwards like a stiff-jointed marionette. Something compelled his arms into motion, and Maddix picked up his sword.

Locked within his own skin, Maddix screamed and fought, but he was helpless against the magic that possessed him. Maddix's hands gripped the hilt of his sword, holding it out towards the man cowering in a puddle of his own blood.

No. The thought was hazy and unfocused as Maddix's arm rose above his head and came down again. There was some distant pain, but he was more focused on the mess he'd made of the man's chest.

Blood was everywhere: on the street, on the walls of the adjacent buildings—some had even splattered onto Maddix's otherwise spotless uniform. *No*, the thought again, unable to take his eyes off of the corpse. The man he'd killed. *I didn't want to. I didn't want to.*

It didn't matter.

The creature turned towards Maddix again, and somehow, beneath the smoky darkness and glowing red eyes, he could see a pale scar slicing the demon's upper lip. Then, he couldn't see at all.

THE DEMON LET him go three days later. Sometimes he was conscious, trapped in that tiny corner of his mind. The creature made him watch, forced him to see himself being moved like a chess piece and unable to stop it.

He killed three more people while the demon controlled him, and every time he woke up, there was more blood on his hands. Maddix was sure the nightmare would never end, and he would be the demon's puppet until starvation or exhaustion killed him.

On the third day, Maddix opened his eyes, and the demon was gone. His body was his own again, and after almost three days of numbness, every breath was agony. His stomach cramped as he tried to move, sending shooting pains through his midsection. Maddix groaned, clutching his midsection. He tried to shout for help, but his voice would not obey him. Minutes after waking up, Maddix succumbed to unconsciousness with his face tilted towards the sky.

Maddix was half dead and covered in the blood of the people he'd killed when he was found lying unconscious in the street. When he finally came to, he was bound and chained in a windowless room, dripping with the freezing water that had been used to rouse him. Two Guardsmen glared down at him, the rage in their eyes reserved for the worst kinds of carrion scum.

He had been charged with multiple counts of murder. Under the demon's control, Maddix had killed four people in cold blood. He tried to tell them about the demon, tried to explain that he had been possessed. He was a victim in this too. They had to believe him—he was one of them for the stars' sake!

They didn't. Nothing in the Three Kingdoms had the ability to climb into a man's mind and take over his body, not even the witches. The very mention of that kind of Darkness was blasphemy.

"You're a disgrace to the uniform," the Guard snarled. Maddix tried to protest, but the man drove his fist into Maddix's gut, and the air exploded from his lungs. He spent six days in that cell before word got back to him. The evidence had been overwhelming and the verdict swift and final. The King himself had passed the sentence, to be carried out at a time of his choosing.

For the murders of four of the King's subjects, Maddix Kell was sentenced to death.

CHAPTER ONE:

JAYIN

Pavaal was humming. A tense, nervous energy hung in the air like smoke. There wasn't a shortage of criminals in the capitol, but public executions had been all but outlawed. Then again, this was the first time a greenblood Guard had ever gone rogue and massacred four people. Serial murder had a tendency to stick in a city's memory, though the actual killings occurred years ago.

Jayin found the hypocrisy laughable. Kids in carrion gangs killed each other every day, and the Kingsguard routinely beat criminals to death in lockup, but the King chose to make an example out of a mad boy.

At first, no one had cared that a dockworker was slaughtered in the street, his body hacked to pieces and left to rot in the gang-infested heart of the capitol. The man was a known gambler and patronized many unsavory establishments in the Gullet. No one batted so much as an eye at his death. But the next day a merchant woman turned up dead, her chest slashed to ribbons. *That* had gotten some attention. Merchants lived comfortably in their riverside villas. Even the least successful ones had lives far better than any inhabitant of the Gull. Though they were in close proximity—in the approximate half-circle that made up Pavaal, their sector wedged between the noble ring and the slums—the merchants didn't fear the violence that stalked the streets as sure as any gang. They were protected.

They were supposed to be, anyway.

Over the next three days, a carrion boy and a witch were murdered in the exact same manner. The Guard had no leads. People began to panic, and it didn't look like the killer was going to stop.

Until Maddix Kell was discovered lying in the street, drenched in the blood of his victims. Justice had been swift. The boy had been arrested and thrown into the deepest hole in the kingdom to rot. Some whispered that he had been possessed, forced to kill by some Dark being, though most maintained that he'd simply gone mad.

What utter nonsense, Jayin thought. There were only a handful of mindwitches capable of possession—only one that she knew of—and Maddix Kell's killing spree had lasted three whole days. Jayin didn't know of anyone who could maintain that kind of magic for that long. Magic only went so far. If someone learned to turn humans into puppets, Jayin would have heard something.

She would already be running.

Just a day ago, the city had buzzed with anticipation for the execution, but overnight the atmosphere had changed. After two years of rotting in the dark, Maddix Kell escaped. Jayin had to appreciate his timing. The King had waited two years to kill Kell—His Majesty was waiting for the perfect time to boost public morale. In these times of hardship, nothing mollified the people like watching a boy hang.

Some said he had acquired magic during his imprisonment and used those skills to get out. The bravest among them suggested he'd been broken out by burgeoning rebel groups seeking to recruit anyone with a score to settle with the Crown. Others, the small number that believed his claims of possession, said the demon had returned to spare him from the hangman's noose.

Jayin kept track of all the rumors—a lingering habit from a different life—but those were especially ridiculous. Magic wasn't a skill to be acquired, and she didn't believe in demons. Even if they did exist, it was unlikely a Dark creature would suddenly find the benevolence to free their former puppet. As for the rebels, they were mad if they would risk the ire of the King—and more importantly, the Kingswitch—by breaking out Ayrie's most famous murderer. Such an open show of defiance could only end one way. Badly.

Absently, Jayin cycled through the Pit's weaknesses and any possible escape routes as she walked through the nearly empty market. With all the talk of an escaped murderer, the Gull was emptier than usual, and the market was nearly deserted. It was a nice change from the overcrowded streets to which she'd grown accustomed. In the last three years, countless people had flocked to Pavaal from the countryside, abandoning their dying farms to find shelter in the cities. There wasn't much to be found

Jayin shook her head, forcing herself to dismiss thoughts of convicts and escapes. That wasn't her life anymore; hunting criminals and convicts wasn't her job. The Palace no longer held her leash—they hadn't for a year—but she could remember the day Kell had been arrested. She suppressed the guilt that weighed on her heart like a stone.

Besides, it wasn't as if she was planning on attending the hanging. The fact that public executions were still in practice was repugnant. The boy was a killer, but that was no excuse to turn his death into a spectacle. The capitol was full of killers, and Jayin knew for a fact Ayrie Palace housed a few of their own.

And to think, Jayin thought, loading her groceries into bags, *these are the same people who consider magic barbarism.*

"Hi, Jay," said a voice at her elbow. Jayin didn't flinch, used to the small boy's presence by now.

"You are getting sloppy," Jayin said. "I'm surprised you're not waiting for me in my kitchen by now."

The boy, Ravi, was one of the dozens of children that roamed the Gull by day. At night, the lucky few took shelter in the temples. The others scurried back to carrion hideouts where they could find a measure of security with the gangs.

Ravi's bright smile lessened, and a faint blush colored the dark skin of his cheeks.

"You changed the locks," he said, the words taking on a petulant edge.

"You picked the last ones," Jayin replied. "But if you're going to follow me home, make yourself useful."

She shifted one of the bags in her arms, careful not to let him touch the strip of naked skin just above the hem of her glove as she dropped the paper sack into his hands. Ravi struggled under the weight for a moment before righting himself. Jayin smiled as she watched him, the stubbornness on his face exclusive to thirteen-year-old boys.

"So, whatcha get?" Ravi asked as they walked into the shop. He handed Jayin her bag of groceries and started poking around as she unpacked.

"The usual ingredients," Jayin said, shaking a jar so Ravi could hear the liquid sloshing around inside. "Virgin's blood." She picked up a container of whitish powder. "Some ground up nixie bones. Be careful with that one," Jayin advised as Ravi peered into a tiny, empty jar. She plucked it from his fingers before he could pry the lid open.

"What's in it?" Ravi asked, standing on his tiptoes to get a better look as Jayin whisked the vial away.

"The soul of a dying sailor," Jayin said, wiggling her fingers and poking Ravi in the stomach.

"Come off it." His dark eyebrows drew together. "No way you got a soul in there."

"If you don't believe me, you're welcome to take a look inside," Jayin said, shrugging. "But if the old man's soul latches onto you, there's no telling what will happen. I heard this one had a liking for *marjan.* He used to eat it on everything. Personally, I love the stuff, but you *dayri* have such delicate palettes."

Ravi made a face, his tongue sticking out as he ran his hand through his dark curls.

"Today's the day," he announced, finding a new topic.

Jayin raised an eyebrow. "Oh? And what day would that be?"

"Today," Ravi said, hopping onto an empty spot on her counter, "is the day you tell me how you got that scar."

Jayin smiled, the small motion only making the mark more noticeable. Ravi had asked about it since the day she first found him in the shop, and Jayin made up a new answer every time, each more ridiculous than the last.

"Pirates," she declared. Jayin drew her thumb over the thin line that carved through the left side of her face, sweeping from just under her eye and splitting her lips. It was a miracle her tongue had survived. "They were harvesting souls and got a little too friendly." She shook her head. "Never was a fan of pirates."

Ravi pouted, folding his arms across his chest. "You'll tell me someday."

"I'll tell you when you earn it," Jayin said, before turning to a safer subject. "And you can start by helping me organize the shop and update my ledger. I'll even give you a bronze." Ravi's eyes lit up at the prospect of earning a coin.

"My numbers ain't so good," he said, his smile deflating by slow degrees. "I don't wanna mess it up."

"How about you try it in pencil first, and I'll check it over?"

Ravi nodded, and Jayin made a mental note to add arithmetic to their impromptu curriculum. Like most in the Gull, Ravi could only read at the most basic level. Over the past few months, Jayin had worked to improve his education. It was an optimistic ambition, but some part of her thought that if Ravi could read and write, he would have more options than being dragged into the gangs.

Jayin handed him the ledger, opening it up to the next blank page. Ravi took it carefully, his eyes solemn, before heading to the furthest corner of the shop to start inventory.

As she stocked the counter, Jayin watched him out of the corner of her eye. His wiry curls bounced as he ticked his head back and forth, tallying numbers and crossing them out again. She didn't think he would try to make off with anything—nothing here was worth much, and with a bronze on the line, it was unlikely Ravi would cut and run. Even so, kids in the Gull grew up quickly and shed their consciences even quicker.

Jayin had known the risks of settling in the Gull when she'd chosen to open her apothecary over a year ago. Newcomers were routinely robbed and bullied into supporting one gang or another. Red Crows, Vultures, Ironbeaks, and Bloodwings, they all vied for territory and didn't care who they killed to get it.

But no one, not the most fearsome of carrions, was willing to cross the Gulwitch. Jayin thought the nickname was a little heavy-handed, but theatricality and violence walked hand-in-hand in this place. Stories and reputation were everything. They were the difference between life and death; the difference between being left alone or having the gangs holding her leash.

Jayin had been collared before. It didn't suit her.

Only two days after she first set up shop, the apothecary had been raided. According to the legend, she hunted for a day and a night before she found the thieves and spelled them into returning the stolen goods. One rumor said she had cursed and enthralled them, so they were bound to do her bidding or die. Another insisted she could shed her human skin to reveal a monster that stood seven feet tall, with magical tattoos that meant ruin to whoever saw them. The newest story was she could kill with a look, her green eyes poisonous to anyone who dared to meet her gaze.

If I were seven feet tall, I wouldn't need a ladder to stock my own shelves, Jayin thought. The stories preserved her safety and status in the Gull, but the reality was much less exciting. Finding the thieves had taken less than two hours, and the carrions had laughed themselves stupid when she'd demanded her wares back. The herbs weren't worth much, but just as the gangs had to hassle newcomers, Jayin had to prove that she wouldn't be pushed around. All it had taken to get her things back was a bit of flash and a few nonsensical words, and thus the Gulwitch was born.

Jayin smiled at the memory. Carrion gangs might run the Gull, but everyone was afraid of witches.

After that, rumors of the vengeful Gulwitch flooded the streets, growing more fantastical with each retelling. As they pinwheeled out of control, Jayin earned a reprieve from the carrions. The stories made customers harder to come by, but for those who couldn't afford medics or expensive *sahir* healers, she was the only option. Home remedies and naturalist cures weren't much, but they were better than nothing.

Jayin had resolved herself to a life of solitude when Ravi started showing up. She tried to chase him away at first, thinking he was one of the scavenger children that scoped out marks or picked crime scenes clean. But he returned the next day, and the next, always watching her with enormous black eyes.

Eventually, she gave up and stopped shooing him out the door every time he dropped by. It was nice to be around someone who didn't look at her with abject horror or thinly veiled suspicion.

Jayin watched as Ravi took stock and made careful notes in the ledger. His tongue stuck out of his mouth as he did the sums, shockingly pink against his dark skin. While he focused on his task, Jayin busied herself by replenishing her store of healing poultices and other powder mixes. She marketed them as magic, but they were just as mundane as most Aestosi. Many *sahir* frowned on selling magic to *dayri*, though there were some that did a booming business in the merchant ring. Technically it was illegal, but in Pavaal, legality had never gotten in the way of turning a profit.

Busy with her work, Jayin barely noticed someone approaching the shop until they were practically in the door

"Ravi," Jayin said coolly. "Mind finishing up in the storeroom?" Ravi nodded, clutching the ledger to his chest and ducking into the back. He knew when to make himself scarce. Jayin couldn't intervene if he pledged himself to a gang without jeopardizing her neutrality, but that didn't mean she couldn't take small countermeasures in the meantime.

Jayin only spared the carrion boy a passing glance as he walked into the storefront, recognizing the crimson Bloodwing tattoos that patterned his skin. He couldn't have been much younger than Jayin herself, maybe sixteen or seventeen, but he was clearly high up in the ranks.

One of the reasons the Guard so consistently underestimated the gangs was because their members were so young. Kids, most of them not even of age, rose through the gangs until they were killed and another child took their place. The oldest carrion Jayin knew of had been twenty-three before he died. Some of them—a rare few—made it out of the game, retiring in comfort to run long cons on merchants and unwary newcomers. But even retired carrions didn't live very long.

This one didn't look anywhere near retirement. He was an enforcer. Big, mean, and stupid, they advanced with whatever streetlord could hold onto power the longest. This one was no exception. He was thick as a tree trunk, all beady eyes and bloody knuckles. It was a wonder he grew to be such a size. Most of the kids running the streets were painfully thin.

Jayin didn't initiate conversation, going about her business until he stated his. Enforcers didn't act unless it was on orders, and there was no way someone with anti-magic sigils tattooed on their shoulders would have any business with a witch. She wondered if he knew sigils were a kind of magic, and they didn't work for *dayri* anyway.

It was unlikely. Aestosi superstitions were boundless when it came to protection against witches. Witches who kept the whole wretched kingdom safe.

"You gotta come with me," the boy said finally, his voice a low rumble. Jayin looked up at him, refusing to break eye contact even when the boy's mouth twisted into a hard line. "The boss needsta see you," he continued, looking away from her.

"If Kane wants to see me, he can come himself," Jayin replied. The boy looked surprised that Jayin knew Kane's name offhand, but she made it her business to know the powerful players in the Gull. The leader of the Bloodwings had a nasty streak a mile wide. He had been a carrion since the tender age of nine, slashing purses before he learned that slitting a man's throat was as easy as cutting his wallet. He was not someone to cross.

Neither was Jayin, and she would not be called like a dog.

"He can't," the enforcer ground out. "He's sick."

"Then take him to a medic," Jayin said, turning her attention back to her work. The Bloodwings had huge caches of coin squirreled away; they could afford someone more qualified.

"We did!" the boy shouted. Jayin's eyes snapped back to him, and she spun a glamor over her skin. Her eyes glowed green, sinking deep into her skull, and mythical tattoos appeared, deep black against her brown skin.

"You"—she said in a voice that promised violence. The enforcer's eyes widened, and he scrambled backward—"should think very carefully about your next words."

The boy swallowed hard. "What's wrong with him ain't physical. It's magic."

"Magic?" Jayin repeated, disbelief coloring her voice.

"He's been cursed."

She doubted that. The Kingswitch banned curse magic years ago, and there were entire squads of witches who monitored all the magical activity in Aestos. If a curse had been cast—especially so close to the Palace—someone would have known about it.

The boy shuffled, rubbing the back of his neck. "We'll pay."

"Yes, you will," Jayin said, but she wasn't thinking about the money. Since Maddix Kell had escaped, it had felt as if Pavaal was holding its breath, waiting for *something* that loomed just over the horizon. Maybe this was it.

Or maybe it was just the beginning.

CHAPTER TWO:

JAYIN

The enforcer let himself out, and Jayin quickly scribbled a note for Ravi, telling him to lock up, before following the carrion boy outside. It wasn't hard to guess where they would go. If Kane really was as sick as the boy said, he would be holed up in Bloodwing territory with a dozen lieutenants by his side. Jayin made sure to maintain her glamor as they walked farther away from her shop.

"Well it's not my taste," she said when they finally arrived at a building by the docks. It was dingy and damp, but well fortified. "But you carrions do love squatting in the dark." His lieutenants glowered at her, but from his bed in the back corner of the room, Kane barked out a laugh.

"Charming as always. You look well, Gulwitch."

She couldn't say the same for him. Jayin barely recognized the wasted figure beside her. His skin was yellow and waxy, stretched thin over his skull. His eyes sunk deep into their sockets and the bones in his collar looked like they might break through his flesh at any moment. Jayin had seen hunger, she'd seen starvation, but this was something different. Even if Jayin thought it was some kind of *dayri* illness, the thrill in her blood told her otherwise. She blinked the world away, allowing her second sight to settle over her eyes. Kane shone with Dark magic, and there was no question that it was killing him.

"Everybody out," Jayin ordered, allowing the world to filter back in.

"We ain't going nowhere," one of the carrions growled and Jayin rolled her eyes at the ham-fisted show of force. Idiots.

"Fine, but if you get spelled, don't blame me." The carrions tensed, torn between their duty to Kane and their fear of magic.

"It's okay," Kane said, waving them away. Reluctantly, his people filed out of the room. "Don't you try anything funny now, Gulwitch."

"Believe me, there's nothing I could do to make this worse," Jayin said. There probably wasn't anything she could do to make it better either. She wasn't a healer, and this wasn't an illness. Jayin carefully peeled away the psychic barriers that separated her from the energy that saturated the air and clung to people like second skins. She tried to be as gentle as possible as she looked for the source of Kane's deterioration. Her eyes fell closed as the pulse of his aura obscured everything around her.

She only searched for a few seconds before her energy brushed against something lodged behind his heart. Something with its hooks in so deep it would be impossible to remove. Something deadly. Something Dark.

Jayin hissed, retracting her magic and throwing the shields back into place.

"That bad?" Kane asked. Jayin nodded. Whatever had been done to him, it was bristling with intention and energy the likes of which she'd never felt before. She didn't know what he'd done to be cursed like this, but Jayin wanted nothing to do with it.

It was time to leave.

"You have a week," she said, not unkindly. Kane was a monster, but no one deserved what was happening to him. What was *going* to happen to him if he survived the coming hours. By her estimate, he'd lose control of his body in three days and his mind soon thereafter. Unless he could find the *sahir* that had done this and have them undo it, the final days of his life would be excruciating.

"Boss!" A slim, shark-nosed girl burst into the room, her eyes wide and urgent. "There's a raid. The Guard is coming."

Jayin's heart stuttered, panic setting in. Without another word, she shouldered past the girl and out the door, weaving through the throng of scrambling carrions. She'd only taken three steps when rough hands gripped the back of her neck. The carrion shoved her hard, forcing her up against the wall before Jayin could so much as reach for her knives.

Always opportunistic, Jayin thought, wrenching her wrists to the right and feeling the cool slide of bewitched steel as it snapped into place. She slammed her forehead into the carrion's nose. He released her, howling and clutching his face, and Jayin drove her newly gauntleted fist into his stomach.

"Next time"—she advised, grabbing his head and slamming it into her knee—"just run like the rest of them." The boy didn't stir. Jayin bolted, winding her way through the emptying streets. She flicked her wrists and grabbed the knives strapped to her forearms, holding them in her hands as she ran. Jayin wasn't going to be taken unawares again.

She was around the corner, just a few blocks from freedom, when a voice sounded from behind her.

"Jayin Ijaad. How nice to see you again."

"Maerta," Jayin said evenly, making sure her face didn't betray her emotions before she turned around.

The witch smiled. "Hello, sweetling. Somehow I knew I'd find you with blood on your face."

"It's how I keep my skin so fresh and youthful," Jayin said, resisting the urge to wipe the back of her glove against her cheek. She inhaled, shaking off the shock of seeing a Palace *sahir* in the middle of the Gull. "You look rougher than I remember. If I didn't know any better, I'd say you were a local."

It was a lie, but it had the desired effect. Maerta's eyes glittered, and the tiniest hint of a frown pulled her mouth down at the corners. She was the Kingswitch's second, his right hand, born and raised in the Palace. If all the inhabitants of the Gull pooled their money for a month, they still wouldn't be able to afford the tonic she used to keep her mane of chestnut curls in place. Her red satin dress was worth more than all of Jayin's profits since she set up shop.

"Charming as ever," Maerta said, her voice measured. "I'm glad your time away hasn't dulled your wit."

"It hasn't dulled my knives either," Jayin replied, spinning her ring daggers around her thumbs. "Now if you'll excuse me, as much as I would love to catch up, I don't like you."

"Ah yes, your penchant for *dayri* weapons. How quaint. Going back to your apothecary?" Maerta called once Jayin was a few steps away. Jayin froze. "I have to say, I was surprised when you settled in the Gullet. Anyone with your skills could have easily left the city."

"I'm just full of surprises, aren't I?" Jayin said, straining to keep her voice even as her thoughts spun.

She had been so careful; she'd taken every precaution to cover her tracks. But how could she have ever thought she'd be able to evade the Palace? And if they'd known where she was, why hadn't they come for her until now? Jayin thought the Kingswitch would want her back in the fold as soon as possible. Allowing her this little field trip didn't make any sense.

"It's good that you stayed," Maerta said, flicking an invisible speck of dust off of her sleeve. "As it turns out, the King requires the services of the infamous Gulwitch."

Jayin clenched her jaw, her teeth coming together with an audible *snap*. She should have left the city. She should've left the whole blasted kingdom.

"We want you to find Maddix Kell."

CHAPTER THREE:

MADDIX

Maddix was almost to freedom, but he couldn't stop to enjoy it. Not just yet. Not when he was the most hunted man in the kingdom right now.

Information was hard to come by in the Pit, but even from his cell, Maddix knew that the tale of his killing spree had reached every corner of the kingdom. And now, two years after he'd been caught, every lawman in Aestos would be scrambling to collect the bounty on his head. *I'm not going back*, he promised himself. *Death first.*

Death first. Death first. Death first. The words echoed in his mind, beating in time with his heart, and the water dripping off of the damp tunnel ceiling. Maddix let the mantra spur his every step, setting a punishing pace. With every toll of the temple bells, his chance of escaping the city slimmed. He had a three-hour advantage, but even that might not be enough.

Maddix knew every protocol for locking down the city; securing every way in and out of the Pavaal took hours. During his training, he'd participated in countless drills for this very scenario. He remembered scoffing at the idea that the Pit could be breached. It was meant to be impossible. The darkness and isolation drove prisoners mad, and even if they managed to keep their wits, they were still buried underground. There was no way a prisoner could fight their way up dozens of floors to the surface. So Maddix didn't.

He went even deeper. And he hadn't done it alone.

"Home again, home again, what a homecoming Mole shall have," his companion muttered. His voice shivered in the air, echoing against the stone.

For two years, Maddix had only known Mole by the sound of his voice, but in the half-light of the tunnels, he looked like something out of a nightmare. Sallow, off-white skin hung off of his bones, giving the appearance that he was melting. His eyes were black and darting, like a rat's, and the only thing more cracked and yellow than his teeth were his overlong fingernails. The whole effect was made worse by the dim glow of the luminescent crystals that studded the walls, lighting their way. Maddix made an effort not to look at him, afraid that disgust would be written all too clearly on his face.

Despite the man's appearance, Maddix needed him. Mole—Maddix never got his real name—was part of a colony that lived underground, inhabiting the tunnels under the city. His people had been down there for so long that Pavaal had forgotten that they existed. There was freedom in being forgotten, and that freedom had allowed Mole's people to expand within the catacombs as they pleased. The main tunnels were maintained by the city, used for sewage and other waste removal, but hundreds escaped notice, including several that led outside the city walls.

Mole knew which were which. It had taken nearly a year of persuading, but Maddix had finally been able to pry the information out of him. On one condition, of course: Mole wanted his freedom. Maddix's skin crawled to think of what the unnerving little man had done to be thrown into the Pit, and he tried to put it out of his mind. They were bound together, and there was no going back.

Unfortunately, now that they'd reached the safety of the tunnels, Mole would *not shut up*.

Maddix blocked out his jabbering as best he could, trying to focus on the task at hand. One wrong turn and they would never see the light of day. The Undercity was a maze of dead ends and switchbacks. If they lost their way they would wander in the dark until they starved.

Maddix had thought of nothing but escape for two years, but now that he'd done it, fear burrowed under his skin and poisoned his blood. The longer he was free, the more fervently he would be pursued.

Death first.

If he did survive, Maddix knew where he was going. He had been wrong that night two years ago. It hadn't been a demon that'd taken his body from him and forced him to kill those people. Demons weren't real, they were just stories told by people who fell for street magicians' tricks. No Dark being had plucked him out of his own body and turned him into a puppet—it was a witch. The truth was obvious once he stopped and thought about it, and in the Pit, there was nothing to do but think.

At first, the nightmares had damn near driven him insane. Every time Maddix so much as closed his eyes, he saw the swirling Dark of the witch's robes, felt the fiery magic crowd him into the recesses of his own mind. As one year passed into the next, Maddix forced himself to recall that night even in his waking hours. He polished the memories until they shone, and he was certain they were no longer clouded by fear.

Eventually, Maddix recognized the scar on the witch's lip and realized it was the same man who had posed as a Guard. The one who told Maddix he would make rank. It had been a game to him; the bastard *sahir* had mocked Maddix's dream, the dream of a foolish little boy, before he'd ripped Maddix out of his body and singlehandedly destroyed his life.

"You're quiet, boy. Quiet boy, quiet boy," Mole muttered in his slimy voice. Idly, Maddix wondered if all of the tunnel-dwellers spoke in such clipped, unnerving sentences, or if that was particular to Mole. The short man trailed long, crooked fingers over the sickly pale skin on his head. If he'd ever had any hair, it was long gone now, leaving only white fuzz in its place

"Forgive me if I'm not feeling chatty in the middle of an escape," Maddix replied, his hand going to his throat. The Guard had taken the amulet away when they arrested him, and not a day went by that he didn't mourn its loss.

"So untrusting, so tense. Not in the Pit anymore, no? No. Mole will not lead you astray. Trust Mole, yes."

Trust Mole? Maddix barely trusted himself anymore. Two years of being trapped in the dark made sanity hard to come by and faith even harder. Mole didn't seem to take the silence personally and chattered away. Maddix ignored him. He had more important things to think about than the mutterings of a sunlight-deprived madman.

A sunlight-deprived madman who soon began to sing, scraping his nails along the tunnel walls. Maddix wanted to snap at him, but at least Mole wasn't trying to talk to him anymore. Let the weird little man sing; Maddix's thoughts had already left the tunnels behind.

His ambitions stretched beyond Pavaal's borders, all the way to the coast. Maddix had never cared for rumors and stories when he was in the Guard, but in the Pit, they were currency. The only currency. Maddix had paid dearly for a single story, one that woke something within him, something that felt like hope. He'd given everything—not that he had very much when they were all just voices and groping fingers in the dark—for the story of the witchhunters.

They were supposed to have a camp somewhere on the eastern shore, where the ocean faced the witches' homeland.

From what Maddix had learned, they were a small, secret division of people that had taken up against the witch infestation that had plagued the kingdom for so long. Though they were few in number, it was said that they had destroyed dozens of covens throughout Aestos. They had something that took the witches' magic away, some kind of anti-magic weapon. Once stripped of their magic, witches didn't stand a chance.

All Maddix had to do was find them. Which was easier said than done for a fugitive with no way to get to the coast.

He shook his head, pushing his lank hair out of his eyes. It was strange, having to sweep it away in order to see. In the Pit, Maddix had allowed his hair to grow long in order to hide his face from sight. It was a silly, ridiculous thing, but the shred of anonymity helped somehow. And after two years of squinting in the darkness, using his eyes at all was strange. The prisoners who had been there the longest said that they had adjusted to the dark, but Maddix chalked it up to meaningless babble. He hadn't seen the sun in two years and probably wouldn't for a few more days, but even the dim light in the tunnels gave him headaches. Maybe he'd just travel by night and avoid daylight altogether.

So wrapped up with thoughts of finding the witchhunters, it took Maddix several long minutes to realize that they weren't following the path Mole had laid out for them. At first, the slimy little man tried to keep the plans to himself, but Maddix insisted he share the directions, so they could both find their way. Maddix didn't bother hiding his distrust then, and it surged anew as they passed through yet another tunnel he didn't recognize.

As a Guard, Maddix had memorized every street and alley in the city, and during his time in the Pit, he began to do the same with the Undercity. It had taken almost a year, but his map of the catacombs was nearly complete, with a single path leading from the Pit to freedom. Mole was taking them somewhere else, down a path Maddix didn't recognize.

"We're going the wrong way," Maddix said, his voice shockingly loud as it bounced off the stone walls. He winced. Nothing in the Pit was ever louder than a whisper.

"Not wrong way, no, not wrong," Mole said quickly, running his tongue over cracked teeth. "Different, just different. Many cave-ins, tunnels filled with water. Mole has been gone for a long time. We must take a different route."

Suspicion welled in Maddix's chest, but he stayed silent, making sure to keep behind Mole as they walked. He didn't trust the small man, but he didn't have much of a choice if he wanted to get out the tunnels without getting lost or starving to death. He wished he'd been paying more attention to where they were going instead of losing himself in his thoughts. Sometimes it felt like he was just as naïve and idiotic as he had been two years ago.

Maddix kept his eyes trained on Mole as they picked their way over fallen rocks and debris that had been shaken loose from the walls and ceiling.

Perhaps Mole had told the truth about cave-ins.

The thought had barely formed in his head when a shuddering groan split the air. Maddix leaped out of the way, barely avoiding being crushed by a falling slab of stone. He pulled his head close to his chest, barely breathing until the tunnels stilled again.

"Bleeding stars," he swore, coughing and spluttering. Wiping dust out of his mouth, Maddix stood and pulled at the stones that had stacked up, trying to find a way through. "*Skies.*"

Wet blood marked the rocks as Maddix pounded his fists against them. He tried to force the stones away but they wouldn't budge. There was no way back now.

A small, wheezing chuckle rattled out from behind him, and Maddix turned to see Mole smiling. His face looked as if it was splitting in two, revealing dirty, yellowed teeth. They looked sharp enough to tear flesh. Suddenly, the timing of the rockslide didn't seem so incidental.

"What the hell is this?" Maddix demanded, fighting to keep his voice even. He was very aware he'd just been sealed in with a madman without anything he could use to defend himself.

"Stupid boy," Mole said, still smiling that splitting smile. There was a glassy quality to his eyes. "Stupid boy, stupid boy. Freedom for Mole – "

"Freedom *I* gave you," Maddix said, interrupting. It was the wrong thing to do. Mole's eyes slid back into focus, looking Maddix up and down.

"And Mole is very grateful. Boy should be grateful too, grateful, grateful…" His words petered off, and Maddix saw that he'd pulled a long, serrated knife out of his filthy prison uniform. How Mole had managed to hide it was a mystery, and again Maddix cursed himself for being so distracted.

His heart pounded so loud he was sure the tunnel-dweller could hear it, and Maddix tensed, every instinct screaming at him to run. Mole advanced slowly, muttering something about sacrifices and offerings, the knife hanging loosely in his hand. Maddix backed away from him until he felt the press of jagged rock against his spine.

"Grateful," Mole said again and lunged at him with the knife. The world slowed, and Maddix could feel fear thrilling through him like poison, his eyes tracking the knife's movement towards his chest. Ducking to avoid the blade, Maddix dropped his head and slammed his shoulder into Mole's midsection. The little man staggered backward, but he recovered just as quickly, stabbing at him again.

Maddix twisted away, casting around desperately for something to use to defend himself. There wasn't much room in the sealed-off tunnel, and he had barely enough time to breathe before Mole was on him again. The tang of copper and iron mingled with the dust in the air, and Maddix cried out as the knife bit into his skin.

"Falling, bloody *stars*," Maddix swore, gritting his teeth and pressing his palm against the wound. His fingers came away bloody and he rushed Mole again, forgoing defense altogether. "Let *go*, you crazy bastard!" Maddix shouted, managing to shove Mole against the wall.

"Can't go back," Mole screeched, raking his broken nails against Maddix's face. Blood poured into his right eye, and all the wind was knocked out of his lungs as Mole tackled him, knocking them both to the ground. One of Maddix's arms was pinned under him, immobilized under their combined weight. "Can't go back without an offering, can't go back!"

Maddix swore, cursing every star in the sky. His blood-slicked hand caught the knife just inches before it plunged into his chest. Mole's mad eyes were just above him, his rancid breath hitting Maddix square in the face. Somehow Maddix managed to keep the knife away from him long enough to free his arm, and he reached blindly for something—*anything*—he could use to fight back.

His fingers brushed against something rough near the wall, and Maddix yanked it free with all his strength. Blood pounding in his ears, Maddix brought the rock down on Mole's head just as the knife struck true, stabbing clean through his shoulder.

Maddix screamed, and the pain made his vision go dark. He smashed the rock into Mole's skull again and again until long after the little man had stopped moving.

"Stars," Maddix breathed, shoving Mole's body away from him. He scrambled as far away from the body as he could until his back hit the uneven stone of the tunnel wall. His breath came in short, ragged gasps as he took in the ruined mess of a man that had been alive just a moment ago. Mole's head was crushed in, and Maddix could see something grayish oozing out of the crater he'd made with the rock. "*Stars*," he swore again, sliding to the ground and pulling his knees against his chest.

Mole was dead. He was *dead*, and his blood—his *brains*—were all over Maddix's hands.

Maddix didn't know how long he sat there, rocking himself against the tunnel wall, clutching at his throat as if the pendant was still there. As if his star still gave a damn about him.

When the shock finally wore off, all of Maddix's injuries made themselves known at once. His side screamed, and blood wept from half a dozen shallow cuts on his back and arms. Most pressingly, Mole's knife was still in his shoulder, the hilt sticking out sideways like a vestigial limb. It had to come out.

One, Maddix thought. He exhaled, gripping the handle. Pain scraped up and down his spine. *Two. Three.* Sucking in a deep breath, Maddix pulled. The world tilted as the knife dislodged from his shoulder, spilling more blood onto his ragged clothing. He pressed his good hand against the wound, but it wasn't enough to staunch the bleeding.

Cringing, Maddix tore strips from Mole's prison shirt and used them to bandage the wounds. It seemed impossible to think about forging ahead, but he couldn't stay here. He had to keep moving, especially now that there was a body in his wake.

He had to keep going. The dust swirled as fresh air somehow found its way into the tunnel. Maddix inhaled deeply, ignoring his protesting ribs. He clung to the sharp, familiar smell of the dyeing vats and coffeehouses that whispered of home, of freedom. Maddix craned his neck to see a crack in the roof of the tunnel and through it, he could see something winking in the black of the sky—

The stars.

CHAPTER FOUR:

JAYIN

Jayin hated the Pit. It stank of fear and hopelessness, all churning together in the dark. She'd been there before looking for information, though she'd never been there after a convict had escaped, and never with Maerta sniffing disdainfully only a few feet away. The Kingswitch had known better than to partner them on assignments, and Jayin could already feel her patience wearing thin.

This was going to end badly and, most likely, with Jayin's fist becoming acquainted with Maerta's nose. It would be a pity to ruin such a fine dress, but somehow Jayin would suffer through.

"I don't recall it taking you this long before," Maerta commented airily.

Easy for her to say, she wasn't being swamped with every insane thought and suicidal impulse of the monsters being housed here. Jayin gritted her teeth together, trying to focus.

"Maybe your year of living among the rabble has dulled your abilities." She sounded far too pleased at the prospect.

"Or maybe I need to concentrate," Jayin replied, tilting her head up to look the smug witch in the eye. Jayin generally avoided eye contact, but she made an exception for Maerta. The pretty, benign smile was still firmly set in place, but there was an unmistakable flash of panic as Jayin's green eyes met hers.

"The smell of your mistress' perfume is lovely. Does your wife know that you're having an affair? And with a *dayri* too," Jayin said coolly. She raised an eyebrow, looking Maerta up and down. "Really, if you're going to be sneaking around Laurel's back, you might want to do it with someone that doesn't favor floral scents."

Maerta just stared, her lips pursing slightly. Jayin took that to mean she'd won this round.

"Now if you don't mind." Jayin gestured towards the door, and after a minute, Maerta backed out of the cell, leaving the torch behind. Angry, venomous thoughts spilled over her aura like ink, pulsing in time with her heartbeat. Jayin didn't let it bother her. Maerta had always been jealous, especially when it became clear that Jayin had surpassed her as the Kingswitch's favorite.

Jayin shook her head, dismissing thoughts of the Palace. The sooner she found Maddix Kell, the sooner she could disappear, and this time she would vanish so completely they would never find her again. Jayin closed her eyes, pulling down her mental barriers bit by bit and fighting the urge to let them snap back into place. There was no way to focus her perception and no way to streamline it, so filtering through all of the energy in the air sometimes took more strength than she possessed.

Stars, Jayin *hated* the Pit.

The prisoner across the hall hadn't been lucid in thirteen months. His mind was swimming with so much sensory overload it was a miracle the pain hadn't driven him to cave in his own skull. Her head pounded from being so close to him, and she could feel her nerves fraying already. A woman in the cell above was carving up her own skin, her ragged nails clawing deep gouges in the meat of her inner arm. Jayin could taste blood in the back of her mouth, and the skin on her right forearm stung and itched where the woman was pulling her own apart.

"Burning skies," Jayin swore, hanging her head in her hands. She hadn't used her abilities like this since she'd run away. This was a hell of a way to get back in the game. Slowly, she inhaled through her nose, trying to focus. "Breathe," she told herself. "Just breathe." Her voice echoed strangely off the walls.

Jayin turned her attention to the cell's missing occupant and staggered. It was a wonder she had noticed the other prisoners at all. Kell was *everywhere*. His energy clung to every surface, filling the air as if he was standing in the room with her.

And he was scared. He was confused and terrified and *angry*. Furious. Whatever the reason for his escape, Kell wasn't just trying to evade the hangman's noose. He was after something.

"You've got to be kidding me," Jayin muttered, sorting through Kell's residual aura and following his trail into the hall.

"What is it?" Maerta asked.

"How long has this cell been empty?" Jayin demanded, pushing into the tiny space adjacent to Kell's. It was vacant, though it had housed a prisoner just a day ago.

The guard shrugged, looking altogether unconcerned that not one, but two prisoners had escaped. He had the look of a man that spent more time on duty chewing violeaf than watching those under his charge.

"Unbelievable," Jayin growled, snatching the torch from the man's hands and searching the other escapee's cell. There, practically in plain sight, was a hole in the floor easily big enough for two men to fit through. Somehow Kell must have picked the lock on his door and then this one, while his partner worked on the tunnel. And if the smell coming out of the hole was any indication, it led directly to the sewers.

"Do the catacombs run under here?" Jayin snapped at the apathetic guard. True to form, the man only shrugged, and Jayin turned away from him, rubbing her temples.

Jayin had long heard the rumors of whole colonies of people living in the tunnels under Pavaal, but she'd never checked them out. Now it seemed obvious. The Pit was already underground. Kell's accomplice must have known that his cell lay above a sewage pipe, and if the stories about the catacombs were true, there were miles of uncharted tunnels beneath Pavaal. They could already be out of the capitol by now.

"Hold your breath," Jayin said, lowering herself into the hole. There wasn't much by way of a ladder and the smell only got worse as she descended, but Jayin was able to make it all the way to the bottom. "You coming?" Maerta peered down at her, disgust shimmering in her aura. Jayin rolled her eyes.

Of course not.

"Don't get any ideas about making a new life for yourself down there, sweetling," Maerta warned, her pretty features warped in the flickering light from the torch.

"We both know you're more suited to skulking around in the dark," Jayin said coolly, savoring the flash anger that twisted Maerta's mouth into a scowl. "But if I find you a summer home, I'll let you know when I resurface."

Without giving her a chance to answer, Jayin took off down the tunnel. Kell's trail was so easy to follow he could have been leading her himself. His energy took up the majority of her focus, but Jayin was able to sense his accomplice as well.

Something about the second man flourished in the dark. He was slimy as Kell was bright, and his intention wasn't just to escape. He sought violence, keened for it, and suddenly

Jayin knew that she wouldn't like whatever she found at the end of the tunnel.

Time was hard to gauge without the sun guiding her, but it felt like she'd been walking for hours when Jayin found the cave-in. It was recent, within the last day or so, and the trail went straight through. Whatever had happened, it had trapped Kell and his accomplice inside.

"What I wouldn't give for something more than flash," Jayin muttered to herself. Years ago, when it had become clear that she had no physical magic, Jayin learned the use of parlor tricks. Most *dayri* had no idea what real magic looked like, so a few words in the language of the Oldlands and some smoke was enough to fool them. For those not so easily duped, Jayin found that serrated steel was all the magic she needed.

Thankfully, she'd chosen to wear her duster despite the heat of the day. The long overcoat earned her some strange looks in the Gull, but *sahir* were warm-blooded people, prone to chills. It was an old instinct, and one of the few that unified witches these days.

Searching inside one of her coat's many pockets, Jayin pulled out two packets of blast powder and fished around for a light. She used the third packet to fashion a fuse and lit it as far away from the rockslide as she could manage. Jayin turned and bolted, positioning herself well away from the explosion. Still, the shockwave knocked her off of her feet. *Skies*, Jayin thought blearily. *That stuff has kick.*

Jayin peered into the reopened tunnel, shaking off the dizziness and ignoring the ringing in her ears. Miraculously, her torch's flame survived the explosion, casting shadows on the inside of the cavern. The stench was foul, and Jayin didn't need magic to follow the trail to a body. Blood was spattered all over the tunnel walls and floor, originating from two different sources.

Only one was still alive.

Kell's accomplice was small in death, curling in on himself like a child. Half of his head was caved in, blood and brains already congealed on the ground.

Jayin caught her breath, inhaling through her mouth to keep from being overwhelmed by the smell. It took some doing, but she managed to sort through the energy that hung in the air like the stench of the man's corpse. She'd been around plenty of bodies, but this one was different. There was no anger here, no malice, not on the part of the killer. Kell was scared and injured, trying to defend himself. So much of his blood had spilled that it was a miracle he had managed to stay conscious, let alone walk away.

"Where are you going?" Jayin murmured. There was a hole in the roof, no doubt shaken loose by the cave-in. Kell's blood made a clear, obvious path. Jayin breathed deeply, inhaling the fresh air as soon as she was free of the tunnel. She was never going underground again.

If he had any sense at all, Kell was on his way out of the city and Jayin should follow suit. She could find a way to the coast, maybe charter a ship to the Southern Isles. There wasn't any love lost between witches and *dayri* there, but the Southern Council hated the King and Kingswitch more than they distrusted *sahir*.

"Thinking about making a run for it?" Maerta said, appearing by Jayin's side as she brushed sewer muck from her clothes. Jayin twitched, composing herself quickly, and fought the urge to strike out with armored fists.

Maerta wasn't alone. An enormous man loomed slightly behind her, every inch an enforcer and worse, a magical one.

"If I'm being tracked, it's just good manners to tell me," Jayin said. Maerta must have been following her progress aboveground. Probably using the same person that had been keeping tabs on her for the past year. Jayin eyed the enormous man, wondering if she could take out the enforcer before

Maerta tried to stop her. The odds weren't good, Jayin had been on the wrong end of Maerta's magic before. It wasn't an experience she cared to repeat.

"And ruin the surprise?" Maerta asked, raising a delicate eyebrow. "None of your replacements are half as good as you are, but they manage."

"You had to replace me with more than one tracker? That's adorable." And pathetic. They really must have been scrambling once she defected.

Once again, the depth of her naïveté hit her in full force. Jayin should've known they would have people looking for her once she left; she should've known she would be replaced. She never thought they would need more than one person to do her job, but Jayin had also been sure she would be able to slip their net. If there was one thing Jayin was better at than finding people, it was getting lost.

"Kell is headed out of Pavaal."

"Well, then you better get going," Maerta said. Jayin raised an eyebrow. She was allowed out of the city? On her own? "Nel will be accompanying you. For your safety, of course." Maerta gestured to the hulking man by her side.

"Of course," Jayin said, turning her lips up in the parody of a smile. She eyed the enforcer up and down before turning back to Maerta. "I didn't know you needed such extreme security."

"The Kingswitch has concerns about my safety," she said, sniffing imperiously. Maerta fancied herself undervalued and moaned about it constantly. "And despite my recommendation, his protection still extends to you."

"Touching," Jayin sighed, pinching the bridge of her nose. Maerta clearly wasn't going to make this easy, and after slogging through the tunnels for the better part of the day, Jayin was exhausted. "Well, if we're going to find the most wanted man in the kingdom, we'd best get started. Come on, muscles."

Jayin wanted to follow Kell a little further tonight, but there was no way she was bringing Maerta's enormous lapdog back to her apartment. The Palace might already know where she lived, but if anyone from the gangs saw her come back with someone who was so obviously working for the King, there would be nothing to come back to. The carrions would burn the whole place to the ground on principle.

"Stay in contact," Maerta said as Jayin and her new friend turned to go. "Wouldn't want you to get lost again." Jayin bit her lip, fighting the urge to say something she might regret. It was best that Maerta thought she was playing this little game.

"So what's your story?" Jayin asked Nel when they finally stopped to rest. "Sit down, muscles, you're making me nervous," she said, falling into a chair in the crowded dining hall of the Fire and Feathers Inn. Nel glared at her for a moment before following suit. The chair groaned under his weight.

"You're not *dayri*, that's for damn sure," Jayin tried again once a serving girl had taken their order. The food was good here, much better quality than anything Jayin could get her hands on in the Gull. The only thing she missed about the Palace was the food. She still had dreams about Cook Heida's spiced plums. Jayin didn't know what it was about non-witches that made them averse to spices, but *dayri* cuisine was staggeringly bland.

"I'm guessing that you're some kind of kinetic," Jayin said around a mouthful of warm bread. "But if you don't want to tell me, I could always find out on my own. Who knows what kind of secrets you've got hiding up there in that tiny brain of yours."

It was an empty threat. Jayin had no interest in Nel or his secrets, but he didn't know that.

"Kinetic, like you said," Nel rumbled. The thought of her prying into his thoughts was enough to get him talking. Jayin paused, waiting for him to fill the silence. Kinetics couldn't create energy or manipulate elements like elementals; they just used what was already there. On bad days, Jayin would trade everything she had for their more manageable abilities. "Energy absorption and redistribution."

A fancy way of saying that he was very good at punching things.

"Enlightening," Jayin said, and Nel fiddled with his spoon. Clearly, he didn't want to give her any more information. Jayin didn't push, changing the subject. "So what did you do wrong?" she asked.

"What?"

"To get stuck with Maerta. I don't know if you've noticed, but she's horrible."

Nel almost smiled. "She's not that bad."

"You keep telling yourself that," Jain said, raising her eyebrows. There was a reason why Jayin had shouldered the isolation of the Gull so well. Maerta was the Kingswitch's favorite before Jayin arrived, and she did not adapt well to being second-best. The Palace was supposed to be Jayin's home, the *sahir* her family, but Maerta made sure that everyone knew that Jayin was nothing but an upstart, a mongrel from the slums.

Jayin forced thoughts of Marta out of her head. She didn't want to lose her appetite, and this could be her last decent meal for the foreseeable future.

As soon as her plate was empty, she stretched her arms over her head, yawning. "I'm going to bed. Thanks for the sparkling conversation, muscles."

Nel stood quicker than Jayin would have thought possible. Idly, she wondered if she'd be able to loop her arms around his thick neck. Strangulation wasn't her style but it never hurt to have options.

"I'm coming with you."

"Look, I get it. You don't trust me. And considering that you work for Maerta, I don't trust you either. But I'm not going anywhere." Nel glowered, unimpressed. Jayin rolled her eyes, fishing in her coat pocket. "Here," she said, pressing a lock of black hair into his enormous hand. "If you don't believe me, give this to someone with *real* magic and they'll be able to find me."

Nel's scowl deepened. It was a sore spot. Kinetics were widely regarded as the lowest rung on the magical ladder, brutish and only good as battle fodder, though Aestos hadn't seen a proper fight in decades. No one wanted to go to war with a kingdom that fought with magic instead of steel.

"You keep hair in your pocket?" Nel asked.

"It never hurts to be prepared," Jayin said with a wink and smile. "Goodnight, Muscles." She turned away from him, climbing the narrow stairs to her tiny rented room.

As soon as she had locked the door securely behind her, Jayin turned to the window, where a familiar face was pressed against the glass.

"Hiya Jay!" Ravi said, waving cheerfully as if he wasn't precariously perched on a third-story window. He had been following Jayin since she'd gone to meet Kane, something that might have earned him a stern lecture or a boxed ear on any other day, but not today. Today, she needed him. If there was something Ravi excelled at, it was tailing a mark. "Who's the big guy?" he asked as he swung into the room.

"Someone I need to get rid of," Jayin said. Ravi frowned, his dark eyes clouding over with worry.

"You in some kind of trouble?" he asked, teeth worrying at his lip. Jayin felt an unexpected pang of affection at his concern.

"Nothing I can't handle with a little help from my favorite pickpocket," Jayin said.

Ravi nodded seriously as Jayin laid out her plan, which was less of a plan and more of a harebrained gamble, but she was short on time. She'd had to give Nel something so he would let her go upstairs alone, but unfortunately, that something could actually be used to track her. She didn't need that lumbering idiot as well as a team in Ayrie Palace on the lookout, which meant Ravi had to steal it back. Easier said than done, but Jayin knew he was more than capable.

Still, if anything happened to him, she'd kill Nel herself. Her arms might not be long enough to strangle him, but a knife in the gut would do just fine. Jayin forced the thought away; Ravi would be fine. He could handle himself.

The trick to running game was not to rush. Jayin waited ten minutes before shrouding herself in a glamor. She reentered the common room in her disguise and spied Nel playing dice with some men at the corner table. Ravi was nowhere to be seen, which Jayin took as a good sign. She held her breath as she moved towards the door, certain that Nel would spot her at any moment, but he never looked up from the table. The cardsharps cheating him out of his money should thank her for leaving them with such an easy mark.

Jayin didn't drop her glamor until she was well away from the inn. It wasn't much by way of magic, but it made it easy to slip through the darkened streets without attracting attention.

"Stars," Ravi said when Jayin released the magic at their rendezvous point. "Never seen you do that before," he said, grinning. "Appear outta nowhere. I didn't even hear you coming."

"That's the idea," Jayin replied.

"I'll look after the shop for you," Ravi said. His smile dropped, replaced by a look too serious to be on such a young face. "Make sure none of the carrions mess with your stuff."

"You'd better," Jayin said, swallowing the lump in her throat. She wondered when she would see him again. *If* she would see him again. Somehow, Ravi had fit himself into her life, and all at once, Jayin realized that she would miss him.

"Here," Ravi said, unslinging the pack off of his shoulders and handing it to her. "I don't know where you're going, but…" He trailed off, shrugging. Holding the backpack in one hand, Jayin swept Ravi into a tight, bone-crushing hug. Her skin tingled and burned where it came in contact with his, but she forced herself not to flinch as his energy threw itself against her shields.

"You take care of yourself, okay?" Jayin said, letting him go and bending down so that they were eye-to-eye. She didn't have to lean that far. Even at thirteen, he was nearly as tall as she was. "Don't get mixed up in the gangs. And if they give you any trouble, make sure they know you're under my protection."

Ravi nodded, sniffling a little. He swiped at his eyes and turned his face away so she couldn't see the tears crowding on his lower lashes.

"You're comin' back, right?"

"Sooner than you think," Jayin said, feeling her stomach twist a little. Maybe she would be back, but there was no way to be sure. Maerta would have people looking for her, and Jayin would have to put measures into play to make sure the Kingswitch wouldn't cause Ravi any trouble. He was a smart kid, but there was no one in Aestos that matched the Kingswitch's ruthlessness.

"Watch the skies," Jayin said, invoking the old Pavaalian saying. It was a blessing, a prayer for protection.

"Catch the stars," Ravi replied, and then he was gone, as quickly and completely as if by magic. Jayin didn't watch him go. She was determined to make it to the city's borders by nightfall. With any luck, Nel wouldn't notice her absence until sunrise, and then he would be off on a merry chase, courtesy of Ravi.

Jayin didn't waste any time. Maerta's temper was legendary and, worse, the Kingswitch would be furious. Jayin shuddered to think of provoking his ire—again.

She'd known the risks of defecting. No one had ever dared to leave the court once they'd been chosen. There was no precedent, no one's footsteps to follow. Jayin had no idea what would happen if she was ever caught, but she wasn't going to stick around long enough to find out.

The streets were quiet in the merchant ring, and the few people Jayin passed walked by without so much as a glance in her direction. Her glamor was the same as before, encouraging eyes to slide over her as if she wasn't there. She walked through the night, and just as the sun peeked over the horizon, Jayin found another ramshackle inn to hole up in until nightfall. Finally allowing the glamor to drop, Jayin fell onto the narrow bed and was asleep within seconds.

CHAPTER FIVE:

MADDIX

Maddix was moving.

Wheels turned beneath him. Every dip and divot in the road rattled his bones and further aggravated his injuries. Slowly, Maddix sat, using the side of the cart to pull himself upright. The wound on his side throbbed painfully, and his shoulder had begun to burn.

"You're awake," Maddix's companion, a mustachioed man named Kenna, said cheerfully. He and his family—his wife Duli and twin daughters, Je and Indra—were traveling to a pilgrimage site on the coast; the place where the first star was said to have fallen from the sky. According to the story, it was what led the original Aestosi to their land.

Thankfully, the pilgrims had no problem picking up a wounded man off the side of the road and providing him with transport out of the city. When Kenna and his family came upon him, Maddix claimed to be a shopkeeper run afoul of the carrion gangs, and like good holy folk, they offered him a lift beyond the walls.

The Guards hardly spared Maddix a second look when Kenna rode up to the gate in his covered wagon. Most everyone in the country swore by the sky and stars, but once the witches had come from their cursed homeland, the number of those who actually still worshiped the deities in the Above began to dwindle. No one even knew the names of the old gods anymore, if they ever had names. Now, pilgrims were met with rolled eyes and sideways glances.

"Good morning," Maddix managed. He had patched himself up well enough that he didn't bleed to death in the street, but the wounds still hurt like burning heaven. His side wasn't infected, not yet at least, but his shoulder had stopped bleeding and begun to ooze yellow pus. The infection hadn't spread yet, but Maddix wasn't confident his luck would hold. His star had stopped shining for him two long years ago.

"We'll be stopping soon to restock on supplies and get something to eat," Kenna informed him. Maddix nodded, fighting to keep the panic off of his face. He had no idea if the Guard was looking for him outside of Pavaal, but there was no doubt his picture had been widely distributed.

Then again, Maddix and the boy on his wanted posters could've been strangers. His eyes were sunken, his skin sallow from two years underground. His cheekbones jutted out sharply, redrawing the planes of his face in harsh, unfamiliar lines. The one thing that remained was his overlong red-blonde hair.

Stars, he used to be so proud of it. Maddix felt a pang of disgust at the shallow idiot he had been. He used to keep his hair just over regulation length and treated it with all kinds of tonics. He spent hours getting the style just right and made a habit of running his hands through it when he knew girls were watching. Now it was so long and tangled that Maddix simply tied it back and was done with it.

They had been on the road for days, and no one had recognized him, but Maddix still couldn't breathe easy. He kept an eye out for anyone lurking on the roads, anyone who looked at them for too long or seemed suspicious. The longer he evaded capture, the higher the bounty would be. Maddix didn't want to think about what would happen if anyone saw him now. He was in no position to defend himself with a gaping chunk of his side missing and only one good arm. He could hardly walk, let alone fight off a bounty hunter.

Thankfully, none of the other shoppers looked twice as their odd little group shuffled around the market. Even so, Maddix made sure to keep his distance. His sickly pale complexion and oddly-colored hair were in stark contrast to Kenna and his family, whose dark skin and matching eyes spoke of the southernmost region of Aestos. It would be strange for them to be traveling together, pilgrims or not.

If he was spotted, Maddix didn't want Kenna's family getting caught in the crossfire. The girls were only eight and had seen even less of the world than he had. They were sweet and friendly, despite the stranger in their midst. Maddix supposed their religious upbringing lent itself to friendliness and limited fear of any injured passerby they might pick up off the side of the road. Je collected polished stones wherever they stopped and gave the prettiest ones to Maddix. Indra was quiet, happy to stand by her sister's side and simply watch, but she braided Maddix's hair when he stayed still enough to let her. They were good kids.

Maddix kept the four of them in his sight as he browsed textile stalls and the other assorted goods for sale. Part of him wondered if he shouldn't simply steal their horse and be done with it, but he doubted he would get far on horseback with his wounds still unhealed. As much as he itched to run, his best hope was to sit tight and part ways with the family when they'd made it to the coast. He would find his own way from there.

They almost made it. A nondescript man approached Kenna as he paid for the supplies, and Maddix's heart clenched, recognizing the stance of a lawman immediately. Sucking in a panicked breath, Maddix ducked his head, snatching a cap off of a garment stand and pulling it over his hair.

He needed to go. He needed to go *now*. There was no telling if the man was a Guard, local law enforcement, or a bounty hunter, but if there was one of them, surely more would follow.

"Maddix Kell."

Maddix froze at the sound of his own name. He didn't turn to see who had spoken, grabbing the closest thing he could find and hurling it behind him. He didn't get far before rough hands grasped the collar of his coat, and he was shoved up against a wall. Maddix bit his lip to keep from crying out as his injured shoulder was pulled behind his back. Blood trickled onto his tongue.

"Stop drawing attention to yourself," said a low voice, spinning Maddix so he could face his attacker. Maddix blinked, seeing Kenna's face inches from his own. Gone was the smiling, fatherly pilgrim. He'd been replaced with a steely-eyed stranger.

"Bleeding skies," Maddix swore, his voice choked under Kenna's muscular forearm. "You've known the whole time, haven't you?"

Slowly, Kenna nodded. Anger burned under Maddix's skin. How could he be so stupid? He had thought himself so clever, running game on starry-eyed sky worshippers, but Kenna must have been seeking him out. Were those people even his family, or simply props for the ruse?

"What's the play then?" Maddix demanded, trying to keep his voice from trembling. He failed, but only just. "Are you going to hand me over to the man back there? Ransom me to the king?" Maddix had no idea what his bounty was, but he would guess that it would keep whoever caught him rolling in coin for some time.

"Shut up and quit feeling sorry for yourself," Kenna snapped. "I'm not taking you back to Pavaal." He dragged his free hand down his face, looking more beleaguered than threatening. "Curse it all, I'm not authorized for this."

"For *what*?" Maddix hissed. Kenna fixed him with a cool, even stare. Whatever moral dilemma he wrestled with, it was decided now.

"You've been looking for us. I was tasked with getting you out of the capitol in one piece." Maddix's heart stuttered in his chest. He couldn't possibly mean—

Something that felt dangerously like hope shifted inside of him, and Maddix squashed it before it could take hold. Half of the Pit knew how desperate he had been to get information about the witchhunters. The Guard could have easily shared the information with anyone looking for him.

"Prove it," Maddix growled.

Kenna rolled his eyes, slowly bringing his free hand up to tug at his collar. Maddix had never questioned why he buttoned his shirt up so high, but now he could see that it was to hide an enormous tattoo that marked Kenna's skin in white ink. Maddix's eyes followed the swirling design, something strange blooming in his gut. He had seen anti-magic sigils before, but nothing this intricate. It wasn't simply meant for protection; it was a call to battle.

"You're one of them," Maddix breathed. Kenna nodded, slowly withdrawing his arm before a crash shattered the quiet.

"Time to go," Kenna said, breaking into a sprint. Maddix followed without hesitation. His wounds screamed as a weight crashed into him from behind, and he wheezed as the air was driven from his lungs. Something tore in his injured shoulder as he threw up his hands to defend himself.

For a moment, the nondescript soldier was Mole, trying to bash his skull in as a sacrifice to the others who lived in the Undercity. For a moment, the sky above him disappeared, replaced by a stone ceiling Maddix had been sure would be the top of his tomb. Hands closed around his throat and despite his desperate attempts to escape, Maddix couldn't buck off his attacker.

Then the man's weight disappeared, and the market returned. Maddix rolled onto his uninjured side, gasping and spluttering like a fish.

"Get up," Kenna shouted, hauling Maddix to his feet. He grunted with every step, but his movements were so driven by fear and adrenaline that he was able to shove the pain away.

The wagon was already moving by the time they reached it, with Duli and the twins inside. Kenna leaped aboard first and Maddix could barely keep up.

"Maddie!" Indra said in a rare burst of verbosity. Maddix grabbed her hand, managing to swing into the cart. "We've got you, Maddie."

"Duck," Je said, holding something thin and cylindrical in her hands. With practiced aim, she lobbed it over the side of the cart. It bounced twice on the ground and exploded in a plume of smoke and dust. The cloud was so thick it was almost a tangible thing, obscuring their escape from any pursuers.

"You're witchhunters?" Maddix managed, looking back between the two sisters. "All of you?" They seemed awfully young to be handling any kind of explosives, especially with such ease.

"Top of our class," Je said.

"That's enough," Kenna said sharply.

He needn't have worried. Maddix could hardly hear anything besides his own heartbeat hammering against his eardrums. Gently, he pressed his hand to his side. His fingers came away crimson and tacky. He couldn't feel his left arm anymore.

Maddix watched the blood drip slowly from his fingertips to his palm with a kind of detached interest. He must have ripped his messy, homemade stitches, but there was no pain.

There should have been pain. Je and Indra gave him identical, wide-eyed stares, and for a split second, Maddix could swear that there was only one of them in the cart with him. Then the vision faded, and he could see their lips forming his name.

Words spilled all around him, not making it to his ears. He was a stone that split a stream, removed from the voices around him. The world pulsed in time with his heart, slowing with every labored beat. Everything seemed to fade, going quiet and still, and very slowly Maddix closed his eyes and let himself go too.

CHAPTER SIX:

JAYIN

Maddix Kell was dying.

Jayin woke with a start, her mind scrubbed clean save for that single thought. It took a moment before she recognized the bare room of the seedy inn she'd checked into at dawn. Travelling by day was too dangerous, and her glamors required less magic in the dark.

Then the pain set in. Jayin's breath escaped with a hiss, her fingers flying to her throat as her lungs constricted. She couldn't breathe, and her vision immediately began to blur. Her side was a pulsing mess of agony, and she was certain her heart wouldn't be able to take the strain. It felt like she was being skewered through the ribs with a hot poker and her right arm had gone completely numb.

She barely had the presence of mind to try to block out the onslaught when the pain stopped as quickly as it had started. For what felt like ages, she could do nothing more than gasp in as many choked breaths as possible. Her wits returned slowly, and a single thought fixed itself in her mind:

Maddix Kell was dying.

Jayin had long since put her shields back up—she'd even built a few more for good measure—and her path had deviated from Kell's days ago. There was no way she could have still been able to sense him.

And yet here she was, startled awake in the middle of the day by his pain. Unconsciously, Jayin followed the echoes of Kell's energy, tracing his aura outside of her own body before yanking the magic back.

"Don't be stupid," she said aloud. Her voice sounded echoey and strange in the drafty room. She had been on the run for almost three days, trying to get as far away from Pavaal as possible without calling attention to herself. Using her powers now would be like sending up a beacon for anyone watching.

Besides, she had no idea if she would even be able to track that far. She had no touchpoint, no place to start, and Jayin was almost afraid she *would* find him if she bothered to look. She had never come across someone with an aura as strong as Kell's, but even so, she couldn't bear to feel him die—to feel herself dying along with him.

Jayin tossed in the rickety, narrow bed, trying to shove him out of her mind. Kell was a monster, a murderer. Jayin had heard all the stories, and she had been part of the team looking for him before he just dropped out of the sky covered in the blood of his victims. But as she tried to fall back to sleep, all she could think of was his fear and desperation from back in the tunnels. Jayin had hunted plenty of murderers, and Kell simply did not compare.

Then again, she was out of practice. Throwing up another shield just in case, Jayin closed her eyes and forced all thoughts of him from her head. All but one: Maddix Kell was dying, and the tiniest part of her was sorry.

CHAPTER SEVEN:

MADDIX

He couldn't see. For a single, terrifying moment, Maddix was sure he was back in the Pit, but his eyes soon adjusted to the light creeping in from under the door. He wasn't underground, thank the stars. Which begged the question as to where he actually *was*. The last thing Maddix could remember was passing out on Kenna's cart.

Gingerly, Maddix pressed his good hand to his ribs, wincing as pain lanced up and down his side. Someone had cleaned and bandaged the wound, but it still felt like his ribs splintered anew every time he moved. His right arm was bound in a sling, and from what he could tell, the infection had been cut out.

He was halfway through propping himself up on the pillows when a door opened and light flooded into the room. Maddix groaned, throwing his unbound arm up to shield his eyes.

"You," a voice said, not unkindly, "should not be awake yet."

Maddix opened his eyes a crack, wincing when the man turned towards him, but not from the pain. His hand went to his throat before he remembered that his amulet was long gone.

"Sorry, I'm not very pretty to look at." The man's mouth quirked into a small smile. Well, half of it did. The rest only twitched, held down by raised, off-color scar tissue that twisted almost all of his face. Only his left eye and half of his mouth were spared. Maddix didn't move, unsure whether or not he should look away. It didn't look like any other burn he'd ever seen; twisted and writhing in such a way that it looked like the mangled corpse of something that had died on his face.

"Where am I?" Maddix rasped, his voice rough from disuse.

"I'm afraid I can't tell you that," the man said. "But you're somewhere safe."

Maddix didn't know if he believed that. "You're lucky to be alive."

"I feel real lucky," Maddix said, groaning as the wound on his side twinged again. He wasn't going to be running, or even walking, anytime soon. He could barely move without feeling like his sternum was cracking in half.

"You are," the scarred man assured him. "A few more hours and no medic in Aestos would've been able to save you."

They were still in Aestos then. Maddix filed that small bit of information away for later.

"I'm Paxton, by the way." Maddix didn't offer his name, but Paxton didn't seem bothered. "Kenna will be thrilled that you're awake."

"Kenna's here?"

"Yes," Paxton said.

Maddix's mind spun. Kenna was here. Kenna the witchhunter, with his family of witchhunters, who'd been sent to get him out of the Pavaal.

"Good, you're awake."

Maddix's head snapped towards Kenna's voice, moving far too quickly, and he winced. The world spun, and it took a moment to reorient himself.

"Not that there was any doubt. Paxton is our best medic."

"Well, I've found patients heal pretty fast when they get a load of my ugly mug," Paxton said, raising a shoulder and then dropping it. He made an effort to sound blasé, but Maddix could hear a stab of pain in Paxton's voice. "*Cruinniú maith,* Kenna-*láttéow.*"

"*Cruinniú maith,* Paxton-*hælend,*" Kenna replied, inclining his head. Maddix's gaze traveled between the two of them, watching the exchange. Maddix had a basic grasp of the languages spoken in Pavaal, but he'd never heard anything like that. It was a strange combination of elongated vowels and sharp consonants.

Paxton turned to go, leaving Maddix alone with Kenna. The medic raised his hand as if to douse the torch, and Maddix's heart stuttered in his chest.

"Leave it lit," he said, too quickly. He wasn't going into the dark again, not if he could help it. "Please." Paxton nodded and left the fire burning behind him.

"I know you have questions," Kenna said once Paxton's footsteps had faded.

"How did you know where to find me? How did you even know who I was? What—"

Kenna held up a hand, cutting him off. Maddix's mouth snapped closed, but the questions built up on his tongue, piling up one on top of the other. "I'm sorry, but I can't give you those answers. I don't rank nearly high enough. But you're safe here, and soon everything will be clear."

"How soon?" Maddix asked. He should be grateful—he *was* grateful—but the secrecy was beginning to grate on him. Being naïve had destroyed his life once before, and he'd be damned if he let it happen ever again. "Can you at least tell me where I am?"

"You're in our stronghold," Kenna said.

"I made it," Maddix breathed. He could hardly believe it. The thought of finally making it to the witchhunters had sustained him for so long, and a part of him had feared he would never get there.

"You made it," Kenna agreed.

HEALING WAS SLOW going. His wounds were messy and deep, made worse by the shoddy patch job he'd done back in Pavaal, but he was getting stronger. It was a miracle that his shoulder was healing at all. His range of motion was limited, but at least he'd finally graduated from the sling. His side had scabbed and was well on its way to scarring over.

He was confined to the medic's wing, but Maddix was allowed to take walks on his own through the halls. His record was an hour out of bed at a time, but that had been pushing it.

And still, he had no answers. Maddix was trying to be patient, but he'd never been good at sitting still and waiting around. It was something that might have made him an excellent Guard.

Finally, after nearly a fortnight of bedrest, Maddix decided to take matters into his own hands. He wasn't a prisoner, and the guards only patrolled this wing at the beginning and end of the night shift. He had plenty of time.

Leaning heavily on the cane Paxton had provided, Maddix hobbled into the hallway. The lamps were lit, and he took care not to venture too far into the shadows. It took time, but eventually he made it out of the medical wing. He had no idea where he was going, but if no one was going to tell him what was going on, he would find out on his own.

"You should not be out of bed," a voice said from behind him. Maddix had to steel himself from flinching and pulling his wounds open again. Paxton would be furious if Maddix ruined all his hard work.

Maddix turned to see a man dressed all in white in the half-light of the dim hallway.

"My name is Hale. I've been eager to meet you, Maddix Kell."

Maddix eyed the man warily. He was very polite, but Maddix knew better than most what could hide beneath a genteel exterior.

"Generally," the man—Hale—said, unfazed by Maddix's silence, "when someone introduces themselves, it's an invitation to start a conversation."

Maddix hesitated a moment more before speaking. "You know my name, and now I know yours. We have nothing else to talk about." It wasn't true, but two years of prison-bred wariness didn't disappear overnight.

To his surprise, Hale laughed. It didn't reach the pale blue of his eyes. "True, very true. But if you insist on being out of bed, how would you fancy a stroll?"

Slowly, Maddix nodded. He was already trespassing and Hale had made no moves to turn him in. The man walked slowly, allowing Maddix to keep pace as they wound through the identical halls. With every step, more questions stacked up, each clamoring to be asked, to be *answered*. Maddix was almost surprised at how quickly his old curiosity reasserted itself; he would've thought it starved to death in the dark.

"Seems like everyone here knows my story," Maddix said, finally breaking the silence. He had the sense that Hale wouldn't speak again until he did. "But I don't know yours."

"We keep our ears to the ground, listening for anything that the demons might be responsible for," Hale said, pleased. "A Guard going on a killing spree and claiming possession? That got our attention."

But not your help, Maddix thought.

"We've been looking for the witch responsible since word reached us, to no avail. When we heard of your escape, Kenna and his family were our closest hunters. They were sent to bring you to us."

Hale didn't say anything else as they walked through the halls. Maddix tried to memorize the route, noting each twist and turn. He wanted to be able to get out of the compound if need be. One of the doors opened, not to another hallway but the open sky.

"I thought you might need some fresh air, considering everything you've been through," Hale explained.

"You've got no idea what I've been through," Maddix snapped, but his anger evaporated as he walked out onto the balcony. Before him, luminous in the moonlight, lay the sea. Maddix had dreamed of the ocean all of his life. Even as a greenblood Guard he'd imagined one day visiting the shore, maybe settling down in a port town once he grew tired of heroism. For a moment, Maddix stared, mesmerized by the light as it sparkled off the shifting water and turned whitecaps bright silver.

"We were sending hunters for you, you know," Hale said finally, cutting into Maddix's thoughts. Maddix blinked, turning to look at him, this blonde stranger. In the moonlight, Maddix could see an off-white scar carving a line from his temple to the back of his skull. Everyone here had scars, it seemed. He would fit right in. "It took us time, but we verified your story, and once we'd done that, we had hunters sent to the capitol to pull you out."

Maddix had no idea what to say to that. In the Pit, he quickly learned to give up any dreams of rescue or pardon. Those who held out hope for salvation lost their minds even faster than the rest.

"You're going to help me?" Maddix asked. It felt too much like asking for permission, but he couldn't bring himself to care.

"We're going to help you," Hale agreed without hesitation. "Everyone here has been affected by the witch plague in their own way, and each has found a home with us. Some stay for shelter, others to join our army."

"I want to join you," Maddix said without waiting for Hale to ask the question. "I want to fight."

"Then you shall," Hale replied. He sounded pleased, even proud. "You're going to heal and train, and when you're ready, you're going to get justice."

CHAPTER EIGHT:

JAYIN

If Jayin ever saw Maerta again—and it was starting to seem like it would be very soon—she was going to spin a glamor around her so tight the courtier would never find her way back to reality. Let Maerta see how tough she was when the walls started melting around her. It would surely be the last thing Jayin ever did, but she was starting to think it would be worth it.

She had no idea how the Palace had managed it so quickly, but somehow her picture and description had been distributed to every port on the coast. Jayin had almost been caught twice, with and without glamors, and after four days of continuous travel even small magic was hard to maintain.

She was running out of places to hide.

"Stars, help me," Jayin cursed, knocking on the door of a falling-down house that looked like every other on this block. She forwent a glamor altogether, flipping her hood over her hair and hoping it would conceal her face.

The door opened a crack and she barely got out a "Hello, Om," before it was slammed in her face again.

"Om!" Jayin shouted, pounding on the flimsy wood, and very aware that she was making a scene. "Omhinar Sank—" Jayin only made it through half of his—frankly, ridiculous—name before Om opened the door and pulled her inside.

"By Sestia and Horaj, *what* are you doing here?"

"Still swearing by the named gods I see," Jayin said. Om glowered and the candles flickered, sending shadows dancing on the walls.

"What do you want, *sahir*?" Om demanded. Jayin rolled her eyes.

"And still denying your nature. Good to know that some things don't change."

Though he towered over her, Om flinched visibly as Jayin's eyes raked him up and down. He had filled out since she last saw him but there was still something of the shifty-eyed teenager she knew from years before.

"You're just as wrong about me now as you were then," Om said. The venom in his voice didn't keep it from shaking. Jayin bit her lip, guilt weighing her down. She never expected to see him again, especially not with the entire kingdom searching for her. It wasn't fair, but she was out of options.

Jayin had still been training under the Kingswitch when Om showed up at the Palace almost three years ago, seeking sanctuary. Witches weren't trusted by the *dayri* in Aestos, but they were valued. They kept Aestos from being dragged into the war between Vandel and Kaddah—they kept the whole bloody kingdom safe.

Witches born outside of their borders didn't live very long. Om had lasted longer than most. Jayin was only fifteen when he showed up at Ayrie Palace, begging for shelter. He was alone, thin and smudgy, and smoke floated around him like an aura. Om denied being *sahir* until he was blue in the face, but he also had a nasty tendency to set things—curtains, table, and people if they were too close—on fire when he got backed into a corner.

Jayin shuddered to think of what might have happened to his parents, though there were really just two possible answers: one, his witch mother—magic descended from the maternal line—had been killed back in Kaddah, leaving him alone and unprotected; or two, he'd burned them alive. She never asked.

Om had refused the traditional tests to determine his particular type of magic, but the Kingswitch still agreed to shelter him from the Kaddahn queen. He was with them for almost a month, and after several small fires, one of which involved a very angry baker in the kitchens, it was assumed that Om was a Fire Mage.

One of the legends said that Mages were the first kind of *sahir*, and split the known elements between them, one for every corner of the world. Their descendants were few and far between, and they made for valuable allies. Jayin had never met a Mage before. Elementals, their less powerful cousins, were some of the most common witches around, but their powers were just in manipulation. Om and others like him could create their element out of nothing.

The Kingswitch assured Om he would be safe in the Palace, and that they would protect him against any repercussions from his homeland. But then something spooked him, and Om ran despite the Kingswitch's assurances. Jayin was still in training, but she was called on to find him.

And she had.

"Don't. Please." She could remember the way his voice had shaken, just like it was shaking now. Jayin had been eager, running ahead of the team and cornering Om on her own. He looked impossibly young then, ashy hair falling over terrified gray eyes as he tried to find an escape. "Please don't let him."

"Who?" Jayin asked.

"Your king. He's going to send me back to Kaddah. He's—he's going to let them kill me," Om said. In that instant, he was just a boy, alone and terrified.

"The King promised you sanctuary," Jayin said reasonably. She had no reason to doubt what she'd been told. The whole court knew a Fire Mage was among them—he'd been there for weeks. There had been uproar when he disappeared. The King and Kingswitch had been furious. Jayin assumed that it was because they hated to see a good witch go to waste. Not to mention that without control of his magic, Om was a threat to witches and *dayri* alike. There was nothing to suggest that the King would hand him back over to the Kaddahn to be killed and stars knew what else.

"They're going to kill me!" Om shouted.

His hair had burst into flame and he surged towards her, stopping only when Jayin brought a knife to his throat. Heat licked at the back of her hand, but Jayin didn't dare pull the blade away. Most witches didn't rely on *dayri* weapons, trusting their powers to protect them, but energy and glamors didn't do her much good against a physical attack. Jayin learned early on to carry a knife and know how to use it.

"They'll kill me like they kill all of them. If your king sends me back there, they'll take me apart piece by piece while I'm still awake. They'll carve me up until I'm just a pile of meat on a slab."

Om had sucked in a ragged breath, his voice breaking. The fire was doused from his hair, and he stood before her, shaking and smoking. She could see tiny beads of blood where his bobbing Adam's apple had come in contact with her knife.

"*Please.*"

There had been something then, something in his face that made Jayin withdraw her weapon.

"Hold out your hand," Jayin said. Om looked at her, his gaze heavy with suspicion, but after a few tense seconds, he extended his hand. Jayin reached for him, steeling herself for the barrage of energy she was inviting.

There was a beat, and then Om's aura flared out, shimmering and red-hot. It took every bit of her concentration to keep it from overwhelming her. Jayin wasn't nearly as experienced with her powers back then, less able to ferret out secrets, but she could see he wasn't lying. There wasn't a trace of deception anywhere within him, just fear so great it was tangible. It had settled under his heart like a stone and it was killing him as sure as any blade. Breaking the contact, Jayin stepped away from him and turned back the way she'd come without another word.

Just like that, she let him go. For the others and the Kingswitch, Jayin pretended that she'd lost the trail. They had no reason not to believe her; she was young, and it was her first hunt. Her act of mercy set her back months of training, and overnight she became the laughingstock of the Palace. The Kingswitch's favorite failing on her first mission made for juicy gossip.

Sometimes she regretted letting Om escape, but then Jayin remembered the truth in his words and the terror in his eyes, and she bore the punishment and humiliation.

That was the first time she'd defied her mandate as one of the King's chosen *sahir*, the first crack in the foundation of her loyalty. It was not the last.

Jayin shook her head slightly, banishing the memory in time to see something flash in the gray of Om's eyes. Jayin didn't stop him as he shoved her against the wall of the tiny house, one hand wrapped around her throat. Jayin's head hit the rotting wood with a *crack*, and spots crowded her vision. The moment her head stopped spinning, Om's energy flooded in, his touch flattening her shields. Her vision tinted red, and Jayin felt her heart pick up in response to his fear.

"What do you want, witch?" Om demanded. He peered at her through the thick curtain of his hair. "I'm not going back to Kaddah, or your liar king's Palace." His hand began to heat up, still crushing her throat, and Jayin hissed.

"Are you done?" Jayin gasped when Om let up enough to allow her to speak. "Because if I were here to take you back, I wouldn't have knocked on the front door." She grimaced. "Besides, the Palace and I aren't exactly friendly anymore. If you let me go, I can prove it."

Om didn't look altogether convinced, but he took a step back, releasing her.

Jayin sucked in a lungful of air, coughing and glaring her displeasure, but she couldn't fault his reaction. She'd let him go once before, but as far as Om knew, Jayin was still loyal to the Palace and the Kingswitch.

Once she was certain she wouldn't pass out, Jayin raised her right arm so he could see the Kingswitch's mark. What was left of it. The flesh of her wrist was raised and puckered, two shades lighter than the soft brown of her skin. Once, a swirling black mark had signified to all who cared to look that Jayin was the property of Ayrie Palace. Once, she had been proud to be so.

"Apparently," Jayin said, seeing the horror flickering across Om's face, "when the Kingswitch marks one of his pets, he doesn't want it to come off."

She'd tried for weeks to remove the striking tattoo, going to *sahir* and *dayri* alike to no avail. Finally, she'd taken matters into her own hands and drawn a heated fire poker over her skin until burned flesh and twisting scars obscured the Kingswitch's mark. The memory of the pain still made her weak in the knees.

"You left?" Om said, not taking his eyes off of the scar. "Why?"

"Creative differences," Jayin said. "As you know, Ayrie doesn't take rejection well. I'm trying to get out of the kingdom, but every bounty hunter and sailor knows my face."

It took a moment, but Om's eyes went wide with understanding. "You're the one they're looking for?" he asked, open-mouthed and gaping. Jayin shrugged. "The Gulwitch?"

"I always thought that name was a little much."

"How true are the stories?"

"I don't know the latest rumors, but if you've heard that I'm seven feet tall and have thralls of street urchins to do my bidding, I'm sorry to disappoint."

"They're saying you killed people."

"Are they now?" Jayin asked coolly, trying to ignore the flash of rage sizzling under her skin. "I've always wondered what it would feel like to be a murderer. Turns out, it's not that different from being a rogue witch."

"This isn't funny, *sahir*," Om snapped. "At best, you're wanted for deserting. At worst, you'll be executed for murder."

"Well we do make a smart pair, don't we?" Jayin fired back. "A murderer and a runaway Fire Mage."

"*Don't* call me that," Om snarled. The tips of his hair smoked, and she saw that familiar fear in his eyes. He was still the same scared boy she'd walked away from three years ago.

"Look, I—" Jayin said, her anger disappearing all at once, replaced by bone-deep exhaustion. She pressed her fingers against the bruises blooming on her neck. She would have to wear her collar high for a few days. "I'm sorry. I'm sorry I came here and put you in danger again, but I've got nowhere else to go."

"What did you do to make them hunt you down like this?" Om asked.

"I left," she said. "Once you belong to them, it's supposed to be forever, and they're not going to stop until I'm theirs again." For the hundredth time since Maerta's reappearance in her life, Jayin cursed her foolishness for thinking that she could hide in plain sight.

"I'm just trying to get out of Aestos," she said finally. He was her last option. She had nowhere else to go if he sent her away.

"You know what happens to witches in Kaddah," Om said quietly. She did, but he knew better than anyone. "You can't go there."

"I'm good at disappearing," Jayin replied. "It doesn't matter where I go. East, west, to the Isles, or even the colonies. Anywhere is safer than here."

Om didn't speak for a long while and Jayin was sure that he would tell her to get out.

"I work on the docks," Om said, finally filling the silence. Jayin couldn't help but raise an eyebrow at that. Of course, he would spend his days surrounded by water. "I can poke around, see if any ships are leaving soon and won't ask questions, but it'll take a couple of days." He sighed as if resigning himself to something. "You can stay here until then. There isn't much room but—"

"Thank you," Jayin said, cutting him off.

Om shrugged. "I owe you. For before. This makes us even."

CHAPTER NINE:

JAYIN

Jayin slept on the small couch that took up half of Om's tiny living space. He tried to insist that she take the bedroom, but Jayin just waved him off. The instant she sat down on his threadbare couch, she fell asleep in seconds. She woke once in the afternoon to find a thin blanket wrapped around her shoulders. Without so much as sweeping the area for danger, Jayin pulled it up to her neck and fell back asleep.

The sun's first rays were creeping through the windows when footsteps shook her out of sleep a second time. Jayin's heart pounded, alert in an instant. Trying to move as soundlessly as possible, Jayin twisted her wrists and felt the bewitched steel slide into place as she reached for the knife in her boot. Om had insisted that she disarm herself before he allowed her to stay. It was an unrealistic request that Jayin had no problem ignoring.

She inhaled once and burst into motion, throwing herself over the back of the couch. She let her momentum carry her forward where brute strength would not and managed to pin the intruder. Jayin brought her knife up, pricking the hollow of the man's throat and throwing on a glamor to make her seem taller, stronger, fiercer. The Gulwitch's infamous tattoos appeared, dark and dangerous against her skin.

"*What are you—?*" a voice demanded in Kaddahn before switching back to Aestosi. "Stop!"

Jayin blinked, recognizing Om's face above hers. She dispelled the glamor and stepped back, slipping the curved blade into her sleeve.

"I thought I told you no weapons in the house. Where did you even hide that?" Om demanded. Blood pearled on his collarbone. He rubbed his chest where Jayin had pressed him into the wall with her gauntleted hand.

"Can't blame a girl for being prepared," Jayin said.

"Can I blame you for almost taking my head off of my shoulders? And *why* are you wearing armored gloves?"

"They're the latest fashion in Pavaal," Jayin said, rolling her eyes. "Don't be dramatic. Next time don't sneak up on me."

"Don't sneak—" Om parroted. "It's *my house.*"

"And I'm the tiny defenseless witch girl with the might of Ayrie Palace bearing down on her," Jayin replied, stretching her arms above her head. Om glared.

"Defenseless my maiden aunt," he muttered to himself, stalking out of the room into the tiny kitchen. "If your attempt on my life made you hungry, I made breakfast."

Jayin smiled, trailing after him. She helped herself to the food on the stove, savoring a warm meal after weeks of stolen hardtack and half-cooked rations. It wasn't half bad either; world class compared to the slop she'd been eating in the Gull.

"Is there *marjan* in this?" Jayin asked, tasting the familiar spice on her tongue. The same one Ravi had sniffed weeks ago.

"You Aestosi know how to cook, I'll give you that," Om said. Jayin bit her lip to hide her smile, electing not to tell him that *marjan* came from the Oldlands.

Om raised an eyebrow when Jayin stood to get a third portion, but she ignored him. Maybe in his attempts to convince himself he wasn't a witch, Om hadn't noticed how much energy it took to do magic, but she wasn't going to miss an opportunity to eat her fill.

"There's a ship leaving for the Isles in the next couple of days," Om said finally, setting his plate aside. "The captain is *sahir* like you, so it shouldn't be too hard to get you onboard."

Sahir *like us*, Jayin thought, though she didn't say the words aloud.

"You could come with me, you know," she said instead. Om's head snapped up, and he stared at her, unblinking. Jayin felt her cheeks warm at the naked surprise on his face.

"There's no stigma against witches in the Isles. You'd be safer than you are here," she went on, fighting through the discomfort. "You wouldn't have to be afraid of your abilities, or anyone hurting you because of them. I could try to help you control it."

"I don't *want* to control it," Om snarled, all blankness replaced by anger in an instant. "I want it gone, and I want you and your *sahir* lies out of my life."

He stood, shoving himself away from the table and storming out of the house. Only the faint smell of smoke lingered.

Jayin stayed frozen for a long time after he left, cursing herself for her stupidity. She didn't know what she expected. Om had spent the last three years of his life hiding from both the authorities and the power inside of him; of course he'd be angry at her offer. Asking for help controlling his magic meant admitting that it was a part of him. It was always easier to hate something from the outside.

The knowledge did nothing to ease her disappointment. It was selfish to even ask, but the rejection still stung like a slap. She had been on her own for so long, isolated from her people and her culture. Despite Om's insistence he was *dayri*, being with him had been a balm to an ache she'd barely noticed until it vanished.

This is what you wanted, said a small, insidious voice inside of her. *You left of your own free will; you decided to turn your back on your people. If you miss it so much, why don't you let them find you?*

Jayin shook her head as if she could rattle the thoughts away, shoving that voice into the furthest reaches of her mind. She wasn't going back there, not ever, loneliness be damned.

Part of her expected Om to throw her out for her impertinence, but he kept his word, securing her passage on a *sahir* captain's vessel. Jayin barely saw him in the four days leading up to the ship's departure. He left the house before she woke up, and during the few occasions they happened to be in the same room, he wouldn't speak a word to her. Jayin didn't hold it against him. It wasn't fair, reappearing in his life and asking him to uproot everything he'd built here.

For her part, there wasn't much preparation to do. Her belongings fit easily into the pack Ravi had given her, including some meager rations in case the journey went longer than expected.

In one of the few instances where they spoke after her disastrous offer, Om told her the ship would stop at one more Aestosi port before heading to the Isles. Jayin didn't think it would be much of a problem. She could keep her head down while the ship docked, then she would be free. Jayin had no doubt she would be looking over her shoulder for the rest of her life, but it would be a life. It would be *her* life.

On the day of departure, Jayin rose with the sun, not bothering to wake Om. She folded the thin blanket on the couch, and didn't bother looking back as she closed the door behind her.

The captain, a tall sun-bronzed woman, was overseeing the cargo being loaded onto her ship when Jayin arrived on the docks.

"So you're my mystery passenger," the captain said, sizing Jayin up. Unglamored, Jayin didn't cut much of an impressive figure. She looked more like a carrion than anything else with the patchwork of scars crossing over her skin. It didn't help that the captain towered over her by a large margin. "Name's Sinta, and this is my baby, *Stormwind*."

Jayin raised an eyebrow as Sinta patted the mainmast.

"Bold name, considering that a storm could mean death at sea," Jayin said. Sailors were notoriously superstitious, and naming a ship after a squall seemed like tempting fate. Sinta grinned, the corners of her eyes crinkling.

"I'm an elemental," she explained. "Stormwitch. While I'm at the helm, we'll have nothing but clear skies and powerful headwinds." Sinta paused, a wicked gleam in her eye. "Unless I get bored, a'course. Come! Let me show you to your quarters."

To her surprise, Jayin was led to a cabin belowdecks. She'd expected a hammock in the hold with the other cargo, if that.

Sinta laughed, seeing the confusion on Jayin's face. "Nothing but the finest lodgings for the Gulwitch."

Jayin's head snapped up. Om had told the captain Jayin was a low-tier witch seeking passage to the Isles. If the captain knew the truth—

"Don't look so struck," Sinta said, tossing the long braid of her gold hair over her shoulder. "I make it a point to know who my passengers are."

Jayin's fingers twitched, gathering up magic around her.

"Peace. You've got nothing to fear from me."

"Prove it," Jayin said, stretching out her hand. She wasn't willing to lower her shields in a harbor filled with people, so she would suffer through physical contact. Just this once. Sinta raised an eyebrow but pressed three fingers to Jayin's palm anyway. It only took a cursory search to see that the captain was telling the truth, and Jayin pulled away before all of Sinta's secrets could come tumbling out.

"You are spectacular, aren't you?" Sinta murmured, flexing her hand. "Satisfied?"

"Satisfied."

"Good. Now if you'll excuse me, I've another passenger to greet. I think you two know one another."

Another passenger?

Jayin followed Sinta after a beat of silence. A familiar figure was climbing aboard the gangplank as Jayin reemerged on the deck. A figure with long, ashy hair and steel-gray eyes.

"Om?" Jayin said before she could stop herself. Om's eyes flashed to hers and a rueful smile touched his lips.

"Hi," he said, rubbing the back of his neck uncomfortably. "If it's not too late, I thought I would take you up on your offer. Being a dockworker isn't much of a life."

"Are you sure?" Jayin asked softly.

"Well, considering he's already paid his way, I'd say it's a little late for a change a' heart," Sinta cut in. She frowned, leaning close to Om and sniffing his coat. "Try not to burn down my ship, aye firebrand?"

"She likes to know who her passengers are," Jayin said conspiratorially as Om blinked, surprise flickering across his face. The ship hadn't set sail yet, but he looked a little seasick.

"So serious!" Sinta said, clapping Om on the shoulder. "You're not the first passenger I've had with a penchant for fire, and you won't be the last. One of my own crew is a firewitch," she said, pointing to a burly man doing something complicated with a coil of rope. Om watched the enormous sailor, looking interested in spite of himself. "Now, I suggest you two stow your belongings. We're setting sail soon."

CHAPTER TEN:

JAYIN

Being aboard the *Stormwind* was unlike anything Jayin had ever experienced. She'd traveled all over Aestos in search of runaways and criminals, but she'd never made it to the ocean. The Kingswitch usually sent mercenaries and bounty hunters if a convict made it beyond Aestos' borders. Jayin used to think he valued their safety in kingdoms less friendly to *sahir*, but she knew better. The Kingswitch didn't want his pets escaping.

Now, Jayin wished she'd gotten her sea legs before running for her life. After having solid ground under her feet for eighteen years, the constant rocking of the ship was playing havoc with her stomach.

Om, for his part, took to the open ocean almost immediately. Jayin shouldn't have been surprised considering his work on the docks, but it was still odd to see a Fire Mage striding the upper deck of the ship like he'd been born on board. Jayin was not so adaptable. During the first few days of the journey, she only ventured outside the stuffy walls of her cabin to throw up over the side of the ship.

"What are you supposed to be?" one of the sailors asked the first night Jayin wandered abovedecks. The open air was biting and cold against her flushed skin. She'd already vomited her meager supper into the sea and nausea still roiled in her stomach. It wasn't doing much for her temperament.

Jayin didn't look at the man, casting her eyes to the heavens. She hoped he'd get the hint and leave her alone. She didn't need an audience when she was sick—again.

"You don' look much like a rogue witch," the sailor tried again.

"What's a rogue witch supposed to look like, *dayri*?" Jayin spit. She didn't need her powers to know there wasn't a drop of magical blood in him.

"We were expecting someone, you know. Someone more." The man's eyes raked her up and down. "Not a slip of a girl who can't keep her food down."

Jayin knew she should ignore him. She should just go back to her cabin and pray to the stars that tomorrow she might be able to eat a meal without losing it to the rolling of the *Stormwind.*

Instead, she turned to face the man head-on. Jayin was used to being underestimated—it had been an asset more than once—but it still grated on her nerves. And with bile burning in her throat, she wasn't in the mood to suffer insults at the hands of a sailor who wouldn't know a shadowitch from a kinetic.

"Sorry to disappoint," Jayin said shortly.

"Don't provoke her, Zed," Sinta said, coming up behind them. Jayin didn't react, but Zed snapped to attention. "There's more to her than meets the eye."

Jayin fixed Sinta with a cool, even stare, disliking the captain's willingness to hint at her identity. There were some things Jayin preferred to keep to herself. She didn't know if tales of the Gulwitch had reached Southport, but Jayin wasn't willing to take the chance.

She wasn't willing to let the sailor's insolence go unanswered either.

Jayin paused and gathered her magic, weaving it carefully, making sure to get the details right. When she was finished, there were two captains standing on the deck. The real Sinta crossed her arms, looking amused, while Zed's mouth dropped open. Jayin suppressed a laugh, mimicking Sinta's pose down to the enigmatic smile. Sinta grinned and Jayin matched it, following the other woman's movements.

"It's like looking in a mirror," she said, raising her hand and dropping it. Jayin followed suit.

"I think I make a more convincing you than you do," Jayin replied.

"Bleedin' skies," Zed gaped. "How are you doin' that?"

Jayin turned, still wearing her captain's disguise, and sized the man up.

"How are you doin' that?" she repeated, glamoring her voice to match his. Zed blinked, suddenly staring himself in the eye. Jayin laughed as his mouth dropped open and let the glamor slip away, but by then she'd attracted the attention of the crew. They shouted out suggestions and Jayin slipped in and out of glamors to uproarious applause.

Eventually, the sailors dispersed at Sinta's orders, going back to their posts. All except for Zed, who lingered a moment longer.

"Try climbing up to the crow's nest," the sailor suggested. "It might help wit' the seasickness." He ambled away after that, leaving Jayin alone on the deck. Jayin had no idea how climbing to the highest point of the ship would help, but without the distraction of magic, her stomach was roiling once more.

Slowly, Jayin pulled herself into the rigging and began to climb. The wind bit at her with icy teeth, and by the time she reached the crow's nest, Jayin was convinced Zed was trying to punish her.

This high up, the rocking of the ship was magnified tenfold, and the tiny wooden platform pitched so violently Jayin was sure she was going to be thrown into the sea. She clutched the mainmast with trembling hands and closed her eyes to keep from looking down. Heights had never been much of a problem, but this was something new altogether. It was terrifying, it was nauseating, it was—

Quiet.

Jayin could hardly feel the energy of the crew up here, and at such a height, her magic soared farther than ever before. Jayin inhaled through her nose, a small, incredulous smile spreading on her face. She'd never known the world could be so gentle after living in crowded, aura-choked Pavaal for so many years. Emboldened, she stepped away from the mast and threw her arms wide, embracing the wind as it lashed around her.

She lost track of the time spent in the crow's nest, but when her feet finally hit the deck again, they were steady. Compared to the crow's nest, the ship was blessedly solid, and Jayin found she could roam freely without her stomach heaving. Reveling in her newfound freedom, Jayin walked every inch of the ship, exploring everything, and when she finally found Zed, she thanked him for the advice.

"Guess we both learned something new today," the man said with a wink. Jayin decided she liked him.

Once she didn't spend every waking moment in her cabin, Jayin quickly won her place amongst the crew. The journey to Aestos' southernmost port took a little over a week, and Jayin was eager to make up for the time she'd lost hiding below deck. She bounced between crewmembers, picking up whatever skills they had to teach her. Tying knots, unsnagging sails, taking watch shifts, Jayin tried her hand at it all. But she quickly found her favorite place to be was up in the rigging.

There was something intoxicating about being up so high, the wind whipping color into her cheeks and teasing her dark hair into a mad tangle. With nothing but the sky above and sea below, Jayin breathed easy. There was nothing to be afraid of, no one who wanted anything from her, no noisy auras screaming for her attention. More often than not, Jayin woke up in the crows' nest instead of her tiny wooden cabin. She'd slept under dozens of different roofs in her life—from twisting, glittering gold arches to leaky slats that barely kept out the elements—but Jayin preferred the stars.

At night, after the day crew had eaten, they entertained themselves with stories, demonstrations of magic, or competitions. Jayin was often called upon to glamor herself into members of the crew. The other firewitch, Massimo, created brilliant displays of brightly colored flame. Some of the *dayri* played instruments or showed off their sleight of hand. One night, one of them offered to teach Jayin how to protect herself.

"I've got it covered, thanks," Jayin said, not bothering to move from her perch atop three stacked barrels. She had snagged the blankets from her cabin and dragged them onto the deck to make a nest. The men teased her, calling her a little bird, but Jayin didn't mind.

The sailor, an enormous, muscle-bound man named Quintin, raised his bushy eyebrows. "Your tricks and disguises won't do you any good in a fair fight," he insisted.

Jayin snickered. "Good thing I don't fight fair then. And I can take care of myself." Stars only knew she'd been doing it for years.

"I wouldn't push it," Om advised from his place at the back of the crowd. Jayin turned her head, a small, startled smile quirking her lips. Om almost smiled back. It was good to see him on the deck with the other sailors; for most of the journey, Om had kept to himself. The only time Jayin saw him was when he was with Massimo, quietly learning how to control his magic.

"Prove it," Quintin challenged. Jayin shrugged, rising from her perch. "I'll even lend you a blade."

"I don't need it," Jayin said, very aware of the fact that they had the attention of the entire crew. She kept perfectly still as the sailor unsheathed the sword at his hip. Moonlight glinted off of the massive blade. Quintin swung it in an enormous arc, hard enough that the sword whistled as it split the air. Jayin didn't flinch, but a burst of doubt blossomed in her chest. Quintin was huge, towering over her by at least a foot, and probably outweighed her by a hundred pounds.

Well done, Ijaad. Way to keep your head down. For someone who was meant to be lying low, she was spectacularly bad at walking away from a fight. Jayin chalked it up to her time with the carrions.

"Come on then," Jayin said, watching Quintin swing the sword again. He advanced, hesitant. Then, with a roar, he drew the weapon over his head. Jayin waited until the very last moment before raising her hand. A *clang* echoed across the deck as Quintin's sword sparked off of her magicked gauntlet. By the time he regained his balance, Jayin was armed, two ring daggers spinning around her thumbs.

"Cheap tricks and pretty daggers ain't much use against a sword," Quintin said, slashing at her. Jayin blocked the tip of his blade with the hook of one knife and forced it away with the other before falling into a roll. She used the momentum to slip past Quintin's guard and sprang up, stabbing at his side. The tip of her knife sliced through his tunic, barely nicking the skin.

"First blood to Jayin," Sinta announced.

"Big heavy sword isn't much good against pretty daggers," Jayin said, throwing one of her knives in the air and catching it again.

To her surprise, Quintin laughed, deep and full-bodied. All of the tension drained away, and Jayin grinned as the sailor charged at her again. She'd already proven herself, now the fight was just for fun. They danced across the deck, trading blows and blocking them in equal measure. Quintin's reach and strength far outmatched Jayin's own, but she could dart halfway across the deck before he took a single step.

Finally, Quintin forced Jayin against the railing and she leaped onto the edge as he slashed at her. She reached for her third dagger—a straightblade, not curved like the others—and threw it with all her strength, a final bid at gaining the upper hand. Cursing, Quintin ducked, only to lose his footing and hit the deck with an almighty crash.

"The match goes to Jayin!" Sinta announced and the crew roared. Jayin whooped, but her moment of victory was short-lived. The *Stormwind* pitched forward and she slipped, tipping over the railing.

"Jayin!" Om shouted. His hand shot out, and he grabbed hold of her sleeve before gravity could claim her. "I got you," Om said, pulling her back to the safety of the ship. Her legs gave out the moment her feet hit the deck, and she collapsed into a pile of shaking limbs. Jayin exhaled, leaning her head back against the banister.

"Well fought!" Quintin shouted, extending a hand and hauling Jayin to her feet. "How many of those do you have on you?" He handed the straightblade back to her and she pocketed it with trembling hands.

"You will never know," Jayin said breathlessly, her heart still pounding. "I need to keep an edge somehow."

"How about you keep your edge without throwing yourself overboard," Om muttered.

Jayin grinned at him, her fear giving way to euphoria. There was something about a good fight that made everything else disappear. All the energies, the auras, the noise, it all vanished into the background as her focus narrowed on the next move, the next strike.

"I second that," Sinta said. "Enough entertainment for the night." She clapped her hands and the crew dispersed, a few stopping to congratulate Jayin on her way back to their posts.

"You're mad," Om said. Something almost like silence settled over the ship as the sailors went about their duties in the lantern-lit darkness. "I mean, I knew it when you let me go, but now I'm certain."

"So defecting from Ayrie, living in the slums for a year, and crawling to your doorstep, none of that tipped you off?"

"No, it was you almost pitching yourself into the sea to win a fake sword fight that did it," Om said.

"That felt pretty real to me," Jayin replied.

Om rolled his eyes but he was smiling. "How many knives *do* you have on you?" he asked, his voice lighter than she'd ever heard it. Jayin pulled down her sleeves to reveal twin sheathes strapped to her forearms, each one holding a curved dagger.

"But what about—" Om started before Jayin raised a hand to shush him. She lifted the hem of her shirt to reveal three more stashed in her belt, along with the parrying knife in her right boot and two more blades hidden in her overcoat.

"That is excessive."

"A girl's got to be able to defend herself," Jayin said, shrugging. Om chuckled. "How's it been working with Massimo?" she asked, taking a brave stab at a dangerous topic and hoping he wouldn't snap at her like before.

Om didn't answer for several long seconds before he stretched out his arm. A fireball bloomed in his palm, casting flickering shadows over his face. It moved and danced across his skin like a living thing before Om closed his fist, extinguishing the flame.

"I have to use his flint," Om said. "But he's helping."

"It's beautiful," Jayin said softly. "You see that, right?"

"I'm starting to," Om said, his light eyes on her. His eyebrows furrowed, and he looked away, suddenly fascinated with his fingernails. Jayin didn't need magic to know what he would ask next. Part of her wanted to encourage the curiosity, but Jayin had hidden her powers for so long that talking about them made her twitchy.

"This is what I look like."

Om's eyes snapped to her as she answered his unspoken question. I'm sorry," he said quickly. "I thought—"

"Glamors take energy," Jayin explained. "I could keep a full disguise on for a day or two, but it would burn me out."

Jayin tapped her wrist, the skin shimmering before her scar reappeared. Of all of the marks that crisscrossed her skin, it was the only one she hid from sight. Sinta might have known Jayin was the Gulwitch, but none of the sailors could know she was a Palace *sahir*.

"I can maintain small ones for as long as I need. Can't have the crew knowing I'm one of Ayrie's pet witches."

"Used to be," Om corrected gently. Jayin didn't bother disagreeing with him. She couldn't tell him that there were still mornings where she woke up and was surprised not to find herself in Ayrie. Worse, in that moment between sleeping and waking, sometimes she even missed it.

"Aren't you going to ask how I found you?" she asked.

"I think I've exhausted my credit of rude questions for one evening," Om replied. He was giving her an out. She should be grateful.

"I can sense energy," Jayin said instead. Om raised his heavy eyebrows but didn't stop her. "Auras, signatures, the soul, whatever you want to call it. Once I know someone's energy I can follow it, and that's how I found you." It felt strange, telling him this. She half expected him to shout at her again.

"What's it like? Your magic?" Om asked, his curiosity getting the better of him.

"Loud," Jayin replied. "Painful." Before she could control it, it was as if every person for miles was screaming at the top of their lungs. She knew where they were, what they were doing, their thoughts, feelings, secrets—everything. There had been so much it all blurred together into a haze of pain. It was agony she wouldn't wish on anyone.

That was how the Kingswitch found her. Many young witches were discovered before their powers emerged and they were taken to the Academy, so they could learn to control their abilities. Some, like Jayin, were found after their magic manifested. Most were helped to undo any damage their powers might have caused before going to the Academy. After the healers helped ease the pain, Jayin was brought directly to the Palace to begin her magical education.

Stars, she'd thought herself so lucky, so blessed. The Kingswitch never recruited so young, usually selecting exceptional graduates to join him at Ayrie. Jayin was the first to be plucked off of the streets and brought to the Palace.

"I'm sorry," Om said finally.

"It's not your fault," she replied. "Besides, it doesn't hurt anymore." Unless she accidentally touched someone, then all hell broke loose. Jayin still hadn't managed to build a shield that could withstand physical contact.

"But it does hurt? Every time you use your abilities?"

"Not anymore," Jayin said. Lie. "I've got shields up to keep everything from getting too overwhelming."

"Shields?"

"Psychic barriers," Jayin explained. "They help with the noise."

As she spoke, it occurred to her once again how little she knew about her own magic. She spent years in the Palace experimenting, trying to find the boundaries, and Jayin had finally thought she knew the extent of her powers until Maddix Kell shattered every assumption she'd ever made. She hadn't sensed him since that night when she was sure he was dying, but there was some part of her that kept tabs. Somehow, she knew he'd pulled through.

Jayin blushed, realizing how invasive her abilities sounded. She ran her fingers through the thick mane of her hair, trying to work through the tangles and failing.

"No wonder you ran away," Om said finally. Jayin was startled a little, quickly composing herself so the surprise didn't show on her face. "I mean, they wanted you to use your magic for them. They wanted you to hurt yourself."

He was trying to make her feel better, but Jayin felt a weight settle in her stomach, and for the first time in days she felt seasick.

"Right," Jayin said, looking away from him. She wished it were that simple. If *only* it were that simple. "What are you going to do once we reach the Isles?" It was an obvious change of subject, but Om didn't seem to mind.

"I don't know," he said, but he didn't sound altogether worried about the prospect of not knowing. "I'll probably find some other firewitch who can help me control my powers. Maybe stay with Massimo for a while. He's a decent teacher and doesn't ask a lot of questions."

Two very important qualities, the latter even more so. Even in the Isles, someone with Om's abilities could be in danger.

"What about you? What are the Gulwitch's grand plans?"

"I think I might ask Sinta if I can stay on the crew," Jayin admitted, voicing the tiny thought she'd been turning over and over in her mind since she'd won the battle against the rocking of the *Stormwind*.

"You know you'd actually have to work," Om teased. "Not just play around in the rigging."

"Did you just make a joke?" Jayin asked, knocking her shoulder into his midsection.

"It has been known to happen," Om replied. "I think this life would suit you. You fit here, and it's quiet."

Jayin gave a small smile, touched he would think of that. Of her comfort, as if it was something that mattered.

"Not necessarily," Jayin said, the smile growing. She pointed at Zed, who was unsnagging the mainsail. "That man has one of the loudest auras I've ever heard."

He had nothing on Maddix Kell, but Zed had brushed against Jayin on the first day of their journey and his energy had buzzed along the outskirts of her consciousness ever since. Her shields managed to keep out his thoughts for the most part, but she could still sense him hovering on the edges of her second sight.

"Really?" Om said, his eyes lighting up. Jayin nodded, prodding at Zed's energy. It didn't take much for his secrets to come tumbling out of his head. Jayin stopped herself before she found anything too damning, but it still felt like an invasion, and a wave of guilt crashed over her.

"I—" she started, before she snapped her mouth closed again. "I shouldn't have done that." Jayin ducked her head.

Stars, she really was stupid. She was so excited to be with another *sahir*, so eager to show off that she'd gone and sifted through someone's mind. It was everything she'd sworn not to do, and she had done it without a moment of hesitation.

"Jayin," Om said, but she stepped away, trying to put some distance between them. It felt like his aura was expanding, surrounding her. Heat seared her lungs, making it hard to breathe. Burning, *bloody* skies, this was why she was better off alone. "Jayin." Om reached out, his hand brushing her wrist, and Jayin's world exploded into shades of red.

The contact only lasted a moment before she ripped her arm away, but she wasn't fast enough. Om's thoughts burned through her shields before she could stop them. His fear was still trapped behind his heart, freezing him from the inside out, but more recently there was something warm. Hope. Hope that was directly linked to her, which was so wrong that Jayin felt her stomach turn.

"Don't touch me."

"I'm sorry," Om said, taking a step away from her. "I shouldn't have—I'm sorry."

"What's going on in your head is your business," Jayin said, her voice clipped and cold.

"I'm sorry," Om said again. "I didn't know."

Neither had she, for a long time. There was no one with magic like hers, not anywhere. The Kingswitch had searched all of Aestos for a witch whose abilities resembled hers, but there was no one to be found. From the moment her magic manifested, Jayin was destined to be alone.

"Did I hurt you?" Om asked, snapping Jayin out of the swirling mess of her thoughts.

"No," Jayin said quickly. Something flared in Om's eyes and his mouth pressed into a thin line.

"You're lying."

Jayin shook her head. "We're heading to port tomorrow," she said. "We should get some sleep while we can." She walked away from him without another word, the answer to his question echoing in her mind:

It always hurts.

CHAPTER ELEVEN:

MADDIX

Maddix scrambled to his feet before charging back into the sparring ring. Metallic *clangs* shivered in the air as his blade met his opponent's, his shoulder barely twinging as the force of the blow vibrated down his arm.

He'd put on weight since his arrival at the witchhunter stronghold. His wounds had healed up nicely, thanks to Paxton's tireless work and constant insistence Maddix stay in bed. Which he never did, but his side hurt less and less as the days went on, offering only minor complaints. His shoulder was another matter entirely, but after a month, Maddix couldn't stand to be trapped in the medic's wing a moment longer. With Hale's blessing, Maddix threw himself headfirst into training.

Paxton nearly had a fit when he heard, but Maddix was eager to begin. That eagerness soon resulted in bruises and sore muscles, but it didn't deter him. These people were warriors, every one of them. Even those who hadn't earned their marks bore scars from one skirmish or another. Many were refugees like him, hurt by witches in the past. They came to the compound looking for shelter and to learn how to defend themselves.

Everyone in this place had their own horror story to tell, and though Maddix's infamy was well known in the capitol, with the witchhunters, he was just another recruit. Hale promised Maddix's identity would be safe for as long as he was with them. Sometimes he thought he heard his name whispered in the halls, but the murmurs dissipated the moment he turned the corner. He ignored the prickling on the back of his neck, chalking it up to two years of paranoia.

He was part of something again, something bigger than himself. Something important. Maddix couldn't remember the last time he had been given anything without something demanded in return, but at the compound he was fed, clothed, and given a warm bed to sleep in. He was protected.

So he worked hard. He trained until he could barely hold a sword before falling into bed each night, exhausted, and doing it all again the next day. Hale promised he would have their support when he went after the witch who ruined his life, and then it was up to him whether or not he would stay.

For his part, Maddix had already made up his mind. Once the witch was dead and burned, Maddix would stay with the hunters and join their ranks. He would help make a safer world, one cleansed of the *sahir* and their poisonous influence.

And he was learning more than just how to fight. The witchhunters had a language all their own, one they claimed was pure Aestosi. Kenna said when the witches came from their Oldlands, they brought their savage language with them. The original witchhunters were descendants of a race of native Aestosi who'd sworn themselves to the protection of the kingdom. They called themselves *helwyr*, the hunters. They had their own words for witches too: *Valyach*. It meant demons, bastards, invaders; every insult or slur ever used against the witches all rolled into one. They weren't just lazy and pampered, gifted with luxury because of their magic; they were monsters in human skin, cursing the Three Kingdoms with every day they drew breath.

Valyach. Maddix committed the word to memory and vowed to use it.

Any time not spent sleeping or training was devoted to studying the hundreds upon hundreds of books the *helwyr* had collected over the decades. The volumes detailed a history that had been hidden from view for centuries: battles waged in secret to keep past Kingswitches out of power, uprising and insurgencies, and attempted coups, all of which eventually led to their retreat to the outskirts of the kingdom. But the hunters never gave up the mandate of their forefathers, pledging to keep protecting the people of Aestos from the *valyach.*

When Maddix asked why they hadn't allied themselves with the rebel groups that sought to overthrow the Kingswitch, Hale only scoffed, his white-blue eyes flashing with contempt.

"The rebels only seek to topple a corrupt ruler pulling the King's strings. They think the *valyach* should be allowed to remain in Aestos. We do not."

In the ring, another *clang* rang out, and Maddix staggered backwards before readjusting his grip on his sword.

"Come on, keep your guard up," said Maddix's opponent, a woman named Misha. She was one of a continuous rotation of sparring partners, each with a different style or skill to teach. Misha favored twin blades, longer and more sharply curved than any Maddix had ever seen. What she lacked in brute strength she made up ten times over in speed, and the dual blades made it nearly impossible to get close enough to land a blow.

Maddix shook his head, swinging his sword in a heavy arc. He held his own for a few moments before Misha gained the upper hand again, her swords clashing against his. She spun, and Maddix's head snapped back as her elbow connected with his jaw. Stars danced on the outskirts of his vision, and when they cleared, Misha was standing above him, and his sword lay discarded by his side.

"Well done," Misha said, extending her hand. She pulled him to his feet and clapped him on the back.

"You're coming along," Kenna said, appearing outside of the ring. Je and Indra were nowhere to be found, but Maddix knew that the children trained in a different section of the stronghold. They'd come to visit him a few times in the infirmary, still braiding his hair and gifting him with polished stones. Maddix still had a hard time thinking of them as warriors, but for a war that had been waged for centuries, training started young.

"She still beat me," Maddix said, spitting blood out of his mouth. His jaw ached.

"If you'd won after so little training, I would have accused you of being *valyach*," Misha joked.

Maddix smiled wanly, biting the acidic comment on his tongue. He didn't begrudge their paranoia, but he wouldn't stand to be compared to the same creature who had doomed him.

"Kenna's right, you're coming along very well," Misha said, oblivious to Maddix's sudden anger. "Let's go again."

"Actually, Hale needs to see him," Kenna interrupted smoothly. "If you don't mind me borrowing your practice dummy?"

Misha smiled, inclining her head.

"Is everything okay?" Maddix asked, ducking out of the ring. Hale hadn't asked to see him personally since the night Maddix slipped out of the infirmary.

"I'm sure it is," Kenna said. "But I don't ask questions. You must learn to do the same if you wish to remain with us."

Maddix nodded, snapping his mouth shut. He knew pledging himself to the *helwyr* was dangerous. The only way that they could all stay safe was if the information was compartmentalized. Maddix understood that, but he couldn't help wanting to know as much as possible in order to protect himself. He had earned that much.

Hale, it seemed, disagreed. He'd made it clear in the beginning that the answers to Maddix's questions had to be earned, and Maddix chafed against the imposed ignorance. It was his one point of contention, the tiniest hint of rebellion, and the *helwyr* commander had made it clear if Maddix had no intention of following the rules, he was welcome to try and find shelter elsewhere.

That had shut him up, but the curiosity hadn't gone away; Maddix had simply gotten smarter about it. He learned what would and wouldn't be told to him outright, and anything he couldn't learn from Hale or Kenna, Maddix searched out in the *helwyr*'s hundreds of books. It was time-consuming, but he wasn't willing to be caught unaware. Not again.

"Maddix," Hale said when they entered his study. It wasn't large, and the space seemed smaller with the weapons that lined the walls. Ancient books were stacked on every available surface in precarious towers that threatened to topple at the slightest provocation.

Hale sat, ramrod straight and white-clad, in the middle of the chaos. There was something *tense* about the man, as if a collection of razor wires stretched beneath the surface of his skin. "Welcome. Please sit."

Maddix slid into the chair on the opposite side of the desk, folding his hands neatly in his lap.

"What's this about, sir—er, *dryhten*?" Maddix asked once the door was closed, stumbling over the witchhunter honorific.

"I've been tracking your progress," Hale said. Thankfully, he ignored the slip. "You're doing well."

"Thank you, sir."

"We've gotten a tip," Hale went on, "that a ship sailing under a *valyach* captain will be arriving in Southport tomorrow. A witch onboard might be able to help you."

"Help me?" Maddix repeated, balking at the idea. He was here to catch and kill witches, not bring them into the fold. "How?"

"From what we know, it can track people. I'm assembling a team to head down there, and I want you to go with them."

Maddix blinked. He hadn't expected to be sent on a mission, not so soon in his training. Two years in the dark hadn't been enough to completely erase the skills he'd cultivated in the Kingsguard, but he was far from peak form.

"If our source is correct, this witch is trying to leave the kingdom. This might be our only chance to apprehend it, and your best chance to find the *valyach* who made you a murderer."

Slowly, Maddix nodded, his fingers worrying the spot on his throat where his pendant used to lay. The magnitude of this mission wasn't lost on him. This was his chance. This witch was his chance at vengeance, at *redemption*. Slowly, he forced his hands still and tipped his head up to look Hale in the eyes.

"I won't let you down, sir."

CHAPTER TWELVE:

JAYIN

Jayin slipped onto shore the minute they lowered the gangplank of the *Stormwind,* vanishing down the winding streets of the port town. It only took a few moments for a headache to form, pulsing behind her eyes as the town's energy clamored for her attention. She didn't fight the current of people as they milled around her, allowing herself to be swept away from the ship and the fiery figure that watched her disappear. She roamed mindlessly through the throngs of people, catching snippets of auras and emotions, but nothing stuck. Jayin let it all wash over her, absorbing nothing.

Until Zed disappeared. In the space of a breath his buzzing energy vanished, leaving a black hole in her second sight. Jayin staggered at the loss, abandoning caution for a moment to seek out the rest of the crew.

Four of them, including Zed, were missing. The signatures she did find were soaked in blood. Jayin didn't take the time to do a head count; she was already moving, sprinting back to the docks.

It was a massacre. For a moment, she couldn't see through the violence, unable to distinguish the attackers from the crew, but she *did* see the bodies. Zed and Massimo lay sprawled on the dock, reduced to empty husks.

Footsteps. Jayin spun to see two strangers charging at her, both brandishing weapons. Without taking time to arm herself, Jayin slid to her knees, slamming a gauntleted fist into the first man's kneecap. He swore, nearly falling on top of her. Jayin freed one of her knives from its sheath and drove it through the man's chin.

The assailant crumped, and his companion roared, swinging his sword so close it tore the thin fabric of her shirt. Jayin rolled backwards and spun onto one knee. She threw her arm out, hurling a straightblade with all of her strength. The man collapsed as the blade punched through his chest.

Freeing her blade from the man's sternum, Jayin turned in time to see another attacker take Sinta by surprise. The man, enormous and tattooed, lodged a double-bladed axe into Sinta's side. The captain pressed her hand to the wound as if she could hold herself together before her legs gave out, and she collapsed in a broken heap. Her insides spilled onto the dock with a slick sound. Sinta did not move again.

"No!" Jayin shouted, throwing herself back into the mob. She only made it three steps before she was blindsided. Something—energy, magic, *something*—ripped through her shields, and Jayin screamed, going to her knees. She clapped her hands against her ears, her voice going hoarse as her second sight dissolved into a landscape of pain. Black spots crowded in her periphery, and she could barely force herself to breathe, let alone fight back. Whatever this was, whatever Dark magic, it was going to kill her.

Somehow, through the barrage of pain, Jayin sensed someone advancing.

"*Valyach* scum," snarled the figure above her. His rage gave her a lifeline, something to hold onto though the agony that tore at her with psychic claws.

Jayin had enough presence of mind to dodge the boot aimed at her midsection, scrambling to her feet and slashing wildly with one of her remaining knives. Her assailant laughed at her pathetic attempt to defend herself. Jayin spun back to the ground as a fist clipped her jaw. This time the boot caught her in the stomach, and she went flying. She struck something on the edge of the dock, the back of her head crashing into the sturdy wood, and for a moment the mental pain lessened as she hovered on the edge of unconsciousness.

"Jayin!"

She couldn't tell if the voice was in her head or not, but she recognized the red aura in her second sight before the world exploded. Jayin pulled her knees into her chest, ducking her head to avoid the flames. After a moment the heat abated, and warm hands hauled her up with murmured words of apology.

Om.

Jayin forced her eyes open, finding some last reserve of strength to stand up under her own power as Om helped her hobble towards the safety of the ship. The tips of his hair were smoking, threatening to burst into flame.

"Om," Jayin wheezed, sensing energy flare behind them. Om reacted before his name was fully out of her mouth, shoving her forward and turning towards their attackers. The air rippled around his hands before they ignited. Fire spiraled in two concentrated beams and somewhere, someone screamed as their skin blackened and peeled from their bones. Om turned back to her, and Jayin could sense more than see more men approaching from behind.

"Om!" she screamed, but it was too late.

Jayin saw the point of the sword before anything else. The blade erupted from his chest, slick with his blood before it was ripped away, leaving a crater in its wake. Om choked, blood dribbling from his lips, and his hands scrabbled uselessly at the hole in his chest. His eyes found hers as he fell, his aura flashing with relief. *You're okay.*

Screaming wordlessly, Jayin threw her knife with the last of her remaining strength, stabbing Om's killer clean through the throat. The man gasped, clutching at his neck as he died. Jayin didn't wait to see his energy extricate itself from his body.

"Om," she whispered, falling to his knees beside Om's broken form. His limbs sprawled in a haphazard heap that reminded Jayin of the stick insects boys used to dismember in the Gull. "Om, please talk to me. Please." His eyes were open, but he didn't see her.

"You saved me," Om said, blood tracking down his face "Now I saved you." He inhaled, his breath rattling in his lungs. "You were right about me—about magic. You were—" His voice gave out, and Jayin felt hot tears spilling onto her cheeks.

Sucking in a deep, pained breath, Jayin pressed her fingers against his cheek. His aura was weak, but it was still there.

Please don't leave, Jayin thought desperately. *Om, please stay with me.* There was no response, none by way of words at least, but Om moved his hand to cup hers. She winced, the pressure in her head almost unbearable, but didn't pull away.

Jayin was so focused on keeping Om with her she didn't notice the others approaching. One of them grabbed her, and she spun, her rage igniting in her bones as surely as any flame. The man's aura was pulsing and dark in her mind's eye, and Jayin threw her hands out instinctively.

The man flinched, expecting some kind of magical attack, and his face twisted into a sneer when he realized she was defenseless.

Then something changed. In an instant, the man's energy spanned the divide between her two sights, bursting into physical existence. Jayin could feel it under her fingers, whispering like silk. She didn't waste time asking questions, her body moving of its own accord.

Distantly, she could hear the man howling as she tore him apart. When the last shreds of his aura were gone, the man dropped like a stringless puppet. Jayin whirled on the others, intending to destroy them, but the pain in her skull tripled.

Jayin swayed, and the world tilted, the ground rising up to meet her. As she lay on the bloodstained deck, the last rational part of her mind wondered if this wasn't the way she'd always known it would go. That she would die bloody, surrounded by fallen friends.

At least, she thought hazily. *At least* he *never found me.*

Jayin choked as a heavy boot crushed her throat, unable to so much as flinch away. She was out of knives, out of strength, out of time.

Don't. The word might have been in her head or spoken aloud, Jayin didn't know. Whatever the case, it stopped them. *We need this one.* Jayin wished they would leave her to die with Om and the rest of the crew, but it didn't seem to be up to her.

The world spun in a whirlwind of red, gold, and blue, and Jayin couldn't force her eyes to focus before blessed darkness finally claimed her.

CHAPTER THIRTEEN:

MADDIX

Wagon wheels rattled over the pockmarked road, the only sound from their broken company as they made their way back to the *helwyr* stronghold. The way to Southport had been marked by songs and raucous laughter, but now their procession was as solemn as a funeral march.

Your fault. Your fault. The words wore a track in his head, drumming in in time with his heartbeat. Several of their horses were without riders, trailing behind the remaining hunters, their footsteps heavy as if they too felt the loss. At the very back of the caravan was a prison wagon. A *helwyr* stationed in Southport had provided it, and within the bars, the witch lay in a hazy sleep. They took turns watching her, but Maddix knew she was his responsibility. He rode beside the cart, unable to stop looking at the creature in the cage. Whoever she was, the witch had seen battle. They'd found eight knives on her person, each sharp enough to kill, and her gloves were bewitched to become armored at her command. Pale scars distorted her dark skin, creating a map of old wounds. Privately, Maddix didn't know why she bothered. She didn't need mundane weapons to kill; he'd seen what she did to Helleck at the docks.

The witch twitched in her sleep, and Maddix signaled for the caravan to stop. The sedative was powerful, but *valyach* metabolized chemicals much faster than normal humans. It wasn't worth the risk.

"Check the collar," ordered one of the hunters, a woman named Barra. She'd been promoted when their previous leader burned to death. Maddix shuddered as he clambered into the wagon, thinking of how Durem had screamed as his skin bubbled and blackened. The scent of charred flesh was still stuck in his nostrils. He rattled the brass lock on the witch's collar, careful not to let his skin brush hers.

Their nightly camps were as silent as the days' travel, the silence only lifting when one of the hunters announced shift rotations. When he wasn't on watch, Maddix made it a point to sleep as far away from the witch as possible, but one night he woke up to the sound of a girl crying out. The next morning, the *valyach* was still unconscious, but fresh bruises bloomed on her dark skin.

Maddix didn't ask.

The damnable quiet made it all too easy to replay the battle at the docks over and over in his mind. Maddix had seen magic before in the Gull, little displays to dazzle tourists that spoke nothing of true power. Every time a cloud passed over the sun he flinched, expecting magicked lightning to split the sky. Even their cookfires reminded him too much of the two firewitches and the screams of the hunters who'd burned alive, roasting in their skin.

But as terrifying as the other witches were, they had nothing on the creature that rode in the prison cart. Maddix had never seen anything like her—he hadn't even thought such magic existed. She'd killed one of the hunters with a gesture. In an instant, he'd been reduced to meat and bones, stripped of anything that made him human.

The sun was just beginning to peek over the horizon when a shout shattered the silence. Maddix's eyes flew open, the nightmare fading. Around him, the other *helwyr* charged to their feet and through the haze of confusion, the cry was repeated.

"She's escaped!"

Maddix fumbled for his sword as Barra barked out orders. The *helwyr* scattered, sprinting into the forest to reclaim the lost witch. He crashed through the trees, trying to ignore how the shadows seemed to reach for him. Every rustle of leaves sounded like Mole's rasping voice, calling for his death, demanding his sacrifice. Maddix clenched his hands around the hilt of his sword to keep them from shaking.

It's not real, he told himself. *It's not real.*

Wind gusted on the back of his neck, and Maddix whirled, smelling Mole's rancid breath. He swung his sword and a flock of birds burst from the underbrush, shattering the illusion. There were no ghosts in the woods, no tunnel-dwellers that lurked in the shadows. It was just his imagination.

Here!" one of the hunters shouted, his voice echoing off the trees. "I've got her!"

Maddix exhaled, forcing thoughts of ghosts and molemen from his mind. He was *helwyr*, and he couldn't go to pieces whenever it got a little dark.

He raced towards the sounds of voices, of shouts and grunts of pain, to find the witch kicking and struggling in the hunter's arms. One of his hands was clapped around her mouth, and he swore as she bit him hard enough to draw blood.

"*Valyach* bitch!" the hunter—a man named Wulf—snarled, dropping the girl. She scrambled on her back, bruised and bleeding from shallow cuts on her neck and face. "Oh no you don't!" Wulf shouted, grabbing her wrist before she could get away. He twisted her arm behind her back, and the witch hissed through her teeth.

"Stop!" The word was only halfway out of Maddix's mouth when Wulf brought the hilt of his sword down with bone-shattering force. The witch screamed, the only thing keeping her upright was the grip on her wrist. Maddix rushed forward, plunging a syringe into the girl's neck. Her eyes rolled, and she went limp.

"If it tries that again, I'll break both its legs," Wulf promised, spitting. His face twisted with revulsion. "You carry it back. I ain't touching that thing."

For the rest of the journey, Maddix doubled the dose of sedative in the witch's system, and there was at least one hunter with eyes on her at all times. They couldn't risk her getting free again. If the silence had been forbidding at the start of their return trip, it was downright oppressive now, and Maddix knew he wasn't imagining the poisonous glances shot his way.

They made it back to the *helwyr* compound two days later, met with a solemn kind of celebration. The mission had been a success, but it had come at a terrible cost. Seven dead. Seven *helwyr* fallen, and all to get the witch for him.

Maddix couldn't help the guilt churning inside of him and was quick to transfer the blame onto the *valyach*. Of the seven hunters killed, she'd killed four.

"You need to be debriefed," Kenna said, appearing in the crowd and beckoning to Maddix. He was grateful to the intervention. Witchhunting was a dangerous business, but he knew the others blamed him for the deaths of their brothers and sisters. The whispers that had followed him since the beginning became more pointed, accompanying sharp glances and angry eyes.

Maddix spent the next several hours being asked question after question in a tiny room that made it hard to breathe. *What happened? How did the plan go wrong? What were the natures of the* valyach *killed? Was there anything else he could have done? Was he sure?*

Finally, *finally*, Maddix was released.

Hale was waiting for him.

"Walk with me." It wasn't a request. "How are you feeling?"

"Tired," Maddix answered honestly. "If I may ask, sir, how long until the *valyach* is ready to help us?"

Now that this was in motion, he was eager to continue. He wanted to prove this wasn't all for nothing.

"That is entirely up to it," Hale said. Maddix looked at him strangely. "It isn't the first *valyach* to assist us, and it probably won't be the last, but we've found many of them need a bit of training before they're manageable. The sooner it proves itself, the easier this will be."

Hale clapped Maddix on the shoulder. "But don't worry, if this one is as spineless as the others, it should only take a couple of days."

It took more than a couple of days. Kenna tried to assure him things were progressing well, that this *valyach* was just a little tougher than they'd expected. He was also explicitly told to stay out of the dungeons where the witch was being held. Maddix chafed against the restrictions but did as he was told.

Another five days passed without any progress.

Once, Maddix would have balked at flaunting a direct order. Once, he had been a star-eyed boy with dreams of grandeur and glory, and it had gotten him thrown into the Pit. If he could do something to make the witch talk, he was going to do it, orders be damned.

CHAPTER FOURTEEN:

JAYIN

Jayin woke to footsteps. It was a nice change of pace from her previous wake-up calls of ice-cold water or a blow to the stomach. As best as she could tell, she'd been imprisoned for over a week, though she didn't know how much time she had lost on the journey from Southport to her new dungeon home.

Dried blood was crusted on her skin from half a dozen shallow cuts all over her body, and her arm was mottled with purple bruises where it'd been broken. One eye was so badly swollen Jayin could barely see, and if the pain in her side was any indication, she was sporting a few broken ribs. Despite all of it, she still didn't know what they wanted from her. She didn't even know who *they* were. Her captors asked no questions, made no demands, just dealt in pain.

Worst of all, they'd neutered her magic. Jayin learned quickly not to use her powers—if she did, the collar around her neck choked her until she passed out or let the magic go, whichever came first. She'd chosen unconsciousness more than once.

The first day, Jayin thought they were going to kill her. She wanted to let them. Every time she closed her eyes she saw Om dying in her lap, his energy guttering out in her second sight. He'd saved her, risked everything—his anonymity, his safety, the life he'd built in Aestos—and in return, Jayin had gotten him killed.

The dungeon door swung open, and Jayin tensed, all thoughts of Om vanishing in an instant. Her heart picked up, fear chilling her blood.

"Bleeding stars," she swore. Through her one good eye, she recognized the figure walking towards her. Even with her magic suppressed, she would know him everywhere; his face had been featured on wanted posters for years. "Maddix Kell."

He started, surprise flitting across his face before he composed himself. "How do you know my name?" Kell demanded, crossing his arms over his chest.

Because I'm the one who caught you, Jayin thought, remembering the day she'd found him. The Kingswitch had been pushing her hard to find the rogue Guard, harder than he ever had before, but there was nothing. No trail, no aura. It was as if he'd just vanished. Then, after almost a week of aimless searching, he appeared out of nowhere, half-dead and covered in blood.

His aura hadn't hurt so much then. Jayin wished she'd noticed, wished she'd known there was a *dayri* walking around Pavaal with the power to cut through her defenses like a knife through silk. Maybe she could've done something about it with enough time and forewarning.

Maybes didn't do her any good now.

Jayin rose to meet him, standing as straight as she could manage. The chain around her ankle didn't allow for much range of motion, but she was small enough to stand to her full height.

Kell looked different than she remembered. There was something behind his eyes, as if he'd traded despair for something else. Fanaticism, perhaps.

Whatever it was, whatever was driving him, it was the only thing keeping him going. He wasn't the emaciated husk he should've been after two years in the Pit, but he still had a starved look about him that showed in the hollows of his cheeks.

"How do you know who I am?" Kell barked.

"All of Pavaal knows who you are," Jayin said, injecting as much scorn into her voice as she could. He knew she was *sahir*, but he didn't have to know she was the one who'd caught him. Somehow she didn't think knowing that would improve his opinion of her.

Jayin's legs trembled, threatening to give out, but she refused to fall in front of him. He was unsure of himself, that much was obvious, and Jayin intended to press any advantage she could find.

"You're the poor Guardling who lost his head and killed four people."

"Shut up," Kell said, and Jayin had to tilt her head up to look him in the eye. She sneered, moving as close to him as her chains would allow, gratified to see him flinch away from her. His hand went to his throat before he dropped it again.

"Why?" Jayin challenged. "Afraid talking about them will call their ghosts to you? If you didn't want to be haunted, you shouldn't have killed them."

"Shut *up*," he said again, fists clenching at his sides.

"They were people," Jayin went on as if he hadn't spoken. "They had families that cared about them. Do you have any idea how many lives you ruined, you starcursed—"

"Shut up!" Kell shouted, and then he was moving. Jayin bent her knees, trying to ignore the pain that burned through her muscles.

Anger made Kell sloppy and stupid. Even as weak and hurt as she was, Jayin managed to slam the top of her head into his jaw. He staggered backwards, off balance, and Jayin dropped into a crouch. She swept her leg out, knocking his feet out from under him, and pounced, wrapping her chains around his neck.

The door burst open and men poured in, alerted by the crash.

Here comes the cavalry, Jayin thought, pulling the chain tighter. Kell choked, brushing her bare skin as his arms flailed. Her second sight erupted behind her eyes, Kell's energy blotting out everything else and redrawing her world in strokes of white-hot pain.

The leather around her neck constricted, grounding her. Jayin hissed, shoving the boy away from her. She fell to her knees as her magic fizzled out again, and the collar loosened enough for her to suck in a single, desperate breath.

"How dare you raise your hand to one of us?" Jayin forced herself not to flinch, recognizing the voice of one of her torturers. She didn't have time to brace herself before a booted foot caught her in the chest. "Filthy *valyach*," the man spat, kicking her again.

Valyach. Jayin wheezed out a breath, blood speckling her lips. The word tickled something in the farthest reaches of her memory; a story she hadn't thought about in years. Dread pooled in her stomach and Jayin steeled herself to keep it from showing on her face.

"Oh how the mighty have fallen," Jayin wheezed, tilting her head up. The hunter was a ghost, washed-out except for his ice-blue eyes. They were flinty and hard, narrowed with contempt. "The great and terrible *sahirla* reduced to torturing a lone witch. Pathetic"

She smiled unpleasantly, baring her teeth. There wasn't much of a chance she would get out of this alive, but she'd be damned if she cowered before these monsters before they killed her.

The *sahirla* were a ghost story, a fairytale that witch mothers told their children to scare them into behaving. *Don't be naughty or the* sahirla *will get you. Do you know what happens to bad children who don't eat their vegetables? They're given to the* sahirla.

Jayin had always thought they were a myth, an imaginary group of old-fashioned madmen who spoke antiquated Aestosi and hunted witches for sport. She never imagined that they were real. Not only real, bit active on the outskirts of the kingdom.

"Oh, wait," she continued despite the anger growing on the hunter's face. She forced a laugh. "You were run out of Ayrie Palace, and then we replaced you. Funny how those things happen."

At first Jayin was sure that the hunter would strike out at her, but the rage on his face quickly cooled into something icy and cruel.

"And you'd know all about that, wouldn't you?" he said softly. "You're one of the Palace's pets. Or do you prefer to be called the Gulwitch?"

Jayin's heart dropped even lower. There was no way he could know that, just like there was no way the witchhunters could've known where she was. Unless—

"Maerta," Jayin whispered, understanding dawning.

"You creatures even turn against each other. You're disloyal, dishonorable animals."

"And yet here I am," Jayin snarled. "Alive and kicking, while seven of you died like cowards. The proud *sahirla*, begging for their lives from a—" Jayin's words died as a fist met her stomach, driving all the air from her lungs. Blow after blow rained down with pause or hesitation. Jayin squeezed her eyes closed and tried to brace herself, but it wasn't enough. She was breaking. She was broken.

She was dying.

"*Dryhten*," Kell's voice broke through the ringing in her ears. "Sir, stop—you're killing her! Hale!"

"We'll find another," the hunter—Hale—said, his voice horribly even. "If these animals can't be trained, they're no good to us. There will be another that does what it can do."

"No," Jayin rasped. The word stung her throat, scraping against the shards of glass lodged beneath her skin. She spat blood out of her mouth, struggling to meet the hunter's eyes. "I am the only one."

"It's lying to save its own skin," Hale insisted. She could see the indecision in the hunter's eyes before her own fell closed.

"The mighty *sahirla*. No wonder you died out."

She was adrift, numb and nerveless. Her second sight spluttered back to life for a single second, and the dungeon was aglow with Om's fiery aura.

I'll see you soon, Jayin thought. Her injuries and exhaustion finally caught up with her, and she finally faded away.

CHAPTER FIFTEEN

JAYIN

Water dripped onto her fingertips, a slow, rhythmic reminder she was still alive. Jayin hovered on the edge of consciousness for a long time before resurfacing. She didn't open her eyes at first, allowing her other senses to filter back in their own time. Someone had begun stitching up her wounds, and her ribs were set and bound. A thin cot rested between her and the cold ground, though her hand was still firmly chained to the wall.

A door creaked and light footsteps echoed inside the chamber. Jayin opened her eyes slowly and sucked in a breath. She saw the scar before the man, a twisting mass of dead tissue that obscured over half of his face. Her own was barely a scratch by comparison.

"That looks like it hurt," Jayin croaked.

The scarecrow jumped at her voice, the instruments in his hands falling to the ground with a clatter.

"You don't get scars like that from any natural fire."

He didn't answer, hurrying to pick up the items he'd dropped. His hands shook so badly the metal rattled.

Slowly, careful not to pull any of her stitches, Jayin sat up as much as her restraints would allow. She leaned on her elbow, looking the scarecrow up and down. He didn't look like much. In fact, he shared almost nothing with his *sahirla* brethren besides the scar. No wicked tattoos crawled over his skin, marking him as one of their killers.

Good. The advantage was hers.

"So you tangled with a firewitch and lost, obviously. And you're not a fighter, so the *sahir* is still alive. You're hiding then." Jayin nodded, leaning in towards him. "Would you like know a secret about witches? We never forget a face."

Jayin surged forward as much as her restraints would allow, snagging the scarecrow's sleeve before he could scurry out of the way. He froze, a mouse caught in the claws of a hawk.

"Careful. I know your face now."

There was a beat of heavy silence, and then the sound of the dungeon door slamming as the scarecrow fled. No doubt he thought himself lucky, escaping a brush with death at the hands of the rabid witch.

Idiot.

She had no interest in killing a man so scared he couldn't look her in the eye. She was, however, interested in the pins holding his ratty coat together. Jayin rolled the stolen needle around in her hands, feeling better now that she had some semblance of a weapon.

Finally, when her internal clock told her that the moon was high in the sky, Jayin wiggled the pin from under her hand and went to work on the cuff binding her to the wall. It took some doing but eventually the clasp sprung free.

Thank the stars, Jayin thought, rubbing some feeling back into her wrist. The room spun as she sat up too quickly. Jayin gritted her teeth, fighting through vertigo that willed her to lie back down again. She didn't have time for fainting like a damsel. Her odds of a successful escape were slim as it was, and dwindling with every wasted second.

The last thing was the collar. The lock that kept it in place was even easier to pick than the cuff and with a soft *click*, it popped open. Jayin tore the leather away from her throat and tossed it away, thankful to be rid of the wretched thing.

Free of the collar, magic sparked in her veins, familiar and with none of the violence from the docks. Snatching a scalpel from where the scarecrow dropped it, Jayin gathered her magic to herself and faded from view.

Inhaling deeply to steady her heart, Jayin crept through the stone halls, her footsteps hardly making a sound. That she'd been left unguarded was not lost on her. It smelled like a trap, but Jayin wasn't willing to wait around.

It felt like she'd been moving through the compound for hours when she finally sensed the sky beyond. There was just one more room to go through. One more occupied room. Jayin clenched her teeth, slipping the scalpel up her sleeve before she pushed the door open. She expected an attack.

She didn't expect applause.

"Well done." Jayin couldn't help the shiver that went through her at Hale's voice. The *sahirla* was facing her, smiling a joyless smile as if he'd won some private wager. Clearly, he had been waiting for her. He stood on a dais in the middle of the room, softly backlit like some kind of avenging warrior. Directly in front of her exit.

The display was suddenly, terribly familiar. For a moment, Hale's face was replaced by another, his hands outstretched to her to welcome her back. Jayin shook her head, blinking away the vision.

"Honestly," he said. "I didn't think you would make it out so quickly."

"Well I'm just full of surprises," Jayin said, searching around him. She poked at his defenses, hissing when the energy reverberated back at her. It was almost like what she'd felt in Kane's chest back in the Gull, the Darkness that was killing him. The backlash was identical.

"As are we," Hale replied, forcing Jayin back to the present. She abandoned searching him, eying him with newfound wariness. It was time to leave. There was nothing to stand in the way of her freedom. Nothing but Hale, but this was one fight Jayin was looking forward to. After everything he'd done to her, it was time for her to pay it back in kind.

Hale snapped his fingers and auras appeared out of nowhere. Witchhunters.

Jayin whirled, trying to keep all of them in her sight, but there were easily two-dozen hunters. She cursed, forcing herself to keep her face unreadable. How had they shielded so many people from her? It took her a moment to notice the glittering white jewels that studded the walls—the same jewels that adorned her collar.

"Is this all for me?" Jayin asked, crossing her arms. She would not show fear, not to these monsters. "You lot really know how to make a girl feel special." She smirked, all bluster and Gulwitch arrogance. "Or like you're scared of her."

"We are *helwyr*, and we are not afraid of a creature like you," Hale replied stiffly.

"Big talk from a group of zealots who were run out of Pavaal a hundred years ago," Jayin replied offhandedly, wondering if she could somehow use Hale's distraction to her advantage.

The thought had only just entered her head when her mind splintered into fragments. She pressed her teeth into her lip to keep from screaming and bit down so hard she could taste blood in her mouth. This time, there was no question where the pain was coming from. Some twisted part of her almost longed for the collar so she wouldn't have to suffer the pain of Maddix Kell's aura. Her fingers tightened around the scalpel, longing to throw it.

"Big talk indeed," Hale said, laughing. Jayin swayed on her feet but managed to stay upright. Kell joined Hale up on the dais, a pupil at his master's side, and the two of them looked extraordinarily smug.

"What are you?" she demanded, looking him straight in the face.

Kell's eyes widened, and he quickly turned to Hale to gauge his reaction, his hand going to his throat and tapping a nervous rhythm.

Jayin didn't give him time to recover. "I've been all over this kingdom, and I've never felt anything like you. Whatever you are, it sure as hell isn't *dayri.*"

Kell's face paled, and Jayin felt a vindictive surge of satisfaction. If she was going to die here, she was taking him with her. She forced a laugh, turning her attention back to Hale.

"You all think you're so much better than we are, but you're the one with some Dark creature in your midst."

She shot Kell one last mocking grin before Hale gestured to one of the men. Jayin fell hard as her knees were kicked out from under her, not bothering to use the scalpel to defend herself. It wouldn't do any good now.

The pain abated as soon as she was dragged out of the room, and Jayin allowed herself to be hauled back into the dungeon. She had no idea what she'd just set in motion, but she hoped it might unsettle them enough to give her an opening. The *sahirla* would never let an accusation like that go unanswered, and while they were dealing with Kell, she would make her own escape.

And this time, she was going to burn it all down.

CHAPTER SIXTEEN:

MADDIX

Maddix watched as the witch was dragged away, fear blooming in his heart. The witch called him Dark. In a room full of *helwyr*, she'd likened him to the very monsters he'd sworn to destroy.

"Hale," Maddix said finally, breaking the tense silence. "*Dryhten.*"

"Peace, Maddix," Hale said, raising a hand. "We'll discuss it later."

The words did nothing to soothe his fears. Slowly, the *helwyr* started to disperse, and Maddix followed suit. Part of him wanted to follow the witch down into the dungeon and demand an explanation. She was wrong. She had to be wrong, and more importantly, she had to tell the others it was a lie.

Maddix didn't follow the others, balking at the thought of being alone with any of them. He ducked out into the training yard, more to avoid the other *helywr* than anything else.

The night was clear, and Maddix could see the stars dotting the sky, the swollen moon hanging high above the horizon. Maddix grabbed his sword from the rack and squared off against one of the practice dummies. He didn't line up his stance or practice form, just slashed and stabbed until he was surrounded by hacked pieces of wood, and his arms ached from the strain.

"Your form is sloppy." Maddix whirled, moving the sword in a high arc. Hale's white uniform glowed in the moonlight. Maddix quickly relaxed his stance.

"I'm sorry," Maddix said. Again, Hale held up his hand, and Maddix fell silent.

"I wanted to speak to you away from the others," Hale said.

"You have to know that anything out of the *valyach*'s mouth is a lie," Maddix said. The words sounded rehearsed, too strained to be honest.

"Of course," Hale said peaceably. "But you understand, we cannot let such claims go unanswered. Especially from a witch with its kind of abilities."

"But—"

"Kell. If you are innocent, you have nothing to fear." Maddix's blood chilled in his veins. He'd heard those words before, when Guards interrogated Gull rats. The accused didn't always make it out in one piece.

"I don't," Maddix insisted, trying to iron away the edges in his voice. He knew what would happen if they thought he was a *valyach* spy. The proof was in their dungeons: tiny, half-dead, and somehow still fighting.

"We shall see," Hale replied, and for the first time, Maddix understood the whispers that followed Hale like a shadow. *Dead-eyed. Coldblooded.* Now, with those white-blue eyes turned on him, he finally understood. "Don't wander off. This is a compound full of *helwyr*, after all."

The chill in his blood froze over completely. Maddix knew a threat when he heard one, but Hale turned away before he could respond.

"Oh, and Maddix," Hale tossed over his shoulder. "Be careful. You'll find that this world is a very cold place without us."

Hale thought he was a spy. The thought struck Maddix as sure as a bolt of lightning. How could he not suspect? A *valyach* known for prying secrets from men's heads—a *valyach* necessary to his revenge, whose capture had led to the deaths of seven hunters—had called him Dark in front of half the hunters in the compound. More than that, Maddix had managed to escape from the most secure prison in the kingdom after killing four people and claiming he'd been possessed. Taken together, it sounded just mad enough to be some kind of harebrained scheme to earn a place among the *helwyr* only to destroy them from the inside.

Please help me, Maddix winged a prayer skyward as he wove his way through the halls. If there was any star in the sky that hadn't completely forsaken him, now would be the time to show itself.

"Paxton," he said by way of greeting, arriving in the medical wing. The healer turned, his face going pale when he saw Maddix at the door. Word traveled fast. "Paxton, it's not true, what the *valyach* said. I'm not like her."

"O-of course not," Paxton replied, half of his face trying to smile and failing.

"I'm *not*," Maddix insisted, taking a step forward. Paxton flinched, scurrying back until he hit the wall. His skin was so pale the scar looked gray in comparison. "Paxton, it's me."

"I know that," Paxton said. "I do, I know that." He was lying, but Maddix didn't have the time to stand around and try to convince him otherwise.

"Look, I'm sorry," Maddix said, putting his hands up in surrender. "I was just looking for some blister salve." He flexed his right hand so Paxton could see where the skin had bubbled and calloused. The healer nodded jerkily, turning to scrounge around in the cabinets. As soon as his back was turned, Maddix lifted the keys off of the ring on his belt. Paxton had access to the dungeon where the *valyach* was being held, and after Maddix broke in the first time, the door had been locked tight.

Paxton didn't so much as twitch at the sudden lightness at his hip, and Maddix pocketed the keys without a sound. Picking pockets was practically a sport for boys in the Gull, and Maddix learned like the rest. Now he wondered what might have happened if he'd joined a carrion gang like all the others. Maybe he'd be dead. Or maybe he'd be retired by now in one of the river mansions, having grown tired of robbing the Gull blind.

"Here," Paxton said, handing over the jar.

"Thank you," Maddix said, turning to go.

"I hope—" Paxton said haltingly. "I think you're one of us." He wouldn't, not after what Maddix was about to do. The idea was completely mad, but if there was another choice, Maddix couldn't see it.

There were four guards posted at the dungeon door, but he'd expected that.

"Hale—*dryhten* sent me," Maddix said with as much cocksure arrogance as he could muster. They nodded and let him inside. He snapped a salute and closed the door behind him.

The *valyach*'s eyes were closed, but Maddix had the sense she knew he was there. She could pretend to be asleep if she liked. Frankly, he preferred it. Her gaze was unnerving, too bright and too green to be quite human. The collar was back on and her hands were shackled behind her back, connected to the wall by a length of chain.

"How's it feel?" she asked. Maddix jumped. "To have a whole building full of fanatics think you're a threat?"

"You *are* a threat. You and all your kind," Maddix shot at her. The *valyach* opened her eyes, sizing him up.

"Why are you here?" she demanded.

"You're going to tell me if they think I'm a traitor, *valyach*."

"*Sahir*," she corrected sharply. "I'm *sahir*, not *valyach*. That word died out with the witchhunters' usefulness." Maddix felt his hackles rise, but it wasn't the time to argue semantics. "And why would I help you?"

"Because if you do, I'll get you out of here."

The witch hesitated. For a single moment she was just a girl, bloody and exhausted. Then that moment ended and the witch was on her feet. The manacles clattered against the stone and a scalpel glittered in her freed hands, winding through her fingers like magicians' playing cards.

Maddix stiffened, putting distance between them, but she only rolled her eyes, cutting through the collar in one swift movement. As soon as it was off, her face twisted and she tossed the studded leather at him.

"Bleeding stars," she huffed, rubbing her temples.

Maddix scowled, his mouth mashing into a thin line. "Get on with it."

The girl waved her hand at him, gesturing rudely before her eyes unfocused. "They're looking for you," she said, still somewhere he couldn't see. "Hale and a woman named Misha. She likes long walks on the beach and has two very scary swords. And he's a sadistic bastard who is definitely thinking of throwing you into the cell next door."

She could be lying. She could be telling him what he wanted to hear to force his hand.

The *valyach* seemed to sense his hesitation. "The scarecrow medic with the burn on his face? His name is Paxton, and he got his scar because he decided to get involved with a firewitch's fiancé. The fiancé's name was George and poor Paxton doesn't think he'll ever love anyone again. You stole his keys. Naughty."

"Enough," Maddix said. Her eyes slid back into focus.

"Good timing, because the guards are starting to wonder why I'm not screaming."

"I'll give us a distraction," he whispered. *Us.* The word burned on his tongue. He hated having to ally himself with her, but he didn't have any other choice. Part of him knew that by escaping with the *valyach*, he was proving himself a turncoat. But if he stayed, Hale would have him questioned or tortured for answers he couldn't give. Maddix had already played the part of scapegoat. He wasn't interested in reprising the role.

"Everything alright in there?" one of the men asked when Maddix opened the door.

"She got loose," Maddix said, injecting as much panic into his voice as possible. The soldiers rushed into the dungeon to find that the *valyach* was gone. In her place was a serpentine monster with burning black scales. The creature laughed, the sound of boulders breaking. In his hand, the collar's white stones glowed and the illusion melted away.

"Are you just going to stand there and gawk? You stole those keys for a reason, let's go!" the *valyach*. She took off running without waiting for an answer, and Maddix trailed after her, shoving the dungeon doors closed and locking them behind him.

"Wait!" Maddix shouted. "What are you *doing*?" He demanded when he found her trying to pull one of the torches off of the walls.

"We need a distraction," she said, finally prying the torch free. Her eyes were luminous, manic in the firelight and through the mottled bruising, a long-healed scar slashed through the left side of her face. She didn't wait for him to reply before running off again. "I need to pick up a few things," she shouted without breaking stride.

Cursing the whole blasted lot of them, Maddix raced after her. *The armory*, he realized when she didn't immediately head towards the exit. She was going to the armory.

"They're all looking for you," she said when the weapons vault was unguarded. "Thanks for being so popular."

The idea of running around with an armed *valyach* made his stomach turn, but it also gave Maddix an idea of his own. As the witch girl vanished, Maddix went looking for something Hale had told him about in passing, something that might save his life.

"I love shopping, don't you?" the witch asked, reappearing. She tugged a pair of black gloves over her hands, the same pair the *helwyr* had confiscated. Maddix hauled a sword off the wall, the other objects settled firmly in his pocket. Before he could stop her, the witch dropped the torch. The flames caught.

Above them, an alarm shrilled, reverberating through the compound. The *helwyr* knew the witch had escaped. This little detour may very well have killed them.

"They're coming," the *valyach* said, palming two wickedly hooked knives. For the first time, she looked nervous, and with the fire already burning behind them, they didn't have very many places to go. "You got an idea, traitor?"

He had half of one, and he didn't like it.

"Come on," Maddix said, breaking into a dead sprint towards the yard.

"Oh no," she said, guessing his plan the moment they stepped out onto the training ground. The stronghold was perched on a cliff over the sea, and the yard was little more than an outcropping of rock that had been sanded flat. "No way."

"Don't tell me you can't swim," Maddix panted, trying to convince himself that he wasn't about to get the both of them killed.

"There's a difference between being able to swim and surviving a fifty-foot drop," the *valyach* objected, her voice rising in pitch.

"I thought your people didn't feel fear."

"*My* people aren't suicidal," the witch shouted.

"Well then you're welcome to try your chances with the hunters."

"*Kell!*"

Maddix whirled to see Hale walking out onto the grounds with a small army of *helwyr* at his back. Misha stood to his right, swinging her two swords and looking grim. It was nice to know not everyone wanted his head on a pike, but Misha would kill him without a second thought if Hale ordered it. Her loyalty, unlike his own, was unquestioning.

"Your actions betray you, just as surely as you have betrayed us," Hale said. He didn't even have the decency to look disappointed. "You could've been the very best of us. I had such high hopes for you, but I guess we'll never know."

He signaled with one hand and Maddix could hear the distinct sound of a bowstring being drawn. Without pausing to take a breath, Maddix dove. Relief bloomed in his heart when there was no shock of impact, no pain.

The archer missed.

"Oh."

The word was impossibly loud in the silence, and Maddix turned to see the *valyach* stagger back a few steps towards the edge of the platform. A crossbow bolt was lodged deep in her chest, and blood soaked into her filthy shirt anew. Her eyes were hazy and unfocused, but somehow, they managed to find him. "Watch the skies," she said softly, pressing two fingers to her heart and stretching them out to him.

Catch the stars.

The witch's eyes hardened and she looked away from him. In an instant, the girl disappeared, consumed by column of emerald flame. Maddix ducked wildly before the vision cleared. Half of the *helwyr* hit the ground and the others followed when a second explosion shook the compound—a real one. Smoke billowed into the sky, blotting out the sun.

Maddix shook his head, fighting through the dizziness as he tried to find the wounded witch.

She was gone, vanished like so much smoke, and she had given him the chance to do the same. Maddix didn't waste another second. He leaped over the railing, throwing himself into the empty air. His heart jumped into his mouth and time slowed around him. He pulled his arms over his head, bracing himself before he crashed into the sea. There was a single spike of mind numbing pain and then nothing.

CHAPTER SEVENTEEN:

MADDIX

He came to a moment later, spluttering as he breached the surface of the water. Maddix sucked in a single panicked breath, disoriented by the movement of the ocean before the waves pulled him under again. Fighting against the sucking tide, Maddix forced himself to stay above the water. He hadn't survived a drop like that just to drown now.

The current had floated him away from the *helwyr* compound, well out of range of their arrows. No doubt they would be sending scouts to scour the beaches, but Maddix had a head start and planned to be well away from them by the time they could organize a search.

All he had to do was get to shore. Thanking the Guard's insistence that all their recruits learn how to swim, Maddix paddled towards what spit of land he could see. Something bobbed in the waves, catching his eye. The *valyach*. Without pausing to weigh the alternatives, Maddix dove towards her, grabbing her arm just as the ocean pulled her down. The arrow was still lodged between her ribs and Maddix knew enough to be grateful. If it had come out, she would have bled out into the water and there wouldn't be hope for either of them. He needed her. "Breathe," he commanded, as if his words made some kind of difference. "Come on," he urged, pounding on her chest. "Come *on*!"

Maddix wedged the crook of his elbow under her body and pressed hard on her chest, as far away from the arrow as he could manage. For a moment there was nothing, then the witch's eyes opened and she jerked away from him, cursing.

"It *hurts*." She winced and Maddix felt an inexplicable flash of guilt. "Help me." The *valyach* stilled, allowing Maddix to pull her close. By the stars she was small; Maddix could nearly wrap his arm around her torso.

Together, they managed to half-swim, half-float to shore. Once or twice, she forced them to change course, and Maddix didn't have the energy to disagree with her.

Somehow, they managed to get to land. Maddix crawled onto the sand on his hands and knees, practically dragging the witch behind him. Skies of the Above, he was tired. Despite the exhaustion weighing down his bones, Maddix knew he had to keep moving. The *helwyr* wouldn't be far behind.

"I'd hate—" the *valyach* sputtered, her voice tinier than she was. "I'd hate to…bother you but—" She inhaled deeply, a rattling, choking wheeze, and all at once Maddix remembered the extent of her injuries. "I think I'm dying."

She said it matter-of-factly, but there was a tremor of fear there that Maddix knew too well. There were nights in the Pit, endless nights, where he was certain he was going to die without anyone to mourn him. But now was not to the time to feel sentimental. He needed her alive. All of this was pointless if she died on him.

"Stay awake," Maddix said, trying to sound more confident than he felt. Murmuring an apology, Maddix lifted the witch into his arms and walked into the tiny port town they'd washed up alongside. The streets were all but deserted, but the few onlookers stared when they saw him. Maddix didn't blame them. He was sopping wet, dressed in training garb from the *helwyr*, with a dying girl in his arms. They stood out.

"Take a right," the witch whispered. Maddix obeyed, adjusting his route until he found himself in front of a tiny storefront. Not bothering with politeness, Maddix banged his fist on the door.

"Who under the—" A stooped old woman came to the door holding a lamp.

"We—she—needs your help," Maddix said.

"Go to a medic," the old woman said, waving her hand in dismissal. She began to close the door.

"Ayanara Awsley," the *valyach* croaked. The old woman stopped short. "I know you're no friend to the King…or the *sahirla.* I…" Her voice broke off.

"They're trying to kill us," Maddix said, not specifying who in particular. He could let the old woman draw her own conclusions. "Please. She's dying and if you let her, then they've won."

He had no idea if this woman could even help them—by his estimate, she looked well past her usefulness—but the *valyach* wouldn't have brought them here without a reason. The old woman hesitated a moment longer before ushering them inside. Maddix had to duck to fit in the doorway.

"Put her on the table, quickly," the old woman ordered. As he did so, she lit a few lamps, and he could see that the small space was cluttered with old books, papers, odds and ends, and yellowing bones. Something was bubbling in the corner, belching fumes into the air at odd intervals.

She was a witch. Of course she was. Why would a *valyach* turn to anyone but one of her own? Maddix's skin crawled, and he had to force himself not to leave the way he'd came.

"If you're going to be in my home, you're going to be useful," the old woman told him. In the dim lamplight, Maddix could see that her eyes were white and crisscrossed with scar tissue.

"You're blind," Maddix blurted. His nerves were too frayed to bother with niceties. "How under the sky can you heal her if you can't even see?"

"I see more than you. Old Aya knows that only foolish boys think only those with eyes can see."

"But you *can* save her," he insisted.

"Only if silly *dayri* stop talking and help me instead."

Maddix bit back his retort, resolving himself to being pushed around by two *valyach* in one day. Aya didn't spare another moment with talk. Faster than he would've thought possible, she pulled the arrow out of the *valyach's* chest. Maddix pressed bandages to the wound to staunch the bleeding, unable to stop himself from staring. Her lower body was a mess, new and old injuries coming together in bloody map on her skin. Whoever she was, whatever she'd done for the Palace, the witch was no stranger to violence. No wonder she'd lasted so long under Hale's ministrations.

She was lucky. Had the arrow struck any lower it would have pierced her heart and there wouldn't be hope for either of them.

Old Aya was a whirlwind of movement and surprisingly quick for her age. He had no idea what she was doing and didn't care to ask. All he wanted to know was if it was working, and every time he asked, the old witch whacked him on the back of the head with her bony knuckles. Maddix quickly stopped asking, though he still earned himself a rap to the skull when he took a moment to roll up his damp sleeves and pull his hair into a messy knot.

Finally, after the sky knew how long, the old woman proclaimed she had done all she could do. Maddix's shirt clung to his skin from the heat inside the hut. He could feel the magic soaking into his every pore as he breathed in the smoke and incense in the air. He felt dirty, like he needed a long, hot bath, but after everything he'd gone through tonight, he wasn't letting a little magic scare him away.

"It is up to her now whether she lives or dies," Old Aya announced, settling herself in a chair next to the table. "Your friend is strong. What is her name? I wish to add her to my prayers."

Maddix didn't know *valyach* prayed to anything. He also didn't know the girl's name. It hadn't seemed important while they were escaping certain death. Old Aya murmured something about stupid *dayri* before handing him a cup of steaming liquid.

"Here," she said, and as tired as he was, Maddix didn't think before accepting it and taking a sip. The drink tasted strange and burned like *arak* going down.

"What did you give me?" he demanded, trying to rise to his feet.

"You need rest," Old Aya said, nodding her head. "And you need to heal. You will sleep now." Maddix didn't have a choice. His eyelids grew heavy as soon as the words were out of the witch's mouth, and part of him was grateful.

MADDIX WOKE TO a nearly empty room. Sunlight streamed in through the small window, only adding to the heat inside the shop. He rubbed his eyes, trying to locate what had woken him when he saw the figure on the table stir.

"Skies above," the witch breathed. She turned to look at him and Maddix found himself relieved to see those green eyes. Old Aya's healing seemed to have worked; the worst of her injuries were healed, though the scars would remain. Even the bruises on her face were little more than shadows and without them the slash on her face was thrown into sharp relief. "Let's never do that again."

Maddix didn't know if she was referring to the escape, the jump, getting shot through the chest, or all three, but he was only too happy to agree. Her eyes closed again, but something told him she would pull through. His hands fiddled with the white stone on his neck Old Aya had given him the night before. The pendant wasn't an adequate replacement for his amulet, but it was a comfort nonetheless. Besides, Maddix had long suspected his black star had turned on him.

The worst was by no means behind him, but he still had a chance of accomplishing what he had set out to do all those weeks ago when he escaped from the Pit. The witch was alive. She was alive and mostly healed, and she would help him find justice.

"I always hoped they were wrong about you," the witch said.

Guilt rose in Maddix's throat like bile and he swallowed it back down. He shouldn't feel guilty.

Before she could see what he was doing or move to stop him, Maddix fished inside his pocket, thanking the stars that they survived the leap into the ocean. He locked one of the cuffs around his own wrist before clasping its twin around hers.

"What are you doing?"

"I need a witch that can do what you do," he said, trying to emulate Hale's haughty arrogance. This is what he needed her for; he shouldn't feel anything less than triumphant that his scheme worked. She stared at the band encircling her wrist, understanding and anger dawning on her face in equal measure. "You're going to help me find the witch who made me a murderer."

CHAPTER EIGHTEEN:

JAYIN

She was a fool. Bleeding, falling stars, she never should have gone with him. She should have gotten out of the *sahirla* compound on her own like she'd planned. But no, this accursed boy offered her a chance to escape and she'd jumped without thinking of the consequences. Of course he would want something from her. Why else would a baby witchhunter go to such lengths to save one of his sworn enemies?

"Take it off," Jayin ordered. She felt better than she had since the *sahirla* ambushed Sinta's ship at Southport, but she was still far from whole. Even if she was strong enough to force his hand, she had a sneaking suspicion it wouldn't do her any good. Not if the metal band was what she thought it was.

"I can't do that," Kell said. He almost sounded sorry. Almost wasn't good enough. "You're the only one."

Jayin cursed herself again. She had no reason to expect fair play from the likes of him, even after he'd saved her life. He was a liar and a criminal, someone with the skill and sense to escape the most heavily guarded prison in Aestos. Those things taken together made for a guilty man.

Even if his claims of possession were real, and not just the ramblings of a boy gone mad in the dark, Jayin couldn't go back to Pavaal. Maerta had tried to have her murdered. Going back there would be suicide—for both of them.

"What you're asking is impossible," Jayin shot at him. Her chest ached, and when she pressed her hand against the bandages her palm came away sticky with blood. "If either of us are seen in the capitol, they'll throw us both in the Pit."

That was if they were very, very lucky. No matter where she went, there would be people who wanted her because of what she could do, but Jayin would die before she ever went back to the Palace. And he was Maddix *bloody* Kell, boy murderer and the most wanted criminal in Aestos. If either of them wanted to keep their heads on their shoulders, they needed to get out of this blasted kingdom, not head into the heart of it. If Kell had any sense at all, he'd do the same.

So far, he hadn't shown much by way of sense.

"You're a fool," Jayin said, suddenly exhausted. She laid her head back, staring aimlessly at the ceiling. She couldn't stand the sight of him.

"As soon as we find them, I'll let you go." There it was again, the hint of childish naïveté that should have been burned out of him years ago.

"We'll never get close," she said softly. Someone would see them, try to stop them, or kill them to collect their bounties. And if the bracelets were what she thought they were, they were both going to die well before this little adventure concluded. The thought was so bleak she almost laughed.

"What?" Kell demanded.

"You've tied yourself to the most dangerous *sahir* in Aestos," she said. "And I am now bound to the most wanted criminal. We're going to die bloody."

And no one would mourn them. Ravi perhaps. Jayin's stomach twisted at the thought of him. He'd never know what happened to her. Maybe Om might have been saddened to hear of her passing, but he was gone. She could still feel him hovering on the outskirts of her second sight, a reminder.

Jayin was leaving quite the trail of bodies behind her, and now she was being forced back to the place where it all started.

"Let me show you something," Jayin whispered. Kell eyed her warily. As fast as she could manage, Jayin ripped the white crystal off of his neck. She tried to brace herself, but it didn't do any good. His energy was weaponized, a blunt instrument that destroyed her shields as if they were made of glass. Beside her, Kell fell to his knees, clutching his head and screaming as her pain echoed inside his skull.

"What under the stars?" Ayanara demanded, bursting into the room. Jayin didn't fight when she took the necklace and looped it back over Kell's neck. She uncurled her fists one finger at a time to keep her hands from shaking. "None of that. You both need to heal. And *you*, girl. Old Aya doesn't know what to make of you, but you won't live much longer if you don't get those gifts of yours under control."

"We're not going to live long anyway," Jayin replied.

"Live or die is up to you, but there will be no petty tomfoolery under Old Aya's roof. Not when you are both guests here."

Jayin muttered a half-hearted apology before turning her face to look at Kell again.

"You sure you want to be linked to me?" she asked. He was the initiate; only he had the power to remove the cuff. Until then, she would feel his pain and he'd feel hers. They would live and die together. It was a brilliant way to compel her help and an equally brilliant way to get them both killed.

At least I won't have to glamor my skin anymore, she thought bleakly. The bracelet was just wide enough to hide the telltale burn from the world. It was a small consolation.

"I don't have a choice," Kell said. "Once he's brought to justice, I'll let you go, I swear."

Brought to justice. That was the biggest farce of all. Jayin thought after everything Kell had gone through at the hands of the King's so-called justice, he should know better than to put his faith in the courts. But clearly, she was wrong.

"Enough talk," Old Aya insisted. "You two must heal, or all my work will be for nothing, and I hate wasting magic. Hush."

Jayin shot Kell one more poisonous glare before turning her back to him and closing her eyes. Just an hour before, she wouldn't dare to sleep with a baby *sahirla* so close lest he slip a dagger between her ribs. Now he couldn't.

"Thank you," Jayin said later, once she'd woken up again. Kell was still asleep, passed out in the chair next to Jayin's table. Old Aya was standing over a steaming cauldron of something, and for once, Jayin wasn't cold. The warmth and magic made her feel at home, safe the way the Palace used to. "For helping me." A potionwitch was a lucky find, especially in a place like this. Not as effective as a healer, but damn close.

"You know many things, young one," Old Aya said. It wasn't the answer Jayin was expecting. Slowly, she sat up on her elbows, facing the blind woman. "I have seen much in this lifetime, all kinds of magic, but nothing like you. Old Aya would remember."

"I've heard that before," Jayin said, wincing as she sat up. Her injuries throbbed, but she had laid down enough for a lifetime. She was tired of being hurt. "Have you always been blind?"

It was a rude question, Jayin realized when Aya didn't answer right away, but she'd been a prisoner and lived with carrions for too long to bother with politeness. She'd never been good at playing courtier, much to the Kingswitch's dismay.

"You could find that out yourself."

"I don't do that," Jayin said.

"You did last night."

"I didn't have a choice," Jayin replied, feeling defensive. "I was dying, and I needed to find someone who could help me."

"So your powers allow you to find Old Aya, but you draw the line at gleaning my secrets? Why?"

"It hurts," Jayin said honestly. She checked to make sure Kell was truly asleep before going on. The less he knew about the extent of her powers, the happier she would be. "If I don't protect myself it's all so overwhelming I can't keep up. Sensory overload," she said, remembering when she'd said the same words to Om.

Jayin felt a stab of anger towards Kell and the whole cursed lot of the *sahirla.* They thought that they were ridding the world of monsters by killing her people, but with every life they took, the more monstrous they became. She hoped their starcursed compound was still burning. She hoped they burned with it.

"So you are content to render yourself powerless in order to avoid pain. Pain is a part of life, child."

"Not like this," Jayin insisted. "When I was young and couldn't control my abilities, I thought it would kill me. It was like having acid poured into my ears." If the old woman didn't believe her, Jayin welcomed her to try it out for herself. She'd given Kell the opportunity to see things her way, though she still didn't know what it was about his aura that made it so agonizing.

"My sight was taken from me as a little girl," Aya said abruptly. "I am very old, and I have seen much of this world. But not with my eyes." She sighed, settling into the armchair by the fire. "When I was young, the *sahirla* were still a force to be reckoned with in Aestos."

They still are, Jayin thought. She had the scars to prove it.

"They roamed this kingdom in packs, searching out and killing any witches they came across. My family was new to Aestos, immigrants from the Oldlands—"

"You're from the Oldlands?" Jayin interrupted. She'd never met anyone from their ancestral home before. Travel between the two lands had been nearly impossible for a hundred years.

"Yes, child. I am much older than I look, though I do not think that means much anymore. Your generation is so different than my own. You live so rashly and die so young. You have forgotten how long our lives can be. I was just a baby when my parents brought me to this land. They thought it would be safer for us. From what, I never knew. I still do not know, but the rumors are many and terrible."

Jayin had heard them as well. The Oldlands had always been a topic of interest for her, one that was infuriatingly difficult to learn about. Only the Kingswitch had the answers she sought so eagerly, but he had always rebuffed her attempts to pry them out of him. Some people said the land itself was dying, driving the last of the witches to the Three Kingdoms before it vanished altogether. Others claimed that whatever had blessed the *sahir* with their gifts had somehow come alive and hunted them for their power. *Dayri* whispered that their Dark deal was up, which is why their numbers seemed to be dwindling and the Oldlands were barred to them. Jayin didn't know the truth.

"No one in our village escaped the slaughter," Aya went on, oblivious to how Jayin's thoughts spun away to rumors of the Oldlands. "Save for Old Aya, of course, but the encounter left me blind. I was just a child, but I managed to find my way to Pavaal, and petitioned the then Kingswitch to help me avenge my family." The old woman sighed, pain evident in every line of her face. "They told me that witchhunters were a necessary evil, and I should consider myself lucky to be alive. Then they turned me away. I was a child, an orphan, ripped from my parents and my sisters, and they left me out in the cold to fend for myself."

Jayin knew the anger in Aya's voice, knew the sting of betrayal from the people she'd been taught to trust. The Kingswitch was supposed to look after them, but the title came with a power that corrupted and turned his interests away from the good of the *sahir*, and instead to whatever would keep them by the King's side. Jayin had learned that the hard way.

"I'm sorry," Jayin said. She'd grown up without a family, so she had no idea what it was like to lose one. But it couldn't be anything less than devastating.

"It's in the past," Aya said, waving a bony, veined hand. "The very distant past. Sometimes I think our longevity is a curse." Jayin wondered what it would be like to live for centuries, seeing wars come and go, rulers rise and fall. If Kell had his way, she wouldn't have the chance.

"I doubt I'll live long enough to compare," Jayin said, not bothering to keep the bitterness out of her voice. Aya was a stranger, but she'd done more for Jayin than those who had known her for years. "Have you been around long enough to know how to break the bond on these?" she asked raising her wrist. Aya's knobby fingers drifted over the cold metal band and after a moment she shook her head.

"Old Aya does not know how to break such an enchantment. Your lives are bound until the bracelets come off." Jayin knew as much, and yet hearing it said aloud sent a thrill of fear through her blood. She wasn't ready to die. She hadn't been at the *sahirla*'s compound, and she wasn't ready now.

Stars, she just wanted to go to the Isles like she'd planned. Or perhaps join a crew and spend the rest of her life at sea, where no one wanted anything from her. Not the Kingswitch, not the *sahirla*, not Kell. No one.

She was only eighteen—ancient by the Gull's standards and infantile by the *sahir's*. There was an entire world she hadn't seen yet. Even if she spent the rest of her life looking over her shoulder, waiting to see the telltale colors of the King's men, at least it would be her life. At least she would be *living.*

"He will not betray you, whatever you think of him,"

Jayin shot Aya a sharp look. "He already has. He's *sahirla.*" Jayin wanted to slit his throat and be done with it but there was no way to do it without dying along with him.

"The *dayri* is not one of them. I would not have allowed him into my home if he were. I do not know what he is." The blind woman paused, threading her fingers together. "It seems that you two are creatures without equal, bound to one another. It is interesting."

That wasn't the word Jayin would use.

"It is time for me to rest," Aya said, abruptly. "You should as well. You have a long journey ahead of you, and many hardships." Shuffling to her feet, Aya patted Jayin on the head and disappeared into a back room. Jayin didn't move for a long time before finally taking Aya's advice and trying to sleep.

CHAPTER NINETEEN:

JAYIN

This time, when Jayin opened her eyes, Kell was awake.

"Good morning, traitor," Jayin said, not bothering to ease the cranky bite in her voice. Never in her life had she enjoyed mornings, and weeks of imprisonment and torture hadn't changed that. He stared at her oddly, his blue eyes still clouded with sleep. "What?" she snapped.

"Your hair," he said. Jayin glared, daring him to say another word. Her hair, which had hung nearly to her waist, was gone. With one of her knives, she'd sheared it off without bothering to look in a mirror. It wasn't pretty, but her head had been matted with so much blood and seawater that it was unsalvageable. Now her hair was cropped short in the back and lighter than she'd ever felt it.

"You found me based on a description," Jayin said. She shook her head, tossing the new, uneven bangs out of her eyes. "I'm not walking back to Pavaal looking like I used to, and neither should you."

"Children," Aya said, emerging from her back room. "You will need these." In her hands were two identical packs, one for each of them. Jayin dug around in hers to find a week's worth of provisions, a sleeping roll, as well as several knives to replace the ones she lost and a belt to conceal them. Aya had already outfitted them with traveler's gear to replace the sopping wet—and in Jayin's case, bloody—clothes they'd worn to her door. Jayin's new coat didn't have half as many pockets as her old one, but it would do.

Jayin caught Kell looking at her, his hand worrying the stone around his neck.

"What?" she snapped, pulling on a fresh pair of gloves and tucking the new daggers into her belt.

"Do you really think you need so many knives? That seems excessive."

That's excessive. Om's voice echoed in her head. Jayin inhaled, trying to keep herself from flying at him. The thought of Kell and Om having even one thing in common made her stomach turn.

"Your *sahirla* friends thought so too," Jayin said. She made a show of spinning one of the new knives around her thumb. "Right before I gutted them." Spots of color appeared on Kell's cheeks, and he took a furious step towards her.

"None of that here," she said sharply, her knuckles connecting with Jayin's skull. Jayin cursed, rubbing the bristly hair on the back of her head. "You are still in Old Aya's house and you will be civil." Aya muttered something else, but Jayin couldn't make it out. She doubted it wasn't complimentary. "Now, you must leave. I have done all I can for you."

Jayin was sorry to go. She would miss the tiny house and the warmth and magic curled in the air. Maybe, when all this was over, she would come back. Aya had years worth of stories to tell, and Jayin wanted to hear them all.

"Thank you," Jayin said, surprising even herself by pulling the old woman into a hug. Aya was only just taller than she was, and it was a strange thing to be the same size as someone. Jayin was used to being dwarfed.

"Try not to die, yes? I will be upset if you waste all of my hard work."

Jayin nodded, biting her lip. Kell was already waiting outside, the pack slung over his shoulders and stolen sword at his hip. The white gem gleamed against the pale column of his throat.

"Come on then, traitor," Jayin said. "It's a long way to Pavaal and I'd like to get this suicide mission on the road."

"Are you always so cheerful?" Kell asked as they started walking.

"Only when I've been kidnapped by a simpleminded murderer with a death wish," Jayin replied without missing a beat. He didn't answer.

It was slow going, but at least they would have plenty of advance notice if the *sahirla* were coming. Jayin used a tiny part of her power to scour the land, searching out hostile witchhunter energy. Her only advantage was Maerta probably thought she was dead, killed by the *sahirla*, so there was no need to go to such lengths to conceal her powers. She wouldn't be sending up magical flares anytime soon, but it was better than traveling like a *dayri*.

"We should get off the streets," Kell advised as the sun started to set, breaking the silence that had held since Old Aya's.

"There's still plenty of ground to cover."

"Not if you want to stay out of sight, *valyach*," Kell insisted. "The *helwyr* do sweeps at sunset."

Helwyr, *valyach*, he kept using the words like he knew what they meant. Jayin shook her head. It wasn't worth explaining, not to him. He'd sought them out. He escaped from the Pit just to join them. That was fanatical dedication if she'd ever seen it, and Jayin didn't have time to try and recondition a zealot.

"Play along," she hissed, pulling him into a dingy inn off of the main thoroughfare. Jayin looped her arm through his, careful to keep their skin from touching. "Hello," she said brightly to the man behind the desk.

"What can I do for you?" the innkeeper asked. "Are you looking for a room?"

"Two," Jayin said, pulling an exaggeratedly mournful face. She pulled Kell close, ignoring how he stiffened in discomfort. "I love this man with all of my heart, but stars does he snore."

The man behind the counter smiled. "I know what that's like." He leaned towards her conspiratorially. "My wife is the prettiest little thing you've ever seen, but she snores like a sailor. Here." He handed them two separate keys. Jayin thanked him before leading Kell up the stairs.

"What was *that*?" Kell demanded as soon as they were out of earshot.

"You're saying you want to share a room?" Jayin deadpanned. "With me?"

"No, but—"

"Then shut up and you're welcome," she cut him off, pushing into her room and slamming the door behind her. Stars. They'd only been on this little adventure for a day and she was already exhausted.

Jayin locked the door firmly, weaving tiny amounts of magic into the door. It wasn't much, but it would give her a split-second head start in case someone came too close.

Even after she'd settled on the bed, Jayin couldn't sleep. She lay awake, tossing and turning on the soft mattress. After sleeping on the stone ground of the witchhunter's dungeon and Old Aya's table, the plush mattress was stifling.

Eventually, Jayin pulled the blanket and pillow off of the bed and settled herself on the floor. Her arm was bent under her head, fingers wrapped around a ring dagger. She should kill Kell now, while he was sleeping, and be done with it. Her days were numbered anyway and there would be one less *sahirla* maniac in the world. She should slit her own throat and expedite the process. Jayin sighed and rubbed her temples, trying to force the idea out of her head.

Her dreams were bloody.

THEIR ROUTINE DIDN'T vary after the first night, walking from sunup to sunset and only taking breaks at midday to eat. Aya's rations lasted a little over a week, but they soon resorted to stealing.

"It must be nice," Kell said when Jayin tossed him his share. Walking into the shop unnoticed had only taken a whisper of magic, and Jayin wasn't willing to risk exposing Kell. She didn't want to think what would happen to her if he were captured while still wearing the cuff. "Being able to disappear."

"I don't disappear," Jayin growled, tearing at a hunk of bread with more force than strictly necessary.

"And yet I've seen you change your shape," Kell pointed out, a mouthful of food.

Jayin rolled her eyes. "That's not how it works."

"Then how does it work?" Kell insisted, oblivious to how quickly Jayin's tolerance was waning. "Come on, *valyach*, what could be the—" The rest of the question died on his lips. Jayin surged forward, pinning him to the wall with a gauntleted hand and bringing her dagger to his throat. She could feel the prick of steel against her own skin and ignored it.

"I," she snarled, her face so close to Kell's that she could feel his aura even with the stone, "am *sahir*, you stupid, ignorant boy. And your heroic witchhunter friends aren't *helwyr*, they're *sahirla*. Using a dead language and insisting on *cleansing* Aestos doesn't make them pure. It makes them monsters." She straightened up and slipped the knife back up her sleeve. "I've spilled enough witchhunter blood to know their blood is as red as mine, and if you call me *valyach* again, I'll spill yours too. Cuff or no cuff."

She didn't wait for him to answer, tucking her meal into her pack and stalking off. She didn't bother looking over her shoulder. He would follow her. He didn't have a choice.

For days they walked without speaking, barely looking at one another. Kell trudged behind her, always warning of the sunset sweeps before Jayin found them somewhere to stay. The best places were inns or hostels, and the worst, abandoned, half-destroyed structures that barely kept out the elements. Those nights, they slept in shifts. Jayin sat with her back to Kell during her watches, trying to ignore the way he thrashed about in his sleep. She knew enough about nightmares to recognize the symptoms.

"Why aren't you looking for him?" Kell asked her one morning. It was the first time he'd addressed her since she'd threatened him. Jayin dragged her hand down her face. It was too early for this.

Because I don't believe he exists. "We're too far away," she said instead. They were still days away from Pavaal, and Jayin wasn't willing to use her powers from such a distance.

"I thought you could find anyone, wherever they were."

Jayin sighed, blowing out her cheeks in irritation. "I can, but thanks to you and your homicidal friends, Ayrie thinks I'm dead. Right now, that's the only thing keeping the Kingswitch from finding and killing both of us. I'd like to keep breathing, thanks."

"What does that—"

"You really have no idea how magic works, do you?" Jayin snapped.

"Magic is power," Kell supplied. *Bleeding stars is he* jealous*?* "It's the only reason you witches think you run things."

Magic is pain. Jayin didn't bother correcting him. Let him think what he liked.

"Yes, well, the big bad witches who run things want my head on a spike, and I'm a fan of living."

"How does a coddled Palace witch end up with so many people wanting her dead?" Kell asked, changing track.

"How does a Guardling go completely mad and murder four people?" Jayin shot back.

"If there was anyone else—" he started. Jayin cut him off again.

"But there isn't, is there?" she asked coldly. "That's why I'm stuck on a death march with the dumbest skiv under the stars and not some other *sahir*. That's why you didn't kill me."

Kell's blue-eyed glare softened into something that might have been shame, but Jayin had already turned away.

That night, they found a busier inn than the others.

"Aren't you coming?" Kell asked when Jayin didn't follow him up the stairs.

"No," she said shortly. "We need money." Jayin gestured to the card tables in the tavern connected to the inn. She couldn't keep wasting magic on stealing meals for them every day.

"I'll come with you," Kell offered.

"You're a wanted felon, and I'm the one who can sharp," Jayin said. How he failed to understand how little she wanted to do with him was beyond her. "Go to bed, traitor."

"Deal me in," she said, sitting at one of the card tables. A portly, balding man looked her up and down, his lip curling.

"You know how to play Dead Man Sevens?"

"Do you?" Jayin fired back.

"Deal the girl in," said another man, this one with sandy hair and dark eyes. "She's allowed to lose her money just like everybody else."

Jayin inclined her head and accepted the cards as they were dealt to her. Sevens was a game she knew well, one she used to play with the other *sahir* in the Palace. Until they realized that she was sharping them and banned her from playing. It wasn't her fault. At least, it wasn't at first. Divining the other players' cards took so little magic Jayin hardly realized she was doing it. Before she got caught, Jayin learned a thing or two about cheating. In the Gull, knowing how to sharp had come in handy when money was tight.

The trick was not to win every hand. Jayin knew if she won too big, too quick, it would be suspicious, and these didn't seem to be the types of men to take kindly to being sharped. Especially since two of them were cheating themselves. Jayin didn't mind, allowing herself to be played for a couple of rounds. Then slowly, one card at a time, she started winning her money back. By the end of an hour, Jayin had tripled her *lira*. It was enough to get them to Pavaal, and if she survived this, to the Isles like she'd planned.

"I'm out," Jayin said finally, setting her cards down and scooping up her winnings.

"Don't tell me you've given up on us," the dark-eyed man said. He had nervous hands, fiddling with his cards or the hem of his sleeve. "You're the only interesting one here, and by far the prettiest."

Jayin raised an eyebrow. "I know when to call it a night," she replied. She thumbed the trigger on her forearm sheath. The man's aura was sugary, cloying and sticky like molasses.

"Come on," he insisted. "Let me buy you a drink."

"I hate to break it to you," Jayin said. "But I'm married."

"Bachelors everywhere weep at the loss of you," the man said. He took a step closer, and Jayin lowered her shields, seeking him out. There was something *off* about him. She'd just found the answer when something pinched her side. "You know, you're very good," the man said. His voice began to morph, lowering in pitch, and around her, the room began to spin.

She needed to go, but she couldn't remember why. Some small part of her mind seemed to realize she'd been drugged and she tried to stagger away or call for help, but the poison stole her voice.

"Easy there, love," the man said, steadying her. The moment his skin touched hers, Jayin remembered.

"Bounty hunter," she slurred.

"Man's gotta make a living." The swirling was giving way to nothingness, and Jayin fumbled for a dagger. "Ah ah, none of that. Don't want anyone getting hurt, do we?" the man said, pulling her hand away.

"You're making a…mistake," Jayin mumbled. Her head felt too big, too heavy, and she had no choice but to lay it against the man's chest.

"I don't think I am," the man whispered, pressing his lips to her temple. Jayin flinched violently, shoving away from him. She managed to stand up straight and take a single step under her own power before she earned another sting for her efforts.

"Get *away* from me," Jayin said, swinging her fist.

He laughed, batting her hand away. "You're trouble, but I think you'll be worth it."

CHAPTER TWENTY:

MADDIX

The witch was gone. She was gone. Vanished in the night. Maddix knew he should have stayed with her, but he hadn't wanted to test his luck. Even with the bracelet, the look she'd given him promised violence. So he'd gone to bed and let her out of his sight like a fool.

And now she'd run away.

Maddix hadn't bothered waiting up for her, shutting himself in his room and trying to get as much sleep as possible. The witch never voiced a word of complaint as they trudged through the countryside, but Maddix knew he was slowing. For such a small person, she seemed to have reserves of energy the rest of them lived without.

They barely said two words to one another, and Maddix told himself he didn't mind. He was too busy planning ahead. Once this was all over and done with, he had his whole life ahead of him. There was a whole world out there, and he'd spent enough of his life trapped in one place. He wanted to see Vandel and the Isles. Maybe leave the Three Kingdoms altogether and travel to the colonies across the sea. He would go everywhere and see every corner the world had to offer.

But he would never get the chance if he didn't find the skyforsaken witch that was his only chance at clearing his name.

"Hey," Maddix said to the barman behind the counter. "I'm looking for my, uh, my wife?" He tripped over his words, trying to remember the story. "She was playing cards last night. Small, dark, short black hair. Long coat. She probably won a bit of money."

"Aye, I remember her." The man gave him a pitying look and Maddix's stomach swooped. "I think yer girl might be stepping out on you, laddie."

"What do you mean?"

"I saw her leave with one of the regulars. A man named Oskar, he plays cards a couple of nights a week. She looked like she'd drunk her weight in whiskey, swaying all over the place."

"Can you tell me where to find him?" Maddix asked, not bothering to hide the desperation in his voice. Let the barman think he was an idiot newlywed looking for his missing wife, maybe it would garner him some sympathy. "Please. I think she might be in trouble."

"Far as I know, Oskar's got a place on the edge of town. Real run down, near the water. Yer girl might be there."

The house was exactly as the barman had described, a rickety shack at the river's edge that looked like a strong gust of wind might blow it over.

Please, please, please, Maddix prayed as he crept to the side of the house. No sound came from inside, and he couldn't see anyone from his vantage point.

The lock on the door was easy to pick and the door itself was practically falling off of its hinges. Maddix let himself in, barely breathing in case he wasn't alone, but it didn't matter. The place was empty. Dust and debris piled under the broken windows, and winding vines snaked in through the gaps in the walls. Something shifted against the wall, and Maddix whirled, his hand flying to the sword on his hip. A single piece of paper was tacked to the wood and Maddix's heart plummeted as he recognized the face peering back at him. The witch wasn't as hard around the eyes and her hair was longer, but it was undeniably her.

Maddix cursed, ripping the poster down.

She'd been taken then. The bounty hunter must have recognized her in the tavern. Or perhaps her magic had made a trail straight for them. It didn't matter now; she was gone and he had to get her back.

"Falling *skies*," Maddix swore, putting his fist through one of the crumbling walls. He cocked his fist again before something tugged at his wrist. Maddix went still, his eyes flicking down to the cuff.

Again, the bracelet pulled at him, more insistently this time. Slowly, step-by-step, Maddix allowed himself to be led along by the strange tug in his gut. It wasn't physical, he realized after a little experimentation, but something else, something deep inside of him. When he went in the right direction, the pull lessened.

Fiddling with magic had never served in the past, but he couldn't go forward without her. Maddix was the one who'd dragged her on the path back to Pavaal. He was the one putting her in danger. He needed her. She was the only one who could help him, and he wasn't willing to give up on two years of planning because someone had stolen his guide.

Maddix quickly realized following on foot was impossible. Whoever had her, they were moving fast, and he couldn't keep up.

He needed a horse. Maddix sidled up to the first barn he saw and made easy work of the lock. The only horse in the stable, a whickering palfrey, snapped at him, but allowed Maddix to bridle her once bribed with an apple.

Maddix's hand went to his throat as he rode out of town as fast as he could, praying against all odds that no one would notice him on his stolen horse. For once, his fickle star shined in his favor; the town was practically deserted. The farmlands had been dying for years, and every spring more and more people crowded into the cities to find jobs and shelter as their crops withered. The more hopeful among them remained, waiting for help that would never come. Maddix set a hard pace, trying to close the gap between them as quickly as possible.

Then the witch woke up.

His arms burned even though he wasn't bound, and his head snapped to the side from a stinging backhand. She was definitely awake and fighting. As promised, Maddix could already feel bruises forming, mottling his skin black and blue. After the second slap, Maddix thought of maybe taking the bracelet off, to spare himself pain. But then he wouldn't have any idea how to find her and nothing to go by.

The connection pulsed insistently as he got closer, turning off of the main road onto a path so overgrown with weeds it was hardly visible. That, he supposed, was the point.

Carefully dismounting, Maddix tied the palfrey to a tree and left her with the last of the water from his canteen. Maddix had one hand on his sword as he made his way forward, the connection thumping inside of him like a second heartbeat.

Whoever had taken her—this Oskar—had a serious liking for rundown buildings. This one was in even worse shape than the other, and Maddix could hear voices coming from the inside.

"So what's the plan here?" the witch asked as Maddix crept towards the structure. "Because right now, I'm not impressed."

Stars, Maddix thought desperately. *Stop talking.*

"Been kidnapped before, have you?" a thin voice replied. Oskar. Maddix moved around the building, looking for a way inside.

"I've seen my fair share of scum," she said. "And as far as monsters go, you do not measure up."

"It's not me you should be worrying about, love," Oskar said, and even from outside the walls, Maddix could hear the man's leering smile. "It's the people I'm going to sell you to." The witch sucked in an audible breath. "*Sahir* fetch such a wonderful price."

"Your buyers are going to be very disappointed then," she said without inflection. The witch was an impressive liar, but Maddix could feel his own heart pick up in response to her fear.

Stepping over bits of splintered wood and broken glass, Maddix picked his way through the house. He was sure Oskar would hear him, but the man seemed too busy grandstanding to notice much else.

The witch was facing him, tied up in a chair with her arms wrenched behind her. A white stone hung around her neck.

Her eyes widened as she saw Maddix through the walls and he quickly put a finger to his lips. *Distract him*, he mouthed. Hopefully, she'd keep talking and give him a way to get Oskar out of the room. Maybe then he could slip in and free her without the man noticing that he was there.

He should have known better.

The witch started laughing. She looked half-mad, tied up and helpless, obviously disarmed—her knife belt lay discarded in a corner though her magicked gloves remained—cackling like a moon-struck loon.

"Have you lost it then, love?" Oskar asked. His fingers tapped an anxious rhythm against his leg. Maddix understood the feeling. The witch had that effect on people.

"No, but you're about to." He had no idea how she'd managed it, but suddenly she was free and moving. She sprang at Oskar, and Maddix took it as his cue. He burst into the room, brandishing his sword. For a moment, they had the advantage. The witch was adhered to Oskar's back like some kind of Dark monkey, her arms wrapped around his throat.

Maddix was able to back him into a corner before Oskar shook the witch off. He threw her away from him, and she went flying, hitting the wall with a *crack*. White stars danced in Maddix's vision, and he nearly went to his knees as the pain reverberated up his spine. Out of the corner of his eye, Maddix could see the girl's motionless body, her limbs splayed wide. *Please be okay*, he thought, forgetting if she'd died on impact, it would've killed him too.

Oskar snarled, swinging his sword down. Maddix parried the blow. Not fast enough. The blade cut him high on his leg and blood gushed. "You should not be interfering in my business."

The clang of metal shivered through the air and with every blocked strike, Maddix felt himself slowing.

He wasn't aware that the crystal around his neck had come loose until pain exploded in his head. Maddix didn't even have time to scream, his knees giving out beneath him. He was able to hang onto his sword, but he was in no shape to fight, not with splinters of agony ripping inside of his skull.

Somewhere, he could hear the witch hissing ragged curses. Maddix had just enough presence of mind to be grateful she was conscious

"Freaks, both of you." Oskar pulled his sword back and Maddix closed his eyes, bracing for impact that never came. His blade clattered to the ground, landing just shy of Maddix's midsection.

The witch's voice sounded above him, furious and vengeful. "*Khayald*." The word was an accusation, a condemnation, a death sentence. Her hands were outstretched, fingers twitching, and Oskar screamed like he was being ripped apart. "You want a monster? I'll give you one."

"Stop," Maddix ground through clenched teeth. Through the splitting pain in his head, he managed to stand. Darkness swirled around the witch's hands, twisting between her fingers. "*Val*—stop! You're killing him."

"I mean to," she said. Her voice lost its anger, leaving only perfect, terrible calm behind. She clenched her fist and, what was left of Oskar fell, hitting the floor with a heavy *thump*. His skin was gray, mouth was stretched into one last, eternal scream. Maddix sucked in a breath, a vision of the souls trapped in the Dark witch's robe rushing to the forefront of his mind.

"Put this back on," the witch ordered, tossing him the white gem necklace. As soon as it touched Maddix's skin the pain in his head vanished, taking the vision with it. He snuck a glance at her hands but there was no trace of Darkness left.

"What did you do to him?" Maddix gaped, rubbing the back of his hand against his forehead. The thing on the floor hardly looked human.

"He deserved it," she said, not looking at the corpse as she retrieved her black duster from its discarded place in the corner. She clenched and unclenched her fist, and Maddix felt a rush of gratitude for the cuffs that bound them. However he died, he didn't want to go out like Oskar.

"No one deserves that," Maddix said. "A sword in the back would've been kinder."

"I did not mean to be kind," the witch said. Her shoulders slumped slightly, weighed down by some unseen load. "He was like me."

"What?"

"He was *sahir*," she said, rounding on him.

You animals even turn on each other. Hale's voice echoed in his head. Fire burned emerald in her eyes and Maddix had to steel himself from backing away from her.

"A witch, capturing and selling his own people. To the *sahirla* to be killed for sport or rich *dayri* who want magical slaves or to Vandel or Kaddah to be taken apart. I did not mean to be kind. I hope he burns."

He'd assumed Oskar was a bounty hunter, someone after Jayin for the reward. Not this. Nothing like this.

"He deserved it," she repeated, her voice ragged. Maddix had a sudden, ridiculous impulse to lay a hand on her shoulder. He balled his fists by his sides, telling himself it wasn't worth losing a finger.

"Let's get out of here," he suggested when he couldn't stand the silence any longer.

The witch didn't say a word, ducking her head so he couldn't see her eyes. It was odd to see the sun waiting for them outside after everything that had happened. It felt like it should have been the dead of night not early evening with the sky still a cheerful blue above them.

The witch followed him out of the shack, making a small noise of surprise when Maddix didn't immediately walk away. Instead, he fished in his bag for a book of matches and offered them to her. She took them without a word, and within minutes, the dilapidated house was ablaze with Oskar's corpse still inside. They stood and watched it burn for a long time, neither speaking until the girl spat on the ground. It was more blood than saliva.

"Jayin," she said without expression.

"What?" Maddix said, his eyes still on the fire.

"My name is Jayin." She stalked away from the burning building, a dark smudge against a backdrop of smoke and fire. Jayin. The name echoed in Maddix's ears. It was too delicate for her, too soft to belong to this girl with her daggers and scars.

The palfrey wasn't waiting where Maddix had left her, the reins bitten clean through. No doubt the animal had panicked when she saw the fire. He hoped she would find her way home and sent silent thanks down the road where her hoof prints led.

He and the witch—*Jayin*—walked without speaking to one another. Maddix found himself as half of a duo shrouded in tense silence, making their way to the next town as if this day had been just like all of the others. As if Jayin hadn't been kidnapped by one of her own people intent on selling her to whoever could pay. As if she hadn't just killed someone.

When he was young, Maddix entertained himself with notions of the glory of battle, of proving himself through the trials of war and blood. And then, as a greenblood Guard, he knew he would kill, and see his comrades kill. It was a part of the job, a part of life. Death was something he knew and understood.

But not like this. The way she killed was like nothing Maddix had ever seen. Again, he heard Hale's voice hissing in the back of his mind. Unnatural. Evil. *Dark*. She had killed Oskar with little more than a gesture and sheer force of will.

Maddix liked to think he was above the death and violence that had been a companion since he was small. Even after the witch had taken his body from him and used his hands to kill, Maddix never thought of himself as a murderer.

Until Mole. He tried to think it was self-defense, how he'd smashed the small, strange man's head in until Maddix was covered in blood and brains. Maybe it was. But when Maddix thought about that night, the memories were so saturated with fear and anger he didn't know if he had been just protecting himself or if the years in the Pit had finally turned him into a monster.

Monster. The witch had called herself the same.

And so they walked, with Oskar's pyre still burning behind them. A pair of monsters, on their way back to the city that created them.

CHAPTER TWENTY-ONE:

MADDIX

Maddix was sure his feet were going to be nothing more than bleeding stumps in his boots by the time they stopped walking. Jayin insisted they walk through the sunset sweep to make up for lost time, and the moon was high in the sky by the time she found them someplace to sleep.

"One room," the woman in the lobby snapped. The boardinghouse was a lucky find, and it was even luckier the doors were still open at this time of the night. "Only got one left."

"I'll go somewhere else," Jayin said. "Take the room."

"You're no good to me if you pass out from exhaustion," Maddix said. She didn't respond, simply lifted one shoulder and let it drop. Maddix took it as acceptance.

The room was smaller than most. Jayin's hand lingered on the doorknob for a moment after it was closed. Maddix imagined he could feel the magic sizzling in the air, but it was as silent as ever. He collapsed into a rickety chair by the window, his injuries making themselves known all at once. The wound on his leg was the most pressing; it wasn't deep, but Maddix wasn't willing to take any chances.

"You're doing that wrong," Jayin said, as if he was doing it in purpose to spite her. Maddix didn't respond, very aware of her bright eyes on him as he bandaged the wound.

"Stars, you're useless," she said after a moment, throwing up her hands and stalking towards him. "Here. If you wrap it wrong, you'll cut off the circulation." Maddix held very still, unsure. Jayin's teeth worried her bottom lip as she tied off the bandages, her fingers expertly avoiding his skin even with the gloves. The frustrated line of her brow smoothed by slow degrees as she worked. Not for the first time, Maddix's gaze was drawn to the scar that traced down her cheek and bisected her lips.

"Can I ask you a question?" he asked.

"Depends on what you ask." It wasn't a no.

"Where did you get that scar?"

Jayin shook her head. "Wrong question." She stood, arranging her bedroll on the floor. Maddix supposed the bed was his, then.

"Thank you."

Maddix was nearly asleep when her words broke the silence. He blinked, barely recognizing her. The witch's face was open, honest, unlined by pain or anger. She looked young. "For getting me out of there."

"You're the only one who can find him," Maddix said. Something flashed across the witch's face and something slid behind her eyes, as quickly and surely as a curtain being drawn. She turned her back to him and didn't speak again.

Maddix didn't sleep. He slept so rarely these nights, plagued by nightmares that lived in the dark. There was a reason the Pit was such an effective prison. Without light or hope to stave off the darkness, inmates went mad. Most killed themselves. Maddix couldn't decide which nightmare was worse, reliving Mole's murder or running headlong through the dark, knowing Hale's cold, hungry eyes waited for him if he faltered. Sometimes they swirled together in a terrifying, senseless jumble, and Maddix woke with his heart pounding so hard he was sure his ribs would crack under the strain.

"What is wrong with you?"

Maddix froze at the sound of Jayin's voice. He knew that his restlessness sometimes woke her, and he considered it a kindness she never said anything. Apparently that line of credit had dried up.

"What?" Maddix asked, feigning sleepiness. Jayin glared. The wide-eyed girl from before was gone, vanished as if she'd never existed.

"*Dayri*," she said, scrubbing the back of her hand over her eyes. "Remember if you keel over from exhaustion, so do I, and I refuse to die because you can't sleep."

"I'm trying," Maddix said. "But—" He clamped his mouth shut, wishing the word unsaid.

"But what?" the witch said. She was a circling shark, and his weakness was blood in the water. "What, is the bed not comfortable enough for your tender sensibilities? Or are you worried I'll shiv you in your sleep? Because you took care of that when you leashed me like an animal."

"The dark," Maddix snapped, louder than intended. "Remember I spent two years in pitch blackness, waiting to be executed at your king's pleasure, *witch*."

He expected her to snipe or shout, but she didn't take the bait. Instead she sat up, facing him.

"He's not my king," she said.

"You could've fooled me."

Jayin pinched the bridge of her nose and sighed. "Close your eyes," she ordered.

"Why?" His suspicion gave the word teeth.

Jayin only rolled her eyes, raising her hands. Maddix didn't look away as she inhaled; the air shimmered around her as if the witch was giving off heat. A soft gold light gathered on her skin, turning it to glowing bronze and highlighting her scars in molten silver. It only remained for a second before the light pulled away and floated into the air. Maddix gaped, openmouthed, as the magic chased the darkness away. "How are you doing that?" Maddix asked once he could find his voice again. It shouldn't be possible, not while he wore the stone.

"The *sahirla* don't know as much about magic as they think they do," she said. Maddix didn't miss the satisfaction that colored her tone. "And I'm not the Kingswitch's pet anymore either." Jayin pulled at the silver cuff, revealing raised, puckered scar tissue encircling her wrist. Even bathed in golden glow, the ruined skin was hard to look at. The burn was clearly self-inflicted, done with a shaking hand. Whatever mark had been on her wrist before, the witch was determined to destroy it.

"I need you too," she said. "I hate silver." She almost smiled, her eyes clear and spectacularly green in the magic's light. Maddix tried to find the words to thank her. Something bloomed in the air, arching between them, trying to take shape. Something as fragile and delicate as spun glass. Something—

You wouldn't thank an animal. Hale's voice rose up in his mind. *Don't forget what she is.* Maddix wanted to agree with him, but somehow, he couldn't reconcile his hatred with the girl who was giving him a light in the darkness.

"Go to sleep, *dayri*," Jayin said before he could sort out his thoughts, and the moment shattered. The witch turned away from him without another word, without giving him the chance to try to pick up the pieces. Maddix held his breath, sure the light would flicker and die with the witch's ire. But it remained, floating above him like a miniature sun, and for the first time in weeks, Maddix slept.

CHAPTER TWENTY-TWO:

JAYIN

Something was coming. Call it intuition or paranoia, but something wasn't right. She could feel it with every step closer to Pavaal, dogging her footsteps. At first, she assumed it was guilt prickling on the back of her neck, but the traitor had gotten what he deserved. Wherever Oskar was, she hoped he was still burning.

Whatever was causing the nagging sensation, she wished it would try to kill them and be done with it. Waiting had never been her strong suit.

"What?" Kell asked, raking his fingers through his wet hair. The sky was black, the moon obscured by thunderclouds. She'd found them an abandoned barn where they could hole up until the storm cleared, but it was starting to look like they'd be there all night. "You've been acting strange for days. What aren't you telling me?"

Jayin shot Kell a look, pulling her knees up to her chest. The damp duster around her shoulders did little to keep out the cold. She wanted to tell him to skiv off, to stop pretending that he knew her.

The weight of the matchbook in her pocket stopped her. She could still see the flames burning when she closed her eyes, erasing the *khayald* from this world. It wasn't much, but it was enough that she swallowed her acidic comments.

"Something's wrong," she said, struggling to find words.

"Besides the torrential downpour and the bounties on our heads?"

Jayin glared, her indulgence of him drying up almost instantly. She scrubbed the back of her hand over her eyes, pulling her coat tighter around her shoulders. "I can't tell if you think you're funny, or if you're just as stupid as you look."

Kell raised an eyebrow. "Right, says the girl who looked like a drowned cat."

"Are you adding cat-killing to your list of crimes, convict?" Jayin replied, self-consciously running her fingers through her jagged bangs. "You don't look much better."

His hair was out of its usual knot, hanging loose to his shoulders, red-gold and sopping wet. He'd already shucked off his soaked shirt and hung it over a wooden beam, revealing a lean chest cut in hard lines and dotted with old scars.

"Let's assume your feeling has nothing to do with my style choices," he ventured. Jayin didn't miss how he bit his lip to keep from laughing.

"I'm starting to think that it might," she replied.

"Jayin," Kell said. Hearing him say her name was still odd, though he didn't use it very often. It was almost too familiar, and the strange way it sounded on his lips set her teeth on edge. At least he'd stopped calling her *valyach*.

"It's been easy," Jayin said finally. "All of this. It's been too easy."

"You mean besides the *val*—" Jayin glared at him. "The witch who kidnapped you? What was it you called him?"

"*Khayald*," Jayin said, her mouth twisting into a scowl. "Blood traitor." In the Palace, they probably called her the same.

"Right, besides this kobold character who tried to *sell* you?"

"*Khayald*," Jayin corrected. "That wasn't supposed to happen."

"You think any of this was supposed to happen?" Kell insisted, his eyebrows furrowing. "We escaped from a *helwyr* compound by jumping into the ocean. We should be well beyond dead right now."

Jayin shook her head. They'd walked for miles without seeing so much as another person, let alone the *sahirla.* There should be soldiers, bounty hunters, *someone* looking for them. It was as if their way had been cleared, smoothed by some divine hand.

"I am a Palace witch and former *sahirla* captive," she said. "And you are a convicted murderer and traitor to your zealot witchhunter friends. Besides one rogue witch who came across me by accident, we haven't been spotted or seen."

"I thought you were taking care of that?" Kell asked. "Finding us safe routes."

"I can hardly find you half the time and I'm sure your friends have much more sophisticated anti-*sahir* talismans than a rock on a string. It's not foolproof, what I can do. It's just magic."

Kell ogled at her, his hand going to his throat. "*Just* magic?"

Stars, *dayri* really didn't know anything.

"Yes, just magic," Jayin repeated like she was talking to a simpleton. "I'm just saying there should be more patrols, more people. Our faces should be everywhere. We should've been *seen.*"

"You're right," Kell said finally, still worrying the pendant. He inhaled through his nose, his pale chest expanding. "Why do I feel like we've been jinxed?"

Jayin raised one shoulder and dropped it. Dread settled deep in her bones, weighing her down, and leeching away her strength. Kell didn't look much better. For a single moment they were united as exhaustion took its toll.

"I'll take the first watch," Kell offered, rubbing at his eyes.

"No, it's fine," she said, standing up to work the kinks out of her legs. Her shirt was almost dry and she could sleep under her coat.

"Jayin." There it was again. He drew out the first syllable of her name, letting it hang in the air. "You're tired, and you're no good to me if you burn yourself out."

Jayin scowled, the fleeting sense of camaraderie vanishing in an instant. She moved to brush past him, and Kell caught her arm.

She moved without thinking, ripping Kell's hand away from her and bringing a hooked blade to his throat. Jayin was only touching his shirt, but the close proximity made her head throb.

"Do not touch me," she hissed, dragging him down by his collar. She was close enough to see the hint of gray in his eyes and smell the homemade soap he'd used to wash his clothes a few days before. "It'll hurt both of us, but I bet I'll handle it better."

"Stars, are all of you like this?" Kell demanded when she released him. He didn't move away from her, standing his ground. "Or am I just lucky to be stuck with the single most emotionally stunted witch in this skyforsaken kingdom?"

Rage flared hot in her belly, and Jayin's grip tightened around the knife's handle. "You're the one with the taste for bondage jewelry," she snarled. She waved the cuff at him, the silver glinting like her blade. "If you want a kinder, gentler *sahir,* let me go and hunt another one. That is what you *sahirla* do, isn't it?"

"I need you," Kell said. He sounded earnest, as if that somehow made it better.

"Stop *saying* that!" Jayin shouted, spinning and hurling one of her straightblades in one movement. Kell ducked just in time to keep the knife from plunging through his forehead. It struck the wall instead, the handle quivering from the force of the throw. A tiny, horrible part of her wished it'd struck true.

"What is *wrong* with you?" Kell demanded. The blood drained from his face, leaving it ashen. "I die, you die, remember?"

"Let's be very clear," Jayin said, her voice icily calm. "You do not need me. You need my magic, and you've made it very clear what you and your antiquated band of witch-hunting crazies think of my people. You hate us until you need us, but we're disposable. Work animals for you to use and then put down."

"I didn't—"

"I am not a tool in your arsenal." She looked him up and down, raking him over. "Want to know the saddest part?" she asked. "You actually think you're different."

The *sahirla*, the *khayald*, they saw her as something subhuman, something to be used, but at least they were honest about it. Kell had the audacity to treat her like a person while leading her by the nose to her death.

She saw something flash in his eyes, too quick to place before it was gone. It didn't matter, she told herself. She didn't care about his comfort or his feelings. He'd be just as bad as Hale someday. He'd be worse. Grabbing her coat and throwing it over her head, Jayin stalked outside, heedless of the pouring rain.

"Jayin!" Maddix shouted. She ignored him. It was better when he just called her *valyach* like the rest of them. Stars, she'd been so stupid, thinking maybe he might be different. Bringing her to Old Aya, calling her by name, the matches, they were all just ploys to make her more willing to help him.

Kell didn't follow her, and Jayin didn't turn back. It was wet and freezing, but she couldn't stand the thought of being near him. She wandered aimlessly, following stray bits of energy as they swirled in the air, until she heard the rattle of wagon wheels.

Pulling her hood firmly over her hair and spinning a quick glamor to distort her appearance, Jayin crept forward. There were people everywhere, milling about in the darkness. It felt like a village, but it wasn't stable, wasn't permanent. She didn't feel any *sahirla* but there were too many auras to be sure.

"Excuse me, mister," Jayin said, fixing an embarrassed smile on her face as she approached a man on horseback. "I've been hearing the commotion for days and wanted to see what was going on."

"In the rain?" the man questioned, but it was more indulgent than suspicious.

"Mama always said I was too curious for my own good."

"It's for the protection of the people," the man said. "These are dangerous times, what with killers and rogue witches running free." He waved a hand and through the rain Jayin could see the beginnings of a massive structure jutting up into the sky. Soldiers strutted along its length, their auras coiled like springs, waiting for violence. A wall. It was a bloody, starcursed *wall.*

A weight dropped into Jayin's stomach. One day more and they would've walked right into it.

"It sure is big," she said, tilting her head up and squinting at the top of the wall. She was playing the country bumpkin a little too heavily, but the soldier didn't mind. The wall wasn't even completed, and the structure dwarfed anything she'd ever seen outside of Pavaal.

"It's going to keep the whole inner kingdom from outlanders and murderers. Rebels too." Jayin's heart sunk even further.

"Can I…?" Jayin hedged. She was pushing her luck and she knew it, but she needed to know more. "Can I see inside?" The man didn't answer for a moment and Jayin looked away, trying to seem abashed. "I'm sorry," she whispered. "Never mind."

"I'm sure it couldn't hurt," he said finally, grandly dismounting his horse and handing the reins off to another worker. The man slung his arms around her shoulders and Jayin had to fight the urge to shrug him off.

Jayin allowed herself to be led towards the massive structure and crowded into a rickety box at its base. The man pulled a lever on the side of the box and it lurched into motion, pulling them skywards. Jayin's breath came in a surprised huff and the man laughed.

"You get used to it," he promised. Jayin wasn't sure she wanted to. The box opened on the top of the structure, and even in the rain she could see for miles. While the soldier chattered on about the miracles of modern science and the blessings of architecture, Jayin threw her abilities as far down the wall as she could reach—

—And reached Kaddah. The wall stretched all the way to Kaddah. Om's birthplace, the sworn enemy of Vandel, and whose anti-*sahir* practices made the *sahirla* look like amateurs. Some people said any witches found within their borders they were enslaved for their magic. Collared and tortured until they couldn't remember their own names. Others disagreed, describing the dungeons as massive experimental chambers, and said that the Kaddahn were trying to steal the *sahir*'s abilities and bottle them.

"Burning skies," Jayin murmured.

"What was that?" the man asked. His voice was small and far away, unimportant. Something caught her attention as she drew her power back in. A blank space where there should have been something. Panic settled behind her heart, slithering through her blood like tar. Even with the stone, Jayin had only felt malevolence like that from one person.

"Well, well." Jayin froze at the sneering voice. "I wondered when you were going to show up."

Hale. Even in the rain, the *sahirla* was dressed in all white, and his milky blue eyes fixed on her. His thin mouth was twisted into a smile, and Jayin could see a white gem glittering at his throat.

"Sir?" the man asked, snapping a salute. He wasn't a witchhunter, but he deferred to Hale. "Do you know this girl?"

"Know her?" Hale purred. "She's the witch we've all been trying to catch."

"Imprisonment didn't take before." Her voice trembled slightly, but she was more concerned with cobbling together an escape plan than putting on a brave face. She was alone, outnumbered, and fifty feet up. The last time she jumped from this height it had almost killed her, and even then she'd jumped into the ocean. There was nothing but unyielding stone below her now.

"You were more resourceful than I anticipated," Hale admitted with a shrug. "And you had help. Where is Maddix Kell? I thought he'd want to keep you close, what with the bond and all. Don't think I didn't notice when those cuffs went missing. Clever, tying you to him in order to compel your help. But I take comfort in the knowledge that he'll feel everything I have planned for you."

"I'll be sure to tell him you send your love."

Hale signaled and the soldier's hand clasped around Jayin's arm. She didn't hesitate, bringing her knife up in one fluid motion. The hand hit the ground with a wet *thump*. The man screamed, clutching the bleeding stump to his chest as he went to his knees.

"You do like those knives," Hale said, stepping around his bleeding comrade. "I'll be sure to remember that when we get you back to the stronghold."

"Not going to happen," Jayin hissed. All eyes were on them now, and she knew she only had a second before the soldiers converged. Jayin threw her arms wide, gathering as much magic to her as she could and hurling it away from her.

Bright green flames erupted on the far side of the wall. The glamor was sloppy and imperfect but it was enough. The cry spread to all of the workers, and the wall shook under the weight of dozens of booted feet. Jayin used the chaos as cover, diving into the panicked crowd.

"The witch!" someone shouted as Jayin shoved past him. She ran until the rickety platform gave way, leaving a gaping hole with nothing to catch her but the empty air. She'd have to climb.

You can do this, Ijaad, she told herself, peering over the edge of the wall. *You've been captured, tortured, shot, drowned, and saddled with the biggest idiot in Aestos on a suicide mission. You're not going to fall to your death.* It wasn't much by way of a pep talk, but it was enough to get her moving.

"Ah, ah, *valyach*," Hale said, appearing at the top of the wall. He was holding a crossbow, the same kind that had put a bolt through her chest at the witchhunter's compound. "You didn't think it would be that easy, did you?"

"And I didn't think you were that stupid," Jayin said. Her voice was tight, and she could already feel the muscles in her arms cramping from clinging to the side of the wall. Hale's head cocked in benign confusion, still aiming the crossbow at her. "If you shoot me now, I won't survive the fall and you'll kill Kell along with me. We both know that you need to use him as an example of how *sahirla* traitors are handled."

Jayin didn't wait to gage his reaction. She threw all of her weight off of the wall, hands grasping for a rope dangling just out of reach. The air shifted by her arm, and the crossbow bolt lodged in the wall, missing her head by a hairsbreadth.

Her palms burned as the cable slid through her hands. She landed hard, the impact reverberating all the way to her hips.

As soon as her feet touched the ground she was running, sprinting headlong away from the wall. Jayin weaved as arrows sailed past her head, not stopping until she was well out of range. She couldn't go back to the barn without leading them straight to Maddix. Instead, Jayin found a place to hide, slipping into an old barn that had been reclaimed by the elements. It was half-collapsed, barely big enough to squeeze into.

The wall seethed like a disturbed anthill, but Jayin didn't dare to move. People—soldiers, worker, *sahirla*—ran around everywhere, searching for her. Twice she could feel the blank space where Hale's aura should be, too close for comfort. Jayin buried her head in her arms, barely breathing until he moved on.

Finally, just as the sun was starting to rise, Jayin dared to move from her makeshift hiding spot.

"Where the *hell* have you been?" Kell demanded the minute Jayin staggered inside. He took a step towards her as if to crowd her into a corner before thinking better of it. Smart boy. "I thought you, that you—"

"If I'd been hurt, you would've felt it," Jayin said, not bothering to keep the bite out of her voice. She'd been up all night after barely getting away from Kell's sadistic witchhunter mentor; she didn't have a lot of patience to spare. "And you'd better be careful, convict, or someone might think that you care."

"I—"

"Remember how you said we'd been jinxed?" Jayin said, cutting him off. She didn't have time for half-baked apologies. "I found the jinx."

CHAPTER TWENTY-THREE:

MADDIX

A wall. A great, big, skyforsaken *wall.* In the time it had taken them to get this close to Pavaal, fifty feet of wood and stone had been constructed to stop them.

Skies.

"Then let's go around," Maddix offered once she'd finished with her explanation. Jayin shook her head, her movements jerky and stiff.

"If we go around," she said slowly, "then we have to go through Kaddah, and if I go to Kaddah, I won't make it out. And you need me, remember?" Maddix bit his lip to keep from using those words to reassure her. The last time he tried she'd nearly carved him a second smile.

He should have gone after her. He should have proved she was wrong—she had to be wrong. But Maddix let her go, and he kept the bracelet on. He was still using her. Shame bubbled up inside him, and Maddix tasted the acid of it on the back of his throat. Maybe he *was* worse than Hale.

"So what, magic is outlawed in Kaddah. It's practically outlawed here. How will they even know you're there?" Maddix's patience was waning, worn thin from the stress of the night.

"I don't know," Jayin answered, the words sharp and bitter. "Witches who go into that place don't come out."

"So you have no proof? Nothing that says we won't be able to just waltz in. How do you—"

"Because Om told me!" Jayin shouted. She glared at him like she meant to say more before something splintered in her gaze. Her hands trembled, and she slid down the wall as if her legs couldn't support her any longer. Maddix could only watch, horrified, as she collapsed in on herself. He didn't know what to do, what to say, and settled for pacing, his hands flapping uselessly by his sides.

"He survived half of his life in that skyforsaken queendom, and then I got him killed." The words were so soft that Maddix wasn't sure he heard her correctly. Jayin lifted her head and he tensed, readying himself for an attack.

"You were there," she said, not looking at him. "He was trying to protect me." Maddix struggled to stand his ground as he recalled the firewitch from the docks.

He waited for her to turn the blame on him, to call him *sahirla*, traitor, any number of names before threatening to gut him like a carp. But the words didn't come, and Jayin simply stared through him, trapped somewhere he couldn't reach.

"I killed him," she said finally. Tears glittered on her cheeks. "He survived Kaddah and he survived the Palace, but he didn't survive me."

"It wasn't—" Maddix started, but she cut him off before he could finish. He wished he'd let her say the words. He was glad she stopped him.

"No one knows how the Kaddahn can sense magic, but they can. And the moment a witch steps over their border, they send in kill squads. However they do it, it's real."

"So we go through," Maddix said, scrambling for some kind of solution. Anything to erase the terrible, glassy-eyed look from her face. "You said that the wall is only half finished. It shouldn't be too hard to get through."

"Hale is there," Jayin said. Maddix's blood turned to ice. "I think he's working with Ayrie to get the wall built. There's no other way that he'd have the authority or manpower to get it done so quickly."

"And you didn't think to lead with that?"

He found it hard to believe she could forget the man who'd tried to kill them both. Maddix had thought Hale was going to be his mentor, that he and the other *helwyr* were the keys to his vengeance. Stars, he really was a stupid, naïve boy, thinking that he would be able to carve a place out for himself in the world after everything he'd been through, everything he'd done.

"I was a little preoccupied," Jayin replied. She shifted and it was only then Maddix saw something dark dripping from her fingers.

"You're bleeding," he said. He hadn't felt her get hurt. How was that possible?

"I'm fine," Jayin insisted, but Maddix felt the throbbing pain as she finally noticed it herself. Slowly, she shucked off her duster and he could see the long gash on the inside of her arm. Shock was a powerful numbing agent, but that looked like it hurt.

It *felt* like it hurt.

"Let me," Maddix started. "I mean…" He knew better than to try to order her to do anything.

Jayin nodded and stretched out her arm so he could look at it. The cut was bloody but shallow. It didn't need stitches.

"How didn't you feel this?" Maddix wondered aloud as he cleaned her arm. They winced at the bite of antiseptic.

"I was trying to climb down a wall and convince Hale not to shoot me in the head. Forgive me if I didn't have time to worry about a graze."

"This is more than a graze," Maddix insisted. Blood seeped through the bandage faster than he could wrap it.

"I've had worse," Jayin said. Maddix didn't doubt it. He'd seen the mess of scars on her abdomen, souvenirs of the witchhunters and whatever she had done for the Palace. Her arms and back bore evidence of violence too, thin pale slashes and punctures that had long since healed. Maddix wondered why she kept them, when a Palace healer could simply magick them away.

"I'm sorry about your friend," Maddix said after a few moments of tense silence.

"You didn't kill him," Jayin said. "If you did, we wouldn't be having this conversation, and I'd probably still be a *sahirla* captive." She paused before laughing to herself. Maddix couldn't tell if it was the stress of the night, blood loss, or a mixture of the two. Perhaps she was just mad. "Stars, he would've hated you."

"Why?"

"You're crazier than I am," she said with a small, unlikely smile.

"No one's crazier than you," Maddix said.

"Says the convict dragging us back to Pavaal." She sat back, leaning her head against the barn wall. "Where we will be captured or killed." The small smile was still there, but Maddix's heart twisted at the exhausted bleakness in her voice.

"We're not going to die," Maddix insisted, but he didn't sound sure, even to himself. With the wall and Hale's reappearance, their odds of survival had gone from unlikely to dismal.

"See?" she said. "Crazy."

"I'll break the link," Maddix said. Jayin's eyes found his, and he saw his own surprise reflected there. "If anything happens, I'll break it. You're not going to die on my behalf, I promise." He didn't know why it was so important that he say it. Maybe he was trying to convince her he wasn't the same as the other hunters.

Maybe he was trying to convince himself. It was amazing how quickly allegiances shifted when the people he'd broken out of prison to find were the ones trying their best to kill him.

"Don't make promises you can't keep."

"I don't intend to."

"He *really* would've hated you," Jayin said.

"Smart man."

"Smarter than me," she agreed. "Smart enough to keep his head down and stay put when he had the full force of Ayrie Palace bearing down on him."

Just like that, Maddix understood. She must have convinced Om to leave whatever hole he'd dug and leave with her, and that's why he was on the docks when the *helwyr* ambushed them. He was never meant to be there.

"If I ask why he was a fugitive are you going to threaten to stab me?" Maddix tried.

Jayin took an uneven breath. "He came for sanctuary, but the King was going to give him back to Kaddah, so he ran. I was ordered to find him, and then I let him go."

"Why would you do that?"

"Because he was scared, and you can't fake that kind of fear." Her mouth turned down and she closed her eyes. "Your *sahirla* friends would've loved him. A witch afraid of his own magic."

"They're not my friends," he insisted. "They're trying to kill me too, remember?"

"But you wanted to be one of them," Jayin said. She didn't sound angry anymore, just tired. Somehow, that was worse. "You use their bastard language, abide by their prejudices, and have no problem using my people to get what you want." Absently, she ran her fingers over the silver cuff, tracing swirling designs on the metal. Maddix was starting to hate the sight of it. More than that, he hated that he wouldn't take it off. He wasn't willing to give up his vengeance so easily.

"I just…" Maddix stood. Guilt and shame roiled inside of him. This rabid need for justice had sustained him in the Pit, but now— "I never wanted any of this. Do you think that if I hadn't been attacked, I would give a damn about witchhunters and runaway *sahir* and a war that most people don't even know exists? Witches *ruined* my life, and all I want is to prove that I'm innocent."

"*Dayri* don't have a monopoly on suffering," she said. "I've suffered plenty at the hands of my own people, and you don't see me joining up with lunatics."

"No, you just ran away," Maddix snapped. If they'd destroyed her life just like they'd done to him, he couldn't understand why she wouldn't want to fight back. "At least I'm trying to do something about it."

Slowly, Jayin stood up, fixing him with a dark green stare.

"Then we'll find a way through."

CHAPTER TWENTY-FOUR

JAYIN

They left the barn at sunset. Jayin wanted to leave earlier, loath to stay in one place with Hale searching for them, but Kell insisted. He took watch as she slept, his eyes on the door and his sword held in his lap.

"You know," Kell said, kneeling to pick the lock on an abandoned farmhouse. Heading into the town beside the wall was a risk, but they needed information and this was the closest crossing for miles. "When I set out to clear my name, I didn't think it would involve adding to my criminal resume."

"You're a regular carrion," Jayin said, wishing he'd move faster.

"What would you know about it?" Kell asked, pushing into the house. Jayin didn't bother telling him that she probably knew the Gull better than most Guards. She followed him inside and searched around to see if the previous owners had left anything behind. The activity at the wall had brought this town back to life for the moment, but it wasn't enough to stave off the degradation of the countryside in its entirety.

"This'll do," she said finally. The windows were boarded up and the door locked. It would be a fine place to plan their next move. Hopefully, Hale wouldn't be looking for them in the town anymore. Coming here so soon after she'd been seen was absolutely mad. No one would expect it.

Or so she hoped.

She was bandaging the wound on her arm when something flared in her second sight. For a moment the aura was Om's, red and scorching, before reality reasserted itself. Whoever the energy belonged to, they were terrified—and they had magic.

Jayin was moving before she could think it through, leaving her arm half-unbound as she ran out the door.

"Jayin!" Kell hissed behind her. His voice was an inconsequential buzzing in her ears, easy to ignore. Jayin wound her way through a tangled warren of alleyways and roads, trying to catch up to the witch.

"*Jayin*!" Kell's voice came again, this time accompanied by a sharp tug on her sleeve.

"Let *go*," she snarled, whirling on him. She didn't have time to explain herself, not when Jayin could feel the witch's fear in her blood.

"What under the stars are you doing?" Kell demanded.

"There's someone out there," Jayin said, ripping free of his grip. The witch's aura was getting further away, and now Jayin could sense the dead space of *sahirla* in pursuit.

"I don't know if you've forgotten, but those someones want us dead."

"A witch, you *dayri* idiot," Jayin snapped. It explained how the wall had been built so quickly. The witchhunters had kidnapped another witch—or several—to do their work for them. "They've got a witch, and if they catch her—"

For a moment, Kell hesitated. In that moment, Jayin hated him all over again.

"I know what happens if they catch her," he said finally. He gestured down the alley. "Lead the way."

Jayin didn't waste time thanking him. She could hear Kell's footsteps behind her and that was enough. Jayin followed the girl's aura easily, as if there was a path laid at her feet. She hadn't used her abilities like this in months, but in the moment, she didn't care.

She'd almost caught up when the ground beneath her feet turned to putty. Jayin staggered, arms pinwheeling as she tried to regain her balance. Her boots were encased in ankle-deep mud and no matter how she struggled they refused to come free.

"I'm not going back," said a voice from the shadows. "You won't take me back there."

Earthwitch, Jayin thought. She turned to face the girl, but the mud crawled up her body until she was immobile from the neck down.

"Wait," Jayin said. "I can help you."

"No!" the girl cried. Her amber skin was caked with dirt and ash. The bags under her eyes spoke to sleep deprivation. The witch balled her hands into fists, and then Jayin hissed as the mud turned to solid stone. Her chest constricted and she couldn't draw breath without her lungs burning in protest.

"Jayin—" Kell said, finally catching up. He skidded to a stop, taking in Jayin's earthen cocoon and the witch who'd trapped her.

"Stop!" the girl said, her voice trembling with rage. The earth sucked at Kell's boots until he too was forced to be still. "You wait there. I'll get to you once I'm done killing your friend."

The witch raised her hand and Jayin groaned as the vice tightened around her.

"Hey, hey, stop!" Kell said, far too loud to be safe. His voice was tight with Jayin's strain. "Let her go and take me, okay? You don't want her."

"Why not?" the witch snarled.

"Because I'm *sahirla* and I've been using her just like they used you."

Jayin tried to open her mouth to stop him, but her voice had abandoned her.

"See?" he said, pulling at his sleeve so the witch could see the silver cuff around his wrist. "This is one of the weapons in the *sahirla* vault. Everything that I feel, she feels, but I'll take it off if you let her go."

"Why would you do that?" the witch asked, her black eyes slitted with suspicion.

"Because I promised she wasn't going to die on my behalf, and if you kill me while I'm wearing it, you'll kill her too."

"You're lying."

"I'm not," Kell said. "And if I were, hunters would be swarming this place, and you'd be in chains. Let her go and take me."

Don't! Jayin tried to shout but she couldn't force her lungs to cooperate. The witch relaxed her hand and the vice disappeared, sinking back into the earth. Jayin pitched forward, sucking in as much air as she could. Her head spun, but she managed to keep her footing

The witch wasn't paying her any mind, too focused on Kell to see Jayin pull one of the knives out of her belt. The dagger was in the air before the girl could draw breath, spinning hilt over the blade, and she crumpled as the handle collided with the base of her skull.

"Jayin, what—" Kell started, coming up behind her. Jayin spun to meet him, her fist connecting with his cheek. Pain radiated down her own neck and her head snapped to the side from the force of the blow.

"What were you *thinking*?" Jayin demanded, spitting blood out of her mouth. Thankfully she hadn't used the gauntlets. "She would've killed you!"

Kell blinked at her, confusion furrowing his eyebrows.

"I thought," Kell started. "You could've run." The truth of his words hit her like a blow.

Why didn't you run? whispered a voice inside her. *This is what you wanted; this was your chance! Why did you save him?*

She didn't have an answer.

Jayin shook her head, trying to clear it. "I'm not letting another witch become a murderer on your account."

The words fell flat, but Kell didn't comment, instead walking to the witch's prone form and gathering her into his arms.

"What are you doing?" Jayin asked. Kell raised an eyebrow.

"Bringing her back with us," he said, as if it should be obvious. Jayin scouted the area around them, seeking out hunters as they made their way back to the hideout with the stolen witch. She glamored the three of them, but it was luck more than magic that delivered them to their destination safely.

"I'll take the first watch," Jayin said as Kell set the girl down on his bedroll. She spun her knives around her thumbs, watching how the blades glittered in the half-light and steadfastly ignoring the way Kell stared.

"Jayin, what did I do?" he asked, sitting down next to her. Stars, she hated how he said her name. "I thought—"

"I don't want you dying for me either," Jayin said. The worst tumbled out in a rush, sounding like a confession.

She couldn't look at him without seeing Om's body, bloody and broken on the dock that was supposed to lead them to freedom. She raised her hand, showing the cuff and trying to steady her voice.

"We've come too far." She understood he had never planned to take the cuff off. It was the only thing binding them together, and as he was constantly reminding her, he couldn't do this alone.

"I saved her for you," Kell said. "To prove to you—"

"Prove what?" Jayin growled. "That you're stupid enough to throw your life away after *everything* we've done to get you back to Pavaal? Does none of this matter to you?"

"To prove that I'm not like them!" Kell said so sharply Jayin's words died on her tongue. "Stars, Jayin, do you think I like the way you look at me? Do you think I don't *know*?

Behind them, the girl shifted, and Maddix rose to his feet.

"I'll sleep in the other room. It's probably best that the first thing she sees isn't…me."

Part of Jayin wanted to insist he stay. *Why*? asked the insidious voice inside her. Again, Jayin didn't have an answer, and Kell was gone before she could make sense of her warring impulses.

"Where…?" the girl asked, and Jayin forced herself to refocus.

"You're safe," Jayin said. "But if you turn your magic on me again, you won't be." The girl paled. Fear froze her aura and turned her blood to ice. "What's your name?" Jayin asked, trying to smooth the edge out of her voice.

"Kaolin," the girl said. "Who are you?"

"Jayin Ijaad. I'm *sahir* like you."

"Jayin…" Kaolin repeated, her eyes widening. "The explosion. That was you?" Jayin nodded, a glamored plume of emerald flame erupting in the air between them.

Kaolin jumped, the fire reflecting in her dark, slanted eyes. "If you can do that, why didn't you just blast through the wall?"

"Because it's not real," Jayin said, and the fire guttered out. "Illusions are all I have. Good for distraction, not so good for demolition."

"But—" the girl asked before something seemed to occur to her and she froze, looking around. "Where is he? The *sahirla*?"

"He's still here," Jayin replied, trying not to let her irritation twist in her stomach. "I would appreciate if you didn't try to kill him either."

"Why?" Kaolin demanded. "He's one of *them*."

"Actually, he's not," Jayin interrupted. "They want him dead too, so for now we're on the same side."

"But—"

"Enough," Jayin said sharply. "Kaolin, please." The "please" seemed to give Kaolin pause. "We need to get through the wall."

"There's no way through," the girl replied without hesitation. "I—they made me… It's not possible. They will kill you if you try to cross."

And I'll die if I go around, Jayin thought.

"They've tried before," she said. The arrow scar pulsed like a second heartbeat, like a reminder.

"I made the walls," Kaolin admitted, ducking her head. "They're reinforced by magic and guarded day and night. Even if you try to go through where it's not finished, the *sahirla* will find you first. I'm sorry."

"It's not your fault," Jayin said. Kaolin flinched.

Jayin closed her eyes, her anger melting away. How could she fault the girl for doing what Jayin had done for years—simply trying to survive? Kaolin had no reason to trust Kell, and after everything she'd been through at the hands of the *sahirla*, trust would be tantamount to suicide. Stars, *Jayin* barely had a reason to trust him.

"Kaolin, listen to me. None of this is your fault. The hunters are monsters, and one day they're going to get everything that's coming to them."

"I just want to go home," Kaolin whispered.

"And where's home?"

"The colonies. My parents sent me to train at the Academy, but I never made it." Pain twisted the girl's delicate features, and Jayin's fists clenched by her sides. "They took me on the road. I—I was traveling with other witches from outside of the Three Kingdoms and they—" She exhaled, her voice breaking. "I'm the only one they kept alive."

"I was on a ship to the Isles," Jayin said, not looking at her. "A friend and I—another witch—were looking for a fresh start. We were going to go somewhere no one would ever find us. But the *sahirla* had a different plan. They killed him right in front of me."

Jayin took a shaky breath, feeling the remnant of Om's aura in her second sight, as if talking about him called his spirit to her. "You can go home," she said, an idea springing to life. "I know someone who might be able to help you, we just need to get you far enough away from here that they'll stop looking."

"They'll never stop," Kaolin whispered. "They're never going to let me go."

"Yes, they will," Kell said, reappearing. Kaolin stiffened, gathering her magic like a shield. "Believe me, they want us more than they want you."

Jayin couldn't disagree. Hale knew that they were close; he knew that they would try to cross the wall. He wouldn't risk losing them by chasing after a single runaway witch.

"I can get you as far as the next town, and then you need to find your way to Southport," Jayin said. "Do you know where that is?" Kaolin nodded. "Good. When you're there, find an old woman named Ayanara Awlsley and tell her that I sent you. She'll help you get home."

Jayin stood but Kell was quicker.

"I'll take her," he said. "It's too dangerous for two of you to be out in the open. I'm not a witch; no one will look at me too closely."

"Kell…" Jayin said, battling between suspicion and concern. For all his talk of wanting to save Kaolin, he was still, well—

"Jayin, please," Kell said. "Let me do this." *For you.* The words rang in her ears, unspoken but heard.

"Fine, but I'll be watching," Jayin said, tapping her temple. "Both of you." She turned back to Kaolin. "You're going to get home, okay? You're going to put all of this behind you and no one is ever going to hurt you again. You remember who you're looking for?"

"Ayanara Awlsley."

Jayin nodded. "Good."

"Come on then," Kell said briskly, his hand on his sword. "We need to get moving before they do another patrol."

"Watch the skies," Jayin said, the words coming before she could stop them. Kell nodded and Jayin watched as the two of them wound through the streets before disappearing from her sight. Her magic flared, following their auras as they walked quickly from the town. Kaolin would be okay, she told herself.

They both would.

CHAPTER TWENTY-FIVE:

MADDIX

Maddix could feel the witch girl's eyes on him as they walked, watching him as they wound through the town.

"Don't you try anything, hunter," Kaolin growled. Maddix swallowed his barbed reply. She had no reason to trust him, but the constant threats were beginning to grate on him.

"If I wanted to kill you, you would already be dead, and I wouldn't bother lying to Jayin about it."

"What does a *sahirla* care about the opinion of a witch?"

"I'm not—" Maddix started. "I've done enough harm." And he would do more. The bracelet weighed heavily on his wrist, a shining reminder of his cowardice. He should've taken it off before, should've just let Jayin go, but he was too afraid. He needed to see this thing through and there was no way to do it without her.

"You really were going to let me kill you, weren't you?"

Yes. "I knew she would stop you." Unfortunately, traveling with Jayin had not made him any more adept at lying.

"Trying to go through the wall is suicide. No one gets through except for the bounty hunters and only because they have the paperwork," Kaolin said after a long, heavy silence. "You won't make it."

"I've heard that before," Maddix said. "And here I stand." The Pit was supposed to be impossible to escape, and he'd managed. The *sahirla* were impossible to find, and yet he'd found them. It seemed that laughing in the face of the impossible was what he was good at. Maybe—just maybe—it would be enough to get them to Pavaal alive.

They almost made it.

"We're being followed," Kaolin said, reacting to something Maddix couldn't see or hear.

"Just keep walking," Maddix said under his breath, but when he turned to look at her, the witch was gone. Of bloody course she was.

Kaolin planted herself in the middle of the dirt road, her arms outstretched and aimed at a wagon that could only be filled with witchhunters.

"Don't!" Maddix shouted, but the word fell on deaf ears. Kaolin raised her fist and brought it down, and Maddix could only watch as the earth erupted under the wagon. The horses screamed as they were sucked into the ground with the cart. "I'm not going back there," Kaolin said. Her voice was clear and unwavering. The back of Maddix's neck prickled and he grabbed the girl's shoulders, forcing her to duck as an arrow flew over their heads. An ambush.

"You won't be going anywhere if you're dead," Maddix shouted. The wagon had been a decoy and he could hear half a dozen footsteps thundering towards them. He didn't have time for any other words of warning before the hunters were on them.

"Traitor!" one of them shouted before Maddix plunged his sword into the man's stomach. *Come up with a more creative insult*, Maddix thought, yanking his sword free and spinning in time to block the next attack. Through the magic of the cuff, he felt Jayin's heart accelerate, but he didn't have time to wonder what was happening on her end, busy with his own battle.

By the time the dust cleared, his arms were bleeding from a dozen shallow cuts and surrounded by bodies. The witchhunters he hadn't slain were nothing more than earthen statues, solid and suffocated by Kaolin's magic.

"Why did he call you a traitor?" she asked, nudging the man's corpse. "I thought you were supposed to be one of them."

"Because—" Maddix started, before he heard a telltale whistle in the air. "Move!" he shouted, leaping in front of the witch.

Something silver flickered in the edge of his vision and there was pressure against his chest, but no pain. No impact. When he opened his eyes, the arrow was broken on the ground, snapped cleanly in two.

"Come on," Maddix said, not wasting time to thank her for deflecting the arrow. He grabbed her hand and ran towards the overturned cart.

"What are you doing?" she asked.

"Get on," Maddix said, slashing at the leather tying one of the horses to the cart and swinging Kaolin onto its back. "Ride as fast as you can as far as you can. Get to Southport. Find Aya." He smacked the horse's rump, and it erupted into a wild gallop.

Kaolin shouted something back to him, but the words were snatched away by the wind.

Maddix took the long route back into town, every nerve stretched taut as he surveyed for more hunters. Most of the townsfolk had been recruited to work on the wall, but there were enough milling about to make him twitchy. He couldn't risk exposing Jayin by going straight back to their hideout, but staying out in the open was begging to be spotted.

"Get outta the way!" a man barked from behind. Maddix ducked his head, stepping to the side to allow him to pass. A man staggered to keep up, connected to the soldier's horse by a long coil of chain.

Bounty hunter, he thought, watching as the man showed their papers and the doors behind the checkpoint opened.

No one gets through except for the bounty hunters and only because they have the paperwork. Kaolin's words echoed in his ears. Maddix hurried from the checkpoint before anyone noticed him loitering.

"What *happened*?" Jayin's voice appeared a second before she did, the stone around his neck wiping away her magicked disguise. She fell into step beside him, her hood flipped up to hide her face.

"We ran into some trouble," Maddix replied out of the side of his mouth. "But she's safe and on her way to Southport."

Kaolin would be fine, Maddix was sure of it. He pitied anyone who tried to stop her now. The girl's magic was terrifying.

"Where are you going?" Maddix asked when Jayin didn't head to their safehouse.

"The *sahirla* tracked Kaolin to the house," Jayin whispered. "I had to get creative." Maddix was almost afraid to ask what that meant, choosing instead to follow in silence as Jayin led them to a rundown hostel only a mile or so away from the wall.

Maddix was worried about hiding in plain sight, but he trusted Jayin not to walk them into a trap. The tiny inn was so filthy and rundown he doubted they'd seen business in weeks.

"Stars," Jayin said, pushing open the door to their room. "The orphanage was nicer than this," She sucked in a breath, her eyes snapping to his face. It was a slip, her first, and Maddix wasn't going to be the one to break the silence. "Don't look so surprised, *dayri*."

"I just thought—" Maddix started, quickly composing himself to hide his shock.

"That I grew up in a manse in the outer ring, with servants to wait on me hand and foot?"

"I didn't know that there were witch orphans too." With how they prized their magic, Maddix couldn't fathom *sahir* parents giving up their child. Besides, he'd heard more than one person call her Ayrie's favorite. How did an orphan wind up at the Palace at all, let alone their favorite pet?

"I knew there was something familiar about you," Jayin said with the ghost of a smile, and Maddix realized he'd given himself away as well. "We can always recognize our own."

"Southside," Maddix managed, still reeling. "That's where I grew up."

"North," Jayin replied, and Maddix marveled at how close they'd been as children, orphans living with dozens of other unclaimed kids just across the river from one another.

"I thought I was one of you for years." Jayin said without prompting. Maddix had to bite his tongue to keep himself from asking a thousand questions. Even after a lifetime of living side-by-side with witches and his education at the *helwyr* compound, there was so much he didn't know.

There was so much about *her* that he didn't know.

"I lived in a room with eight other girls until the Kingswitch took me to Ayrie. I'm just much a dockrat as you."

"How?" Maddix asked. "How did you know you had magic?"

He expected her to snipe at him, not turn her head away.

"Because I thought I was dying," she answered, spreading her bedroll onto the filthy floor. "And then he found me."

For someone who'd been rescued and thrown into a life every orphan dreamed about, Jayin's voice didn't hold a lot of gratitude for the Kingswitch. For the hundredth time since he met her, Maddix wondered why she'd run away. Or who she was running away from.

He had a hundred questions, a thousand, but Jayin was done talking. Maddix stayed awake long after her breathing evened out. He stared at the rotted ceiling, wondering about corruption that lurked beneath gilt floors and how it was starting to seem like nothing he'd ever believed about the *sahir* was true.

"No," Jayin said the next morning, before he'd managed to explain even half of his plan. He knew she'd react like this, but it wasn't as if they had any other options. "Not a chance, convict."

"It'll work."

"It's a death sentence."

"This whole thing is a death sentence, isn't that what you've been saying this entire time?" Maddix asked. Jayin paced, her movements jerky and stiff

"If anyone's got those anti-*sahir* charms, this whole thing falls apart," she said finally.

"If we stay here, they'll find us, and you're the one who refuses to go to Kaddah."

She turned to him, glaring.

"If you have a better plan, I'd love to hear it." Maddix challenged. His hand went to the jewel at his throat, worrying the stone.

"This is a terrible idea." She was right, of course.

"I know," Maddix said, steeling himself. "Let's get it done."

CHAPTER TWENTY-SIX:

JAYIN

Jayin had been told her entire life she was mad. Before they knew she was *sahir*, the medics thought her pain was caused by some kind of Dark possession. At the Palace, older witches scoffed at her recklessness but whispered worriedly about the things she could see inside their minds. Mind reader and secret stealer. The Kingswitch's favorite, the King's pet. Eventually, the words lost all meaning.

Kell's plan redefined madness, even for her.

"We're going to die," Jayin hissed. Her head ached from the strain of glamoring Kell around the stone. To curious onlookers, he was one of dozens of soldiers milling around the wall. Jayin allowed herself to be dragged behind him, disguised as a stocky man who stank like the bottom of a bottle.

The plan was a simple on, and in a *sahirla*-free world, it might actually work. Jayin could fabricate the credentials and keep them from being detected. But Hale knew they were coming, which meant there would be an untold number of people walking around with those starcursed gems.

"How about you concentrate on magic, and I'll worry about getting us through? Stars, I thought you Northside kids were tougher than this," Kell whispered. Jayin almost laughed and forced herself to swallow the sound.

She dug her elbow into Kell's ribs, using the pain's echo to refocus. She still didn't know if telling him about Northside was a mistake, but if her concentration wavered now, it could kill them both.

Some part of her worried he might use it as leverage. Another part marveled at his unexpected empathy. They'd practically grown up in the same place, only separated by the river that bisected the city. In a different life, they might have grown up together.

Who would she be without magic? She wouldn't have pursued the Guard, that was for sure. After years of living under the matron's thumb, she wouldn't subject herself to a career of taking orders. She might have joined one of the gangs, recruited for her skills with a blade. Maybe she'd already be dead. Maybe she would be running things.

"Hold," a soldier ordered. Jayin snapped out of her thoughts, focusing her attention on him and searching out what he expected to see in order to let them pass. "Papers."

Kell handed over a blank sheet they'd stolen this morning and Jayin projected the correct information, plucked freshly out of the soldier's head. The man nodded after briefly inspecting the paper and waved them through.

"That went better than I expected," Kell murmured.

Jayin rolled her eyes. "You are the most infuriating kind of optimist." The fact that he could remain so after everything that had happened to him was beyond her.

"And you are ten pounds of surly in a nine-pound bag, but here we are," Kell replied easily. Once again, a laugh bubbled up inside her and she shoved it back down. *Don't be an idiot.* "Come on, we're almost through."

As Kell marched her through the inner chamber of the wall, Jayin let her power flare out, searching for the empty spaces that meant there were *sahirla* about. Suspicion prickled under her skin, the sense of unease deepening the closer they came to the other side. The wall should be crawling with witchhunters. Someone should have seen through her glamor by now.

"I have a bad feeling about this," Jayin murmured as they crossed through the second checkpoint.

"Me too," Kell started before words hiccupped and died on his lips.

"Stars, sometimes I hate being right," Jayin hissed, dropping the glamor. It wasn't worth maintaining anymore.

"Ah, our guests of honor have arrived," Hale said, stepping into the middle of the chamber. A chamber studded with white gems. "I'm impressed you made it this far."

Jayin should have it seen coming from miles away, but she'd been too focused on searching out individuals to notice the gaping void in her second sight.

"Look at that," Jayin said, forcing her voice to remain even. There had to be two-dozen soldiers waiting for them, all masked and armed to the teeth. Jayin sized them up. She didn't like their odds. "The zealot thinks we're impressive. High praise." Hale's smile twitched, but the smug look remained in place.

"You two make quite the pair." He turned to Kell. "Oh, Maddix. You could've been such a wonderful *helwyr*. But here you are, allying yourself with one of these animals. I'll be sorry to hear when it kills you."

I am not an 'it'! Jayin wanted to shout. She bit her lip so hard it bled.

"You look real broken up about it," Jayin said.

"Enough from the *valyach*," Hale said, raising a hand. Burning skies, Jayin hated that word. Her lip curled over her teeth in a snarl. "Let's get this over with, shall we?"

Knives appeared in Jayin's hands, and Kell ripped his sword from its sheath. They stood back to back and for the first time, Jayin could sense something in his aura besides pain. He was ready to die by her side. But they wouldn't go down without a fight.

Something shifted inside of her, a magical spark that shouldn't have been possible with so many of the gems studding the walls.

"Run," Jayin whispered to Kell. He stiffened, his muscles tensing. "Run as fast and as far as you can and then take the necklace off."

"Not a chance."

Hale motioned his hand forward and the soldiers advanced, pressing in on them from all sides.

"Then this is going to hurt," she warned, pulling off one of her gloves with her teeth. The second their skin touched, pain bloomed behind her eyes and the strange power surged with it.

Jayin fought through the haze of pain and threw her hands out in front of her. Auras disintegrated under her fingertips, blowing away like ash. Jayin killed five soldiers before Kell ripped his hand out of hers, shoving her hard.

The air beside her shifted, and Jayin moved just in time to avoid the head of a double-bladed axe plunging into her skull. Her movements were uncoordinated and sluggish, slowed by the ringing in her ears. Jayin rolled out of the way, her knife sliding cleanly into his ribs. The soldier fell and Jayin threw her shields back up, lurching into the fight. The chamber erupted into chaos, and it was all she could do to stay standing as the soldiers converged in a tide of violence and steel. Time dissolved into chaos, the space between each heartbeat seeming to go on for hours as her knives flashed. The air was thick with blood, and Jayin lost track of Kell until he grabbed her sleeve and hauled her back the way they came.

"That door was open the whole time and you tell me now?" Jayin panted, doubled over. Soldiers pounding on the door.

"I was a little busy trying to keep you alive," he protested, slamming the heavy bar down and pressing his back against the doors. It wasn't going to hold for long.

"There's got to be another way out," Jayin said, casting about for something, *anything*.

"Well if you have any brilliant ideas," Kell said through gritted teeth, "now would be the time."

Jayin didn't answer, her gaze landing on a stack of abandoned supplies. *Please, please, please*, she thought, pawing through the pile.

"Jayin," Kell said urgently, but she ignored him, grabbing as many thin logs as she could carry. "What are you—*Jayin*!"

"I'll be right back," she promised, sprinting as fast and as far as she could. This side of the wall was as empty as before, presumably because the bulk of the soldiers were on the other side trying to break through. As soon as she was far enough away, Jayin set up three of the blasting sticks against the wall and set a small fuse of flash paper. She lit the flame and took off again, setting two more charges before she made it back to Kell.

"What were you—" he started, before an almighty crash shook the wall. Jayin ducked for cover, throwing her arms up against the debris that rained down.

"Running now, talking later," she said.

For once, Kell didn't argue. Two more explosions shook the earth and within minutes Jayin could hear shouts and footsteps echoing behind them. Her little trick with the blasting sticks wasn't as effective as she'd hoped. Hale was persistent, that was for damn sure. She and Kell had slipped through his fingers twice. Jayin was willing to bet he didn't want it to become three.

"Turn!" Jayin shouted, sprinting into one of the mechanized boxes. Kell followed and she threw the lever as soon as he was inside.

"Bloody skies," Kell swore, pressing himself flat against the walls of the box as it lurched skyward.

"You'll get used to it."

"Explain to me how this is better?" Kell asked as they stepped out into the open air. The wind howled, threatening to pitch them over the edge.

"No soldiers, no fire, no Hale," Jayin said, ticking them off on her fingers.

"No way down."

"At least I did something," Jayin snapped. "Now cut that," she said, pointing. Maddix severed the cable it in a single swing and the box plummeted to the ground. It wouldn't keep the soldiers off of them forever, but now they had a head start.

"Keep up, convict," she said, picking her way along the top of the wall.

Kell muttered under his breath but followed her footsteps.

"Impulsive, irresponsible, *incendiary*," he groused just within earshot. Jayin tried to ignore him, scouting ahead.

"Stars, are all Guardlings so whiny?" she demanded without looking back. "If you want to take your chances with Hale, be my guest."

"I'm not *whining*—" Kell started, but his words faded as something in her second sight caught her attention. An archer.

"Move!" Jayin shouted. Even as the word left her lips she knew it wouldn't be in time. She wasn't fast enough.

Jayin reached out her hand. Something flickered to life around Kell's body, glowing like a silver sun. By the time her vision cleared, Kell was staggering on the edge of the wall. The arrow was broken at his feet.

"Kell!" she cried. The world seemed to slow as he tipped over the edge. For a moment, it looked like he might regain his balance, but then gravity claimed him. "*No*!"

As he fell, Jayin could almost imagine that Kell pressed two fingers to his heart, and then stretched them out to her.

Jayin moved without thinking, throwing herself off of the wall after him. Her heart leaped into her mouth as she fell, air whistling in her ears until she managed to grab hold of a stray rope. It slowed her descent, but Jayin still hit the ground hard. She rolled, absorbing the impact before scrambling to her feet.

"Kell," she said, forcing herself to breathe as she approached his body. The glow was nothing more than a dim flicker, winking out between one breath and the next. Jayin pressed two fingers to his neck, hardly daring to hope. There was nothing. No pulse. No heartbeat. "Kell," she tried, louder this time. "*Maddix*! Bleeding skies, if you die on me, I'm going to kill you."

She drew her fist over her head and pounded it against his chest. Once, twice, three times, until finally she could feel his heart stutter back to life. The breath rattled from his lungs and he groaned.

"Stop that," he mumbled without opening his eyes.

"*Dayri* idiot." Jayin sank to her knees, laying her forehead on his chest. She barely felt the pain, her heart beating in time with his.

"Let's never do that again," Maddix breathed. She almost laughed, exhaling shakily. Maddix grabbed her sleeve, careful not to brush her skin. His gray-blue eyes found hers. "Jayin."

She waved off his thanks, interrupting as something much more pressing occurred to her.

"I didn't feel it," she said. It was a fifty-foot drop. Miraculous survival or not, she should have felt the impact. Maddix lifted his arm for her inspection, a small smile on his lips. His wrist lacked a certain cuff.

"I told you I'd take it off," he said, slowly pushing himself up. Jayin just stared at him. He'd thought the fall would kill him, and he'd taken the precious few seconds he might've had left to free her.

"I don't know what you did, but it saved my life," Maddix said, still smiling.

"I didn't—" Jayin started before startling to her feet. This time she was ready. "Duck!" she ordered, a knife in her hand and thrown before the word was out of her mouth.

Twenty feet away, a soldier crumpled. The hilt of her dagger sprouted from his neck.

"Stay here," she said, darting forward to retrieve it.

"You're never…getting out of here…alive," the soldier gurgled. Bloody foam speckled his lips and dribbled into the sand.

"I've heard that before," she said, pulling the blade out of his neck and wiping it clean on his jacket. "And I'm still here."

"Come on, convict," she said, pulling his arm around her shoulders and helping him to his feet.

"You called me Maddix before," he said. "I think you're going soft on me."

"And you're soft in the head," Jayin replied. She let him lean on her, trying to ignore the ache behind her eyes.

Jayin's nerves pulled taut as they hobbled towards freedom. They weren't moving fast enough, and if it came to a fight, Jayin was on her own. Maddix's movements were sluggish and he could barely walk, let alone swing a sword.

"Stars," Jayin swore as a volley of crossbow bolts flew over their heads. Archers were assembled on all sides but one, and it only took a moment to realize where the open path led.

Kaddah.

Jayin swore, skidding to a stop. Om's energy flared in her second sight, a beacon of fear and warning. Hale was herding them into the accursed queendom where she would be killed just as surely as if the hunter did it himself.

"What are you doing?" Maddix demanded, pulling her against the wall and bracing himself so they were chest to chest. Jayin's head throbbed. "Now is not the time to be standing still."

"It's Hale," Jayin said, her voice shrill with panic. "He's forcing us across the border. I can't go to Kaddah, Maddix. I *can't*." Another arrow whistled past their heads and Jayin sucked in a breath. Maddix crowded close, covering her body with his own. The archers were getting bolder.

"I'm not seeing a lot of other choices here," he said tightly. Jayin could feel him wince, and she smelled blood. She hissed a breath, not bothering to hide her fear. If they crossed the border, a simple scratch would be the least of their worries.

Jayin tried to look beyond the cage of his arms, searching out escape routes, anything that would allow them to get through. She could set another fire, she could go out swinging, she could fight her way out.

"Jayin, we don't have any other choice."

"I'll die there," she said, dread weighing in her stomach like a stone. "I'll die in that place, and they'll drain my magic and sell me for parts."

"Nothing is going to happen to you," Maddix said, his voice low and steady.

"You can't promise that."

Maddix grabbed the collar of her coat and used it to tilt her face up, forcing her to meet his gaze. "I am not going to let them hurt you, I swear. I'm going to keep you safe."

Jayin flinched away from him, doubt blooming in her heart.

"Jayin," he said, reading her thoughts on her face. "Stop it. Pavaal or no Pavaal, we need to go."

Pavaal or no Pavaal. He could be lying, she knew that, but the words gave her enough strength to pull herself together.

“If I die, I will haunt you for the rest of your life,” she swore. Maddix smiled grimly and pulled her forward by her sleeve.

“I expect nothing less. Now run, before we’re both ghosts.”

They ran.

CHAPTER TWENTY-SEVEN:

MADDIX

The Kaddahn countryside looked overwhelmingly familiar. There were the same rolling hills, spare trees, and dirt roads. They didn't meet much by way of resistance crossing over, but Maddix assumed Hale had ensured that. If what Jayin said was true, they wouldn't last long anyway and the witchhunters would be rid of the both of them. Maddix preferred to take his chances in another kingdom than go back and face whatever Hale had in store.

By his side, Jayin clenched her hands into fists. She hadn't stopped fidgeting since the moment they had crossed the border, and her skin was sickly, sallow and bloodless.

"You need to breathe," Maddix said.

"I'm actually trying not to," Jayin said through her teeth.

"Well if you don't exhale soon, you're going to pass out, and I'm not carrying you the rest of the way." He took a round stone out of his pocket and handed it to her. "Here." Jayin blinked at him, her eyes enormous and brilliantly green. She looked more like a startled deer than a person.

"Where did you get one of these?"

"Fell off the wall the same time I did," Maddix said. "I thought it would help." He didn't know how the Kaddahn could sense magic, but at the very least the stone might be able to give her some peace of mind.

"Thank you," she said softly, turning the stone over in her hands before pocketing it. "You realize we're going in completely blind, right?"

"Yes," Maddix replied with all the confidence he could muster. Jayin was jittery enough for the both of them. "But I can now safely think about how annoying you are without the chance of your overhearing me."

"That's not—" she started, but Maddix cut her off before she could launch into a lecture about the intricacies of magic.

"And short. Annoying and short."

Jayin almost smiled.

"And I doubt the wanted posters were distributed over the border, so you and I are officially free," he added.

"You're free," Jayin corrected. "I feel like I'm inhaling through a straw."

"But you're still breathing," Maddix pointed out.

"There's that optimism I know and hate."

"I don't see you volunteering any good cheer," Maddix said. "So I have to be cheerful enough for both of us."

Jayin elbowed him in the stomach.

They hadn't seen anyone since they entered Kaddah, but the kingdom was nearly twice the size of Aestos, without much by way of resources or farmland and a much smaller population. It wouldn't be long now that the hills merged into gray deadlands. Maddix had heard stories that Aestosi witches had cursed the countryside on the King's orders. The curse remained for a hundred years until Kaddah could barely feed its people. The famine left them vulnerable and Vandel had capitalized on that vulnerability.

Guerrilla warfare and underground skirmishes kept the conflict alive, and no-one in either kingdom felt safe. From what Maddix knew, kidnappings and impressments were commonplace as both sides tried to gain an advantage over one another.

He also knew what they did to witches. When Maddix had first heard the stories years ago, he'd applauded the Kaddahn for how they handled *sahir*. He had even suggested they do the same in Aestos. Why would they need the witches if their magic could be bottled and weaponized for soldiers and Guards?

"I say, get rid of the whole blasted lot of them," Maddix remembered saying one night in a bar. His fellow Guardsmen roared their approval. "Who says they should get all the magic to themselves? Give it to us, we're the ones *really* protecting the kingdom."

"What?" Jayin asked, startling him out of his thoughts. She peered up at him, one eyebrow raised. "You look like I feel."

"It's nothing," he said quickly, feeling inexplicably guilty, like she'd caught him in something. He nodded toward the rapidly decaying landscape. "They say that your people are responsible for all this."

Jayin snorted, the thinnest of smiles turning her lips up in the corners. "Honestly, sometimes I wonder how *dayri* have survived this long. You lot will believe anything."

"None of you have the ability to do something like this?" he asked, pointing at a particularly forlorn-looking tree. Maddix didn't know why he was pushing, but listening to her talk helped to keep him out of his own head.

"There are plenty of weatherwitches who could do this to the sky," she said gesturing to the clouds above them. "Maybe certain earthwitches could strip nutrients from the soil, but I can't think of any *sahir* that could create a drought and pestilence at the same time. There wouldn't be any way to maintain it for this long. Magic dies with the witch who cast it."

Most of her words were going over Maddix's head, but he didn't bother asking her to explain.

"Damn," he said, nodding as if she made perfect sense. "There goes the legend of the crooked legion of witches cursing the other kingdoms on the orders of Ayrie. A Kingswitch that corrupts kings, witches, and common folk alike."

The small smile disappeared, and Maddix went silent, suddenly wary.

"I wouldn't rule it out," she said. Maddix didn't press—he knew all too well what happened when he pushed too hard—but he couldn't help the questions that piled up. Who was she running from that had her so scared? She was more willing to face the *sahirla* than go back to Pavaal. Half the time Maddix thought she was trying to get herself killed in order to stay away from the capitol.

The thought made him feel guiltier than ever for dragging her back there.

He'd always seen the witches as lazy, useless aristocrats who lounged in the Palace and looked down on the common folk of Pavaal, or greedy charlatans who sold their magic to fat merchants for exorbitant prices. They were allowed to live because they offered a service and kept Aestos safe from Kaddah and Vandel, but Maddix had always assumed they could be easily dealt with if the King so chose.

Now he knew better. And if the Kingswitch or the other Palace *sahir* had even a fraction of Jayin's stubbornness, they wouldn't go quietly. For the first time, Maddix wondered who was really running the kingdom, the King or his magical counterpart.

"Not going to ask for the dirty details about the Palace?" Jayin asked when he didn't respond, too wrapped up in his questions about Ayrie. About her. "Don't you want to know about how the Palace owned me?"

He did, but her voice had gone to a cold, removed place where Maddix knew he couldn't follow. A place with walls of gold instead of stone.

"Would you tell me if I did?"

Jayin was silent for a long time before she answered, tracing patterns on the cuff. A jagged edge of scar tissue peeked out from beneath the silver. "Probably not."

"And as much as I'd love to lose a hand, I know better than to demand answers from testy witches."

"Please shout that a little louder, I'm not sure they heard you in Vandel," she griped, but there was no heat behind it.

They came upon a border town minutes later and Maddix's curiosity was pushed into the back of his mind. Maybe Jayin's paranoia was rubbing off on him, but he didn't want to give anyone the opportunity to overhear them. Just in case.

"We can stay here," Jayin said, gesturing to a small inn with so much confidence that Maddix's eyes snapped to her.

"What are you doing?" She narrowed her eyes at him. "You can't"—he looked around significantly—"*you know.*"

"I'm not," she said, still eying him like he'd grown another head. "I was born in the Gull, remember? I know how to case a mark."

"Case a mark?" Maddix repeated, fighting the urge to laugh. "Skies, you sound like a carrion. I used to arrest people like you."

He said the words without thinking, then froze as they washed back over him. Maddix made it a point not to talk about his life as a Guard. It hurt too much, the reminder of everything he'd lost and could never have again. Even if they caught the witch that had taken his life from him, he'd never be able to go back to the way things were. The knowledge didn't make it any easier to think about.

"You would've been one of the good ones," Jayin said without looking at him. "And the stars only know how few good Guards there are left in Pavaal."

Before he could answer, she knocked her shoulder into his chest. He froze, unwilling to spoil the moment. She was softer somehow, some of her jagged edges smoothed away. Still, he knew thinking Jayin was harmless because she wasn't sporting a scowl was like calling a wildcat a kitten because it had sheathed its claws. Best to tread carefully, but Maddix found he liked this Jayin. He liked her smile, the one that didn't promise bloodshed.

"Of course," Jayin continued, almost teasing. "You wouldn't be good enough to catch me, but still good." He couldn't stop himself from staring.

"So you were some kind of criminal, is that it?" Maddix asked, trying to match her tone.

"Absolutely not. I ran a shop."

Maddix snorted, choking on his laughter.

"Why is that funny?"

"Ran a shop? You?"

"What's wrong with running a shop?"

"That has to be the single most mundane job in the entire world. And you are…not…" Maddix trailed off.

Jayin raised an eyebrow, her green eyes missing nothing. "I'm going to take that as a compliment," she said. "Now if you're done making snide comments, we've got to pretend to be normal."

Despite being so deep in enemy territory, Jayin was still the better liar. She smoothly checked them into the inn, spinning a tale about being travelers passing through. They'd gotten into the habit of sharing a room instead of making excuses for their own. Two people traveling together but sleeping separately was suspicious, no matter how many lies Jayin told to explain it away.

"I'll take the floor," Jayin offered, closing the door behind them.

"It's alright," Maddix objected.

"Maddix, don't be stupid," she insisted. "You fell five stories. Take the bed and shut up. It's too soft for me anyway."

"Too soft she says," Maddix grumbled, but he was distracted by the way she said his name.

"Shut up and go to sleep," she said, grabbing a pillow and blanket and making a nest on the floor. Maddix didn't know how she managed it, but she was asleep within minutes.

It took him much longer. He'd gotten used to Jayin magicking the darkness away, the sphere of light floating like a personal sun. Maddix fought against the ice crawling under his skin, desperately trying to keep his breathing even.

"There's no one there," he said. The echo sounded like voices, hissing back at him. *Traitor*, they whispered. *Murderer.*

No, Maddix thought, trying to plead with the spirits, his hands fisting in the sheets. *No, I'm not—I'm innocent!* He tried to move, to snap himself out of it, but he couldn't move. The shadows solidified, forming familiar faces—Mole and Hale, both reaching for him. Behind them, the demon lurked, its eyes glowing like coals.

"No—*no*. Stop! Please!" The words were his, but the voice was unfamiliar. Maddix's eyes opened and the shadows were just shadows. No figures skulked in the dark. "*Stop!*"

"Jayin," Maddix whispered, finally recognizing her voice. He leaned over the bed. "Jayin wake up. You're having a nightmare. Hey," he tried again, reaching out to shake her awake. He should have known better. A gloved hand gripped his wrist and pulled him onto the ground in a single motion. Maddix blinked, and she was on top of him, straddling his hips with a knife in each hand. Her eyes were empty, her pupils blown so wide he could see himself reflected in the black.

The knives plunged towards his chest. Maddix threw his arms up, barely catching her wrists in time. "Jayin!" Maddix said, too loud. She blinked and the daggers slipped from her grip.

"I'm sorry," she whispered, horror dawning in her eyes. She scrambled away from him until her back hit the far wall. "I'm sorry. I'm sorry."

"It's okay," he said, trying not to think about how close she'd been to gutting him. "It was just a nightmare."

"I can't breathe," she whispered, pulling her knees close to her chest. Each word sounded like it was being wrenched out of her. "I'm sorry. I hate this place."

Jayin exhaled shakily, and Maddix searched for the words to comfort her. Outside their window, something popped like—

"Get down!" Maddix shouted. He pulled Jayin to the floor and flattened his body over hers as something crashed through the window. The cannonball rolled to the far end of the room before exploding into a whirl of fire.

Maddix tightened his arms around Jayin, ducking his head to shield her from the blaze. Something buzzed under his skin, dizzying and warm like the first sip of *arak*. He pushed himself to his feet, dragging Jayin with him. The fire raged, spreading the walls to the ceiling in an instant, but the blaze passed them by. Maddix didn't know how Jayin was doing it, but if she was using magic, they needed to go. Now.

"Is it just me," she asked, breathless, "or did we just walk into another warzone?"

"Stop it," Maddix barked, ignoring her question. The faint silver glow framed his vision. The entire building was on fire, its patrons streaming onto the streets like ants from an anthill.

"Stop what?" she demanded, sprinting alongside him as they burst onto the street. Three more buildings were ablaze, and men in armor rode through on horseback, cutting down anyone in their path.

A raid, Maddix realized. A Vandelian raid. Skies, of course it had to be tonight of all nights. His star really had gone dark on him.

Maddix had to leap aside to avoid being trampled, and hot blood splashed onto his face. A woman slid to the cobbled streets, nearly split in two. Jayin screamed, moving before Maddix could stop her. She launched herself onto the soldier's horse, her blade gleaming in the firelight before she opened his throat. Jayin flipped off of the saddle, landing neatly beside the soldier's corpse. She stalked back to Maddix's side, hissing in the *sahir* language.

"Stop what?" she asked calmly, flicking her knife to the side. Blood spattered onto the street.

"Using magic," he said. He swallowed hard. "They can track it here."

"I'm not using magic," she insisted. Maddix was about to reply when another soldier came galloping towards them, sword in hand. This time, Maddix was ready, parrying the man's thrust. He spun onto his knees, and slashed at the horse's legs. The poor creature fell immediately, crushing the man beneath its bulk. Jayin finished them both off.

They only made it a few steps farther before more men poured into the streets.

"I'm not using magic," Jayin said again, her eyes on something in the distance. "But she is."

Maddix wouldn't have noticed the woman, a hunched-over old crone, until she opened her mouth. The air distorted like heat from a flame and the soldiers in the woman's path crumpled like paper dolls.

"I thought that was impossible."

"Apparently not." Jayin managed before two soldiers set upon them again. Maddix lost track of her as he focused on his own adversary. "Oh, to the Dark with it," she cursed and then her hand was at Maddix's throat, snatching the stone off of his neck.

Jayin hardly winced, throwing her arms out in front of her. She cut down soldiers the instant they appeared, and Maddix had no choice but to follow as she created a path through the teeming streets.

Footsteps. Maddix whirled, sword in hand, but it was as if his head had been filled with cotton. The world slowed to a crawl. An old woman stood over him. She was dangerous somehow, but Maddix didn't know how. The cobblestones felt cool again his cheek. He couldn't remember falling.

The world resumed its previous speed just in time for him to watch Jayin turn and shout something. It might have been his name. Maddix didn't mind. Everything had gone quiet and peaceful.

Jayin reached out to him, and Maddix tried to reach back, but his arms wouldn't move. She might have run to his side, but Maddix's world had already gone dark.

CHAPTER TWENTY-EIGHT:

JAYIN

Jayin watched Maddix fall, unable to stop the old witch as she turned her magic on him.

"Maddix," she cried, but it was too late. He was already unconscious, his breathing slow and even. "Maddix, wake up." She shook him, but he didn't stir.

"We must go," the old witch said, laying a hand on Jayin's shoulder. She recoiled, bringing her knife to the woman's throat. The witch reached for her magic and Jayin pressed the blade in further.

"Touch me again and I'll carve out your larynx," Jayin hissed. "What did you do to him?"

"He is *dayri*," the witch said. "He was going to attack you."

"He's *with* me." She didn't have time for this. If the stories about Kaddah were true—if even half were true—they were going to be set upon any minute.

Just go, a voice whispered in the back of her mind. *Leave him.* Maddix had been nothing but trouble since the day he helped the witchhunters capture her. Stars, that seemed so long ago. A lifetime ago. A lifetime she could have been spending on the Isles with Om, safe and free of all of this.

Jayin's eyes strayed to the cuff on her wrist. The cuff that no longer bound them.

Stars damn it. "I'm not leaving him."

"But you are—"

"Yes, I'm *sahir*, he's not," Jayin said hurriedly. Her heart pounded like it was trying to rip free of her ribcage. "But unless you want all of us to get captured, you'll take us both with you. Please."

The witch had to have a safe place. There was no way someone with her kind of power had survived so long in this kingdom without a hideout.

"Not him," the woman said, gesturing to Maddix's prone from. "No *dayri*."

"Yes him," Jayin insisted before slipping into the Oldlands language. "*I will reap what he sows.*" She didn't even know if Kaddahn witches spoke the ancestral tongue, but it was worth a shot.

"*His actions, your consequences*," the witch said, replying in kind. Jayin nodded. Anything Maddix did, any rule he broke, was her responsibility. She knew how dangerous it was to vouch for him, but she was out of options.

It was an old *sahir* custom and common in the carrion gangs. Both factions lived with a sense of honor, a code of conduct that could never be broken. The Kingswitch vouched for each and every one of the witches that were brought into the Palace, and for that, they owed him a debt. For all of the *sahir*'s elitism and arrogance, they were nothing more than a gang. An aristocratic, magical bunch of carrions.

The witch snapped her fingers and Maddix rose slowly to his feet.

"Hey," Jayin said, her voice heavy with relief. Maddix didn't respond. His eyes were open but unresponsive, pupils blown so wide she could hardly see the blue of his irises anymore.

"He will not answer, and he will not remember, but you will be able to lead him. We must go. Now."

"Come on," Jayin said, taking Maddix's hand.

"He does not hear you," the witch said over her shoulder, weaving through the crowds of people still streaming through the streets. Maddix followed, shambling behind her. His aura was quiet, wiped clean. Jayin pushed away the temptation to read him.

"Where are we going?" Jayin asked as they made their way out of the tiny border town. The surrounding land was dusty and barren. Deadlands. Maddix had been right about one thing; Kaddah was dying.

"Hush, child," the old witch said. She set an impressive pace for someone her age. "Do you have a name or do you just talk and keep company with *dayri*?" Jayin's grip tightened on Maddix's hand.

"Jayin," she said.

"Linji," the woman replied. Something behind them rustled.

"Who is this?" said a voice at their backs. There were knives in her hands before the stranger finished his question. Jayin stepped in front of Maddix before turning to face the tallest man she'd ever seen.

"And why does she have a *dayri*?"

"Evin, good," Linji said. "Come, help an old woman. It's been a very long night."

"Explanations first," said the man, Evin.

Jayin eyed him up and down. He looked like Ravi, or what Ravi would grow up to look like, all pitch-dark skin and close-cropped black curls. Only his eyes were different, gray-gold and unyielding.

"They got caught in a raid," Linji said. She muttered something in Kaddahn, too quickly for Jayin to translate.

After what felt like an eternity, Evin shrugged, gesturing them forward. Holding on the old witch's arm, Evin pressed his hand into a boulder that blocked their path. Jayin felt a flare of magic, and the ground rumbled. The center of the stone shifted and crumbled away, revealing a steep staircase that led under the ground.

"Watch your step," the man said, gesturing Jayin and Maddix ahead. "You're with me, Nana. Can't have our best girl tripping and hurting herself, now can we?"

"Evin, you smooth talker," the old witch said, pleased. Jayin ignored both of them, focusing on the tunnels. Unhewn stone flickered under torches mounted on the walls. She tried to scout ahead, but something was interfering with her magic. She could only sense a few feet in front of her before the connection fizzled and her second sight winked out of existence.

They walked for nearly half a mile before, the tunnel opened into a cavern so enormous it would have housed half the Palace.

And it was filled with *sahir*.

"Bleeding, *bloody* stars," Jayin gasped. There were dozens of witches gathered in the cavern below her. Some were sitting together, laughing and talking; some were even practicing magic. In the middle of Kaddah.

"Impressive, isn't it?" Evin said in her ear.

"How is this possible?" Jayin asked.

"I'm afraid questions are not in this part of the tour," Evin said. "You're lucky we let in a *dayri*-sympathizer. By any means, Nana should have just let him die out there. That's what I—"

Jayin jammed her knife under his chin, the hooked blade poised to yank his tongue out from the outside.

"Shut up before I make you," she said, deadly calm.

"You really do know how to pick them, don't you Nana?" Evin said tensely. "How about you put those down before you hurt yourself, little girl."

Jayin gritted her teeth, forcing her temper into check. "I'm not the one who'll get hurt, I promise you."

"I like her," Linji proclaimed, breaking the stillness. "But Evin is a bit of a favorite around here, so before anyone gets disemboweled, you and your *dayri* should come with me."

He's not my *anything*, Jayin thought. She shot Evin one more poisonous glare before stowing her knife back up her sleeve.

"Come on," she said, taking Maddix's hand again. The old woman led them away from the cavern to a wide tunnel honeycombed with caves. They rounded a corner to a tiny living quarter well away from the others. It was tall enough for Jayin to stand straight, but Maddix had to crouch to fit inside.

"I'm going to have to tell the others about this," Linji said. She sounded amused by the prospect.

"What about him?" Jayin asked, guiding Maddix into a sitting position. "How long is he going to be like this?"

"He'll be fine in an hour or so," Linji said, waving her worry away. "He'll wake up with a headache, but otherwise he'll be all right." She paused, looking between the two of them. "You two will be safe here. Evin has a big mouth but we do not harm our own people, and you've vouched for the *dayri*."

"Forgive me if I don't take that on faith," Jayin replied, playing with one of her ring daggers.

"I don't care if you take it at all," Linji said, shrugging. "But we have only survived here for so long because we know that *sahir* must stand together."

"How did all of you get here?" Jayin couldn't help but ask. "I didn't know it was possible to do magic in Kaddah."

"That is not a question I can answer, but I will send for someone who can. Until then, you should get some rest. I will ensure that you are not disturbed."

Jayin didn't quite believe her, but the old witch seemed to be done talking. As soon as Linji was gone, Jayin settled down on the stone ground. A chill settled into her bones and she sagged as the stress of the night finally set in. Jayin sat close to

Maddix while his aura couldn't hurt her, laying her head on his chest and leeching his body heat.

Somehow, while she was waiting for Maddix to metabolize Linji's magic, Jayin fell asleep. She woke slowly to a comforting weight on her shoulders. Jayin blinked, feeling her skin warm.

"Welcome back," Maddix said when she shifted her head. The weight lifted and Jayin realized that Maddix had been holding her. His muscles were pulled taut, one hand on his sword as if he expected an attack at any moment.

"You had an encounter with a very powerful witch," Jayin said, sitting up. "A sonic. We're underground, and there's a whole network of caves and tunnels. There are witches here, Maddix. A whole coven of us."

He stiffened beside her, and Jayin had to consider that the news might not be as good for him as it was for her.

"That explains why my head feels like it's about to crack open," he said, rubbing his temples.

"That's what happens when you act like a stupid *dayri*," Jayin said, forcing lightness into her voice. She could still feel where he'd held her in his arms. It was distracting.

"Act like a—" Maddix said indignantly. "I was watching your back."

"Now you know better."

"Next time I'll just let you get stabbed."

"Right and you'll be dead within two days," Jayin scoffed. Maddix rolled his eyes, nudging her with his shoulder.

Jayin didn't know where this familiarity had come from, but something had changed. A barrier had been broken and Jayin wasn't sure she disliked it. Everything was different now. With the cuff gone and with the both of them trapped in Kaddah, the things that had mattered in Aestos now seemed insignificant.

"Well, isn't this heartwarming." Jayin's smile vanished at the sound of Evin's voice.

"It's almost enough to make me think that the war might be solved by the power of friendship."

Jayin spat something in the Oldlands language, unsure if he'd understand, but Evin put his hand over his heart.

"That hurts."

"Knives hurt more," Jayin promised.

"I'd take her word for it," Maddix put in.

"Your input, like your presence, is unwanted, *dayri*," Evin said, turning his attention to Maddix. He sneered, lip curling with disgust. Jayin wanted to carve the look off of his face.

"A very special *dayri*, to be vouched for by one of us," said a stately voice. The look slid off of Evin's face and Jayin watched as he schooled his features into a respectful mask, deferring to the newcomer.

The woman was old enough to be Jayin's mother, but carried herself like a soldier, stiff-backed and rigid. There was something in the way she held herself, something familiar.

"You did *what*?" Maddix grabbed Jayin's sleeve.

"Shut up and let me handle this," Jayin replied, her voice low so only he could hear.

"Especially," the woman went on as if neither of them had spoken, "to be vouched for by Ayrie's golden girl."

Jayin's blood went cold. *They know who I am.* Linji said that the witches looked out for one another, but Jayin had spent enough time in the Palace to know all about *sahir* politics.

She'd never been good at politics.

"So you know who I am," Jayin said, trying to sound unruffled. "I don't think it's fair that I don't know who you are."

"Rahael," the woman said. "I run things around here."

"How is *here* possible?" Jayin asked. They hadn't mentioned Maddix by name but that didn't mean his identity wasn't a chip to be cashed in later.

"See for yourself." Rahael extended her hand, palm up.

"You don't want me to do that," Jayin said flatly.

"I insist." Slowly, Jayin took the woman's hand, preparing for the onslaught of energy that would follow. It never came. Instead, there was a fierce tug inside of her and Jayin's legs nearly gave out.

"You're a feeder," Jayin murmured, snatching her hand away. Her shields disintegrated at the woman's touch and energy from every *sahir* swirled in her second sight. She winced, trying to block it all out.

"Here," Maddix said, holding her steady and looping his necklace over her head. The white stone settled on her chest and the noise went completely, blissfully silent.

"Bleeding stars," Jayin hissed, rubbing the back of her hand over her forehead.

"Ayrie's favorite pet nearly faints after losing a little magic?" Evin raised an eyebrow. Jayin wanted to strangle him but she thought she might pass out if she moved too quickly.

"Evin, hush," Rahael said sharply. Now that her vision had cleared, Jayin could see that the witch woman looked a little ill herself. "That is some gift you possess."

"I'm not sure it's a gift at all," Jayin said, still scrubbing at her eyes. "So you use shields to block detections and feeders to siphon magic out of the air."

She'd managed to sort through enough of the energy to see that much. It was a good system. A brilliant system.

"How could you possibly know that?" Evin demanded.

"What's it like being a stormwitch stuck underground?" Jayin asked, raising an eyebrow. Maddix snickered.

"Enough from both of you," Rahael interrupted. "Evin, go. I want to have a word with our guests in private." Evin scowled but did as he was told, shooting Jayin one last glare before slinking off.

"You really do know how to make friends," Maddix murmured.

"Friends notwithstanding, you two are causing quite a stir. Never before have we had Aestosi join us, let alone a *dayri*," Rahael said.

"I gathered," Maddix said coldly. Jayin elbowed him in the ribs. "I'm guessing there are rules that go along with being allowed in your witchy clubhouse."

"Just as I'm sure there were rules to be one of the *sahirla*," Rahael said pointedly. "Oh, yes, I know all about you, Maddix Kell."

Jayin's fingers went to her throat, ready to rip off the gem and grab Maddix's hand if she threatened either of them. Maddix reached for the sword at his hip. Rahael raised a hand, obviously noting their tension.

"Peace," she said. "We have no ties to the Aestosi crown. You're safe here."

"Until you need bargaining chips," Maddix accused. "And then what? You trade us for protection or political favors?"

"You do not know us, so I will choose not to be offended. We do not betray our own for political favors." Rahael said the last words with particular distaste. "Our so-called queen wants us dead, down to the last, so we've had to band together to survive. Jayin has vouched for you, so you will also find refuge here, as long as she allows it. Besides," the woman said with a wry smile, "if we wanted to make a trade with the Aestosi, I think the Gulwitch would do just as nicely as a convict Guard."

"We accept your terms," Jayin said quickly. Stars, did everyone in the Three Kingdoms know who they were?

"Then it's settled. You will have free reign of the compound, but please do not take it upon yourselves to leave. This is not a safe place for fugitives."

"So we're trapped here," Maddix said. Jayin wanted to clap her hand over his mouth. "You can call us guests all you want, but you've taken us prisoner."

He must be shocked at the role reversal, Jayin thought with only a little bitterness, being captured by *sahir* instead of the other way around. She pushed thought away.

"You can choose to think of it that way. But we offer safety and protection so long as you remain here."

"It's fine," Jayin said, shooting Maddix a meaningful look. She knew being stuck underground with a coven of witches made him twitchy, but it was someplace they could figure out their next move. It was selfish, but she was safe here, surrounded by her own people, and she could do magic without fearing for her life.

"I will have a space made up for both of you and someone will be by shortly to show you around." Jayin nodded and Rahael let herself out.

"We need to go," Maddix said as soon as Rahael was out of earshot. "We need to get out of here."

"I know," Jayin said quietly.

"It's—what?" he said, looking surprised that she wasn't disagreeing with him.

"We need to keep moving, but not yet," Jayin explained. "They've got a safe haven and resources we can use. Just until we figure out what to do next."

"They know who we are."

"They know who we are," Jayin agreed. "Because witches are gossips no matter where they come from."

"How do we know we can trust a word they say?" Maddix demanded, refusing to back down.

"We don't," Jayin said. Maddix looked away from her, his eyes clouded. A muscle jumped in his jaw. "And if it turns out that any of them mean us harm, we fight our way out."

She didn't think it would come to that, but as Jayin said the words, she found that she meant them.

"I can breathe here," she said softly.

"Okay," he said finally. "We stay."

Jayin exhaled. "Thank you."

"But stars, that Rahael woman looked like she was going to rap our knuckles."

"My matron liked using her fists," Jayin replied, still turning over their strange similarity in her mind.

Maddix opened his mouth before thinking better of it. "Who's the Gulwitch? I've heard that name before," he asked instead. Jayin blinked before remembering that Hale had mentioned her colorful Pavaalian alias back at the witchhunter's compound.

"Me," Jayin said haltingly. "I mean, it's a name I went by back in the Gull." She shrugged. "I needed a way to keep the gangs off of my back and the whole world is scared of witches. It kind of took on a life of its own."

"You're an urban legend," Maddix said. He almost sounded impressed.

"An urban legend that is trapped underground." She stood. "Might as well look around."

"I thought the matron told us to stay put."

Jayin smiled. "Please. You're a wanted fugitive and I'm a deserter and the ghost that haunts the Gull. Rules do not become us."

CHAPTER TWENTY-NINE:

MADDIX

Being in the witches' underground compound felt like being trapped behind enemy lines. Maddix had been stripped of his sword. They said it was for his protection, in case any of the Kaddahn *sahir* thought that he was a threat. Jayin gave him one of her hooked knives to keep on his person, but the little weapon felt flimsy and small in his hands.

The tunnels themselves seemed to stretch for miles, and Maddix was lost more often than not. It was an endless maze of stone, some of which led nowhere or double-backed to drop him in the same spot he started in. To make things worse, the tunnels shifted every couple of hours, a ward against intruders. It was infuriating, and even after a week, Maddix still had no way to get around without Jayin by his side.

The worst of it was that he still wasn't allowed outside. Maddix spent his nights staring at the stone above him, imaging the miles of stone bearing down on them. The air in the tunnels was stale and close, reminding him too much of the sewers where Mole's corpse still lay. The moleman featured heavily in his nightmares, visiting Maddix in his sleep even with Jayin's magic driving the darkness away.

"You're fidgeting again. Restless?" Jayin said, appearing in the doorway of their tiny living space. Maddix shot her a glare, swallowing the acidic comment on his tongue. Of course he was restless. They'd been trapped underground for days. He felt as if his skin was too tight, constricting his lungs every time he drew breath. He was going mad down here.

"Okay, come on," she said, understanding.

"And go where?" Maddix snapped. "In case you haven't noticed, we're not allowed to leave." He didn't doubt their ability to break out if they so chose, but Jayin seemed content to stay and Maddix had no illusions about his ability to leave without her. She said it herself; he wouldn't last the week.

"You're in a mood," Jayin said. Maddix only noticed the sheath on her back when she slipped the strap off of her shoulder and lobbed it at him. He caught it before it could collide with his forehead, recognizing the weight of his sword. Jayin grinned at the incredulous look on his face.

"How did you get this?" Maddix asked, pulling the blade from the sheath. His mood lifted instantly, his jangling nerves settling again now that he was armed.

"I stole it," Jayin replied as if it should be obvious.

"If any of your friends see me with this, they're going to be out for blood," Maddix said.

"Should make for an interesting afternoon," she replied, twirling her knives around her thumbs and catching them again. "Come on. I'm bored and you're going insane down here. Let's have some fun."

"What did you have in mind?" Maddix asked. He was almost afraid of her answer.

"Fight me." Of course.

"Fighting is your idea of fun?"

"Yes."

"You're mad."

"We've established that."

Maddix hesitated for a moment before standing and shouldering his sword. The tunnels should be empty at this time of day. Without access to the sun, he had no way to gauge the time except by way of meals. Jayin always ate with gusto, laughing and relishing her food all the more when Maddix grimaced at the spiciness.

"This is a bad idea," Maddix said as they walked. He was nagging and he knew it; he blamed it on being underground for so long. Even with Jayin's magic, he didn't sleep most nights, just stared up at the ceiling and wished to be anywhere else.

"We've been acting on bad ideas since this started. Why stop now?"

She had a point.

"Want to make this interesting?" Jayin asked as they entered the main chamber.

I'm about to fight someone half my size, Maddix thought, *in a hidden coven of witches in the middle of Kaddah*. He didn't know how much more interesting he could handle.

"Winner gets to hit Evin in his smug face."

Maddix laughed, a sudden, startled sound. Jayin grinned, the shiny scar that split her lips pulling taut. He liked her smile, Maddix realized with a strange pang in his stomach. It looked natural on her face, so unlike her usual scowl.

Despite his own misgivings about the Kaddahn witches' hideaway, Maddix couldn't deny that it was good for her. The tightness in her voice was no longer there, vanished along with the darkness in her green eyes and the tension she always seemed to hold in her fists.

"Deal," he said a beat too late. Jayin didn't comment, peeking around the corner to ensure that the main chamber was empty before walking inside.

"Ready when you are, *dayri*," she said. Clearly, she wasn't going to attack first. She was small and fast, but he had a much longer reach. Maddix didn't like the way she was looking at him. She held herself still, perfectly relaxed, as if they were just having a conversation and both not holding instruments meant to maim and kill.

Finally, Maddix struck, swinging his sword with both hands. Jayin moved without so much as a sound, neatly dodging the attack before reappearing behind him.

"Stars, that was pathetic," she said, raising an eyebrow. "No wonder the *sahirla* are going extinct if this is how they teach you to fight."

"Where did you learn then?" Maddix asked, swinging his sword in a wide arc.

"The Gull," Jayin answered simply, still sidestepping his every move. She hadn't raised her weapons once. Every time he tried to get close, she just danced out of the way with that little smile on her face.

"That's a story I'll have to hear," Maddix said, trying to keep her talking long enough to gain an edge.

"You have to earn it," Jayin said. Maddix blinked and she was moving. She darted at him head-on, slipping into his guard.

Maddix froze at the cool touch of the metal against his skin.

"And right now, it doesn't look like you will anytime soon."

Maddix didn't wait for her to finish gloating. He grabbed hold of her wrist, for once not avoiding her skin. Jayin winced and Maddix pressed his advantage, lunging while she tried to shake off the sudden deluge of pain. It was a dirty shot, but Maddix wasn't near arrogant enough to think he could beat her in a fair fight. He reached out with his sword to tap the side of her neck but she moved at the last second, hooking her knife around the tip of his blade.

"That wasn't nice." Jayin forced his sword away, ducking well out of range. She paced around the chamber, matching him footstep for footstep, her gaze unwavering. Maddix rocked on his heels as she sprang at him, barely able to block her blows in time.

Stars, she was fast. He only had a moment to brace himself before he saw her knives aiming for him. In a real fight, she would have killed him a dozen times over, and Maddix found himself wondering how she had ended up with a shop in the slums. With her skills, she could've been running the Gull. The Gulwitch could've been a streetlord instead of a phantom.

Somehow, amidst the ceaseless attacks, Maddix managed to throw her off balance. She blocked his sword with both knives and Maddix forewent the blade altogether, shoving her hard. Jayin stumbled, trying to right herself before spinning into a crouch. She threw her leg out, sweeping it in a low arc, and then Maddix was on his back.

"Ow," Maddix groaned. His vision swam, and he blinked to find Jayin kneeling on his chest.

"You're not very good at this," she said, extraordinarily smug. She almost looked happy, with her knives in her hands and spots of color in her cheeks. It was a good look on her, happiness. There was a beat and the strange feeling in his gut surged anew. Something flickered in Jayin's eyes, and she stood in a single, fluid movement.

"You're terrifying," he said, still trying to control his heartbeat. Jayin preened at the compliment.

"Says the boy who looks like a scarecrow on fire," she said, extending a hand and hauling him to his feet.

Maddix snorted. In his mind's eye, he saw an image of her in a different life, a different world, one where she laughed openly and often, and her smile didn't promise violence. One where she didn't have any scars and she'd never so much as heard of the *sahirla.*

"You're no shopkeeper," Maddix said, forcing himself to push away the vision and smile. "You're a carrion." He froze, wondering for a moment if she'd take it as an insult, but Jayin she only laughed.

"Well then come on, Guardling. Arrest me."

It was a game after that. No cheap shots, no tricks, just trading blows and forth for the fun of it. The clang of metal on metal echoed in the stone cavern, and Maddix found himself laughing along with her as they competed.

Abandoning caution, Maddix surged forward, slashing wildly. Jayin pinwheeled backward and would've fallen if strange hands hadn't caught her. She swore and reality filtered back in. They'd attracted an audience; half of the coven was watching them. Maddix immediately raised his sword again, fear buzzing in his blood. There were too many to defend against at once. A tiny noise snapped him out of his swirling panic, and he turned to see Jayin looking at him.

Something was wrong. Her skin was gray, as if all the life was being bled out of her. The witch's hands were still on her skin.

"Let go," Maddix said, raising his sword in a silent, obvious threat. The other *sahir* shifted, and he could hear them closing in behind him. He didn't care. The witch swayed, her eyes slightly unfocused, but she didn't release her grip.

Maddix brought his sword up, pressing it to the witch's throat. Someone shouted in a language he couldn't understand and Maddix felt the bite of magic in the air.

"You're killing her," he said. "And I swear to all the stars, if she dies, you will join her in the Dark."

Finally, the witch blinked and her eyes cleared. She pulled her hands away slowly and stepped away. Ignoring the angry murmurs around him, Maddix pulled Jayin to his side. She didn't seem to notice, her eyes hazy and unfocused.

"Jayin," Maddix whispered, trying to keep his voice from shaking. She looked dead on her feet, and he had no idea how to help her. "Jayin, can you hear me?" She didn't answer, but her eyes landed on something behind him. Maddix turned in time to see Evin striding towards them.

Of course, it had to be him, Maddix thought. The witch's arms were stretched towards them and Maddix pulled Jayin behind him, anticipating an attack that never came. Silver framed his vision, and Evin stopped before he could reach them. Maddix had no idea how Jayin managed it, but there was no doubt that magic was keeping the *sahir* at bay.

"Back off," Maddix snarled.

"You're not permitted to have weapons, *dayri*," Evin said.

"And you lot aren't supposed to harm your own people," Maddix said, gesturing to Jayin. "Looks like we're both breaking rules. Move before I cut you down."

The stormwitch held his gaze before stepping out of the way. None of the others tried to stop them as Maddix led Jayin back through the tunnels to their small living space. The glow remained until they were safe—as safe as they could be in a compound full of witches that he'd just threatened.

Exhaustion settled deep in his bones, but Maddix pushed it aside.

"Jayin," Maddix said softly. Some of the color had returned to her cheeks, but she still looked like she was about to keel over. "Please say something. Please."

She didn't answer, staring blankly beyond him. Her dark hair fell into her eyes, and Maddix brushed it away, careful not to let his skin touch hers.

"I don't know how to do this without you," he admitted softly, looking at the ground.

He wouldn't have gotten this far without her, that he knew for certain. Jayin had saved his life more times than he could count. She could've left him at the wall and taken her chances in the Aestosi countryside instead of following him into Kaddah. Skies, she could've left him in the village when the old witch had spelled him, but she vouched for him in order to get them both to safety. He wouldn't have blamed her if she had left him to die. After everything he'd done it was a wonder she hadn't slit his throat the moment he broke the bond.

But she hadn't. She'd stayed.

Maddix lost track of how long they sat in silence, his mind turning in anxious circles. None of the witches bothered them, but he kept his sword at the ready, just in case. Finally, when Maddix felt like he was about to pass out from exhaustion, a gloved hand slipped into his.

"You're not getting rid of me that easy, convict," Jayin said, her voice rusty and small. "I'm not going anywhere."

Maddix exhaled, feeling as though he'd been holding his breath for hours.

She didn't stay conscious for very long, laying her head on his shoulder before falling asleep.

"I heard the two of you made quite the scene earlier," Rahael said, appearing in their doorway.

"You could say that," Maddix replied.

"My people are alarmed."

Maddix stood, abandoning Jayin's gloved hand to look Rahael in the face. He was tall enough that she had to tilt her head up to meet his eyes, but there was no question of her power.

"One of *your* people nearly killed her," Maddix said hotly. Before the leader could respond, Jayin shifted beside him and all thought of posturing vanished. He knelt back down beside her again, placing his hand over hers.

"Takes more than a feeder to kill me," Jayin breathed. Her eyes opened slowly, focusing on Maddix's face.

"Hey," he said, smiling. She blinked, looking him up and down.

"You look terrible."

"There she is," Maddix said, his voice heavy with relief.

"I win," she said, slowly pulling herself upright.

"Win?"

"I won the fight." Jayin turned her head to look at the witch leader as if she'd just noticed her. "Next time I see Evin I'm going to hit him."

"I'll be sure to let him know," Rahael said, sounding amused.

"So, how much trouble are we in?" Jayin asked before Maddix could say another word.

"You and the *dayri* were armed without permission," Rahael said before turning back to Maddix. "And *you* threatened two of my people. They're scared."

"One of you almost killed her," Maddix said again.

"It was an accident."

He had to bite his lip to keep from saying something foolish. Now was not the time to anger another witch. Jayin was enough for him to handle.

"One more minute and it would've been a murder," Maddix said when he was sure his temper was in check. The leader opened her mouth to reply, but they were both distracted by Jayin trying to get on her feet. She huffed, staggering onto one knee.

"Hey, let me," Maddix said, offering her a hand.

"I'm fine," she said, pressing her palm against the wall and managing to stand on her own. Maddix didn't say anything when she leaned on him, trying to keep as still as possible to encourage her to stay there.

"You need to get that girl under control before she hurts someone else," Jayin said, fixing Rahael with a heavy look.

"That's never happened before," the *sahir* woman admitted finally.

Of course it hasn't, Maddix thought.

"Your magic had an…unforeseen effect."

"Mother always said I was special," Jayin said through her teeth. "You shouldn't have disarmed us in the first place. We didn't hurt anyone, and we've done nothing but keep our heads down. I'd call that a win."

"I'm afraid the others don't agree."

"I'm afraid I don't care."

The *sahir* leader paused, weighing her options, but Jayin spoke again.

"We should go. You've got a lot of hiding underground to do and we're clearly getting in the way of you lot turning into mole people."

Rahael nodded stiffly, any hint of amusement gone in an instant. Her lips pressed into a thin line. "You're right. As soon as you're well, I'll have you escorted to the surface."

"We can go now," Jayin said. She took a step, and Maddix had to lunge forward to keep her from collapsing.

"We'll leave when you're better," Maddix whispered, bending over to look her in the eye. "Don't be stupid."

Jayin held his gaze for a moment before looking away. "Fine."

"I'll have someone sent up to see you soon," Rahael said. Jayin said something in the *sahir* language and the woman paused for a moment before walking out.

"What did you say to her?" Maddix asked.

"I said that hiding like rats isn't a way to live." Her voice was small again. She looked like she was about to pass out at any moment. "Ow." She winced and Maddix helped her back onto the cot.

"You didn't have to do that," he said as soon as he couldn't hear Rahael's footsteps anymore.

"Yes I did," Jayin replied without looking at him. There was still a bite in her voice that he didn't understand.

"You could stay, you know," Maddix offered. He'd been thinking about it for a few days and it made sense. "It's safe and you could be with your people."

"What about you?"

"I'll keep going," Maddix said. "Get to Pavaal on my own."

"You'll never survive."

Probably not. Maddix knew that it was mad to go back in the first place, let alone by himself. But he couldn't let the witch that ruined his life go free. He had to settle the score—he had to at least try. He couldn't live on the run, always looking over his shoulder and sleeping with one hand on the hilt of his sword. That wasn't a life.

"But you can," he insisted. She had said since the beginning that this was a suicide mission. She was right. She'd always been right. "Stay here or go back to Aestos. You don't have to come with me."

Jayin didn't say anything for so long that Maddix had to fight to keep from fidgeting under her gaze.

"Stars, you really are stupid," she said at last. Maddix's mouth pulled into a frown and she went on without allowing him to speak. "I'm here, Maddix."

"I know, but—"

"I'm in Kaddah, A place where my people are rounded up and taken apart to harvest our magic. I'm here."

Guilt roiled in Maddix's stomach. He looked away from her and Jayin caught his hand.

"I'm here because I want to be."

"What happened to me being a *dayri* idiot that was going to get himself killed?"

"That's still true," Jayin said with the ghost of a smile.

"Then why would you stay with me?"

Why was she so willing to put herself in danger? She should be glad to see the back of him. Burning skies, he really was a selfish bastard. Even after everything, he was still using her. He still wanted her with him, even if it meant getting them both killed.

"Because I don't want to run anymore," she said. "And if I stay here, I'll be running for the rest of my life."

"But—"

"Maddix," she said, cutting him off again. "I'm with you and I'm not going anywhere." She smiled tiredly. "Besides you wouldn't even make it out of the tunnels without me."

Relief and guilt warred inside of him. Maddix desperately wanted her to stay here, stay safe, and desperately didn't want to leave without her.

"Ask me again," she said, cutting into his thoughts.

"What?"

"Ask me how I got my scar."

"How did you get your scar?" he asked, obliging

"I was young," Jayin said. "Still at Northside, before my magic manifested. One day I woke up to something yowling outside of my window, and when I went to check, I found baby carrions throwing rocks at a stray cat. They were going to kill it. I told them to stop, and when they wouldn't..." She sighed, throwing an arm over her eyes. "I broke two of their noses and gave another a black eye before they fought me to the ground. I thought they were going to kill me and let me bleed to death in the gutter, all over a stupid cat. But instead, they gave me this. So they would know always know me, they said."

"What happened to the cat?" Maddix asked. It was an insipid question, but he couldn't stop imagining her, beaten and bloody but refusing to back down. Willing to stare death in the face, even then.

"I tried to bring it back inside with me, but my matron found out," Jayin replied. "She broke two of my ribs and drowned it in a bucket."

In that moment, Maddix hated the lot of them. The carrions, the Northside matron, all of them.

"Jayin?" Maddix said after a few minutes. There was no answer, and he turned to see that she'd fallen asleep. Maddix stood, taking care not to wake her.

The story was no comfort to him. If anything, it only tightened the knot in his stomach. He was no cat, and the foes they were up against weren't kids who hadn't yet been jumped into the gangs. If they kept going to Pavaal, she was going to fare a lot worse than just a scar.

Maddix laid his head against the stone wall, his thoughts a tangled jumbled save for one. *Neither of us are long for this world.*

CHAPTER THIRTY:

JAYIN

It took almost a day to sleep off the effects of the feeder's magic. Jayin woke with a start, her magic flaring. For a moment she forgot about the stone around her neck, helping to accelerate the healing, and she panicked.

Maddix was gone. She couldn't feel him anywhere.

"I'm here," he said, his face swimming into focus. His hair was out of its usual bun, wet and hanging to his shoulders. It was darker too, more red than gold. Somehow Jayin was embarrassed she noticed. She reached out a hand as if to cup his cheek, and Maddix stilled.

"Stars, *ow*, what was that for?" he said when she cuffed him on the back of the head instead.

"For being an idiot."

"I'm not sure I deserved that," Maddix said, rubbing the back of his head and handing her a canteen. "How are you feeling?"

"Like I had the magic sucked out of my body by a kid who can't control her powers," she replied. She'd had run-ins with feeders before, but nothing like that. Her shields had gone down and everything flooded in, but only for a second. It was like her magic was bleeding into the air and taking her life along with it. She was dying, right there in the tunnels while half the coven watched.

Worst of all was the cold. Jayin's blood froze in her veins and every heartbeat felt as if it should shatter her frostbitten skin. Then Maddix found her, blue eyes so full of fire that he chased the ice away.

"That sounds about right. Here," he said, passing her a canteen. "The *sahir* are not happy with us."

There he went again, talking about them like they were some kind of team when he'd tried to convince her to stay behind just the night before. Jayin couldn't understand it. He wouldn't even make it back to Aestos without her, let alone Pavaal.

She should be praising the stars to be rid of him—he'd almost gotten her killed half a dozen times and there was no way this wouldn't end bloody—but she had nowhere else to go. Nowhere else she *wanted* to go. No doubt there were Kaddahn ports that chartered ships to the Isles, but even if she could get there without alerting the authorities, the Isles were a distant dream now. This was her reality.

She was tired of running, tired of being on her own. For so long, she thought that she was better off that way, and then Om had come along and given her hope. He'd given her hope and it had gotten him killed. Jayin would be damned if she let that happen to Maddix too.

Besides, it was high time she went home.

Only now, home wasn't a ramshackle apartment over the apothecary in the Gull, but something else entirely. Something she desperately wanted to keep.

"They'll get over it," Jayin said, sipping the water slowly. "Besides, we'll be gone soon." They should have left already, but Maddix made it clear that they weren't going anywhere until she was well.

"Excuse me," a young voice said by the door. "Rahael sent me. I'm a healer."

"You're a kid," Maddix said. The girl couldn't have been older than fifteen, most of her face obscured by shining blonde hair.

"Training to be a healer starts early," the girl said. "But what would you know about it, *dayri*?"

"Watch it," Jayin said sharply, and the girl had the good sense to look abashed.

"Maddix, I'm okay." She didn't want him around for this next part. He nodded, shooting the healer one last look before leaving.

"This is going to hurt," the girl promised. Jayin gritted her teeth. She'd been injured often enough to be intimately familiar with the healing process. The girl laid her hands on Jayin's skin, placing her fingers over the bruises. Jayin winced as fire burned under her skin, scorching away the injuries. The girl's energy slammed against Jayin's shields until it finally broke through.

The girl was terrified. Of Jayin and of Maddix even more. She thought he was one of *them*, a Kaddahn soldier who'd conned his way into their hideout. She was sure that he'd murder them in their beds.

"He won't," Jayin said, answering the girl's fears without thinking. The girl—Maia—looked at her, eyes wide. "He's not one of them."

"How do you know?" Maia asked in a trembling voice that betrayed her age.

"Same way I know that you lost your parents to them, and you're the only healer in this place worth a damn. The other one isn't half as good as you, so don't let him tell you otherwise." Maia was quiet for a while after that, focusing on her work. Jayin tried to keep any more of the girl's secrets from spilling into her head.

"You really think I'm better?" Maia asked softly, taking her hands away. Jayin rubbed her arms, trying to coax the feeling back into them. She could feel Maia's eyes roaming over the patchwork of scars on her exposed skin.

"I know you are," Jayin said before she could offer to erase them.

"You'll be low on magic for a day or so, but you should be fine," Maia said, blushing.

"Thanks."

"You too. For what you said. And uh, for what it's worth, I don't think you're a blood traitor."

Jayin knew that, but it was still nice to hear.

"Oh, and, um, Rahael wants to see you. If you're feeling up to it, I mean—"

"It's okay," Jayin said. She and Rahael had some things to discuss. She followed Maia through the winding tunnels to an unfamiliar sector of the compound.

"I can announce myself," Jayin said when Maia went to knock on a closed door. The girl swallowed, looking relieved. Jayin didn't bother with niceties, letting herself in.

"Do all Aestosi have such bad manners?" Rahael asked when Jayin let herself in. She didn't look up.

"You should come to the Gull sometime."

"Unfortunately, I haven't had the pleasure of visiting your homeland."

"Your son did," Jayin said.

Rahael looked up at her, shock and confusion written all over her usually impassive features. Now more than ever, Jayin could feel Om's ghost hovering in her second sight. He was waiting. For what, she didn't know. Justice, perhaps. Reconciliation.

"What did you say?"

Jayin was walking a dangerous line and she knew it. She inhaled through her nose. It had taken her days, but she'd finally placed why Rahael was so familiar.

Om took after his mother.

"He came to Aestos looking for sanctuary," Jayin said, forcing her voice still.

"You know my son? You know Omhinar?" Rahael's voice wobbled. "I thought he died. There was a fire and he—"

"Caused it," Jayin finished when she broke off. "He was a Fire Mage, one of the most powerful elementals I've ever known."

"Was?"

"He died," Jayin said, each word a knife in her gut.

"How?" Rahael's voice shook, tears shining in her gray eyes. Om's eyes.

Inhaling through her nose, Jayin told the story of how they'd met in the Palace and how she'd let him escape. Om's energy drew closer with every word until Jayin was sure he was about to materialize right behind her.

"He saved my life," Jayin said. "He took me in when I had nowhere else to go and—" She looked down, trying to keep her voice from cracking. "We were going to the Isles, someplace safe. But we were attacked before we got out of Aestos. I—I couldn't—he died."

"He was alive," Rahael said again. "My Omhinar. I thought, I would've—"

"Om thought he killed you," Jayin supplied, trying to somehow make this easier. They didn't agree on much, but Rahael had just learned her son was alive. Or had been, weeks ago.

"In the fire. He blamed himself, so he came to Aestos." And their treacherous liar of a king had nearly turned him back over to the Kaddahn crown.

"Thank you," Rahael said, breaking the cavernous silence. "For being there in his last moments."

"I'm sorry I couldn't save him," Jayin whispered. Suddenly Jayin couldn't look Rahael in the eye. She'd convinced Om to leave the safety of his home and travel with her, and they'd been ambushed by the *sahirla*. "It should've been me."

"You gave him more years than I ever could've hoped for," Rahael said. She should be furious—cursing the day Jayin had ever been born and threatening her, but she was suspiciously calm. "Just tell me one thing. Was it your *dayri*?""

"No," Jayin said quickly. "I killed the hunter that did it."

"Thank you."

"Don't—" Jayin started before something shook the room, nearly knocking her off of her feet. "What was that?" she asked, shaking the dust out of her hair.

Rahael went pale. She stood and rushed past Jayin without answering. Jayin followed, pulling her knives out of her belt. The tunnels, usually so quiet at this hour, were filled with *sahir* racing in every direction. Magic churned in the air.

Without thinking, Jayin sought out the cause of the chaos, before Rahael clamped her hand down on her wrist. Jayin hissed, yanking her arm away.

"No," Rahael said sharply. "They've found us. Don't use magic unless you have to. Be safe, Jayin Ijaad."

The woman disappeared into the crowd, and Jayin was alone. Behind her, the clatter of a sword scraping free. Hostile energy in her second sight. Jayin spun, curved knives catching a spear meant to run her through. Time sped up and her body moved of its own accord, instinct taking over as she fought. Jayin lost track of where her vision ended and second sight began, relying on both to tell the Kaddahn from the *sahir*. Only one rational thought remained as she tore through the tunnels:

She had to find Maddix.

A scream shattered her concentration. Jayin's focus wavered and a masked solider slipped past her guard. She wasn't fast enough; his blade struck true and pain licked up and down her right arm as serrated steel bit into her collar.

She blocked the next attack, crossing her knives to keep the soldier from slitting her throat.

Biting back a curse, Jayin slammed her head forward. The man staggered, blood gushing from his nose. His mouth opened in a surprised 'O' as Jayin thrust her knife under his chin. The soldier crumpled and Jayin took off towards the flash of blonde hair at the end of the tunnel.

Maia was trapped, cornered by two enormous men wielding swords. The girl trembled, holding a knife out in front of her like she'd never used one in her life.

"Maia, duck!" Jayin shouted, throwing a straightblade with all her strength. It struck the first soldier between his shoulder blades. In the space of a breath, Jayin ripped it free and plunged it into the second man's neck. She kicked the back of the second soldier's knees, slashing both knives across his throat as he toppled.

"Are you okay?" Jayin asked urgently, trying to check Maia for injuries.

"I—" the girl stammered, eyes round. Blood streaked across her face and dirtied her hair.

"Hey," Jayin said, grabbing Maia's face with both hands. "Now is not the time to break down." She repositioned the knife between Maia's fingers. "You hold it like this. Go for the face or the neck, not the chest. Make it count."

Maia nodded frantically, and Jayin took her hand before running back into the crowd. Somehow they made it back to Jayin's cave without being trampled or coming face-to-face with another Kaddahn soldier.

"Falling stars in the sky Above, where *is* he?" Jayin swore when the cave turned up empty. "Stay here," she said, turning to Maia. "Do not move, do not try to be a hero, and if someone tries to hurt you, kill them first."

"Please don't leave." Maia's voice shook, terrified tears collecting on her lower eyelashes.

"You can do this," Jayin said. "Stay out of sight."

She didn't wait for Maia to respond, running out of the cave. She turned back for a second and glamored the door so it just looked like the rest of the stone passageway. It was more magic than she had to spare, but Jayin knew that if it came down to it, Maia would be slaughtered in a fight.

"Maddix!" Jayin shouted as she ran against the current of people. Someone slammed into her, sending her flying, and Jayin reached for her magic before seeing that it was just Evin. "Where's Maddix?" she demanded.

Evin's eyes flashed, then he was on her. Jayin had only a split second to brace herself before the stormwitch had her by the throat. She choked, fighting against his grip. The air smelled like ozone and above them, thunder rumbled.

"You," he snarled. "You did this."

Jayin gasped, trying to suck in as much oxygen as possible. Evin's face blurred as black spots appeared on the edges of her sight.

"It wasn't me," she wheezed.

"You and the *dayri* show up, and then everything falls apart," Evin said. Jayin didn't know what was going to make her pass out first, the crushing force on her windpipe or his naked hand against her skin. His energy was as dark as a stormcloud, spitting electricity through her veins.

Her lungs screamed for relief. She kicked and fought, but it wasn't any use. All this time fighting *dayri* and *sahirla* and she was going to be killed by one of her own.

"Step away from her." The voice was hazy, half-imagined. The pressure on her neck released and Jayin crumpled into a heap on the tunnel floor, gasping. Slowly, her vision cleared enough to see Maddix kneeling by her side.

"You okay?" he asked, pulling her to her feet.

"I was looking for you," she coughed.

"You found me. Now we've got to get out of here, come on."

"What did you do to Evin?"

The dark witch was on the ground, his nose bleeding heavily. His gray-gold eyes bore into the two of them, furious but very much alive.

"His face and my fist got into a disagreement," Maddix said. "Sorry I hit him before you had the chance."

"Just this once I forgive you," Jayin said, holding onto him as he dragged her through the chaos. "Maddix!" she shouted, feeling hostile energy heading their way.

A soldier barreled towards them and inexplicably, Maddix turned towards her instead of reaching for his sword.

"Play along," he hissed. He mimed as if running her through and Jayin allowed herself to fall to the blood-soaked ground. "There's more over there!" Maddix shouted. The soldier ran past.

"What—?"

"I'm one of them, remember?" he said, answering the question before she could finish asking it.

"You're not," she said. Not in any of the ways it mattered.

"Yes I am," he disagreed. "Come on."

Jayin wanted to argue, wanted to make him believe her, but they didn't have the time. The tunnels were being overrun.

Through the throng of people, Jayin saw Rahael fighting three soldiers on her own, twirling a double-bladed staff like it was an extension of her body. She was holding them off, but she couldn't keep it up for much longer. More soldiers were converging, their malevolent energy trained on her.

"No," Maddix said, grabbing the back of her coat as Jayin tried to fight her way towards Rahael. Jayin tripped over something—some*one*—as he yanked her towards him. She swallowed a scream. Linji's dead eyes stared up at her, glassy like marbles. Blood matted her silver hair and drew tracks down her wrinkled, unmoving face. Linji. The old woman was the strongest sonic Jayin had ever seen; she should've outlived them all.

She snarled, a furious, wordless cry, ripping her hand out of Maddix's grip and throwing herself into the crowd. She wasn't going to let Rahael die; she *couldn't let her die.* Not now. Not after Linji. Maddix shouted after her, but she ignored him, plunging on.

"Stop!" Maddix said, cutting down a soldier to get to her.

"I have to help," Jayin said, watching desperately as Rahael began to be overwhelmed by her opponents. By her side, Om's ghost burned, demanding action.

"You're going to get yourself killed."

It didn't matter. Om's mother had to live. She had to.

"I don't care," Jayin said, pulling off her glove and taking his hand. Pain exploded through her skull and auras burst into physical existence. Without hesitating, Jayin tore the Kaddahn soldiers apart. She only had one shot at this and she didn't know how much longer her strength would last.

"Don't let go," Jayin ordered. The pain of his touch was the only thing keeping her awake, and she didn't want to know what would happen if she lost consciousness. She clenched her fist and the soldiers around Rahael collapsed, boneless. Dead.

It wasn't enough. Energy flickered in her second sight and Jayin's stomach twisted.

"Where are you—?" Maddix asked as she dragged him with her. Jayin ignored him, blood pounding in her ears so loud that she couldn't hear his words. Finally, *finally*, after stepping over half a dozen bodies, she found the owner of the strange signature.

"*Khayald*," Jayin snarled, recognizing the half-hunched figure as a witch before the anger fizzled just as quickly as it had come. There was something wrong with him. He was broken, his skin hanging off of his bones and his eyes glassy and bright, sunk deep into their sockets.

"Kill them," the witch rasped. "Kill *me*."

Jayin couldn't stop his weak aura from slipping past her ruined defenses. She bit her lip to keep from screaming. They'd had him captive for weeks, torturing him, experimenting on him, and finally using him to ferret out more *sahir*. Jayin pressed her hand to his chest, ignoring the pain that felt like it was breaking her ribs. She had to do something; she wasn't going to let him die with his torturers. But something dark and evil had lodged behind his heart and Jayin couldn't pry it free.

"Please," the witch begged. "*Please*."

"I'm sorry," Jayin whispered. Still holding onto Maddix with one hand, she closed her fist on the witch's energy, snuffing it out.

"Thank you," the *sahir* breathed. His lips turned up into a terrible parody of a smile, and his heart managed one more stuttering beat before it lay still in his chest.

"Jayin," Maddix started, but then she was screaming. Her magic burst out of her, brighter and more terrible than ever before, seeking out each and every Kaddahn in the compound. She marked them in her second sight, lost in the violent whirlwind of energy, and felt them die one by one. It wasn't enough—it would never be enough.

The tunnels were silent and Maddix was still by her side when Rahael found them. Jayin knelt by the broken witch's body, closing his eyes. He was innocent, and they'd turned him into an animal.

"Are you okay?" Jayin asked in a brittle, detached voice as she recognized Rahael's aura.

"I'm fine," Rahael said. Beside her, Om's energy flared once and then disappeared. Somehow Jayin knew it was for good. "Who was he?"

"He led them to us," Jayin said. *I had to kill him*, she thought desperately. *I killed all of them.*

"How?" Rahael breathed, and Jayin knew the question was for her. Rahael's voice was awash with wonder and fear.

"I don't know," Jayin replied. It was the truth. She inhaled shakily, feeling like someone had reached into her chest and was squeezing her lungs with both hands. Her magic guttered like a candle in the wind and Jayin stood, Maddix's hand still in her grip.

A flare of energy. A single soldier still alive.

"Maddix," Jayin gasped, dropping his hand. As soon as she broke contact, the pain stopped, severing her last tether to consciousness. She hurled the last of her straightblades with all of her remaining strength, but not fast enough. The solider pulled the trigger the moment before the dagger struck between his eyes. She tried to move between Maddix and the arrow but she was too weak, too slow. Silver flared and blood dripped from her nose.

The world tilted as she fell. Black spots crowded her vision and her heartbeat thundered in her ears. Voices washed over her but she couldn't make out the words. She was moments away from fading altogether when someone shook her back into her body.

"Jayin, stay with me," a familiar voice said. "Don't fall asleep, okay? Don't fall asleep."

"Maddix," Jayin exhaled. She couldn't see him. The line between her two sights blurred.

"I'm here."

"I'm here too." His eyes were shiny and Jayin's heart twisted to see the look on his face. "Are you hurt? Did they get you?"

"No, I'm okay. Stars, why did you *do* that?"

"I'm not losing you too."

Maddix inhaled and Jayin could see his lip trembling. Slowly, she lifted her hand and cupped his face. The pain was muted and Jayin ignored it easily. He tried to move but Jayin shook her head. Maddix stilled. His eyes looked bluer than she'd ever seen them.

"I don't regret you," she said. Jayin knew she had to get the words out, had to make them count. Somehow she didn't think there would be another chance. "You're one of the good ones."

"Hey, hey. No, stay with me," Maddix said. He held her hand to his cheek, but she was already gone.

CHAPTER THIRTY-ONE:

MADDIX

The world had gone numb. Maddix couldn't feel anything, couldn't see anything, but Jayin's prone body in his arms. He couldn't even tell if she still had a pulse. He didn't know if *he* had a pulse.

"Get away from me," Maddix snarled as witches swarmed around them. They tried to speak to him, but Maddix couldn't hear them over the blood roaring in his ears.

"Come with me," Evin said, appearing out of the crowd. Maddix's arms tightened around Jayin. She was so small, and even unconscious her face was tight with pain.

"Get *off*," he shouted as the witch hauled him up.

"If you don't let the healers help her, she's dead for sure. Stop fighting." Evin replied, hatefully calm. Maddix wanted to break his nose in the other direction.

"Maia!" Rahael shouted, somewhere behind him. Her voice was muted in Maddix's ears. The blonde healer appeared out of the crowed, immediately barking orders. Maddix reluctantly released his grip, and two witches lifted Jayin onto a table. He wanted to stay, to make sure nothing else happened, but Evin hauled him away.

"What are you doing?" Maddix demanded but the witch didn't stop until they were far down the tunnel. "What is *wrong* with you?" he said when Evin finally let him go.

"You don't want to be there," Evin said.

"Yes, I—"

"No, you don't."

"What do you care?" Maddix demanded, rounding on him with clenched fists. Evin had damn near strangled Jayin to death.

"I was wrong," Evin spat. "Happy? I was wrong, and if not for her we'd all be dead. Now believe me, you do not—" His words were cut off by a scream from where they came. Maddix didn't think, making as if to run towards the sound, but Evin held him back. Maddix had never wanted to kill someone more in his life.

"*Dayri*," Evin said, condescension dripping from every syllable. "You cannot help her right now."

Maddix dug his fingernails into his palms as another scream echoed down the tunnel.

"Here," Evin said after the noise died down. He handed Maddix a rag. "You've got blood on your face." Blood from the handprint, the one Jayin had given him. Maddix didn't know if it was her blood or his. It didn't matter.

"Bleeding *stars*," Maddix swore, punching his fist into the wall. The skin over his knuckles split, leaving a bloody imprint on the stone.

Finally, after what felt like hours, the blonde healer came to find them. She looked terrible, pale and haggard, and to Maddix's surprise, Evin swept her into a tight hug.

"Are you okay?" Evin asked quietly. The healer nodded.

"Jayin saved me. She hid me in her room and glamored the door to keep the soldiers away." The healer turned to Maddix. "She's asleep."

"Is she going to be alright?" Maddix couldn't stifle the desperate edge in his voice.

"I don't know," the girl said miserably.

"What do you mean you don't know?" Maddix demanded, taking a step towards her. The girl flinched and a strong gust of wind blew Maddix backwards.

"Step off," Evin growled. "She did everything she could."

"That's not good enough." They had *magic* for sky's sake; they should be able to do *something*.

"She was exhausted and hurt," the healer said so quietly Maddix almost didn't hear her. "She shouldn't have been standing, let alone fighting. The others told me what she did, and I've never heard of anything like it. She was nearly out of magic; it should've been impossible." Maia inhaled deeply. "Jayin's strong. She's going to make it through this." It sounded like she was trying to convince herself more than him.

"But you don't know that. She could be dying in there and you're telling me there's *nothing* you can do about it?"

"If you didn't want her hurt, you shouldn't have dragged her on your little suicide mission, Maddix Kell," Evin said, his land still laid on Maia's shoulder.

Maddix froze, all his anger leaving him in a rush, replaced by open-mouthed confusion.

"Yes, we know who you are. We've known since the beginning. The Aestosi Guard who went on a rampage."

"You know who I am," he repeated.

"A murderer and a convict, chased through your kingdom and into ours. Did you think we're just hiding down here? Burying ourselves away from the world? I didn't want to let you live, but Jayin vouched for you. Unlike the *dayri*, our word means something."

"But you let us stay," Maddix said.

"We let *her* stay," Evin corrected. "And it's a miracle she's still breathing. She might survive this, but she will not survive you." With one last poisonous glare, Evin tugged the blonde healer away.

Maddix watched them leave, feeling the spider web of cracks that had been collecting splinter all at once. He felt like he'd been poisoned, fear and guilt racing in time with his pulse. Dread had lived behind his heart for so long he'd almost forgotten it was there. Now he was choking on it.

Without realizing he was moving, Maddix found himself in the chamber with Jayin. The other witches barely noticed him, busy tending to their dead and wounded.

This could've been so much worse. The coven had been taken by surprise, outnumbered and trapped underground without an escape route. Every witch in the place should have been slaughtered and without Jayin's intervention, they would have been. Maddix still didn't know how she'd managed to knock the soldier's arrow out of the air. It shouldn't have been possible, but she'd done it; she'd saved him again.

"How's she doing?" Maddix asked uselessly, walking up to Jayin's sickbed. Rahael stood watch at her side. He knew the answer, but talking was better than the silence in his head.

"She's stable," Rahael replied. "She saved my life."

"She saved all our lives," Maddix said, trailing his fingers through Jayin's short hair. It was longer than before, hanging further in her eyes. Maddix had never told her how much he liked it short. He should've told her.

"I think the debt's paid," Rahael said.

"Debt?"

"To my son," Rahael explained.

"You're Om's mother," he murmured. "Jayin told me about him. She blames herself for what happened." Rahael's eyes flashed, and Maddix could almost see her son's fire within them.

"I know," the *sahir* leader said. "She shouldn't have used her magic to save me." On that, they agreed. "If she wakes up—"

"When," Maddix interrupted sharply. "She's going to wake up."

"When she wakes up," Rahael amended. "I hope she'll know she's done right by both of us."

"I was there." Maddix didn't know what possessed him to say the words, but they were out in the open before he could stop himself. "I was on the docks where he was killed."

A year ago, Maddix wouldn't have been able to imagine feeling guilt over the death of any witch, let alone one he didn't know. But standing with Om's mother, he felt at fault. He'd been there, he could've stopped it. He could've done *something*, but he'd been too blind. Too ignorant.

"I know," Rahael said, with none of the rage Maddix expected. "We do not fear the *sahirla* like our brethren in Aestos, but we still know of them."

"I'm not one of them," Maddix said, echoing Jayin's words from a few hours before. He didn't know if they were true, but he still had to say it.

"Not anymore." The silence that stretched between them was more deafening than the chaos of the battle. Maddix preferred battle. "She said she killed the man responsible."

"She did," Maddix replied, remembering how Jayin's scream had rent the air and how she'd thrown the knife so hard, she nearly took off the hunter's head. "I'm sorry."

It wasn't enough, not by half, but Maddix didn't know what else to say.

"We trust our own," Rahael said at last. "And she trusts you."

And he'd damn near gotten her killed. He didn't deserve her loyalty, her trust, none of it. That he knew for sure.

Then you know what you have to do.

Maddix took Jayin's hand in his and brushed her hair out of her eyes with the other.

"Take care of her," Maddix said. He heard the ring of finality in his own voice. Rahael nodded, understanding the unspoken words: *don't let her come after me.*

"I'll give you a moment." Even when Rahael left, they weren't alone, but Maddix didn't care about the *sahir* around him. They may as well not have been there at all.

"I'm sorry," Maddix whispered. Jayin still didn't stir. The only sign of life was the faint, steady rise and fall of her chest. "I never should've brought you here. I should never have been on the docks that day."

She could've gone to the Isles and been safe there, never knowing him nor being hurt by the *sahirla.* He wanted to say he wished they'd never met, but it would've been a lie.

Jayin had saved him; she'd taken him away from the witchhunters before they sank their claws in too deep. He could've so easily been one of them—hateful and brimming with misplaced anger and righteousness. He might have been too, if she hadn't barreled into his life and saved him from a world of fanaticism and murder.

"I don't regret you either," he said, finally finding the words. "You're going to wake up, and you're going to find someplace safe, and you're going to live." He squeezed her hand. "You have to live."

The thought of leaving her hurt like an ache in his chest, but he couldn't bear to let her die with him. He'd done enough harm. Maddix squeezed Jayin's hand again and leaned down, pressing a soft kiss to her forehead. Jayin didn't stir. Maddix straightened, burying the childish hope that she would wake and ask him to stay.

"We will take care of her. You are free to go." Rahael said, reappearing behind him. Somehow, her words made the decision final.

"Do whatever you have to do to keep her here," Maddix said. Jayin would want to come after him, she'd want to make sure he was okay even though it could get her killed. He couldn't have that. "Whatever you have to do."

There was only one stop to make, and his things had been ready to go since they'd gotten here. A witch was sent to escort him to the surface and they navigated the tunnels without passing by the main chamber again. Maddix was grateful. If he saw her, he would lose his nerve.

The stone door melted away at the witch's touch. Maddix breathed in his first breath of fresh air in weeks, but it tasted stale, and Maddix found that he didn't want to look skyward. The stars held nothing for him now.

CHAPTER THIRTY-TWO:

JAYIN

The world was black, punctuated only by flashes of light and snippets of conversation. Jayin tried to climb her way out, but the dark's hold on her was unyielding. She didn't know why it was so important to wake up. Jayin had no memories, only the unshakable sense that if she didn't find her way to the light, something terrible would happen.

"Maddix," Jayin breathed, everything flooding back to her the moment she pried her eyes open. The Kaddahn soldier had aimed at him, but then she'd collapsed. "Where's Maddix?"

"Hey, you're up," a voice said, not unkindly. Jayin's heart raced and she started to reach for one of her knives before someone pushed her back down. It didn't matter anyhow. She'd been stripped of her weapons.

"Don't try to move, okay? You're in bad shape."

Jayin ignored him, pushing herself up on her forearms and trying to force her eyes to focus. Her muscles were stiff, as if she'd been still for so long they'd begun to atrophy. She was still in the tunnels, that much was obvious, but they'd turned the main chamber into some kind of sickbay. All around her were witches in various stages of healing.

"Jayin," Maia said, appearing by the table that had served as Jayin's home for stars knew how long. "Oh, thank Horaj you're awake."

"How long have I been here?" Jayin said. Her voice was rough and scratchy. Maia handed her a cup of water instead of answering, but Jayin didn't complain, drinking the whole thing in long, greedy gulps.

"You almost died," Maia said when Jayin finished.

"I figured that bit out on my own." From the way her body hurt, Jayin guessed that they'd had to scrape her off of death's door. "What happened?"

"You saved us."

Not all of them. Not Linji. Jayin hadn't done a tally, but she'd seen enough *sahir* bodies to know that there were too many dead.

"They would've killed everyone," Maia went on, oblivious to Jayin's tumultuous thoughts.

"They killed enough."

"No one would've survived. You saved us."

Jayin wished she'd stop saying that. "Where's Maddix?"

Maia went pale and Jayin's heart stopped. Images of Maddix, bloody and broken, filled her mind on a loop. Maddix, struck through the heart by an arrow she wasn't fast enough to stop. Jayin's chest constricted, her breath hissing through clenched teeth.

"Jayin, I—"

"What happened?" Jayin said, her voice splintering. Without thinking, she grabbed Maia's hand. Energy flooded through her half-built shields and Jayin hissed, recoiling. The pain in her head surged anew, but Jayin had her answer. "He's gone."

Maddix was gone. She should be grateful to know that he was alive, but it felt like there was a boulder compressing her chest.

"He left," Maia said.

"Why?"

"I don't know," she replied, looking miserable. Jayin shifted, trying to sit up straighter. "Hey! No, no, no," Maia cried out, and the other healer reappeared to push her back down.

"Get off me," Jayin snarled, but her head was swimming, and she could barely keep her eyes open. Before she could so much as reach for her magic, something was slipped around her hand and her powers went dark. A leather band clasped around her wrist and settled next to the silver cuff. She hadn't taken it off.

"What are you doing?"

"Jayin, if you use too much magic, it could kill you."

"I have to find him," Jayin said.

"He's gone," Maia said more harshly than Jayin had ever heard her. "He's gone, and there's nothing you can do about it. If you overexert yourself, you're going to die."

She didn't care. In that moment, Jayin didn't care that her life hung in the balance. She had to find him.

"Take it off," Jayin ordered. Maia's jaw set.

"You're going to hurt yourself," Maia said. Jayin didn't disagree, but she knew that saying so would do nothing to help her case.

"I swear to every star in the sky if you don't take this thing off of me I'll—"

"You will do nothing," Rahael said, walking into the chamber. Her tone brooked no argument. "You're hurt and you will do as Maia says until you are well again." Jayin wanted to argue, but she didn't think she would be able to sit up again without passing out.

"Is he okay?" Jayin asked, her eyes finding Rahael's. "Please."

"He was when he left," Rahael said finally. The admission did nothing to soothe Jayin's fears, but Rahael wouldn't say anything else about it, leaving Jayin in Maia's care.

Healing was slow, even with her magic locked away and accelerating the process. It was days before the healers allowed her to walk on her own and even then she was still heavily supervised. Rahael was worried she would try to leave the second someone wasn't looking.

It was a fair assumption. Jayin had every intention of leaving the moment her watchdogs so much as blinked.

"Look who's on her feet again," Evin said one day when Jayin was taking her daily walk around the compound. There was another witch tailing her, trying to be discrete and failing.

"If you ask me if I need help I will gut you," Jayin sniped. Bed rest had done nothing for her temperament, but at least she had her knives back.

"I wouldn't dream of it," Evin said without blinking. "You look like hell."

"And you are charming as always," Jayin replied, but she wasn't altogether unhappy to see him. Too many *sahir* had been killed in the attack, and Evin was a powerful witch. He was needed.

"You know, Maia won't shut up about you."

"Probably complaining about the worst patient she's ever had," Jayin said. It didn't surprise her that the healer had confided in him—she'd heard the story of how Evin rescued Maia from Kaddahn mercenaries a few years ago. Near death experiences had a tendency to bring people together.

Jayin would know.

"She thinks you should stay," Evin said without preamble.

"I'm not staying."

The tunnels had been refortified since the soldiers found them, and thoroughly spelled to prevent another breach. There were as safe as they could be, and with Maddix in the wind, there was no reason to stay any longer than she had to.

"What is out there for you?" Evin pressed. "You're wanted in your kingdom as a deserter, and the *sahirla* want your head on a spike."

"Now you're just flattering me," Jayin said, wishing she could move quickly and leave him behind. Even when she was whole he'd be able to run her down.

"This is serious."

"Do you hear me laughing?" she said, unable to keep the edge out of her voice.

"He's not worth it." There it was, the reason why he was here. "That *dayri* is not worth dying for."

"His name is Maddix," Jayin snapped.

"Right, Maddix Kell, convict and murderer," Evin said bitingly. "What a worthy person to waste your life on."

"Does it make you feel superior?" Jayin asked, just barely reigning in her temper. "Thinking that you're better than him?"

"Better than a *dayri* criminal? Yes."

"You know," she said, curling her hands into fists. "I spent some time with the witchhunters back in Aestos. If you could convince them you didn't have magic, you might just get along." She didn't wait for him to respond, hobbling away as fast and with as much dignity as she could.

"You'd choose him over your own people?" Evin shouted after her. Jayin didn't answer, just turned the corner and left him behind.

Maia tried to convince her next. Jayin was expecting it but the healer was harder to dismiss outright.

"You'll be safe here," Maia said softly. "You can help us, and we can help you."

"Maybe I'll be back someday," Jayin said, but it was a pathetic excuse for an answer. She'd said the same words to Ravi all those weeks ago and hadn't intended to make good on that promise either.

“I don’t want you to go.”

Jayin wished she could say the same, but she was tired of being underground and hiding from the world. Traveling in either kingdom was terrifying; it was life and death, but at least it was living. It was breathing fresh air and seeing the stars at night instead of stone ceilings. It was fighting for her life and the dizzying, intoxicating relief that came with each new sunrise.

“I can’t stay, Maia.”

She had been ready to go for days, just waiting for an opportunity to slip away. She suspected they were purposefully keeping her longer than she needed. It had been almost a week and Jayin shuddered to think of Maddix’s head start. He could have already crossed the border for all she knew.

“You’re leaving then,” Rahael said, meeting her in her own quarters. Jayin didn’t answer, pulling her coat tight and slinging the pack over her shoulders. When it was clear Jayin wouldn’t be swayed, Maia had made sure she had fresh supplies before the girl had pulled her own disappearing act.

“You know this isn’t what he wants.”

Jayin’s heart squeezed painfully in her chest. “What do you mean?” she said, schooling her features into a nonchalant mask.

“He left. Without you.”

“We’re safer together,” Jayin said obstinately. It wasn’t much by way of an argument, but it was all she had.

“He doesn’t want you following him,” Rahael insisted. It felt like all the air had been sucked out of the room. “Jayin, be realistic. Your *dayri* left while you were unconscious, without a note or an explanation. If he cared, he would’ve stayed.”

Jayin inhaled sharply, trying not to look as if she’d been struck.

“I don’t believe you,” Jayin said.

"Here," Rahael said, extending her hand, palm up. "My magic won't affect you while you have the stone, but you will be able to see the truth."

Slowly, Jayin pressed two fingers against her skin.

"Where are you going?" Jayin heard Rahael's voice say. It came from far away, distorted through the memory. Jayin could see Maddix through Rahael's eyes. *He was walking away, his sword on his hip and his pack settled firmly between his shoulder blades. He didn't answer her.*

"Jayin is healing," Rahael went on. "She could wake up any time."

"I can't wait anymore," Maddix said finally. "And she'll only slow me down."

"You need her for what comes next."

"There are other witches. Besides, I'm not going back to Pavaal. There's nothing for me there," Maddix said. His face was hard and unfeeling; he looked like he had back at the sahirla's *compound.*

"She'll never forgive this," Rahael called as he turned his back to her.

"You people do know how to hold a grudge," he replied, cold. "I won't take it personally."

Jayin watched him leave from Rahael's point of view. The memory ended, fizzling out. Something broke inside her, something she'd held close and quiet for so many weeks. It shattered into pieces, the jagged edges tearing into her. She could taste blood on the back of her tongue, but all her wounds had healed.

"I don't believe it," she said again. How could she argue? Jayin had seen it with her own eyes.

"He left you behind," Rahael repeated, a touch of sympathy in her eyes.

He left me behind, Jayin thought, trying to steel herself. She knew this might happen; she knew they would have to go their separate ways, but never like this. She never thought he would leave while she was unconscious, sneaking out like a thief in the night. Stars, she'd been foolish, thinking that he had changed—thinking that he might have cared for her. She had been carrying on like a stupid, lovesick little girl.

She had let him in, she'd trusted him, and he played her like the most naïve of marks. Worst of all, she'd let it happen. Jayin believed him when he promised to keep her safe, and now he was gone. The jagged thing in her chest twisted and Jayin didn't push it away. She needed to feel this; she needed to remember this hurt.

It wasn't a mistake she would make again.

"Fine," Jayin said, looking Rahael in the eye for the first time. She was freezing over, ice crawling through her veins. The cold lodged behind her heart, weighing it down like a stone.

"Are you—?"

"Perfect."

She still wasn't going to stay. They'd made it closer to Pavaal than she ever thought they would, and some small, stubborn part of Jayin wanted to see this thing through. She'd gotten out of the capitol once, she could do it again. Besides, she had a promise to keep. Somewhere in the Gull, Ravi was waiting for her to come back. She could abide another broken promise, not now. And with the wall blocking her way to the ocean and half the kingdom out searching for her, she needed a place to lay low and plan her next move. No one in their right mind would go back to the place where they'd been caught, so no one should be looking for in her Pavaal.

"You should remain here," Rahael tried. "Wait a few more days and make sure you're healed." Jayin shook her head.

"No," Jayin said shortly. "I've stayed too long already."

"Jayin—"

"I'm not going to look for him. I left people back in Pavaal." She'd been responsible for Ravi, and she'd left him without a thought to the consequences. "I need to make sure they're okay."

Finally, Rahael inclined her head. "Be safe. Keep the bracelet on until you're out of Kaddah and they won't be able to find you."

"Thank you."

There wasn't anything to say after that, and Jayin didn't bother with any more goodbyes, finding her way to the surface without incident.

Jayin wouldn't be sorry to be free of Kaddah. If she never had to step foot in this skyforsaken queendom again it would be too soon.

THE ROAD WAS long and dark, and without magic to guide the way, Jayin had to rely on the coarsely drawn map Rahael provided. The lack of auras was disquieting, like only being able to see in two dimensions. More than anything, Jayin yearned for the distraction of filtering out energy. She had to keep herself from expecting to see Maddix beside her. The more she pushed him away, the further the ice froze inside her. Soon she would be nothing more than a statue.

Above her, the sky was clear, and the stars glittered brilliantly, but Jayin didn't so much as look up.

For so long, she and other Aestosi had sworn by the stars, seeking them out for comfort and guidance. Some saw them as ancestors that looked down on their living family and provided counsel. The more religious worshiped the stars as all-seeing deities that shaped the course of human life. Jayin had never believed in gods, whether they were named like in Vandel and Kaddah, or unknowable in the Above. She'd never looked skyward for answers to life's unanswered questions.

The stars had been her hope. Proof that there was always something to light the way, even when the night was blackest. It seemed stupid now, after what she'd been through—Om's death, her capture by the *sahirla*, the Kaddahn raid, *Maddix*—that she'd held onto the stars for so long. They were just pretty, twinkling lights in the sky, and she didn't need them.

Not anymore.

CHAPTER THIRTY-THREE:

MADDIX

The road was quiet. For the first few miles, Maddix looked over his shoulder constantly, expecting to see the dull blue uniforms of the Kaddahn infantry. They had no reason to follow him, but months of paranoia and a well-developed persecution complex were hard to shake. Every sudden sound was a bowstring pulling taut; every rustle in the bushes was an ambush.

Worst than expecting an attack was expecting Jayin. The loss of her dogged his every step, and Maddix had to force himself not to turn back. She was safer without him, he knew that, but that didn't stop him from missing her.

It doesn't matter, he told himself, over and over, as if he could somehow make it true. He was going to finish what he started, but he wasn't going to put her life at risk to do it. Had the witch not plucked Maddix out of his body and used his hands to kill, none of this would've happened. He never would've been arrested, or found the *sahirla.* He never would've met Jayin. Somehow, foolishly, he couldn't bring himself to regret that.

Maddix shook his head, trying to force the thoughts of her out of his head. If he didn't make it to Pavaal, none of this mattered anyway. Some part of him, no matter how small, hoped that maybe one day they would find each other again. His name would be clear and they could go somewhere where no one knew either of them. The Isles, perhaps. Or maybe they'd charter a ship, set sail, and never come back to the Three Kingdoms again. Maddix had always wanted to see the world. Maybe they could see it together.

For now, he had to stay alive. There was no use planning if he died on his way back to Aestos. Maddix kept to the Kaddahn side of the border for as long as he could, walking as fast and as far as he could during the day and finding someplace to sleep when the sun went down. After two years in the Pit and weeks on the road with a surly witch, he wasn't picky about where he made camp.

Where he could, he slept with the lights on or else left fires burning. It was a poor substitute, but he would learn to make do. On nights when voices hissed in his ears and he couldn't shake the nightmares, Maddix did sword drills until he could barely stand.

Mole, Hale, Jayin, and the Dark witch all swirled together behind his eyelids whenever he tried to close them. Maddix gritted his teeth, hacking through his shadowy enemies. He could feel eyes on him as he practiced. *Get it together.* He couldn't go to pieces without her to light his way. He had to get by on his own now.

It was only when the bushes rustled behind him that Maddix realized the watchful eyes might not be in his head.

Maddix spun, holding his sword out in front of him as he prowled through the scrubby underbrush. He didn't relish fighting, not like Jayin, but his blood called for action, for movement. Anything to keep him out of his own head.

"Who's there?" Maddix called. Something shifted in the trees and Maddix advanced, his sword held tight in both hands. He drew it over his head before a tiny, petrified squeak stopped him in his tracks.

"Maia?" Maddix said, recognizing the blonde witch crouched in the bushes. "What are you *doing* here?"

"I was following you," she said. Her voice shook and her eyes tracked his sword as he sheathed it.

"Bleeding skies—*why*?"

"I came to bring you back," Maia said, crossing her arms over her chest. The effect was made less impressive by the twigs stuck in her blonde hair and her quivering bottom lip. Blood crusted on her cheek, a souvenir from trampling through the woods.

"I can't go back."

"You have to!" Maia said, raising her voice loud enough that Maddix clapped his hand over her mouth and hauled her inside the ramshackle structure where he'd made camp. Half of the roof was caved in, but it was as good a shelter as any. "Jayin is going to get herself killed trying to come after you, and you don't even care," Maia accused when Maddix finally released her.

"She's not going to come after me," Maddix said. He didn't know what Rahael had done to convince Jayin not to follow him, but he knew it would break her heart. Which meant Maia had put herself in danger for nothing. "I'm taking you back."

"No," Maia said. Her chin jutted out stubbornly. "Jayin almost *died* for you and—"

"I know!" Maddix said, so sharply that Maia flinched. Maddix pinched the bridge of his nose, taking a deep breath. "I'm sorry. She's not safe with me and I…" He trailed off, not trusting himself to speak. "I just want her to be okay."

Slowly, Maia nodded. "I thought—"

"Tomorrow, I'm taking you back."

"You have to come back with me now."

Maddix had to steel himself from snapping again. "Maia. You're tired, and if neither of us gets any rest, we're not going to make it."

"But—"

Once, just once, Maddix wanted to meet a levelheaded witch who actually had some regard for their own safety. He was starting to think they didn't exist.

"I'm taking you back in the morning," he said firmly, handing her his coat. "Here, you can sleep on this."

After a long moment, Maia took the coat and settled on the uneven floor. She curled into a ball, tucking her knees up to her chin just like Jayin used to do. No doubt Maia thought that mattresses were too comfortable as well.

Maddix waited until he heard Maia's breathing even out before he allowed his eyes to close. His nightmares made for light sleeping and soon a small sound outside woke him. Maddix rose silently, gently tapping Maia to wake her. He pressed a finger to his lips and she nodded, blinking the sleep from her eyes. He couldn't see anything outside the walls, but he knew better than to allow that to soothe him.

"Get your stuff," Maddix whispered. Maia handed him back his coat and pulled her pack across her shoulders.

"What is it?" she murmured. Maddix couldn't answer for sure, but something was amiss.

"Come on," he said, pushing her in front of him and holding his sword ready. The sun was still low in the sky, but he couldn't shake the feeling that they were being watched.

"Maia," he said softly once they were well away from the house. Something was different about her and it took him a moment to realize that the cut on her cheek was gone. Healed, as if it had never existed. She followed his gaze, her hand going to her face.

"I healed it," she said, answering the unspoken question. "I didn't mean to, I just—"

Maddix swore under his breath, trying to keep his panic from showing and spooking her. They were in trouble. Maddix handed Maia one of the knives that Jayin had lent him, placing it in her hand so that she was holding it correctly.

“I know how to use it.” Maia’s jaw set.

“Let’s hope you won’t have to,” Maddix said. “Hide the knife in your sleeve and give me your hands.” Maia shot him a questioning look, but she didn’t argue, allowing him to tie her hands loosely in front of her. He looped his necklace over her head, cutting off her magic.

“What are you—?” Maia asked, her voice thin.

“Quiet,” Maddix hissed.

Soldiers came upon them just minutes later, their weapons drawn.

“Can I help you?” Maddix asked, finding the seed of arrogance Hale had planted and bringing it to the surface. He looked every inch a *dayri* bounty hunter, marching a witch captive to her doom. He surveyed the soldiers coldly, arching a superior eyebrow and wishing for Jayin. She had always been the better actor.

“We’ve been tracking a disturbance,” one of the soldiers said, stepping forward.

“No kidding,” Maddix said, rolling his eyes. He nudged Maia and she took a staggering step forward. “This one got away from me.”

The leader looked him up and down, his lip curling. “And you are? Not Kaddahn, surely.”

“Aestosi.” Maddix didn’t bother to lie. They wouldn’t believe he was one of their own and claiming Vandel as his homeland wouldn’t help the situation any. “She’s worth a great deal of coin to me, so I would appreciate it if you stopped wasting my time.”

“How does an Aestosi witch end up here?” the soldier pressed, clearly trying to trip him up.

“You should get out some more, friend,” Maddix said, adding Evin’s condescension to Hale’s haughty arrogance. The soldier scowled. “The Aestosi king decided to build a wall around the capital. You're welcome to go take a look if you don't believe me. It's enormous, you can't miss it."

The soldier hesitated for a moment more before waving them on. Maddix snapped him a single, mocking salute before marching Maia past. For just a moment, Maddix thought that they might get away with it. The air shifted behind them and the hair on the back of his neck stood up.

"Move!" Maddix shouted, slicing the rope around Maia's wrist and pushing her out of the way. One of the soldiers stabbed at his midsection and Maddix whirled, freeing his sword in a single movement. He parried the blow and struck back in kind, forcing the soldier back. His focus narrowed, the world shrinking to his opponent, the screeching of metal, and the bright, hazy instinct to survive. Maddix slashed at the soldier in front of him, severing the woman's hand from her wrist and ran, plunging into the forest after Maia.

Something slammed into him from behind, and Maddix lost his sword as he collapsed to the ground in a violent tangle of limbs. One of the soldiers pinned his arms and Maddix cursed as his shoulders strained in their sockets. The soldier flipped him onto his back and then there was a forearm pressed against his throat, crushing his trachea. Maddix wheezed, the remains of his breath escaping with a rattle.

"Aestosi scum," the soldier snarled and Maddix managed to free himself for long enough to suck in a single lungful of air before a fist clipped his jaw and he saw stars. *He's going to kill me*, Maddix thought blearily. After all this time, after the Pit and the *sahirla* and the wall, he was going to be killed by a Kaddahn soldier.

The sky had a cruel sense of irony.

"Get away from him!" a tiny voice shrieked. There was a flash of silver, and hot blood splashed onto Maddix's face. The pressure against his throat lifted. Maddix's vision cleared by slow degrees. The man went limp, blood running from his ears and mouth. A knife protruded from his neck. Maddix pushed the soldier's body off of him and tried to sit up before he heaved. Vomit and bile hit the forest floor in a wet, stinking mess.

"Are you okay?" Maia asked, going to her knees beside him. He felt the unmistakable tang of magic in the air and batted Maia's hands away.

"Don't do that," he said. His voice was a strained whisper. "They can track magic, remember?"

"They already found us and you need help," Maia said, pressing light fingertips to his neck. Magic prickled under his skin and he could feel the bruises beginning to fade.

"That's enough," Maddix said when he felt whole enough to stand. There would be more soldiers on their way. "Come on." He took her hand they both started running.

"We're going in the wrong direction," Maia protested as Maddix dragged her through the woods. "The coven is the other way."

"So are the people with swords that want to kill us."

"But we have to go back!"

"If we go back, we'll lead the *dayri* right to the rest of them. So stop fighting me and *run*."

Miraculously, Maia didn't argue, sprinting alongside him. There was no way they were going to outrun a whole squadron of soldiers. There was one way they might be able to get away clean, but it was a bad idea. Jayin would've smacked him over the head and called him *dayri* idiot, but she wasn't there, and they didn't have any other choices.

"Where are we going?" Maia asked when Maddix started to lead them towards the border.

"Somewhere you won't get skinned alive for being a witch," Maddix said.

"We can't leave," Maia said, guessing his plan immediately. All the blood drained from her pale face, leaving her skin the color of parchment. "We can't leave Kaddah."

"We can't stay here either," Maddix insisted, not understanding her hesitation. She wasn't the one wanted for murder in Aestos. "I will bring you back I swear, but if we stay here we're dead."

She looked terrified, but clenched her jaw and didn't argue.

Making their way across the border wasn't nearly as difficult as Maddix might have thought—Kaddah simply didn't have the manpower to fight an underground war against Vandel and patrol every inch of their lands. Besides, Aestosi witches knew better than to venture here, and the superstitious Kaddahn rarely visited Aestos, where *sahir* were free citizens.

Maddix doubted the soldiers would risk the ire of the King—and more importantly, the Kingswitch—by following them out of Kaddah. If they were caught, it could start a second war, and fighting against an army of witches was suicide.

So was going back to the place where Maddix's face was plastered on wanted posters and every bounty hunter in the kingdom knew his name, but if there was any other way, he couldn't think of it.

This will work, he promised himself. It had to work.

They made it to the Aestosi countryside without incident, but Maddix insisted that they keep moving, wary of soldiers stumbling across them by accident. The one good thing, the single bright spot in the disaster of the last few hours, was at least they were past the wall. Pavaal was only two days' walk away.

It was the worst kind of tease, being so close to his destination after weeks of travel only to have to go back and start over again.

"Is this Aestos?" Maia asked softly after an hour of walking in silence.

"The one and only," he replied, not bothering to mask the bitterness in his voice. Home sweet home, where he was a wanted man and the witch who destroyed him walked free. "Just a little further," Maddix promised. They needed to find someplace to make camp soon or he was going to have to carry her the rest of the way.

Thank the stars for drought, Maddix thought as they came upon an abandoned farmhouse.

"Why doesn't anybody live here?" Maia asked as Maddix ushered her inside. As soon as he deemed it secure, they split up, looking for supplies. There wasn't much to find, just a few strips of nearly unchewable jerky and empty tin cans.

"Farms aren't producing anymore," Maddix replied, checking the locks and shuttering the windows. "So people have to move." Farmers who'd worked the land for generations fled the fields as their crops withered and their livelihoods died. Over the past two years, hundreds of people left their family farms to try and find work in the capitol.

He didn't tell her that there were rumors that witches were killing the land on the Kingswitch's orders. For years, he'd believed the stories, repeating them like gospels. Maia didn't need to know how recently he'd hated her people.

"I thought Aestos was supposed to be a safe haven," Maia said. "Someplace magic is allowed and nobody is afraid." It was a nice story, no doubt facilitated by Ayrie to boost their standing in the Three Kingdoms. Too bad it wasn't true.

"Sorry to disappoint," Maddix said, a muscle jumping in his jaw. He didn't bother explaining that things were as bad here as they were anywhere. *Sahir* may not have been hunted outright, but he knew Hale and the other witchhunters were more powerful than they seemed. The wall was proof of that;

without support from the Crown, it never would have been built, let alone so quickly.

Maia didn't push, and Maddix gratefully let the subject drop. There were two moldering mattresses on the second floor of the farmhouse, and he pulled them both into the kitchen.

When that was done, Maddix went to work securing the perimeter, pulling empty cans out of the dusty pantry and stringing them up on the old clotheslines that lined the property's southern border. The windows in the kitchen let them see out to the front yard and if anyone approached the house from the back, they'd hear them coming. It wasn't much and not nearly as good as magic, but might give them a head start that could save their lives.

"Maddix?" Maia whispered as they both settled down in the kitchen. Maddix had locked them in and his back rested against the door. "I'm sorry. I know it's not safe for you here."

"Just go to sleep," Maddix said, trying to be comforting. "We'll wait it out for a few days and get you back home."

"Maybe Jayin will still be there," Maia said, sounding so hopeful Maddix fought the urge to flinch. He scrubbed his hand over his face. He hated that Maia had come after him. He hated that he'd left in the first place.

Most of all, he hated himself for hoping the same thing. Jayin had no reason to ever want to see him again. He was selfish, a fool and a hypocrite, and for the first time, he understood why she had so often cursed his optimism. It was going to get him killed.

But even that didn't stop him from hoping.

CHAPTER THIRTY-FOUR:

JAYIN

Jayin ducked into an alleyway as booted footsteps sounded behind her. She had no idea what had gotten the Kaddahn so rattled, but there were soldiers everywhere, prowling border towns and crossings. Looking for something. Or someone.

Part of her, the tiny part she hadn't managed to lock away completely, whispered that it might be Maddix. He was a wanted fugitive, and with his fair skin and red-gold hair, he didn't exactly blend in with the Kaddahn peasantry. The voice urged her to investigate, and Jayin's heart squeezed at the prospect of finding him. What she would do when she found him, she couldn't say for sure. Most of her wanted to see how easily he walked away with her knife buried in his thigh.

The tiny voice wanted something else entirely.

In the end, rationality won out and she picked her way around the roaming packs of soldiers. The stone around her wrist allowed her to pass through without her magic giving her away and no one noticed a small girl skulking about. Travelling without her second sight was like walking around with her eyes closed, but she preferred hiding her magic to losing her life.

Jayin crossed into Aestos as soon as she could, unwilling to remain in this starcursed queendom for a minute longer than necessary.

The wall loomed behind her, so tall that Jayin could see it from miles away. It jutted into the sky, an ugly gash in the countryside. Not for the first time, she wondered about the *sahirla*'s contact in the Palace. They had to have one, or the wall wouldn't be possible.

Absently, Jayin stroked the ruined skin of her wrist where the Kingswitch's mark used to be. Stars, she'd thought herself so blessed to receive it. She had been so young.

From the day she'd entered the gilded halls of the Palace, all she wanted to do was belong. She was younger than most of the other witches, all of whom had been recruited from the Academy. The moment a *sahir*'s abilities expressed themselves, they were educated in magical history and taught how to control their magic. In pureblooded witch families, it usually happened when a child was six or seven.

Jayin had been eleven when she'd been plucked out of the gutter and brought before the Kingswitch. He told her that she was different, unique. He'd filled her head with thoughts of grandeur and promises of a home, a *real* home. He said that the witches in Ayrie would be her family. She should have known it was all lies.

For years she believed she was special, the Kingswitch's personal student. At first, Jayin had loved the attention. She was young and powerful, and there was no one in the whole of the kingdom whose abilities matched hers. But as time went on, the glow of being the Kingswitch's favorite wore off and reality set in. None of the other witches would go near her, whispering that she was cursed and Dark.

Now, wandering through the countryside, she was alone once again, more alone than she'd ever been as a dockrat in the Gull or in the Palace. Maybe it was better that way.

Jayin didn't waste any time, walking until she could hardly stand before finding a place to sleep. She took off the bracelet the moment she was on Aestosi soil and used her magic to avoid anyone that might be in her path.

She didn't bother staying in the small towns that dotted the road to Pavaal. In fact, she skirted them altogether, camping in fields where she wouldn't be spotted. It was best for her to be on her own from now on. Jayin didn't know if the Kingswitch was still searching for her, but she wasn't willing to take the risk.

The trip to Pavaal was much faster than it might have been with Maddix by her side, but Jayin stopped as soon as she saw the capitol on the horizon. She'd been away from civilization for so long she didn't know how to be around so many people at once. Even from the outskirts, she could feel the hum of the city. Jayin wanted one more night of pure air before she started having to filter out half a million civilians' worth of energy.

Not for the first time she yearned to be back on the *Stormwind*. If this mission didn't end with her head on a spike or facedown in the river, she was going to find a ship and never come back to dry land again.

Jayin watched the stars as they rose in the sky, fiddling with the silver cuff on her wrist and tugging at it so it hid her scar. She should get rid of it. She should've gotten rid of it the moment that Maddix severed the connection. And yet, Jayin couldn't bear to leave it behind. She dragged her fingertips over the cool metal until she fell asleep with the bracelet tucked under her cheek.

PAVAAL WAS THE same, but only on the surface. Jayin could find her way around blindfolded, but there was something wrong with the city's energy. Only the smell was familiar, the rotten stench that always seemed to emanate from the rancid river. It took her only a moment to forget what clean air tasted like.

"Hey there, pretty lady," a low, oily voice came out of the dark. She wasn't even in the Gull yet. Stars, this city really was rotting if slummers were starting to infest the merchants' safe streets.

Jayin rolled her eyes, knives in her hands before the man could say another word.

"Do you know how to use those, green eyes?" he leered.

"Come find out or walk the other way," Jayin said without blinking. After the *sahirla*, there weren't many people left in the kingdom that gave her reason to fear. The bald man sneered, advancing with far too much confidence. Jayin ducked underneath his reaching arms, her knife flashing in the sunlight before it severed the man's hand from his wrist. His scream shattered the air and the man fell to his knees, clutching the bloody stump.

"Next time, think twice," she said, kneeling beside him and wiping her knife off on his shirt. "Or I'll be back for the other hand."

The man sobbed and Jayin walked away without sparing him another glance, leaving him bleeding on the cobbled streets.

"It's good to be back," Jayin muttered to herself, twisting the hooked blade in her hands. Some things never changed.

Jayin didn't go home at first—she didn't even know if she had a home to go back to. It didn't seem possible, but she actually missed this place. The Gull was ugly and violent, but she had built something here. Something that was hers and hers alone, without the taint of Ayrie or the Kingswitch on it. If the shop had been looted or her apartment ransacked without the infamous Gulwitch to protect it, she didn't want to know just yet.

The streets were emptier than she'd ever seen them, especially for the daytime. Only fools and carrions were out at night, so those who carved out lives in the slums did so in broad daylight. But Jayin only saw a handful of people as she prowled through the familiar streets, searching for a place to hole up while she figured out her next move. Everything was quiet and Jayin's skin started to prickle when three carrions appeared in front of her. Twice in one day. It was almost like the city was welcoming her home.

Oh Jayin, how we've missed you. Now you must die.

The carrions looked different. Something in their eyes and auras was jagged, desperate. There were three of them and only one of her; they should have been vibrating with confidence. Instead, they almost looked scared.

"Let's not do anything stupid," Jayin said carefully, holding her hands out in front of her. She didn't want another bloodbath, not against kids.

"Give us your coin or we'll kill you."

"Sorry to disappoint, but I've got nothing."

The carrions swore, prowling closer, but it was obvious that their hearts weren't in it.

"Fine," Jayin said, pulling out her knives and spinning them around her thumbs. The display didn't stop them—

But something else did.

Smoke filled the street, blotting out the muted sunshine, and then there were voices all around them. Something rumbled and flashed, and Jayin shrouded herself in glamor.

"You know better," a voice said out of the gloom, mocking and undeniably female. "These streets are protected."

Jayin paused, not recognizing the voice or the signature. Was this a new player who'd risen since Jayin had left?

"We ain't afraid of you!" one of them shouted at the empty air. The tremor in his voice said differently.

"Leave now and I'll let you live," said the disembodied voice.

"You don't control us, witch." *Witch*? This wasn't magic, not by a long shot. But carrions had always been stupidly superstitious, and they had no practical knowledge of magic. Easy marks for a *sahir* imposter.

"And you don't cross the Gulwitch without paying the price," the voice said. Lightning flashed and steel *clang*ed as the carrions' weapons hit the streets. The boys were gone by the time the non-magical dust settled.

Jayin's head spun. She knew that she was infamous in the slums, but she'd never gone so far as to claim territory. She certainly didn't go around terrorizing carrion gangs and rescuing civilians.

"Grab their weapons," a girl said, appearing on a window ledge. Two identical, impossibly young boys clambered to the street, scooping up the knives the carrions had left behind. "Come on guys, let's go home."

"Where'd that girl go?" one of the twins asked. Their friend slid down from the ledge with impressive agility, her braids swinging around her head.

"If she's smart, she's on her way out of the city by now." The girl looked barely over twelve years old, but she was clearly the leader of this little trio. "It's a good thing we were here or she'd be dead."

She was very confident, and Jayin admired that. But there was also no way this girl, even as talented as she was, was running things. Jayin reinforced the glamor as she walked behind them, wary of being spotted.

The kids didn't go very far, ducking into a building only a few blocks from her old place. Jayin slipped in before the door could close behind them, staying in the shadows. This was proving to be an interesting little detour.

"R!" the girl shouted. Her voice echoed off the walls and Jayin could sense over a dozen people in there with them, all of them children. Jayin inched forward, craning her neck to see who was coming down the stairs.

"Well, well," a voice said before Jayin could take another step.

The doors of the building flew open behind her, and a tall figure strode inside, flanked by the most carrions Jayin had ever seen in one place. She spotted the marks of at least three different gangs, and yet they seemed to be working together. What had *happened* while she was away?

"This must be where the Gulwitch and her charges rest their heads."

It took Jayin a moment but she recognized the leader, the man who'd spoken. He was a turncoat Guard who'd betrayed his mandate to run with the gangs. There was more money in murder than in keeping the peace.

Jayin's blood boiled. If any Guard should be thrown into the Pit to rot, it was him.

"You're not welcome here," the same voice echoed from the shadows, but no smoke or flash accompanied the words. They hadn't expected to be followed home. "Leave now and we'll let you live."

"I hear you," the Guard said, his head swiveling from left to right, "but I don't see you. You know, we're starting to think that there's not a drop of magical blood in this stinking place." His eyes glittered. "Let's spill it all, just to be sure."

"You want magic?" Jayin shouted, glamoring her voice so that it rang through the building like rumbling thunder. She prayed that whoever these kids were, they'd get the hint. "I'll show you magic."

She ran into the center of the floor, her glamor filling the room, all glowing eyes and terrible tattoos. The disguise came naturally, settling over her skin like battle-worn armor. Jayin stretched the illusion as far as it would go, blotting out the dim light that filtered in through the high windows. Emerald flames erupted all around her.

Finally smoke filled the room and Jayin scaled back her magic. Before she could try another trick, flash-bombs erupted at the doorway. In the darkness, she could feel the intruders' panic and fear. Hoping the kids could keep up the charade for a bit longer, Jayin bent the glamor of herself over until she loomed over the Guard. His eyes bulged and all the blood drained from his face.

"I know you, Mal Thane," she said. "I know where you live, where you drink, where you hide your money from your own people. I know where your wife and child sleep at night, and if you cross me, I will make you watch as I take it all from you. And when you have nothing left to lose, I will peel the skin from your bones."

The Guard made a tiny, terrified noise, and then he was gone without so much as a word, leaving the carrions behind. Jayin opened her mouth, spitting acid-green flame. By the time the smoke cleared, the rest of them had fled as well.

Jayin made sure that they were all gone before dispelling the glamor. She thumbed the triggers of her arm sheaths, ready to defend herself at a moment's notice. She didn't know how these kids, whoever they were, would react to her little magic show.

"Jayin?" a voice came out of the gloom. Jayin's heart jumped as she saw a familiar face coming towards her.

Ravi. He ran at her, launching himself into her arms and wrapping his own around her midsection.

"Hey there kiddo," she said softly when they finally broke apart, "You've been busy."

"You came back," he said. His voice was small and tears gathered on his lower lashes. Stars, he looked so young.

"I told you I would," Jayin said. The words tasted like acid, like guilt. She never meant to come back.

"Burning stars," the girl with the braids whispered. "You're her."

"But you've been doing a very good job pretending to be me," Jayin observed. The girl blushed. "So are you going to introduce me or what?"

"Guys come on out!" Ravi called. Slowly, fourteen dirty, suspicious faces revealed themselves. Most of them had that shifty, waifish look that had taken hold of the Gull and at least four sported carrion tattoos.

"I told you she was real," Ravi said proudly. Jayin had to fight to keep from squirming under their scrutiny. There were a few moments of tense, awkward silence before Ravi spoke again. "I guess you want some answers," he said almost sheepishly, rubbing the back of his neck.

"How about we take a walk?" Jayin suggested, a little twitchy from being inspected by fourteen pairs of eyes. "See how the old shop is holding up."

Ravi nodded, obviously sensing her discomfort.

"Alright, the show's over!" Ravi said to the crowd. "We got work to do." There was a sigh from the kids, but none of them argued, slipping out of the building in pairs. Smart policy. The streets had never been safe for kids, and now things seemed worse than ever.

"They're going to want to talk to you," he warned once they'd all gone. The girl with the braids lingered a little longer than the others, her dark eyes narrowed.

"You cut your hair," Ravi said as they made their way through the streets. Jayin brushed her fingers through her bangs. She understood his hesitation. She'd been gone a long time, and there was no telling how much she had changed since Ravi last saw her.

"And you started a gang," Jayin replied, trying to set him at ease. She scrubbed at her eyes, trying to familiarize herself with the auras in the building. Being outside was a relief. "I thought I told you to stay away from carrions, not start recruiting."

Ravi blushed, ducking his head like he used to when she scolded him. Some things stayed the same. "S'not a gang."

"Sure looks like a gang," she replied, tapping the top of his head. Privately, Jayin was happy he hadn't grown. Another lasting bit of normalcy.

From the outside, the shop looked miraculously intact, but Jayin couldn't help but hold her breath as she pushed the door open. Everything looked how she'd left it. Herbs, poultices, satchels full of mundane and magical ingredients alike, they were all still there. In fact, it looked like someone had restocked at least once. A thin layer of dust had settled over everything.

"I kept everything running as long as I could," Ravi explained. "I, uh, I lived in your apartment too. Me and a few others until there were too many of us. We kept the doors open for as long as we could, but then things got bad."

"What happened?" Jayin asked. "I mean, the gangs coming together, you amassing kids and rescuing people off of the street…." It was something out of fairytale. Heroics had never gone far in the Gull.

"Things changed when you went away," Ravi said. "People started getting sick. Real sick, and none of the healers could do anything to stop it. Carrions, merchants, dockmen, old, young, it didn't matter. The whole place went mad."

"So how did you get the idea to bring me into it?"

"Only thing that scares people more than a plague is a witch." Ravi shrugged. He ran his finger along the dusty counter, writing his name with a bitten nailbed. It's how he learned to write, drawing the letters with his fingers before graduating to ink. "The gangs were pulling in anyone they could and killing everyone else. When they finally made it here I borrowed some of your flash and scared them off." He smiled a little, but it was a small, barely-there thing. "I couldn't keep it up on my own so I started recruiting. Zia, Palla, Dej, those were the first three, and then it kind of spiraled."

"Kane," Jayin said after a long moment. The Bloodwing leader was the first thing that came to mind. Stars, Jayin hadn't thought about him since Maerta showed up in the Gull. "Did Kane get sick too?"

"Yeah, he was one of the first."

Jayin's blood cooled in her veins. Whatever had made Pavaal sick wasn't mundane. She'd felt the strange magical reverberation in Kane, and when she'd turned her power on Hale so long ago in the *sahirla*'s cage, then again in the *sahir* who'd led the Kaddahn into the tunnels.

"It burned through here like a fire and then stopped like nothing had even happened. But by then it was just one gang and us, trying to survive." Ravi continued, his voice weighed down. He seemed to have aged years since the last time she saw him.

"Stars, I missed you," she said, wrapping her arm around his shoulders and pulling him close. She set her chin on top of his curly hair and didn't say a word as his thin shoulders shook with silent sobs. She waited until the trembling subsided, rubbing her gloved hand on his arm.

"I thought you died," he whispered finally. "Before things fell apart, there were people looking for you everywhere. They said you were a deserter, and when they stopped looking I thought they'd killed you."

"I don't plan on dying anytime soon," Jayin promised.

"I'm tired, Jay," Ravi said after a short, heavy silence. She could tell. His energy was heavy with a burden she couldn't imagine. "They need me to keep them safe and I don't know how much longer flash will work."

"It's okay," Jayin said, turning to him and tilting his head up so he was looking her in the eye. "You don't need tricks anymore. You've got me. I'm not going anywhere."

CHAPTER THIRTY-FIVE:

MADDIX

There was something wrong with Maia.

Maddix had woken up before the sun to scout the area, careful not to wake her, but when he returned it was clear that they weren't going anywhere. The young *sahir* was on the floor a few feet away from her mattress, curled into a tiny ball. It looked like she'd tried to move before falling over. Her face was bloodless, and when Maddix put his hands on her skin, her forehead burned. He managed to get her back into bed, but the fever was burning through her.

"Maddix?" Maia said weakly, rousing from the haze.

"Hey," he said, pressing a cool towel to her forehead.

"I'm sick," she said.

"It's probably just a cold," he assured her. All Guards had basic medical training—sicknesses spread through their barracks like lice in the Gull—but he hadn't seen anything like this. Yesterday Maia had been fine. Today she could hardly move.

"I'm *sick*," she said again. "I'm a healer. We don't get sick."

"We'll get you another healer," he said bracingly, rewetting the cloth and mopping at her brow.

Maia shook her head, tears shining in her bloodshot eyes. "I won't make it back to the others in Kaddah."

"Then we won't go to Kaddah," Maddix said. They were only a day or two from Pavaal, and the best healers in the kingdom lived in the capitol. If Maia could hang on for a little while longer, he could get her there.

Fear bloomed in his chest as Maddix thought of finally returning to Pavaal. He had been trying to get back for so long—it was the reason he joined the *sahirla,* how he found Jayin—but now that he would be there in only a few days time, all the revenge-born bravado disappeared, leaving nothing but fear behind. Skies, he was scared.

"No," Maia said, guessing his idea. "They'll kill you."

"Only if they catch me," Maddix said, forcing a smile. He wished he were a better liar.

"But—"

"If I let anything happen to you, Evin and Rahael will hunt me down and kill me anyway. Besides, I've gotten used to having you around."

Maia tried to smile, but it was weak. She was fading quickly.

"You just get some sleep, okay?" he said, but she was already snoring. Maddix made sure the house was secure as he slipped out and walked to the nearest town. It wasn't much, just a few small shopfronts and a tiny inn.

After doing a quick sweep to make sure no one would spot him, Maddix broke into the barn outside of a ramshackle inn that hadn't seen business in months. There was no way that Maia would be able to walk all the way to Pavaal, and even if she could, Maddix didn't think she would last the time it took to get there on foot. So, in broad daylight, he walked out of the barn with a horse and a cart in tow.

Everyone knew things were getting bad, but Maddix didn't realize exactly *how* bad. It looked like something had come down from the sky and struck down the land and people alike. He wondered how long it would take to reach the cities, if it hadn't already.

He would find out soon enough. In a few days he would be back, with only the barest shred of a plan and a dying witch to worry about. He never should've left the *sahir* in Kaddah. He never should've gone on this harebrained mission in the first place.

For so long, Maddix thought that if he found the witch who was responsible for killing all those people and somehow force them to confess, he could have a life again. A real life. He could live free, not constantly on the run and looking over his shoulder. Even after everything, he still believed the courts would set things right. But looking at the deserted road and the ruined farms all around him, doubt surged anew.

Jayin would've been unbearable, knowing he finally agreed with her bleak opinion of the Crown. She never would've let him hear the end of it.

I miss you, he thought. *I hope you're safe.*

Maia was still asleep when Maddix returned. He tied the stolen horse to the back fence, well out of view of the street, though somehow he doubted that anyone was going to come looking. He pressed a fresh towel to her forehead and drew the sheets up to her chin.

There wasn't much else he could do, so Maddix busied himself with readying the cart for travel. As he worked, he couldn't help but think back to the last time he'd traveled with an injured witch.

Jayin had been half-dead and bloody. She scared him more than he was willing to admit. And she was still the most beautiful person he'd ever seen, he just didn't know it quite yet. He should've seen the strength and the pride in those green eyes and realized that everything he had ever believed about witches was wrong. He should have known better.

Maddix wondered if she would miss him. If this went badly, the news of his capture would reach every corner of the kingdom. Maybe it would find her too. Would she mourn, even after everything?

I don't regret you. Maddix could hear the words as clearly as if she was standing right beside him. That had probably changed now that he left her behind. Still, Maddix hoped. It was selfish—*he* was selfish—but somehow the idea of marching into the jaws of the capitol was more bearable if he imagined that she forgave him.

Just the knowledge that Jayin was still out there—ferocious, magical, beautiful Jayin—made it easier. He'd done one thing right. He hadn't gotten her killed along with him. It wasn't much, but it was enough. It had to be enough, or Maddix wasn't going to make it within a mile of Pavaal.

Jayin was enough.

CHAPTER THIRTY-SIX:

MADDIX

They moved as soon as Maia woke. She could hardly stand, but Maddix helped her into the cart, where he'd laid as many blankets as there were left in the house.

"Where did you get all this?" she croaked as Maddix got her settled as comfortably as he could manage.

"I stole it," he admitted.

"I thought you used to be a Guard," Maia said with a shaky smile that Maddix suspected was more for his benefit than anything else.

"Lawmen make the best criminals," Maddix said, making sure everything was secure before they started off. Maia had plenty of food and water, though Maddix noticed that she hadn't eaten a thing since she'd fallen ill. "Maybe when we get to the city and you get better, I'll show you how to pick a lock."

"I know how to pick a lock."

"Well, then we'll rob a shop. You can have the whole Pavaalian experience. It'll make a great story to tell your friends when we get you back home."

"Okay," she said softly, but he knew she didn't believe him.

"Yell if you need anything," he said before mounting the horse and setting off. They made much better time than they would have on foot, even hauling the cart. As they came closer to the city, the streets began to fill with merchants and travelers, and soon the desolation of the fields vanished altogether.

Maddix rode through the night, eating his rations on horseback without stopping to rest. He hadn't slept in days, but Maia didn't have time for him to stop. Besides, the closer they came to the city gates, the more his blood thrummed with adrenaline. By the time Maddix spied Ayrie Palace looming grandly on its cliff above Pavaal, it felt like he'd never sleep again. His hands shook and he clenched the reins tighter in his fists to steady them.

"So this is Pavaal," Maia said as they rode through the merchant sector. It was quiet, too quiet for the daytime. Maddix had never heard the city this quiet, without the noise of vendors shouting their wares or locals bustling from place to place.

"Yes," Maddix said, keeping his eyes on the road. Something slithered beneath the city's surface, a moment of calm before a riot. Or after one.

"It smells." Maddix almost smiled as he helped her out of the cart. They hobbled into an old guardpost between the merchant sector and the Gull. It had been abandoned for years; during training, Maddix and his classmates used to sneak out of the barracks and meet there to drink smuggled *arak*.

"It does," he agreed. "But it has the best healers in the kingdom.

"I'm the best healer in Kaddah, and I can't fix me," Maia said shakily. Her condition hadn't improved. Her skin was gray and waxy, stretched too tight over her skull. Her eyes were red-lined and clouded. And her hands shook constantly, like she was having some kind of fit.

"I'm going to get some help," Maddix said, setting her up in a sheltered corner. It wasn't immediately visible from the door and close to the back exit. Maia didn't have much strength left, but she should be able to make it out if things went sideways.

"You should get some sleep," Maia advised. "You've been awake for too long."

"I'm fine," Maddix replied. "How about the best healer in Kaddah lets someone take care of her for a change?" Maia smiled a little, and Maddix ruffled her blonde hair. "I'll be right back."

"Be safe."

Maddix tapped the sword on his hip by way of answer before slipping out the door. Closer to the Gull, more people were on the street, but they kept their eyes trained on the ground. No one so much as glanced at him. Apprehension hung over everything like ash after a fire. The Gull was holding its breath, but Maddix had no idea what it was waiting for.

Something terrible, no doubt.

Worse, the local healers had vanished. Maddix checked shop after shop, but each and every one was abandoned. Whatever had happened, it had send the *sahir* running. He took what he could from the dusty shelves, but without magic he didn't know how useful the items would be. Maybe Maia could talk him through it.

He was running out of places to check when he remembered Jayin. It was a wonder he'd managed to forget her for even a minute. She'd run a shop in the slums. An apothecary. He had no idea where it might be, but she said it was squarely in gang territory. Clearly, she'd had a death wish long before meeting him. Who would choose to live in the Gull, of all places, let alone in the middle of the three neighborhoods that were so contested? The streets might as well have run with blood. It was suicide, and yet she had chosen to live there in order to flee from the Palace.

In the end, it wasn't all that hard to find. There were only so many places that matched her description, or herbal shops in this part of the city. The storefront was deserted and the air inside stank of must. Maddix didn't stay for long, grabbing anything he might be able to use and stuffing it into his pack

There was plenty left, untouched by carrions. Perhaps the legend of the Gulwitch was enough to ward away thieves. Maddix rubbed the back of his neck, shivering. It felt like some part of her was still there, haunting the little shop like she was haunting him.

The only evidence that the shop wasn't completely abandoned was a name written in dust on the counter. Ravi. It was a given name, not a ridiculous carrion moniker. Idly, Maddix wondered who this Ravi was, and why he would bother scrawling his name on the counter without stealing anything.

Maybe he knew Jayin, from before. It was a nice thought, that there was someone in this stinking place that knew and remembered her, Maddix said a silent prayer that whoever he was, Ravi was safe too.

"Take one more step, and I put this through your neck.".

Maddix stilled, turning to see a girl no older than twelve pointing a knife at him. Stars, he hadn't even heard her approach. Her eyes were enormous, throwing the hollows of her face into sharp relief. Dozens of thin braids swung around her head as she moved.

"Do you want me to get you a stepstool so you can reach or would that count as moving?" Maddix asked before he could help himself.

"Who are you?" the girl demanded, her mouth twisting into a frown. "What are you doing in Gulwitch territory?"

Maddix blinked at her. Gulwitch territory? Somehow, Jayin hadn't mentioned that her alter ago ran a gang.

"I thought she was a myth," Maddix said dimly.

"You stupid?" the girl snapped, narrowing her eyes. Recognition dawned on her face, quickly followed by fear.

Maddix moved before she could say another word, pushing her aside to get to the door. Her blade bit into his flesh, slicing into his side. The girl shouted for help but Maddix didn't stick around to see who would show up. He had to get back to Maia.

"Maddix, what—" she started as he threw open the doors of the guard post. "They saw you." She paused, her eyes finding the wound on his hip. "Let me."

"There's no time and you need your strength," he said, all but throwing the bag of supplies at her. "That should help, but I can't stay here. If someone finds you, tell them you're protected by the Gulwitch."

"The what?"

"Gulwitch," Maddix said hurriedly. Blood was dripping down his pant leg and his hip throbbed.

"Do you understand me?"

"I'm under the Gulwitch's protection," Maia repeated. Her voice shook. "Please be careful."

"I'll be back as soon as I can," Maddix promised, grabbing the empty bag and rushing back the way he came.

The clattering of hooves and jackbooted footsteps echoed in the street. Evidently, the stillness that had overtaken Pavaal wasn't strong enough to keep him from being pursued.

Maddix ran to the corner of the alley only to find the exit blocked by men outfitted in familiar Kingsguard dress. Cursing, Maddix spun on his heel but even more Guards lay in wait around the corner. Bleeding stars, where had they all *come* from?

Maddix pulled his hood over his hair and secured his sword before leaping for the closest fire ladder and hauling himself through an open window. He pressed flat against the wall on the inside of the building, trying to force air into his lungs. Beneath him, the soldiers marched on the spot where he'd stood just a minute before. He clenched his fists by his sides, his fingernails biting into the meat of his palms. There were too many of them; he couldn't evade them all.

Get out. Jayin's voice echoed in his head He could imagine her beside him, vibrating with violent energy, her eyes glowing with green fire. *Come on,* dayri, *move!* Maddix inhaled deeply and took off again. He made it halfway down the stairs before the Guards stormed the building.

"Stars," he swore. They were going to be on him any second now. He closed the door of the nearest room behind him and pushed an antique chest of drawers in front of it. The single window led into a blind alley. No Guards lurked below—not yet anyway.

Praying that he didn't lose his grip, Maddix slunk out the window and held tight to the frame. There wasn't a fire ladder this time, so he clung to the outside of the building like a spider. He was only a few stories up, but if he fell, he'd break both of his legs. *One*, Maddix counted off in his head. *Two*…

He didn't wait until three before letting go. There were several long seconds of freefall before he caught himself on the next windowsill. He didn't allow himself time to breathe before letting go again. Rain slicked the next sill, and Maddix's stomach bottomed out as his hand slipped. He hung over the street for a single, dizzying second before hauling himself back up. Maddix took a shaking breath, pressing his forehead against the wall before the final drop.

When his boots finally hit the street, silver glowed in his periphery. He blinked and it was gone.

Maddix enjoyed a single victorious moment before Guardsmen poured into the alley.

There were too many. He was trapped. Well and truly trapped with nowhere to go. He didn't have the strength to climb into another building and even if he did, they would catch him before he made it halfway up the wall. Even if he *did* manage to fight his way through the mob, he had no doubt that there were archers perched on rooftops, just waiting to pick him off. Maddix pulled his sword out of its sheath, meeting the first Guards' steel with his own.

Death first. Maddix had made himself a promise when he broke out of the Pit all that time ago. He wasn't going back there, he wasn't ever going back in the dark again. He wouldn't let them have the satisfaction of locking him up for a second time, even if that meant he never took another breath. Even if it meant never seeing Jayin again.

"Maddix Kell," one of the men said, smirking at him as he swung his sword in a wide, showy arc. "We never thought you'd be stupid enough to show your face back here again."

Maddix gritted his teeth, raising his sword to block the man's blow, but he wasn't fast enough. The tip of the man's sword sliced down the inside of Maddix's arm and his weapon clattered to the cobbled street. Maddix didn't let it stop him, rushing into the man's guard and elbowing him in the stomach. The Guard doubled over, but another simply took his place.

The hilt of another sword struck him in the back. Pain and tingling numbness shattered up his spine and Maddix went to his knees, spitting curses. Before he could stagger back to his feet, something pinched the side of his neck. Maddix tried to rise, but his legs had turned to lead. One of the Guards shoved him, and Maddix pitched backward like a wine-soaked drunk. He sucked in a single, panicked breath, trying to force air into his lungs.

Above him, he could hear someone whistle appreciatively. "Ayrie is going to be happy to see him again." Distantly, Maddix felt the toe of a boot nudging his side. "Wonder what's so special that they want 'im alive and not dead."

"Guess we'll find out."

No, Maddix thought, but even as the thought snaked through his mind he knew that it was too late. They had him.

CHAPTER THIRTY-SEVEN:

JAYIN

Jayin told herself that she was overreacting, but she couldn't bring herself to go back to the warehouse. She was hiding. The infamous Gulwitch, scourge of the Gull and Ayrie, slinking about in the dark. Hiding from the kids who swarmed the moment she showed her face. At first, they only hovered at a distance and watched her with wide, rapturous eyes. But at night, assembled back at the abandoned building, they grew bolder.

Sometimes they just wanted demonstrations of her powers—that was easy enough. Jayin could slip on a new skin and be done with it. It worked for few days, but then the game lost its appeal and the witchlings—Jayin still cringed at the name—wanted to know more. Where did she come from? Why did she leave? How had she survived with so many people after her? Why had she come back?

She didn't have the answers, or at least, she didn't have the ones they wanted. They thought she was some kind of hero, the rogue witch that had defied the Palace and the Gull alike before taking on the rest of Aestos. Jayin hadn't told anyone about Kaddah, or the *sahirla*, or—

Or Maddix. The foolish, treacherous *dayri* that had taken her life away and then given it back with both hands.

She shouldn't miss him. Maddix had left her behind when things went sideways; he'd gone on ahead without her because she was going to slow him down. Jayin tried not to think of him. She didn't have time anymore, not with Ravi and the witchlings to contend with. But his absence, his ridiculous optimism and rare smiles, was like a constant ache in her chest. No one said her name like he did. It was a strange thing to miss, but Jayin yearned to hear the clumsy way he overprounounced the syllables, drawing them out too long.

Jayin couldn't tell the witchlings the truth, that she never meant to become some kind of Pavaalian superstition. When Jayin had chased down the carrions who'd robbed her and scared them into giving her goods back, she hadn't intended for it to grow this large. She just wanted to be left alone, not given a nickname and transformed into some kind of boogeyman. She *really* didn't want a gang of children fighting under her banner. Vultures, Bloodwings, Red Crows, and now witchlings. Witchlings who were her responsibility now, whether she wanted it or not.

So Jayin avoided the warehouse. She avoided the kids and their questions and the whispers of *Gulwitch* that followed her wherever she went.

I'm not the Gulwitch! She wanted to scream at them. *My name is Jayin Ijaad, and I can't take care of you.* She could hardly take care of herself. The fact she wasn't dead in a ditch or strung up in some witch hunter's compound was a miracle. A miracle and Maddix.

"Ravi's looking for you," the dark girl with the braids, Zia, said, climbing onto the rooftop where Jayin had been hiding. Of all the kids, she was the only one who didn't seem wholly taken with Jayin. It was refreshing.

"Did he send you to come find me?" Jayin asked, looking at the dusky street. Things had calmed down, but it had been a hive of activity earlier. Some poor bastard had caught the Guards' attention and they'd swarmed like brightly colored insects. There had been so many Jayin and the kids had gone to ground until they withdrew again. Whoever the Guards were after, Jayin pitied them for getting caught, but she had her own people to worry about.

"Nobody sends me anywhere," Zia said sourly.

"No, I suppose they don't," Jayin said. "I never thanked you."

"What?" Zia said and Jayin finally turned to look at her.

"For taking care of Ravi." He was a smart kid, no doubt about that, but he couldn't have done all this on his own. Zia was sharp and capable and obviously very used to being Ravi's right hand.

"Why are you here?" Zia asked. Some of the hostility had drained out of her voice. "The rest of them think you're some kind of savior."

"I'm not," Jayin said, opting for honesty for the first time in what felt like weeks. "I came back because I had nowhere else to go. I never meant for any of this." She paused, standing. "But I'm here now, and I'm going to do whatever I can to keep you all safe."

Zia nodded, and they made their way back to the street in silence.

"Ravi's waiting," Zia repeated when they were about a block away from the warehouse. "I got rounds."

"Watch the skies," Jayin said, knowing better than to tell the girl to be safe. None of them were safe anymore.

"Catch the stars," Zia replied after a moment of hesitation. She pressed two fingers to her heart and held them out. Jayin returned the gesture. It wasn't much, but Jayin felt lighter than before. She may not have made a friend, but something told her that she had an ally.

Ravi was waiting for her when she walked in the door. He looked exhausted after facilitating the evacuation. It was impressive how quickly the kids had vanished, disappearing into the streets until the warehouse looked like the abandoned ruin it was supposed to be. Even with Jayin monitoring keeping tabs in her second sight, she knew how stressful the day had been for him.

"Hey kid," Jayin said, slinging her arm across his shoulders. "You look like something they dragged out of the river."

"I forgot how warm and fuzzy you are."

"That's me," she said, her heart squeezing at his small, tired smile. "You need to get some sleep or you're going to pass out."

"I'm fine," Ravi insisted.

"You're dead on your feet," Jayin said gently. "Don't worry about the witchlings. I'm watching the building." Each of the witchlings glowed brightly in her second sight, marked so she would never lose them. "Get some sleep and I'll look after things," she promised.

Slowly, Ravi inclined his head, knocking his shoulder against hers before retreating to the corner of the warehouse he claimed for his own.

Things were quiet for a while after that—as quiet as things ever were. Pavaal might have changed but the air still hummed with energy. Jayin let it all wash over her, feeling everything and absorbing nothing until a spike from inside the building drew her attention.

Jayin snapped her shields back into place, shaking away the excess magic before pinpointing the disturbance. One of the boys was having a nightmare.

"Hey," Jayin said, placing a hand on the boy's leg. He startled awake and Jayin pressed a finger to her lips. "You're having a bad dream," she whispered. "You're okay."

"Gulwitch," the boy whispered, looking at her with wide eyes. They reminded her of Maddix, or who he might have been before the Pit.

"Call me Jayin, okay?" the boy nodded. "What's your name?"

"Arin."

"Do you want to take a walk with me, Arin?" Jayin stretched out a gloved hand. Arin hesitated but took it, his hand feeling tiny and fragile in hers. They didn't go far, just walked around the block. Jayin didn't try to initiate conversation, content with silence until the boy broke it.

"How'd you know that I was having a bad dream?" Arin asked.

"See that smoke over there?" Jayin said, pointing to the gray tendrils that drifted up in the sky. "People are like fires, and I can see the smoke. Sometimes, like when someone's having a bad dream, there's more than usual. That's how I knew."

"So I'm a fire?"

Jayin nodded, pressing two fingers to his forehead and drawing them back with an exaggerated wince.

Arin's eyes were wide and a smile spread across his face as quickly as the sun appearing from behind a cloud. "Stop that."

"Can't help it," Jayin said, tapping the back of her hand under his chin and pulling it back again. "What's that?" she asked, squinting at the side of his head. "I think—I think there's steam coming out of your ears."

Arin swiped at her, then flapped his hands around his head to dissipate the imaginary smoke.

"There is not," he protested, but he was almost laughing.

"You can't lie to me," Jayin said. "I'm the Gulwitch. You can't lie to the Gulwitch, didn't anybody tell you that?"

"I thought you said your name was Jayin," Arin said.

"You," she said, her smile wavering a little, "are a smart kid."

"You're not as scary as people say you are," the boy went on. "I don't think you're very scary at all."

"What do you think I am?"

"I think you're sad. Like Ravi is sad."

A very smart kid, Jayin thought. She swept the area as they walked, more out of habit than anything else. Something flashed in her second sight, catching her attention like Arin's nightmare, only much, much stronger. Stronger and familiar.

"Arin, I need you to wake Ravi up and tell him to meet me on the edge of the territory." The boy's smile dropped and he nodded. He disappeared without so much as another word, and Jayin took off towards the flare.

She knew that aura, but it was impossible. Angry, violent energy churned in the air. Carrions.

"Bleedin' skies," one of them spat. Jayin could sense four of them from where she was pressed up against an alley wall. This was their turf, and she had no idea how long it would take Ravi to get here. "You said she was askin' for the Gulwitch?"

"Yeah and she looks like she's gonna kick it any second."

"Let's just get this over with then," the first one said and Jayin heard the sound of a sword being drawn.

"Step back and I let you live," Jayin said, spinning her Gulwitch glamor and freeing her knives.

There was a split-second pause and the carrions surged forward, their weapons drawn. Jayin blocked and dodged, making herself look bigger so they were swiping at the empty air. Snarling, Jayin slashed her knife at the first carrion, her blade ripping clean through his stomach. His legs gave out beneath him and he screamed, trying to keep his insides from spilling out.

One of his companions ran at her from behind. Jayin spun and grabbed his arms, leaning forward so that she nearly lifted him off the ground, balanced on her back. The boy swore and Jayin threw all of her weight backward, slamming them both to the ground. She lurched back to her feet, but the boy didn't move, half-crushed. He was lucky the impact hadn't snapped his neck.

By the time Ravi and two other kids showed up, the carrions retreated, pulling their injured comrades away. Jayin barely noticed them, her focus on the prone figure huddled in the corner of the alley. The girl's face was an emaciated mask of its former self and there were two nasty cuts on her cheek, but there was no mistaking the blonde hair or her aura.

"Maia," Jayin breathed, going to her knees at the girl's side. "Maia, how—?" There were so many questions that only the single word came out.

"Jayin," Maia said but her voice was weak. Her aura flickered, guttering like a candle in a strong wind.

"Tell me," Jayin said, but Maia had used the last of her strength.

Gritting her teeth, Jayin took the girl's hand and pressed it to the side of her face. Pain throbbed against the inside of Jayin's skull and with it came fractured images. They all rolled together, nearly impossible to decipher, but when Jayin pulled away her breath caught in her throat and there was only one thing she knew for certain.

Maddix was in Pavaal. And the Guard had him.

CHAPTER THIRTY-EIGHT:

MADDIX

He was awake. Slowly, bit by bit, his senses started coming back to him. Water dripped from the ceiling, and a damp, musty smell clung to his nostrils. Maddix's whole body ached from the beating he'd taken, even the smallest movement feeling as if it was breaking something anew. There was something familiar about the air, something that made him think of darkness and despair and—

The Pit. For a moment Maddix was sure he was back underground, somewhere no one would hear him scream or bother to look for him. But then his eyes adjusted and Maddix could see rays of late-afternoon sunlight shining through a tiny slit in the wall. He was on the surface.

Maddix forced himself to breathe, inhaling shallowly through his nose. Whatever other kind of trouble he was in, he was above ground. He wasn't in the dark, and that was something.

It wasn't much.

His relief was short-lived. It might not have been the Pit, but he was still imprisoned somewhere. There was barely enough light to see by, but Maddix could tell that this new cell was hardly tall enough to allow him to stand. Even if he could, his ankle was chained to the wall behind him.

"Stars," he swore. Mist curled out of his mouth before vanishing. Whatever was keeping the air cold, it wasn't natural.

Outside, the seasons had just turned spring into summer, but within these walls it felt like the dead of winter. He tugged at the iron chain uselessly, but he wasn't strong enough to do much more than rattle it, and every movement set the wound on his hip afire. He should've let Maia heal it when she offered.

Maddix's breath hitched as he thought of her. Where was she now? Had she made it out of the guard post? Had she found the Gulwitch—had she found Jayin's people? There was no way for him to know.

"Stars," he said again, leaning his head back against the wall. He was going to die here, the only question was *when*. He was surprised they hadn't killed him already. Maddix knew that he'd proven himself too difficult to let live, so why they'd bothered to lock him up was a mystery. He doubted he was going to like the answer.

Gritting his teeth, Maddix forced himself not to panic. They were trying to break him, with the cold and isolation. He knew that. That's why the Pit was so successful. Years in the dark, alone except for the voices in your head, drove people mad. He could still hear the screams of the woman in the cell across from him as she tore open her own skin. Absently, he wondered if she was still alive. Probably not. The Pit had a way of making death seem like a welcome respite from endless, maddening blackness.

He wasn't going to let that happen to him, not this time. Not ever. His hands were free, Maddix noted, taking stock. He still had his own clothes, though they were bloodied and torn from days of travel and his unsuccessful escape from the Guards. He was alive.

And she was too.

Jayin was still out there somewhere. The thought of her smile, her real smile, not the glittering snarl she wore so often, helped keep the swirling fear at bay. She was probably on the ocean by now, sailing to the Isles without a single glance back. He liked the idea of her standing on the bow of a ship, the wind whipping through her short hair.

Maddix lost time in the daydreams, but it was better than drowning in his new, terrifying reality. He thought of Jayin and her ship until a sharp sound shook him out of his own head.

"Maddix Kell," said a silky voice, and Maddix found himself looking at a tall, stately woman with inky black hair and a bloody smile.

He was in the Palace then. Maddix filed that information away. He'd spent enough time around *sahir* to recognize the way the air changed around them, and this one looked every inch an Ayrie pet.

"I have heard so much about you," the witch said. Maddix fixed the witch with the coldest glare he could manage. Here, in chains, barefoot and bloody and huddled against the cell wall, he didn't cut much of a striking figure.

"If you're not feeling chatty, I'm sure something could be arranged. Perhaps I should make it a little cooler?"

Maddix bit his lip to keep from cursing and pointedly looked away. Any colder and he'd be hypothermic, and they needed him for something. Why else would they bother letting him live? They wouldn't just let him freeze to death—

He hoped.

"If you don't want to talk about yourself, how about we talk about Jayin?" Against his will, Maddix's head snapped up and the witch smiled unpleasantly. "That got your attention. I've known your little friend for a long time, and frankly, I'm surprised she bothered with you. I always thought she was so much smarter than that." The smile grew and a dark pit churned in Maddix's gut. "Then again, how clever can she be if she came back to Pavaal?"

"She's here?" The words came out before he could stop them and the *sahir* smirked. It looked more natural on her face than the smile.

"In the capitol where she belongs. And do we have plans for her."

Maddix was on his feet in an instant, flying towards the bars of the cell before the chain pulled taut and he went to his knees. .

The witch smiled, her blood-red lips twisting. "How sweet. The convict and the witch who helped us arrest him."

"What are you talking about?" Maddix growled.

"She never told you?" the witch asked, smug. "Oh yes, our Jayin used to be quite the prize. I'm sure she told you what she did for us. She caught criminals. She caught you."

The words were met with a hollow, cavernous silence. Maddix had never found out about the time between when the Dark witch let him go and his capture, only that it had been fast. He gained control of his body for an hour at most before the Guard came for him. But he never thought that the Palace had anything to do with it—in fact, he didn't know that Ayrie had any part in chasing down criminals, besides employing the Guard.

Jayin had made it a point to avoid talking about the Palace except for the occasional scathing remark, but Maddix could've kicked himself for not realizing sooner. Of course she was sent after convicts; she could track people wherever they went. With all that staring him in the face, it was obvious, and he felt like a fool for not figuring it out on his own.

I always hoped they were wrong about you. Maddix had dismissed her remark as the natterings of a girl lucky to be alive. Their time at Old Aya's seemed years away instead of months, but now it seemed strange that she would have thought about him at all before their fateful meeting in the *sahirla's* compound.

Why would an Ayrie witch bother herself with the goings on in the city unless she was directly involved?

Maddix waited for anger to rise up out of the sudden understanding, but it never came. Jayin hadn't known him then, she hadn't known his guilt or his innocence. She was just following orders just as he'd done so many times as a Guard. She gave him another chance at life when fate and the *sahirla* threw them together, a chance not to turn into a witchhunter. Whatever happened before then, he didn't blame her for it.

"You're never going to catch her," Maddix said. His breath clouded on the icy stone. Jayin had survived the Palace, the Gull, Kaddah, and the *sahirla.* She wasn't going to be taken by a self-important Ayrie witch.

"You're wrong," the woman said, serene and utterly sure. She knelt outside of the bars, her dress pooling around her. Sharp nails dug into his chin, forcing him to look her in the eye. "When I first made a deal with that witchhunter—Hale, I think his name was—I thought I would never be bothered by Jayin Ijaad again."

Maddix wrenched himself away, forcing himself to stand despite the chain and the pain in his muscles. Rage burned hot in his blood and for the first time since Maddix woke up in the cell, he didn't feel the cold.

"You set the hunters on her," he snarled.

"Brilliant deduction," the witch replied, looking more and more delighted the angrier Maddix became. He was playing right into her hands, Maddix knew that, but he'd never been good at controlling his temper. "That was the point; I wanted her dead. But you know, I think this is going to be much more fun."

"You'll never get her," Maddix said and spat at her through the bars.

The witch staggered backward, the smug look sliding off of her face. Maddix smiled savagely but his moment of victory didn't last. The witch wiped the blood and spit off of her chin, disgust written all over her harsh, beautiful features. Her sneer was replaced by naked, violent anger.

Maddix didn't have any warning before his world dissolved into a haze of pain. The witch lit a fire under his skin, the flames searing his nerves and charring his bones. He was burning alive from the inside out. Someone was screaming and it took him a few moments to realize that it was his own voice echoing raggedly inside the walls.

He tried to fight through the pain and come back to himself, but as soon as he could gather his thoughts together, another wave of fire scorched through him and they scattered again. His leg was bent awkwardly beneath him where it was attached to the wall and his back arched as he convulsed.

Eventually, the pain stopped, but Maddix didn't notice for a few long seconds, still shuddering from residual shocks. He curled in on himself as best he could manage, every breath feeling like it was splitting him open.

Lightning, the small part of him that remained rational whispered. Not fire, but lightning. Whatever the witch was doing to him, it was deadlier than any natural storm.

"We won't have to get her," the witch said, her voice hatefully soft, almost kind. "Because she's going to come to us on her own."

Leverage, Maddix thought, the realization taking him a beat too long. He wanted to say that she wouldn't risk her freedom for him, that she wouldn't be that stupid, but his voice was gone. The *sahir* had stolen it.

The witch reached through the bars, pressing her hand against Maddix's sternum, and he cried out, trying to twist away from the pressure on his chest. It felt like his heart was going to give out as electricity licked up and down his ribs. He couldn't breathe, he couldn't speak. His bones felt like they were splintering, spearing his lungs.

"And if she doesn't, well, then I'll have my way with you, and believe me when I say that this was just a taste of what I have in store, *dayri*." The witch removed her hand and Maddix gasped, his breath coming back to him in broken, ragged sobs. "Welcome to Ayrie Palace."

CHAPTER THIRTY-NINE:

JAYIN

"Jayin." For a moment the voice belonged to Maddix. Jayin blinked away her second sight, her eyes refocusing slowly. "You okay?"

"Yeah, I'm fine," she said just a second too late to be genuine. Ravi didn't push and a part of her wished that he would. She needed to talk to *someone*, but the witchlings were all too young and too scared. She couldn't burden them with this. "Sorry. Just tired."

Jayin hadn't slept since they found Maia two days ago. She rotated between the warehouse and her old apartment where Jayin had stashed the healer—none of the kids wanted to be around a sick witch, whether or not she was Jayin's friend. Maia wasn't doing well and between taking care of her and the witchlings, what was left of Jayin's energy went towards blind, mindless panic.

Maddix was here, in Pavaal, and he'd been arrested.

Stars, Maddix, she thought desperately. *Why are you even* in *Pavaal?*

In Rahael's memory, he said that he was going to the Isles or the colonies, as far away from the capitol as he could get. She couldn't understand why he changed his plans or how Maia had ended up traveling with him. Maia, who couldn't answer any of her questions because she'd been unconscious since they found her. Maia, who was doing worse than ever despite Jayin trying every trick she knew to stop the sickness from progressing.

It was a creeping, decaying thing, and Jayin felt the same magical reverberation every time she touched Maia's aura. The kids called it soul sickness, and there wasn't a cure.

"You need to get some sleep," Ravi said. Jayin had same thing to him just a few days before. "Jay, I'm serious."

"You've been serious a lot lately," Jayin said, rubbing her eyes like she could force herself to be more alert. "You should smile more, it prevents wrinkles."

"And you only make stupid jokes when you're exhausted," Ravi retorted, not amused. Jayin reached out and tapped his forehead.

"I can already see the crow's feet. It's a shame, you could've been so beautiful."

"Jayin—"

"I can't sleep," she said, any hint of humor vanishing. "I can't sleep until she wakes up. I can't sleep until I know that no one is coming for us."

She couldn't sleep until she knew what happened to Maddix. Jayin couldn't afford to send up a psychic flare this close to Ayrie, but she'd been looking as quietly as she could. All energy lingered, especially from an aura as strong as Maddix's, but there was nothing, not so much as a trace of him. Some *sahir* must have scrubbed the area clean, leaving no residual signature behind, which meant they knew she'd be looking. Jayin didn't know what scared her the most, the fact that Maddix had been taken or that Ayrie knew she'd come back to Pavaal.

"Here," Ravi said, handing her a mug of something. "Drink that. You're going to have a bad taste in your mouth for a few days but it'll keep you up." Jayin took a cautious sip, grimacing as the acrid liquid burned down her throat.

"That is awful," she complained.

"Yes, it is," Ravi agreed. "But it does the job. I stayed awake for almost a week one time drinking that stuff."

She knew he didn't mean anything by it, but she hated the idea of Ravi forcing himself to stay awake. Jittery and tense, with no one to lean on for support. Guilt tasted worse than the horrible drink. She'd left him alone when she slipped away from the Gull, and he turned around and saved over a dozen kids from joining up with the carrions. He was every bit the hero the witchlings thought that she was, and he'd done it all on his own.

"That sounds like a good story," Jayin said, forcing herself to choke down more of the disgusting swill. Already she could feel her heart starting to pick up.

"Not really," Ravi said. "I was so sleep deprived that I almost walked into carrion territory." He paused, thinking. "I wonder what they're calling themselves now. I mean, the old gangs are all gone and everyone who's left banded together."

"That must be a tense arrangement," Jayin said, sticking out her tongue as she took another sip. "How'd you decide to let carrions in?" she asked, trying to come up with anything to keep her mind off of Maddix.

"They were scared," Ravi said, raising a shoulder and dropping it. He settled himself next to her on the floor, his legs splayed out in front of him. He'd grow taller than her soon. "It was mad, Jay. You wouldn't believe how bad things got. Carrions started killing people if they so much as sneezed, so a few of them started jumping ship. By then we were organized and there were enough of us to make a difference." Ravi smiled. "Besides, you're the scariest thing to come out of the Gull in a hundred years. Even when you were gone, you were still keeping us safe."

There he went again, giving her credit she didn't deserve. If Maddix hadn't left her in Kaddah, Jayin wouldn't have ever come back here.

"You're doing that thing again."

"What thing?" Jayin asked, blinking.

"That thing you do when you start feeling guilty. Your nose gets all scrunchy."

Almost unconsciously, Jayin pressed her hand to her nose. "I do not."

"Yes you do," Ravi said, laughing. "You can't try to take all the blame for yourself. There's plenty to go around and if you try to take it all on, it'll crush you. You didn't let anyone down, least of all me."

"When did you get so smart?" Jayin managed after a moment of stunned silence.

"Well one time, this grumpy shopkeeper let me hang around her place so I wouldn't get jumped into the gangs," Ravi said with a grin that reminded her of the easygoing kid she'd left behind.

"Sounds a little far-fetched to me," Jayin said, but she was smiling.

They sat in companionable silence for a few minutes, punctuated only by Jayin's noises of disgust as she choked down the concoction. Then there was a flash of energy and a groan as Maia woke, shifting restlessly on her cot.

"Hey," Jayin said, trying to smile as warmly as she could. Maia's breathing was labored and her eyes took a long time to focus. Jayin didn't bother asking how she was feeling.

"Maddix?" Maia stuttered. Her lips moved but no more sound escaped. Jayin understood and shook her head.

"I don't know where he is," she said, hating how Maia's face fell. "I'm looking, I promise." Jayin knew that her words weren't worth much.

"I'll give you a second," Ravi said, standing. "Drink the rest of that."

Jayin didn't watch him walk out, all of her attention trained on Maia.

"You're safe here," she said softly, taking the girl's hand in hers. "We're doing everything we can to make you better."

Jayin wished that Maddix were around more than ever, if only for the strange effect he had on her magic. If she could somehow manipulate Maia's aura, maybe Jayin could dislodge the darkness that had taken root inside the healer's body.

"Don't think like that," Jayin admonished gently, responding to Maia's unspoken feeling. She was dying and she knew it. Jayin's assurances didn't mean a thing. "You're going to be okay."

The hair on the back of her neck stood up as a horribly familiar aura strode into her second sight. Into the warehouse.

"No," Jayin breathed, her heart tripping. *No, no, no.* She turned her attention back to Maia, but she was already asleep again. Jayin tucked the blanket under her chin and left one of her knives behind, just in case.

Her heart beat like a caged beast as she walked to the warehouse and in those minutes, the distance felt like it stretched for miles.

"Jayin!" a sickeningly smug voice greeted her as she stepped through the doors. Maerta stood in the center of the warehouse, gleaming in all of her Ayrie finery. Her arm looped casually around Ravi's shoulders, the tips of her fingers stroking his collarbone.

"Step away from him," Jayin said, hissing the words through clenched teeth. She knew the damage Maerta could do with the barest flick of her wrist.

"Oh, but your friend and I were just getting acquainted," Maerta said. Jayin wanted to kill her. She wanted to rip Maerta's throat out and watch her bleed to death. See if she was still so smug when she was drowning in her own blood. "I'm sure he's got so many wonderful stories to tell about you. It would be a shame if something were to happen."

She trailed her long, sharp nails over Ravi's neck and Jayin clenched her fists to keep from flying across the room. Ravi winced, his face going tight with pain.

"Stop," Jayin spit. "Let him go."

"You know, I think I will," Maerta said, releasing Ravi and pushing him towards her. Ravi staggered to her side and Jayin pulled him behind her. His hands shook and fear rolled off him in waves.

"Jayin, Jayin, Jayin," Maerta said, her heels clicking as she paced across the warehouse floor. "You have caused us so much grief. Personally, I want you dead." Ravi twitched and Jayin tightened her grip on his arm.

"Well if the *sahirla* couldn't do it, I don't like your chances," she said. Jayin would die before she let Maerta hurt any of the kids, and they both knew it.

"However, the Kingswitch," Maerta continued as if she hadn't spoken, "the man who raised you and gave you everything you ever could have wanted, would rather have you back and in one piece. It would be best if you came willingly."

"And if I don't?" Jayin said but she already knew how this was going to end. Maerta smiled, a mean quirk of her lips.

"Well, then I kill every one of your precious little witchlings and make you watch. And then I drag you back to Ayrie, and I start on your convict friend. Surely you still remember Maddix."

Maerta raised a hand, a familiar necklace dangling from her fingertips. Maddix's energy still clung to it, rising off of the stone like smoke. Jayin closed her eyes, feeling the trap snapping into place all around her. It was over. She didn't have any more tricks to pull or places to run.

"Jayin, don't," Ravi whispered but his voice trembled. Maerta snapped her fingers and Ravi cried out, his legs crumpling beneath him.

"Stop it!" Jayin shouted, falling to her knees beside him. Ravi shuddered, shaking and convulsing. Blood trickled out of his nose.

"Tick tock," Maerta said, walking up behind her. "Give me an answer, or we're both going to watch as his heart stops."

"*Enough*," Jayin said. Ravi's eyes rolled back in his skull, and he twitched once more before lying still. Only the rise and fall of his chest indicated that he was still alive. "I'll go with you."

"What a good answer. Come now, Jayin, the Palace awaits."

Jayin stood on unsteady legs, hating her more than she'd ever hated anyone. Maerta strode away and she had no choice but to follow. Jayin laid her hand on the door, sparing one last glance behind her. The witchlings gathered around Ravi and helped him sit up, all of them watching her with wide, solemn eyes. As she watched, each of them pressed two fingers to their hearts and held them out to her. *Watch the skies.*

Catch the stars, Jayin thought, stretching her hand out to them.

She would need all the luck the sky could offer now.

CHAPTER FORTY:

JAYIN

Maerta spoke as the carriage took them further and further from the Gull, but Jayin didn't answer. Every time the Ayrie witch breathed Jayin choked on the cloying scent of her perfume.

"Your time away really has changed you," Maerta commented as they rode through the golden gates outside of the Palace. "You were never so brooding. And your hair is a disaster. It's a wonder anyone recognized you at all." Jayin swore as Maerta gripped her chin with sharp fingernails. "But there's no disguising those eyes."

"Don't touch me," Jayin snarled, wincing as Maerta's sour energy rolled over her. She pressed down the trigger of her forearm sheath, bringing the blade to the pale column of Maerta's throat.

"Careful now. If I don't come back whole and with you by my side, there's no telling what will happen to your *dayri*." Her eyes flashed. "Maybe they'll give him to the Hounds."

Jayin's blood curdled, and she quickly took the blade away, swearing.

"None of that," Maerta *tsk*ed as they rolled through the Palace gates. "We wouldn't want the Kingswitch thinking your little vacation spoiled your temperament now, would we?"

Jayin bit her lip so hard she tasted copper on her tongue.

Maerta rubbed her hands together gleefully. "Oh, this is going to be such fun."

One foot in front of another, Jayin forced herself out of the carriage and through the yawning mouth of the doorway. Chandeliers shimmered in the midday light and endless decorative hallways greeted them, along with half a dozen Palace guards. They shouldn't have bothered. As long as they had Maddix, Jayin would play nice. The sentries were just a show of force, reminding her where she was and who was in control.

"Where are we going?" Jayin demanded as Maerta began to lead her towards the dormitories.

"You don't honestly think I'm presenting you to the court looking like that, do you?" Maerta sniffed, affronted.

"And you don't honestly think I'm putting up with this charade unless you prove that you have Maddix, do you?" she shot back. Maerta tapped an overlong fingernail to her lip before sighing, shaking her head.

"Fine then, if you insist on looking like a dockrat," Maerta said. Her eyes gleamed. She loved every moment of this. To her, looking out of place here was the worst kind of embarrassment.

I will not show weakness in front of these people, Jayin swore to herself as Maerta marched her towards the viewing hall.

The King and the Kingswitch presided over separate sections of the Palace so *sahir* and *dayri* rarely saw one another. The hall was empty when they entered, save for the Kingswitch's personal guards. The Hounds leered at her, every bit as brutish as she remembered. They'd been with the Kingswitch for as long as Jayin could remember, their terrible magic making them perfect guards and interrogators. Jayin had never suffered at their hands, but that could soon change. Amon and Aema were twins, mindwitches with the ability to pluck out a person's worst nightmare and force them to live it. Not many lasted long under their ministrations.

Jayin supposed she should be honored they thought she was such a threat, but it was all she could do not to be sick right there on the gleaming stone floors.

It was the same. The Palace was exactly the same. Pavaal was unrecognizable, but Ayrie hadn't changed at all, right down to the pulsing energy that made her gag.

"You're looking a little green dear," Maerta whispered. "Feeling anxious?" Jayin didn't answer, forcing herself to swallow the acidic comments that stacked up behind her teeth.

"Where's Maddix?" she demanded, trying to pretend like she had even a little control left. Her skin tingled and itched, magic clinging to her skin and sinking through her pores. Once, it had made her feel safe, at home. Now she just felt nauseous.

"Oh yes, I almost forgot," Maerta said. Jayin imagined slicing the smile off of her face. Maerta gestured to Amon and a hunched figure was dragged into the hall.

"Maddix," Jayin breathed, unable to keep silent.

"Hello again, convict," Maerta said cheerfully. Maddix flinched at the sound of her voice.

"What did you do?" Jayin snarled, whirling on Maerta with murder in her eyes. Jayin would kill her. She was going to gut her like a carp, and then Jayin and Maddix were getting out of here. Jayin had barely touched her knives when Maddix started screaming.

"Come now Jayin," Maerta said, shaking her head like a disappointed parent. "I thought you knew how this was going to go."

"Stop," she said. Jayin didn't know where to go or what to do. She was frozen. "Stop or I swear to the stars I'll kill you."

"And if you don't play nice, I'll kill him," Maerta said. She twisted her hand and Maddix's voice gave out. His screams died in his chest, replaced by a hollow choking sound. "What's it going to be Jayin?"

"Stop," she repeated. Her voice splintered, ripping something inside of her. "*Please.*"

"I'm glad we understand one another," Maerta said primly. All Jayin could hear was the broken sound of Maddix's breathing. "Go, if you must," Maerta said, waving her forward.

Jayin's footsteps echoed off of the polished floors as she ran to Maddix's side.

"Bleeding, bloody, *falling* skies," Jayin swore under her breath. Maddix was on his knees, his arms wrapped around his middle like he could somehow hold himself together. "I'm sorry," she said, whispering the words over and over again. Her hands fluttered around his face, shaking and useless. "I'm sorry. I'm so sorry."

All this time trying not to think of him, all of those wasted hopes that maybe she would find him again, and this is what came of them. She didn't want this; she'd never wanted this.

"Don't," he said hollowly when she tried to brush his hair away from where it hung in his eyes. "Maia?"

"She found us," Jayin whispered. He exhaled, some of the tension draining away. He shifted and underneath his hair, she could see that his face was covered in bruises.

"Jayin, you need to go," Maddix breathed.

"No way in hell," Jayin hissed back. "We've been in worse scrapes than this."

It was a lie, but she prayed he couldn't tell. She had no real confidence that either of them would make it out alive. Maddix's wrists were shackled in front of him—a power play more than an actual attempt to restrain him. Maerta was more than capable of controlling both of them.

She didn't plan on giving her the chance.

Almost imperceptibly, Jayin slid off a glove and extended her hand to him, flipping her palm up. She could get them out of here. She could stop this before it started, but she needed his help—and his permission. It was her fault that he was here, her fault that they were holding him as bait.

"Are you sure?" he whispered, something like hope shining in his eyes. Jayin bared her teeth in a savage grin. Maddix grabbed her hand with both of his and pain ripped through her shields, making way for the strange magic to rise up in their place.

"What a lovely display," Maerta said, smirking. "And holding hands. How sweet."

So arrogant, Jayin thought. Maerta's arrogance was going to get them out of here. She tried to gather her magic but Jayin already had a stranglehold on her aura. The smile slid off Maerta's face as she reached for them and they remained standing.

"What's the matter?" Jayin mocked. "You're looking a little green."

"What did you do to me?" Maerta hissed. Her hands were thrown wide, angled towards them but with Jayin containing her magic, her power couldn't touch them. "Stop this or I'll—"

"You'll what?" Jayin cut her off. "You can't do a thing." *How does it feel?*

"Jayin!" Maddix's voice snapped her out of her gloating, and she turned to see the Hounds lunging for them.

She reached for her knives with one hand but she wasn't fast enough. It didn't matter anyway. Silver sprang into existence around them, more solid than it had ever been. Somehow, while they were behind it, the Hounds couldn't touch them.

"How are you doing that?" Maddix asked, awestruck. Jayin handed him one of her knives and he held it awkwardly in his bound hands.

"I'm not," Jayin replied. "I think…I think you are." She'd had a suspicion since his fall from the top of the wall, but there was never enough proof. Maddix's mouth all but fell open, his eyes flying wide as he moved his arms experimentally. The silver glow responded, stretching at he did.

"That's impossible," he said. Jayin would've said the same if the proof wasn't right in front of her. His aura was the strongest she'd ever felt but magical abilities never manifested this late. Maddix was nearly nineteen. If he were *sahir*, he should've exhibited the signs years ago.

You are two creatures without equal. Old Aya's words echoed in the back of her mind. Jayin hadn't thought anything of them then, but now she couldn't help but think that there was some truth there. There was nothing like either of them in this world.

"Maddix. We'll figure it out later, but now we have to go." Before they lost the chance. Slowly Maddix nodded, squeezing her hand.

"So what's your plan?" Maerta asked and Jayin directed her attention back to her. How very typical. Even rendered powerless she tried to act like she was in control. "There's nowhere we won't find you."

Jayin didn't answer, stretching her arm out and clenching her hand into a first. Maerta choked, going to her knees and Jayin could feel her aura weaken and her heart started to give out.

"Enjoy the Dark," Jayin said coldly.

"Very impressive," said a new voice and Jayin jumped so violently she released Maerta. *No.*

"Jayin," Maddix whispered. It was a question and a comfort, but Jayin could hardly keep herself from screaming. It was over.

"Don't look at him," Jayin whispered, her voice shaking so hard the words barely came out. "Whatever you do, don't look at him." She steeled herself the best she could, positioning herself in front of Maddix before turning to face the Kingswitch.

He hadn't changed. Like the Palace, the Kingswitch remained untouched. He was as striking as ever, with his crimson robes and golden hair. The small smile he used to reserve just for her was fixed on his lips. Stars, Jayin used to love that smile. Now the sight of him made dread coil in her heart.

"Elias," she said, forcing her face into the impassive mask of the Gulwitch. She longed for her glamor, but was already using too much magic as it was. Any more and something would give out.

The smile only widened, the scar on his lip stretching, and his bottle-green eyes crinkled in the corners. He'd once called her impertinent, and Jayin knew that she was the only one bold enough to call him by his given name.

"Is that really how you address your father after all this time?"

Jayin felt Maddix stiffen beside her but she forced him from her mind. She couldn't waver, not now.

"Sir," Maerta started but the Kingswitch raised a hand and she fell silent. Jayin didn't bother reaching for her again, instead conserving her magic. She would need all of it.

"You look different," the Kingswitch said. His eyes—her eyes, too, the ones he'd given her—roamed over her. Jayin had to fight to keep from shivering under his probing gaze. "I hardly recognized you."

That was the point, Jayin thought bitterly. If only it had worked.

"And stars above, what have you done to your lovely hair?"

"*Sir,*" Maerta said more insistently, piqued that her attempted murder was going unanswered. How she hated not to be the center of attention.

"You have new scars, my daughter," the Kingswitch said, frowning as he looked her over.

"You can thank darling Maerta for that," Jayin said, surprised and gratified to see the tiniest bit of surprise in his eyes before it vanished as quickly as it had come. "Or did you not know that she turned me over to the *sahirla* to be killed?"

For a single, ridiculous moment, Jayin felt like a child tattling to her father for being bullied in the schoolyard. She almost regretted the admission as the Kingswitch rounded on Maerta. His pupils expanded, swallowing the green of his irises until there was nothing left but black.

Jayin wanted to shout for him to stop, she wanted to look away, but she was frozen in place, helpless to do anything but watch. The magic in the air was so powerful it was nearly tangible as the Kingswitch speared Maerta with his gaze. There was a single moment of resistance before oily blackness began to spread over her aura like a stain. The Kingswitch held steady, and Maerta's body moved stiffly, out of her control. Electricity crackled in the air, gathering in her palms, and Maerta pressed a hand over her heart.

"No!" Jayin shouted for no other reason than she couldn't bear to watch.

There was a single burst of violent energy and then nothing. The woman crumpled without a sound and Jayin didn't need her magic to know that Maerta was dead.

"How—?" Maddix whispered behind her and Jayin shook her head. The less attention on them, the better.

"With all this excitement I think I forgot to introduce myself to your friend," the Kingswitch said pleasantly, turning back to them like he hadn't just forced his lieutenant to kill herself. His eyes had lost the black tint but Jayin knew that it lurked under the surface, ready to be unleashed at any moment.

"We're leaving," Jayin said. With Maerta gone, this was their best chance, but even then it wasn't good. "Now."

"But you just got back," the Kingswitch said, sounding disappointed, almost chiding. "And I have missed you, Jayin."

She couldn't say the same. She'd spent all this time trying to get away from him and his nest of vipers. Jayin had left because she couldn't bear her father's atrocities and now all she wanted was to get Maddix out in one piece.

"And Maddix Kell," he said. "How I have longed to meet you."

Maddix went still and something flickered on his face.

"Run," Jayin hissed. "Maddix, *run*!" She didn't wait for a response, stepping out of the protection of Maddix's shield and throwing every bit of her magic at the Kingswitch. The world narrowed to just the two of them as Jayin reached for his aura with both hands.

The world blurred away, and all Jayin knew was the energy in her second sight. The Kingswitch's aura was black and corrosive, like something long dead and rotting. She snarled as she came in contact with it, pain vibrating up her arms as she tried to wrestle for control. His energy was oil on water, slipping away before she could get enough of a grip to rip him apart. Somehow, he was resisting her, using his energy to fight and her strength ebbed away with every moment that passed.

"It's a good trick." His voice echoed in her mind and she knew that he hadn't spoken the words aloud. "But I have a better one."

The world shifted and her father's Dark aura stepped from her second sight into reality. Jayin's focused slipped and her vision returned in full, terrible color. She couldn't control him; she wasn't strong enough.

Maddix. Jayin's thoughts immediately turned to him, searching him out. He hadn't made it out of the viewing chamber. Instead he stood a few paces away from her, the silver shield flickering around him. Naked horror was written across his face as he took in the monster her father had become.

For so long, Jayin had only guessed at the Kingswitch's abilities. He never did magic in front of the other Palace *sahir*, but his power was unparalleled. She knew that even as a child with only the loosest grip on her own magic. After years of asking for even the smallest of demonstrations and getting nothing for her efforts, Jayin assumed—like most of Ayrie—he was some kind of mindwitch. It was the best explanation and the only one they were likely to get.

Until Jayin had decided to discover it for herself. She brought him a fleeing criminal, presenting him before the court as she always had, knowing that the convict would be left with the Kingswitch before his sentencing. This one was special. Her father had asked for him personally. Jayin hadn't even bothered discovering his crime; the Kingswitch's word was enough for her.

Stars, she'd thought herself so clever, spinning a glamor so tight she didn't think anyone would be able to see it, not even him. She stood in the shadows and watched as her father's skin split into a swirling, Dark manifestation of the blackest magic she'd ever seen. The criminal had cowered and cried but it hadn't done any good. When he didn't answer the Kingswitch's questions to satisfaction, the man's body was turned against itself.

"Shall I have him cut off his hand?" the Kingswitch had called to her. "What do you think, Jayin? Does that punishment fit the crime?"

Jayin hadn't been able to say a word, fleeing with the man's frantic pleas for help ringing out behind her. She'd vomited into an ancient decorative urn, trying to convince herself that what she'd seen was some kind of illusion, a trick, a test. Anything but the truth.

No matter how she turned over the memories in her mind, there was no doubt that what she saw was real. Her father had tortured a man and laughed all the while. He'd asked her to weigh in on what kind of punishment to inflict next, as if it was some kind of grotesque bonding ritual.

She couldn't escape the sounds of the man's screams, nor the way his energy seemed to adhere to her. She felt his pain as his hands were turned against himself, clawing at his own skin, pulling out his fingernails, and even gouging out one of his eyeballs.

Jayin shrieked herself hoarse, and out of the man's remaining eye, she could see the Dark monster cackling with glee all the while. His red eyes held nothing but joyful malice until finally, the man choked himself to death.

That night, her own throat still burning, Jayin began planning her escape.

"It's him," Maddix managed, his voice all but gone. Her own horror was reflected in his eyes. The silver glow died altogether as panic overtook him. "It's him."

Jayin didn't think, spinning and throwing two of her straightblades with all her strength. It was the last trick she had, and her heart twisted as the knives passed through the Dark figure like he was composed of so much smoke and mist.

"Don't look at him!" Jayin said, sensing magic in the air. Under the hood, eyes glowed red and the smallest sound from Maddix told her that it was already too late.

"Jayin," he whispered and Jayin turned to see him raising the knife she'd given him, pressing the tip of the blade into the center of his chest. "Jayin, I—" he said before his voice choked off. His arms shook as he tried to fight, but the Kingswitch's magic was too strong.

"Stop," Jayin said desperately. Already, she could see blood staining through Maddix's shirt. "Stop it, you skyforsaken monster!"

If Maddix pressed the blade any deeper, he was going to puncture his heart.

"And why would I do that?" the Kingswitch asked. The Dark form was gone, replaced by the golden persona he presented to the word, but his eyes were still flatly black. Maddix's arm stilled but blood rushed down his front and his skin was draining of color.

"I'll stay," Jayin said, the words burning in her mouth. "I'll stay with you, just let him go."

"No, I don't think so," the Kingswitch said, smiling serenely. Green took over the black of his eyes and Maddix collapsed. Jayin twitched, fighting the urge to run to Maddix's side. "He's alive, Jayin. And he'll stay that way as long as you cooperate."

I'll see you burn for this, Jayin thought, tearing her gaze off of Maddix's prone form and forcing herself to look at her father. Jayin used to think he hung the moon. He'd rescued her from the orphanage, taught her that she had magic, a purpose, a *home*. For so long, she didn't think she would ever want anything more than that. Then the Kingswitch revealed to her parentage.

"I have enemies, Jayin," he'd said when she started to ask questions. "If they ever knew that you existed, it would put you in danger. It would put both of us in danger. I did what I could to keep you safe."

Jayin had swallowed the answer without complaint then, but now she knew better. She wasn't sure why he finally sought her out all those years ago but she had no doubt that it was to advance his own power. He didn't give a damn about her. He never had.

"I have terms," Jayin said as steadily as she could manage. She had no more tricks, no chips to cash in. She was in no place to negotiate and they both knew it. But Jayin also knew that he liked to pretend that she was the obedient Ayrie pet, the prodigal daughter who might someday take on his blood-soaked mantle. He would hear her demands.

"What would those be?" he asked indulgently, inclining his head.

"The witchlings," Jayin said. "In the Gull. You don't touch them."

"You know that we don't interfere with the rabble," he replied before pausing. He tapped his finger on his chin thoughtfully. "But I suppose that I can make an exception. The children will not be harmed."

"There's a girl with them," Jayin went on while she still had momentum. "She's sick. You have to help her. *Without* bringing her here."

Maia didn't stand a chance without the healers in the Palace, but Jayin wasn't willing to let what happened to Om repeat itself with Maia. She would never step foot in Ayrie Palace, not if Jayin had anything to say about it.

"We will do what we can," the Kingswitch said. "Anything else?" He was mocking her, but Jayin pressed on.

"Maddix," she started but he held up a hand.

"I'm sorry, my girl, but I've been looking for your friend for far too long to let him go now. But he will remain here. As long as you behave, no harm will come to him, you have my word on that. Are we agreed?"

Far from it, but Jayin didn't have any choice but to nod her reluctant assent.

"Agreed," she whispered. Her voice echoed in the viewing chamber and the enormous room seemed to close in on her like a tomb. The Kingswitch descended from the dais and Jayin had to duck her head to keep him from seeing the disgust twisting her features. He laid a hand on her shoulder and it was everything she could do to keep from flinching.

"Then it's settled," he said, his voice filled with a revoltingly parental kind of pride. "I've missed you Jayin. You're home now."

This is not my home. The words danced on the tip of her tongue but she swallowed them. Home was Ravi and the witchlings, the open sky above her when she slept on the roof of her building, and blue-gray eyes that had seen too much but still shone with hope and laughter.

Right now, Jayin was behind enemy lines and all she could do was keep her mouth shut and bide her time. Because she had to keep her home safe, she had to keep *them* safe.

She would stay. For now. She would play courtier and bide her strength. And then, when her father and his hellish court least expected it, she was going to burn them to the ground.